"You see, I do know what to do with a wife, Cherie."

And Roland grabbed her and kissed her until she couldn't breathe. She fought him at first, but it was useless. His mouth was everywhere—on her mouth, on her cheek, on her neck, and lower. Angelique was sobbing, moaning, "No, no, no . . ."

He smiled tenderly at her flash of spirit, yet his hold on her didn't slacken one bit as he carried her to his bed. "Don't fight me, love," he advised as he set her on her feet. "You'll lose."

Angelique stared up at him. Furious and hurt though she was, she knew that she couldn't deny him his husbandly due. "Now? In the afternoon?" she managed to murmur weakly.

"We've waited long enough, *n'est-ce pas*, my love?" he whispered, reaching for her hair. She caught a sharp breath as he pulled at pins. Her heavy locks tumbled about her shoulders, and he kissed the silken tresses, murmuring, "Ah—*bien*."

His strong hands gripped her slim waist, easily lifting her onto his bed. He doffed his coat, then his hard body followed hers. . . .

~~~

"A beautiful, tender love story . . . will melt every reader's heart, leaving a very warm feeling."

—*Romantic Times* on
Eugenia Riley's *Sweet Reckoning*

Readers Are Mad About The Novels Of Eugenia Riley

"Absolutely wonderful! I was on the edge of my seat the whole way through. I laughed and cried with the characters."

—L.F., Georgia

"Very seldom have I enjoyed a book as much as I did yours. I couldn't put it down."

—J.D., New Hampshire

"Emotionally moving . . . held me spellbound!"

—N.H., Florida

"Refreshing and full of surprises . . . congratulations on what I'm sure will be an award-winning book."

—P.W., Pennsylvania

"A rare story . . . just could not put it down."
—M.F., New Jersey

"I loved it!!! The characters grabbed me . . .
the humor was great. . . . It's the first book in
a long time that I read in one day!"
—G.D.C., California

"Totally captivating! I found myself reading it
instead of cleaning my house."
—Z.N., Mississippi

"Fantastic. Full of clever plots and true-to-life
characterizations."
—M.E.M., Pennsylvania

"A very moving love story. I loved it!"
—L.D., Louisiana

"Wonderful. I loved it! The characters are
realistic and have depth. The love scenes are
very, very well done."
—G.D., Ontario, Canada

Copies of these and other signed testimonials are on file
and may be examined at Warner Books, 666 Fifth
Avenue, New York, N.Y. 10103.

ALSO BY EUGENIA RILEY

Laurel's Love
Mississippi Madness
Sweet Reckoning

Published by
WARNER BOOKS

Angel Flame

Eugenia Riley

WARNER BOOKS

A Warner Communications Company

With love to my daughter, Lienna,
with congratulations on her
graduation from high school.

CHAPTER
One

New Orleans
1850

Sitting in a den of iniquity, Jean Pierre Delacroix heard the voice of an angel.

The summer evening was sultry, the dining room of the house on St. Charles Avenue hazy with smoke. Four men were gathered about the mahogany table, tensely engaged in a game of poker, while overhead, the gaslit chandelier hummed and sputtered, casting its wavering glow over the scene. The men's faces were sweat-glossed and bright from overindulgence; the table was cluttered with cards, ashtrays, an empty whiskey bottle, and grimy glasses. The room mirrored the neglect so evident throughout the house—torn or moth-eaten drapes, frayed upholstery, sagging wallpapers.

Sitting across from Giles Fremont, Jean Pierre was losing, and was rapidly succumbing to a foul humor. He was the youngest of the four players; at twenty-eight, he was doing his best to debauch his way through the vast fortune left him by his dear departed mother. Tonight, Jean Pierre was making some progress in that direction, as his losses were substantial—although he did suspect that the fat commission agent, Etienne Broussard, who sat to his right, had been cheating all evening. By all rights, he knew he should unmask the scoundrel and call him out; yet the loss of a few thousand dollars did not seem worth the risking of his life.

For Jean Pierre Delacroix valued his existence as a libertine far too much.

Jean Pierre knew the evening had become a phenomenal bore, and that he should leave and cut his losses. Yet the soprano voice continued to tantalize him, mesmerizing him, from a distant room. She was humming some sweet, lilting aria that he'd once heard at the opera—Mozart, perhaps? He frowned pensively. As far as he knew, Giles Fremont lived alone. But then who was this mysterious nightingale who called to him, her voice as bright and searing as a flame? He was tempted to stay long enough to find out.

And he knew that, despite the minor setback of losing tonight, far worse indignities awaited him should he venture home early. Frowning over yet another pitiful hand dealt him by Broussard, Jean Pierre recalled the earlier, tactless remarks of his houseguest and cousin, Roland Delacroix. Roland's brutal departing words had been gnawing at Jean Pierre all evening—and, doubtless, not improving his luck at poker in the least.

How dare the man call him a hopeless profligate and a lazy ne'er-do-well! Granted, the labels were accurate, but this time Cousin Roland had breached all limits of courtesy with his crude remarks. Jean Pierre had unfailingly opened his home to his cousin every time the wealthy planter had come to New Orleans on business, and now the man had bitten the very hand that had fed him, declining Jean Pierre's invitation to come along for the evening of cards and dismissing such practices as slothful!

Slothful, indeed! There were definitely some labels he could apply to Cousin Roland—such as foul-tempered tyrant and misanthropic recluse.

Such labels he would apply, were he not a gentleman.

Shuffling his cards in an exercise in futility, Jean Pierre sighed and thought of the old days, when he and Roland were truly friends, before all the laughter left his cousin's eyes and was replaced by that strange, haunted darkness. For a dual tragedy had struck Cousin Roland eight years past; within the space of a mere twelve months, the man had lost both his beloved brother, Justin, and his first wife, Luisa, in unrelated, senseless accidents. Since that time, Roland had seemed little more than a hollow, embittered shell of a man; all he did now was to run his sugarcane plantation, and occasionally conduct business with his factor in New Orleans.

"You in or out, Delacroix?"

The curt words of Etienne Broussard, along with the jingle of coins on the tabletop, roused him from his musings. He stroked his thin mustache and glanced at his hand—a Jack of Clubs and assorted lower cards. He should fold and go home for the night, he thought irritably—Cousin Roland be damned.

Yet still he heard the melodious voice, this time raised in some lovely sacred melody which, owing to Jean Pierre's negligible attendance at Mass, he could not quite recognize. Utterly enchanted by the sweet sound, he turned to his host. "Who is that singing?"

Across the table, Giles Fremont snorted in disdain. Like Etienne Broussard, Fremont was a hefty man; unlike his guests, he had defied decorum early in the evening, doffing his frock coat. Giles had spent much of the game scratching a bulging midsection that protruded even through his shirt-linen.

"The songbird is my niece, Angelique," Giles now drawled contemptuously. "And where is the lazy chit with our refreshments? Did she not indulge night and day in her infernal singing, we would now be served. Angelique!" he bellowed out over his shoulder. "Pray, bring the food and whiskey!"

Jean Pierre scowled at his host. He had never liked Giles Fremont, whose puffy, florid features confirmed an addiction to alcohol. The man was a reputed lecher, and gossip of his randy lifestyle had caused even the libidinous Jean Pierre to raise an eyebrow on occasion. "Angelique?" he now repeated.

"Yes, Angelique—the offspring of my lately departed brother, Samuel," Giles said with distaste.

"Indeed? I was not aware that you had a brother."

Giles shrugged. "Samuel was the black sheep of the family. As a young man, he left New Orleans in disgrace to marry a trashy little Cajun from Bayou Teche. The two of them bought a farm near St. James, where they lived for over twenty years and raised up the girl, Angelique. Then just over a fortnight ago, both Samuel and Evangeline succumbed to Yellow Fever. A distasteful business—their farm was mortgaged to the hilt, and not a penny was left of the estate

after I settled their debts. The sheriff burned all their belongings, as is required in these fever cases. So I was left
with naught but a pauper child to support.''

Jean Pierre felt a rush of sympathy for the niece Fremont
had spoken of so dispassionately. ''The girl is living here,
then?''

''Indeed. And never stops her caterwauling, either. She
was taught by some Italian lady up at St. James—I should
have left the girl with her, I swear. Night and day, the chit
sings or hums. I'm thinking she might be a trifle touched.''

Jean Pierre frowned. ''How old is this girl?''

''Seventeen.'' Abruptly, Giles's features pulled into a lascivious grin. ''Not bad to look at, if you know what I mean,''
he added with a lewd guffaw, elbowing the white-haired
banker, Charles Levin, who sat to his right.

Jean Pierre restrained a shudder as Charles Levin's pale
eyes flashed upward. Levin was tall and thin, sporting a shock
of striking white hair, ruthlessly sharp features and the most
icily cold, remorseless blue eyes Jean Pierre had ever seen.
While many assumed Levin to be a respectable banker, Jean
Pierre knew he was actually a depraved tyrant with a fiend-
ish temper and an attitude toward women sadistic enough to
make Giles Fremont seem a priest by comparison. Married
for over thirty years to a socialite wife who turned her head
the other way, Levin had gone through a string of young
mistresses acquired from Quadroon balls—more than one, it
was rumored, had been murdered by Levin's own hand during
fits of jealousy. Now, the very thought that Levin might be
interested in Giles's niece sent a chill streaking down Jean
Pierre's spine.

Etienne Broussard nudged Jean Pierre, asking again if he
would bid. With a disgusted sigh, Jean Pierre tossed down
his cards. ''Gentlemen, I fold.'' He paused to consult his
pocket watch. ''And if you'll excuse me, I think it's about
time I cut my losses for the evening. I do have a houseguest
waiting for me at home.'' As Levin raised a pale eyebrow,
Jean Pierre explained, ''My cousin Roland is in New Orleans
conducting business with his factor, Maurice Miro.''

''A pity you could not persuade Roland to come along this
evening,'' Giles Fremont commented as he tossed in his bid.

Jean Pierre smiled bitterly. "My cousin from St. Charles Parish informed me that he considers indulging in games of chance to be a slothful practice."

Amid shrugs and deprecating chuckles at Jean Pierre's remark, the bidding was concluded. Despite his urge to leave, Jean Pierre lingered over his whiskey, curious to see if his intuition regarding Broussard's dishonesty would prove true. Seconds later, Etienne's hoot of victory reinforced Jean Pierre's suspicions. Watching the surely cheating Creole gather up his winnings, Jean Pierre said with ill-disguised annoyance, "Gentlemen, I really must be going—"

"Nonsense!" Giles cut in to the younger man. "Don't be a sore sport simply because your luck is down, Delacroix. You must at least join us for some refreshments. Where is that blasted girl, anyway? Angelique!" he again shouted.

And even as Jean Pierre moved to take his leave, Angelique Fremont swept into the room, and the sight of the girl caused him to fall back in his chair.

Out in the butler's pantry at the back of the large home, Angelique Fremont and her uncle's servant, Coco, had been preparing a tray for the men.

Hearing her uncle's voice bellow out her name, seventeen-year-old Angelique frowned, her jaw tightening. Both she and Coco had slaved all afternoon in the oppressive stone kitchen at the back of Uncle Giles's property, preparing hors d'oeuvres for his guests to enjoy this evening. Considering how tricky the cooking had been, Giles Fremont's impatience was not presently appreciated by his niece.

"How does that look, Coco?" Angelique asked, turning to the young mulatress who'd been hovering nearby. Coco was fourteen, pretty and slim—and perpetually nervous as a cat.

"That be fine, mam'zelle," Coco replied, licking her full bottom lip as she studied the collection of finger-foods they had so diligently prepared—including crawfish balls, miniature oyster pies, and stuffed shrimp. "The smell alone makes my innards purr, mam'zelle. Maître Giles, he be pleased."

Angelique smiled back at the negress. "Now I just need to roll the *Bâtons de Noisettes* in sugar. Then I shall take the

tray in.'' Her delicate nostrils flaring in distaste, she added,
"My uncle mentioned wanting another bottle of whiskey.
Will you go to the cellar and fetch it, please, Coco?''

"*Oui*, mam'zelle,'' Coco replied, leaving the room.

Angelique sang to herself as she rolled the small cylindrical
cookies in confectioner's sugar. She heard her voice quiver
slightly on the poignant strains of *Ave Maria*—the sacred
selection so beloved by her parents. Angelique had tried her
best to maintain a cheerful facade ever since she'd come to
live with Uncle Giles in New Orleans, yet it had been so
hard, especially when she remembered her life in St. James,
and the mother and father she had loved so dearly.

Only three weeks past, Angelique had lived blissfully with
her parents on their small farm. Then tragedy had struck in
the perennial form of Yellow Fever—or Bronze John, as the
much-feared malady was called in the region. While Angelique looked on helplessly, both her parents had gone down
with the ailment—coughing, shaking, burning with delirium,
and finally succumbing to the black vomit that claimed the
fever's victims at the end. The hasty graveside service, held
mere hours after their passing, had been a nightmare for
Angelique. Yet her ordeal had just begun, for afterwards, it
was her lot to watch the sheriff burn all her parents' possessions. Even now, remembering how he had hurled her mother's cherished spinning wheel into the cruel conflagration,
Angelique felt tears burning her eyes, and crossed herself in
silent supplication.

And yet she had been raised to believe that death was but
the soul's triumphant entry into life everlasting. Thus she
knew she had no valid cause to mourn her parents' passing
—they were together now, and with God.

This Angelique accepted on a spiritual level. Yet emotionally, it was almost impossible for her to view her parents'
deaths as a victory—and it was far too soon for her to let
them go. Little more than a child herself, Angelique had been
plucked from her loving, nurturing environment in St. James,
then rudely deposited in a strange city, a strange new
home—and at the mercy of her new guardian. She'd never
even met Uncle Giles before he came to St. James to settle
her parents' estate. Now, she knew him to be a temperamental
man who did not abuse her, but who often spoke to her

sharply, drank too much, and gambled frequently. Used to a pious atmosphere, Angelique felt an alien here with her unrepentant uncle, in this purportedly wicked city. And she did not understand the destructive neglect she saw in Uncle Giles' home—the scars on the furniture and rugs, the careless tears and moth-holes on the drapes and coverlets. Back in St. James, her parents' every modest possession had been a treasure to be lovingly preserved.

Nevertheless, Angelique had tried her best to restore order to her uncle's shabby home, knowing that young Coco, as Uncle Giles's only household servant, had borne far too much for too long. As she and the mulatress worked, Angelique often sang to buck up her courage. Singing made her feel closer to her dear parents, and to her music teacher back home in St. James, Madame Santoni. In her occasional moments of despair, Angelique wished Uncle Giles had allowed her to stay on in St. James with Madame. Madame had offered Angelique a home; yet Angelique's uncle had brusquely declined.

"Angelique!"

As her uncle again yelled out her name, a fresh needle of resentment pricked Angelique. She stiffened her spine, dusted off her hands, and picked up the tray. While she did view self-righteousness as a sin, it nevertheless galled that her efforts were being consumed by those indulging in the devil's pastime. Thus, with head held high and shoulders squared, she walked down the narrow passageway from the pantry to the dining room.

At the door to the smoke-filled room, Angelique paused to gain her bearings, frowning at the haziness, the acrid odor of cigars. In front of her, with his back to his niece, sat Uncle Giles; the other three occupants of the table she hadn't met. Two were older men, one portly and the other thin. Yet Angelique's attention was seized by the third guest, a handsome young gentleman who sat directly across from her. The man looked to be still in his twenties—his squarish face was darkly handsome, sporting a trim mustache. Yet he looked unhappy, scowling over his whiskey.

She stepped into the room just as the younger man was getting to his feet—only to wonder why, when he spotted her, he looked stunned and fell back in his seat.

* * *

When Angelique stepped into the room, Jean Pierre could not believe his eyes. The loveliness of the girl literally knocked him back in his chair.

She was a vision, hauntingly beautiful—with the shiniest hair, the darkest eyes, the most perfect features he had ever seen! She was of medium height, her willowy girl's figure graced by the first bloom of womanhood. Her skin glowed with youthful freshness; her honeyed complexion was silky smooth. Her face was delicately etched, graced by high cheekbones, a finely boned nose, a generously lipped mouth, and a firm chin. Her hair was a thick riot of ebony curls, framing her exquisite face and the slender column of her throat. She wore a modest dress of dark broadcloth and bore a tray like a common serving girl—yet she would have looked equally at home in regal velvet, presenting gifts to the crowned heads of Europe.

She paused just inside the door, glancing at her uncle as if to await instructions. Then she turned to stare at Jean Pierre, her lovely dark eyes locking with his for an electric moment. He tried to smile back at her, but found he couldn't, for her look rooted him to the spot. In her eyes he saw anguish and need, and a deep, dark radiance such as he'd never seen before. He felt as if he'd just been seared by a massive flame. There was something so needy, so compelling, yet so pure and glorious in the girl's eyes—

"Well, Angelique, it's about time!"

Giles Fremont's voice, gritty and rude, intruded on Jean Pierre's hypnotic state, breaking the spell the girl had cast about him. He frowned, catching his breath as he watched her turn toward Giles, offering him the tray.

He realized his hands were trembling on the tabletop. *Mon Dieu*, the girl had slayed him! It had been so long since anything or anyone had touched him this way—

Her look alone had humbled him, had made him yearn— almost—to be redeemed.

CHAPTER
Two

"Don't just hand me the tray, girl!" Giles Fremont barked to his niece. "Can't you see that I have guests here who have long waited to be served?"

Jean Pierre felt a rush of sympathy for young Angelique as she glanced about the room with dark, proud eyes; even while Giles was chastising her, her bearing was regal. She stepped forward slowly, offering the tray to Etienne Broussard, and Jean Pierre's heart did a sickening lurch as he watched the merchant's prurient eyes rake over her. Yet while Etienne's gaze was clearly lecherous, Charles Levin's leer could only be called rapacious as he in turn sampled a delicacy from her tray, staring with bald hunger at the swell of her firm young breasts. With strenuous effort, Jean Pierre managed not to leap out of his chair and knock both men to the floor. He realized that his fists were tightly clenched, trembling, in his lap.

Mon Dieu, whence had this righteous wrath sprung up in him, a fierce protective anger he never knew himself capable of?

Then she moved gracefully to his side, offering him the sumptuous tray, and he saw her loveliness up close for the first time. Again, he breathed with an effort. Her eyes, dark and gleaming with tiny flames of radiance, were even more mesmerizing at close range. And nowhere was there a flaw on her skin, or the slightest imperfection to mar her classical beauty.

"*M'sieur?*" she asked shyly, obviously uneasy to have Jean Pierre staring at her so.

Her voice had a lilting quality as sweet as her singing, Jean

Pierre noted. Belatedly, he smiled at her, taking a small oyster pie from the tray. "Thank you, mam'zelle."

"Well, Fremont," Charles Levin was now saying to his host, "aren't you going to introduce us to this lovely young lady?"

Giles shrugged. "Gentlemen, meet my niece, Angelique Fremont," he said offhandedly. Then, catching Levin's menacing scowl, he added to the girl, "Angelique, meet Messieurs Levin, Delacroix, and Broussard."

"I am pleased to make your acquaintance, messieurs," Angelique said demurely, curtsying. Turning to Giles, she asked stiffly, "Uncle, may I go now?"

"Very well," Giles conceded ungraciously. Watching her deposit the tray of food on the table, he added, "But, pray tell, where is the bottle of whiskey I told you to fetch?"

"I sent Coco to the cellar for it," Angelique replied, tilting her chin slightly. "I'll bring it out directly."

Giles harrumphed as his niece swept out of the room. His bulging eyes swept briefly over her departing figure, then he turned, stuffing his mouth with a banana crepe.

"Your niece is quite lovely, Giles," Levin remarked, in a raspily greedy tone that made bile rise in Jean Pierre's throat.

Giles smiled, displaying his rotting teeth as well as oily bits of the crepe which clung to his thick lips. "Like I told you, Charles, not bad to look at, the girl is."

Levin slowly lit a thin cheroot, took a long drag and indolently blew out the smoke. His coldly calculating eyes narrowed on Giles. "What will you take for the girl, Fremont?"

While Giles merely chuckled and waved off the banker, Jean Pierre felt a sharp stab of alarm. Levin was extremely wealthy, and local gossip held that Giles Fremont's fortunes had shifted drastically in recent months due to his increasing addiction to cards and faro. Jean Pierre had an intuition that Levin's seemingly outrageous offer was deadly serious, and he didn't at all like the way things were shaping up for young Angelique Fremont.

"Hey, Delacroix, aren't you taking your leave?" the fat Broussard now taunted.

"I've decided to stay, after all," Jean Pierre replied, picking up his discarded cards from the last round and tossing them to Broussard. While the other three men laughed ribaldly at the younger man's sudden turnabout, Jean Pierre was not the least bit amused.

Momentarily, Angelique swept back into the room with a fresh bottle of whiskey. "Pour me a glassful, girl," Fremont ordered.

"Yes, Uncle Giles." Though Angelique's words were respectful, her young jaw was tightly clenched as she stepped forward, uncapped the bottle and poured her uncle half a glass. Bless her soul, Jean Pierre thought. The girl had obviously been devoutly raised, and now was forced to serve her uncle and his profligate friends like a common barmaid.

Giles Fremont downed his whiskey quickly, then bellowed, "More!"

Angelique calmly poured her uncle another glassful, set down the bottle, and turned to leave. Watching Etienne Broussard's lascivious gaze sweep over the girl, Jean Pierre snapped, "Well, Broussard—aren't you going to deal?"

Broussard shrugged and dealt the cards. In the hour that followed, the men imbibed freely, except for Jean Pierre, who nursed a single glass of whiskey and watched his companions carefully, with rising discomfort. All three, he observed, were becoming quite inebriated—their brightly flushed faces and loud, slurred speech attested to this. And every time young Angelique reappeared in the room—to clean an ashtray or bring more whiskey—the glances of Levin, Broussard, and even Giles himself became more wickedly lewd and insulting. Bawdy remarks invariably followed the girl's departure from the room, making Jean Pierre's blood boil.

Then, on Angelique's fourth visit to the room, the inevitable occurred. As she was leaving, Etienne Broussard reached out and pinched her on the behind.

Jean Pierre saw red. How dare Broussard insult this lovely child! Never in his life had he so vehemently wished that he were carrying a pistol.

Yet before he could react, young Angelique whirled about and slapped Etienne fully across the face. Charles Levin howled with laughter as the girl turned on her heel and swept proudly from the room. Jean Pierre grinned to himself, realizing that the girl was hardly a helpless *enfant*. He was tempted to shout out, "Bravo!" at her spirit, to commend her for giving Broussard exactly what he deserved! The fat commission merchant now sat trembling in outrage, an angry red hand-mark blooming across his pitted, fleshy cheek.

And in that moment, Jean Pierre was struck by another, almost irresistible thought: Wouldn't this slip of a girl be able to stand irascible old Cousin Roland on his ear?

Before Jean Pierre could really contemplate this fascinating idea, Etienne's furious words distracted him. "Giles!" the fat commission merchant barked. "I demand that your niece apologize to me for that affront."

At Broussard's gall, Jean Pierre tossed down his cards and turned on him. "You demand that the girl apologize to you? How dare you insist on reparation, when you're the one who insulted her!"

"How dare I?" Broussard roared back. "That so-called innocent little baggage was swinging her derriere at me, and then, when I gave her her just desserts, she had the gall to slap me."

Fuming, Jean Pierre turned to Fremont. "Giles, have you nothing to say in your niece's behalf? Will you let Broussard's cowardly lies stand?"

Fremont snorted in dismissal. "I agree with Broussard. The girl has insulted a guest of mine."

"Insulted?" Jean Pierre repeated disbelievingly. "Before your very eyes, Fremont, Broussard has just touched the girl in a place where no man touches a lady who is not his wife! And now you're agreeing that he's the injured party?"

Fremont shrugged, poured himself more whiskey and said with a slur in his voice, "I'm not convinced of the girl's so-called virtue in the first place—not considering what a little slut her mother was—"

"I can't believe I'm hearing this!" Jean Pierre cried, gesturing angrily. "You're saying these things about your very own niece—your own blood kin?"

"A fact that I'd just as soon forget," Giles gritted.

"I ask you again, Fremont—how much will you take for the girl?" Charles Levin interjected coolly from the sidelines, the ruthlessness in his voice setting Jean Pierre's teeth on edge.

"You can't have her, Charles," Etienne now countered nastily. "I want to buy her for myself. I'll teach that uppity little Cajun a lesson or two about proper decorum. The first thing I'll do is to take her over my knee and blister that sassy little behind of hers—"

"Forget it, Broussard," Levin cut in evenly. "You know I can outbid you." With a slow, sadistic smile, he added, "Besides, it's quite obvious that the girl needs a much firmer hand than yours. Such willfulness can be mastered with only the proper—shall we say—degree of ruthlessness? Therefore, I intend to see that the girl becomes my property—"

Jean Pierre shot to his feet. "I can't believe I'm hearing this! Gentlemen, we're not talking about some whore from Basin Street!" Whirling on Levin, he demanded, "You're actually trying to buy the girl, Charles?"

"I'd not be averse to making an arrangement in her behalf."

"So she'll end up floating in the canal like your other mistresses?"

Now Levin also stood, his features livid. "I should call you out for that bald-faced lie, Delacroix!"

"Gentlemen, gentleman, sit down!" Giles Fremont half-shouted. "I'll have no challenges issued in my home this evening!"

Glaring at each other, the two men resumed their seats.

"You know, I've been thinking," Giles went on, the gleam of avarice in his eyes betraying his satisfaction with the tension in the room, "that it might be quite difficult for me to give Angelique the advantages in life that I would like her to have. Perhaps, indeed, it might be best if one of you gentlemen should volunteer to become—her protector."

"For the best bid placed on the table?" Jean Pierre asked incredulously. "Where are your scruples, Fremont?"

"And why have you suddenly had this latent attack of morality, Delacroix?" Giles countered nastily. "You've had quite a number of mistresses yourself."

"True. But your niece is an innocent, not a member of the demimonde. We have no right to toy with her life this way."

"And what of her fate if no protector is found for her?" Giles argued. "The girl has no money, no dowry, and I've naught with which to endow her. What future is there for her, then? As a lady's maid? She'd be so much better off as companion to a fine man like Charles here."

Jean Pierre inwardly cringed at Giles calling Levin "a fine man." But taking his cue, Levin replied evenly, "Well-spoken, Fremont." He dragged lazily on his cheroot and added, "I'd like to open the bidding at ten thousand."

"Fifteen!" Broussard cut in angrily, slamming his pudgy fist down on the table as he glowered at the smugly smiling Levin.

And in that moment, something snapped in Jean Pierre. "Enough!" he cried, bolting to his feet. "Gentlemen, I will not stand idly by and let this foul deed be done. Something is lost in us if we are to do this thing to an innocent child." To Giles, he added, "Name your price for the girl."

At once, Broussard and Levin howled their protest. "You just want the girl for yourself, Delacroix—as your own mistress," Broussard accused.

"Wrong! The girl is not going to be anyone's mistress. She is, however, going to be someone's wife." Jean Pierre said the words before he even thought them—yet in making his statement, he realized its truth and saw a solution to the entire dilemma. With a pensive frown, he added, "The man just does not know it yet."

"Enough of this nonsense," Levin snapped to Giles, his casual shrug dismissing the younger man's attempt to circumvent him. "Whatever Delacroix bids for your niece, I'll double it."

"*Sacre bleu!*" Jean Pierre hissed savagely. He turned on Levin, placing his hand menacingly on the back of his chair. With a pitiless smile, he whispered, "Is the girl worth dying for, Charles?"

Levin smiled back with sadistic pleasure. "Are you threatening me, Jean Pierre?"

"Indeed."

"Are you aware that I've yet to lose a duel?"

"Are you aware that neither have I?" Before Charles could comment, Jean Pierre went on, "But even if I should lose this time, be aware that my cousin or my father would swiftly avenge me."

Charles Levin swallowed with an effort. He was a depraved

man, but not stupid, and had no desire to tangle with all three
Delacroix men, who were rumored to be excellent shots, the
lot of them. He shrugged. "Take the girl, then. This entire
affair is becoming an abysmal bore, anyway."

"I commend your wisdom, Charles." Jean Pierre turned
to Giles and repeated with contempt, "Name your price for
the girl."

Giles's grasping mind was humming. "Twenty-five thousand?" he asked, never expecting Jean Pierre to agree.

But the younger man did not bat an eyelash. "It is done."
From his breast pocket, he drew out the bank draft that he
carried for emergency purposes. "You have some writing
implement, I presume?" he inquired of Giles with distaste.

"Of course." Rubbing his hands together with greedy relish, Giles hurried from the room. Within seconds, he returned
and handed the pen and inkwell to Jean Pierre.

As Jean Pierre made out the draft at one end of the table,
Etienne Broussard leaned across the scarred mahogany and
whispered to Charles Levin, "If Jean Pierre's *mysterious*
bridegroom is lucky, the girl will become a wife and a mistress, *n'est-ce pas, mon ami*?"

Charles bit down on his cigar, scowled darkly and didn't
reply.

Jean Pierre tossed the still-wet bank draft at Giles, a vic-
torious gleam in his dark eyes. For the first time in hours,
he drew a comfortable breath—

And in that one moment, he felt redeemed.

CHAPTER
Three

As Jean Pierre's lamplit custom coach clattered toward
home along the stone streets of New Orleans, he sank back

against the richly grained leather upholstery and wondered at the transaction he had just so hastily made.

He'd bought a bride for his cousin Roland! Only, as he'd mentioned to the others, the man did not know it yet!

Had some madness seized him this summer evening? Jean Pierre shook his head and chuckled with self-deprecation. He'd never before thought of himself as a particularly moral man, yet tonight, when he'd realized how three miscreants were plotting to use lovely, innocent Angelique Fremont, some vestige of chivalry had arisen in him and had screamed out, *No, here you will draw the line. This you will not tolerate.* Jean Pierre had found that he simply could not stand idly by and watch the girl become the pawn of one of the two reprobates who had the audacity to bid on her tonight.

Thus, for the hefty sum of twenty-five thousand dollars, he had purchased for himself the right to become Angelique Fremont's protector and to arrange for her a suitable marriage. The money itself was largely meaningless to him, as his mother had left him quite well-endowed.

Early tomorrow morning, Giles would pack up his niece and bring her to meet Jean Pierre at the French market. There she would be handed over—as if she were, indeed, some commodity to be bought and claimed.

Of course, both Broussard and Levin had expressed intense curiosity regarding what "arrangements" Jean Pierre intended to make in the girl's behalf—but Jean Pierre had steadfastly refused to divulge the name of the man he intended for Angelique to marry. Recalling Broussard's snide, overheard remark to Levin, "If Jean Pierre's *mysterious* bridegroom is lucky, the girl will become a wife and a mistress . . .", Jean Pierre had to smile ruefully. The merchant's words had tantalized him to a degree, appealing to his baser instincts. The girl was stunningly beautiful, the fervor in her dark eyes hinting of a passionate nature. Listening to Broussard, Jean Pierre had been momentarily tempted to keep the girl for himself, to make her his own bride.

Yet soon sanity had returned, overruling his wayward senses. Jean Pierre was far too self-honest to subject Angelique Fremont to the dubious honor of becoming his wife. Should he marry the girl, he knew he'd *want* to be a good husband; yet he also realized that he would fail dismally. For he valued his cards, his liquor, and his philandering far too much to ever become the true and faithful mate the girl deserved.

No, somehow Roland must be convinced to marry the girl. It was the only solution. But how? And would the girl really be better off married to his mercurial cousin?

Scowling in the darkness, Jean Pierre gave this question considerable thought. He knew that Roland's first marriage had been disastrous—but then, Luisa had been a flighty creature who seemed to have only a tenuous grip on reality. Since Luisa's death, Roland had regularly sought his ease with a mistress, Caroline Bentley; and while he'd made clear to Jean Pierre that he wasn't in love with Caroline, he'd also remained faithful to the woman over the years.

So the man possessed the ability to be true to one woman, which would be a decided plus for Angelique's sake. But what really convinced Jean Pierre to proceed with his wild scheme was his feeling that what Roland really needed was a wife—the *right* wife this time. While often cantankerous as a mule, the man was also ambitious, hard-working, upstanding—just the type who needed a doting wife to warm his bed and several small children to bounce on his knee.

Only he did not know this as yet.

In time, Jean Pierre mused, young Angelique might even be able to improve Roland's fractious disposition. Of course, that would mean saddling a seventeen-year-old girl with the awesome responsibility of reforming a surly, arrogant, thirty-year-old man. Yet Jean Pierre already knew that the girl possessed mettle. Jean Pierre grinned as he remembered her slapping Broussard, her small, seemingly delicate hand raising a fat welt on the face of that pompous ass. Yes, she would stand up for herself, that one. The flash of spirit he had glimpsed in those dark eyes showed her to be a creature of strong will and stalwart conviction.

She would need every ounce of that will and conviction to contend with Roland.

Bless her heart—it was an underhanded thing he would be doing to this sweet, lost little angel. Yet any guilt Jean Pierre felt for plotting to hook Angelique up with Roland was quickly obliterated by the thought of the alternative the girl would face: becoming the mistress off one of the nefarious types at the card table tonight—of a man like himself, he thought.

No, the girl would be much better off in a respectable— if possibly tempestuous—marriage; and she might well have a few surprises in store for dear Cousin Roland.

Jean Pierre chuckled. Perversely, he welcomed the thought of young Angelique putting Roland through his paces; the girl was so beautiful and engaging, he was sure that in time, she'd have Roland clawing the ground just to kiss her lovely feet. The man could well use just such a humbling, Jean Pierre decided. And he knew that buried beneath Roland's cynical veneer, there was a goodness that he prayed the girl could, in time, bring to the surface. It was even possible that one day, Angelique would give him, Jean Pierre, the gift of a lifetime, returning to him the best friend he'd ever known—his cousin, Roland Delacroix.

Yes, getting the two of them together was the only answer. Yet the dilemma remained, how to get Roland to marry the girl?

He recalled the startling outrage that had arisen in him tonight when he had discovered how Giles Fremont was plotting to use Angelique. Wouldn't it be so much easier to raise such righteous wrath in Cousin Roland?

Jean Pierre lit a cheroot, the glow of the match illuminating his cynically amused expression. A deliciously wicked plot began to form itself in his mind . . .

CHAPTER
Four

Early the next morning, when Jean Pierre half-stumbled into the dining room of his stylish home on Prytania Street, unshaven, bleary-eyed, and still wearing his dressing gown, his cousin Roland was already dressed for the day, sipping his coffee at the Queen Anne table. He noted Jean Pierre's entrance with chilly displeasure.

Jean Pierre's home, which sat at the eastern edge of the American section, actually belonged to his father, Jacques Delacroix; but since the ebullient Jacques spent much of his time traveling Europe, his son had made the huge Greek Revival mansion his permanent residence. This morning, as he stood at the edge of the Aubusson rug just inside the portal to the lavishly furnished room, Jean Pierre looked decidedly unkempt in his elegant surroundings.

Roland raised an eyebrow at the slovenly younger man. "Well, cousin. A bit too much of Giles Fremont's whiskey last night?" he asked in his deep, intimidating voice.

Jean Pierre feigned a wince at Roland's less-than-gracious greeting. He studied his cousin for a moment. Roland Delacroix cut too fine a figure of a man to be such a hopeless cynic. He sat on the east side of the large table, the light from the window behind him glinting down on his thick, jet-black hair. He was a big man, well over six feet tall, with a strong, hard-muscled frame. His face was quite striking— long, well-sculpted, with a straight nose; firm, though sensually full mouth; and startlingly blue, compelling eyes, settled beneath handsomely curved brows. He wore his clothes with unconscious aplomb, and today his stylish black wool frock coat, crisply pleated linen shirt, and black cravat, added menace to his formidable visage.

"Well, haven't you anything to say for yourself, Jean Pierre?" Roland now continued.

Jean Pierre flashed Roland a sheepish grin as he ambled into the room. "You're right, Cousin. I did overindulge again last night."

Roland's reply was a self-righteous grunt as he raised his Sèvres china cup. Jean Pierre was moving closer to the table when a large, smiling black woman ambled into the room. "You ready for your breakfast now, Maître Jean?"

Jean Pierre grimaced at the servant's cheerfulness. "Please, Callie. Coffee alone will suffice."

"*Oui*, maître."

Callie left the room and Jean Pierre gingerly took his seat, sweeping a strand of disheveled hair from his brow. So far, his ruse was working, he noted with self-satisfaction. Roland was accepting that he was miserably hungover, even though he was actually feeling quite in his prime. It had been well worth the sharp sting of soap in his eyes moments earlier to help pull off this charade.

"So what are your plans for the day, Cousin?" Jean Pierre nonchalantly inquired.

Roland smiled ruefully and replied, "Don't worry, Jean Pierre, I'll not impose on your hospitality much longer. I shall conclude my business with Maurice Miro this morning, and then I plan to take him, Emily, and Phillip to luncheon in the Quarter before I catch the river packet home."

"I see," Jean Pierre replied. Jean Pierre knew that Emily Miro was Roland's former sister-in-law. Even though Emily had remarried since her husband's death, Roland maintained a protective interest in her and in his young nephew, Phillip.

Callie now lumbered back into the room with a tray. Jean Pierre nodded as the slave placed before him a steaming cup of coffee. He took a long sip of the strong, chickoried brew, then frowned. "If I may ask, what time are you meeting with Maurice?"

"Not until eleven," Roland replied, muttering his thanks to Callie as the black woman placed before him a breakfast of fat Cajun sausages and steaming coush-coush.

"Splendid, then," Jean Pierre remarked.

Roland's handsome brow tightened suspiciously as he raised his spoon. "Oh?"

Jean Pierre glanced at Roland lamely. "Cousin, I need you to do a favor for me this morning."

"Indeed?"

"Well, you can see that I'm in no shape to venture forth on the streets."

"Yes, I can see that," Roland said dryly.

Jean Pierre feigned a look of great distress. "The problem is, Cousin . . . Ah, there's no way to mince words here, I fear. It concerns a lady."

"A lady?"

"A woman, rather. My new mistress."

Roland snorted in disdain. "Your new mistress? I'd have thought you would have learned your lesson by now, after Emil Darcy practically called you out last year. Wasn't it a little quadroon from the Ramparts that the two of you were fighting over?'' Not giving the younger man a chance to reply, Roland continued scornfully,—''How many mistresses does that make, Cousin? Eight? Nine? I do believe I've lost count.''

Jean Pierre scowled. ''Roland, your sarcasm is of no benefit—''

''But of considerable satisfaction to me,'' Roland cut in with a nasty smile. Indolently, he leaned back in his chair. ''So tell me, Cousin—what quandary have you gotten yourself in concerning this—woman?''

Jean Pierre spoke intently. ''It's really quite a simple matter, Roland. I just need for someone to pick her up at the French Market at nine-thirty and bring her back here.''

Roland roared with derisive laughter. ''You're picking up your new mistress at the French Market—as if she were a slab of meat?''

Jean Pierre placed his hands on either side of his ostensibly exploding head. ''Please, Cousin,'' he whispered in a fiercely trembling tone. ''Your voice does carry quite well.''

''And the depths of your debauchery continue to astound me.'' Roland frowned darkly at the younger man. ''Why not forget this new heartthrob, cousin, and line up for yourself some meaningful endeavor for a change?''

Jean Pierre's hands fell to the table. ''Meaningful endeavor?''

''Yes. Go to work, man.''

''Work?'' Jean Pierre echoed woodenly.

''Work. Make yourself useful at one of the three banks your father owns—or at his cotton commission house—''

''But Roland, all of my father's business ventures are doing quite nicely without me—''

''That's not the point, man. It's the principle of the thing.''

''Principle?'' Jean Pierre repeated sinkingly.

Roland gestured his contempt. ''Far be it from me to attempt to discuss principles with a libertine such as yourself.''

''Roland, please,'' Jean Pierre pleaded. ''None of your moral lectures this morning, pray. My head is exploding, and—''

''And you want me to go pick up your new whore from the French Market,'' Roland gritted.

That barb scored. ''She's not a whore, Roland, she's—''

"Pray tell, what is she, then?"

Jean Pierre thought furiously. "She was—well, associated with Giles Fremont for a time—"

Roland leaned forward slightly, his lips twisted in an expression of sardonic amusement. "*That* reprobate?"

"I see you remember Giles from his New Year's party last year," Jean Pierre said dryly. "At any rate, I met the girl at Giles's gathering last night, and for the right sort of endowment, I persuaded Giles to—"

"You mean you bought Fremont's doxie for your own use?"

"Roland, enough!" Jean Pierre snapped. "I know you're quite disenchanted with me, but that gives you no call to attack this—er—young woman. What if I made such a remark about Caroline Bentley?"

"I'd kill you," Roland drawled with a frightening smile.

"Well, then?"

Roland sighed. "I concede your point. I'll make no more disparaging remarks about the—er—virtue of your new paramour."

"Thank you," Jean Pierre said stiffly. "Will you go fetch the girl from the market, then?"

Roland laughed cynically. "There I must draw the line."

"Roland, I beg you. If you don't go, the young woman will be stood up."

"And whose fault will that be?"

"Not the young lady's!"

Roland scowled, obviously brooding. At last, he asked, "Why did you not bring her home last night? Did Fremont desire her services one last time?"

Jean Pierre inwardly cringed. It *was* a horrifying thought. To Roland he chided, "I thought you promised to make no more derogatory remarks about this young woman's—"

"Very well, very well," Roland conceded wearily. "I'll go fetch the girl." He eyed Jean Pierre with distaste. "Now go back to bed, for pity's sake. You look wretched enough to make the young woman run away screaming for her sanity."

"Thank you, Roland," Jean Pierre replied. "As usual, your kindness is exceeded only by your tact."

* * *

While Roland was preparing to leave Jean Pierre's home for the French Market, Angelique Fremont stood in her small, modest bedroom at the back of her uncle's house on St. Charles Avenue. She'd already said her morning prayers and had breakfasted early in her room; now she stood half-dressed, a loose wrapper thrown over her undergarments. She was busy placing the last of her meager belongings in the worn portmanteau.

She recalled her Uncle Giles's strange, drunken words the night before. Right after his guests had departed, he'd taken Angelique aside. She shuddered as she recalled him leering over her.

"Girl, I've found out that I must leave on the morrow to conduct business in Mississippi," he'd told her, his odious breath scalding her face. "You'll be staying with friends of mine here in New Orleans while I'm away. Be packed and ready first thing in the morning. You can take Coco with you."

When Angelique had tried to question her uncle regarding these sudden and bizarre arrangements, he'd thrust her aside roughly. "Enough! I'll not listen to your whining tonight, girl!" he'd snapped, staggering for the stairs.

Angelique frowned at the memory. Uncle Giles was so often impatient with her, and when he drank, he became downright mean. She recalled how her father—God rest his soul—had once told her that he never touched alcohol because he feared a predilection toward its abuse ran in his family. Uncle Giles was certainly a victim of that malady; knowing this, Angelique tried to regard her uncle with Christian charity.

Yet it was hard not to feel some resentment toward him. After all, she'd been staying in his home for less than a fortnight, and now he was foisting her off on some other family! She sighed. Why had Uncle Giles brought her here, anyway, if he intended to shuttle her about like yesterday's newspapers?

She blinked at a tear. There had been so much change in her life in so little time. It seemed like only yesterday that she had been sitting at home serenely carding cotton or spin-

ning thread with her mother. How she missed her parents—
her father's kindness and wry humor, her mother's warm
smile, the sound of her singing in the kitchen or out in the
garden. Often, Angelique and her mother had sung together
as they did their chores.

Yet on her own she was, in a cruelly short period of time.
In a way, she was glad she would be staying with her uncle's
friends for a time, for sometimes, she caught Uncle Giles
looking at her in the most unsettling way. In those same
moments, he would treat her with an almost nauseating kindness, and his breathing, his voice, would grow labored, raspy.
Sometimes she feared he thought of himself as anything but
her uncle.

Angelique was wondering dismally what her future would
bring when a knock came at her door. Before she could even
answer, Giles Fremont stepped into the room, his clothing
rumpled, his features puffy from overindulgence the previous
night. Angelique whirled to face him, stunned that he would
burst in on her this way.

As Angelique blushed and tugged together the edges of her
thin wrapper, Giles caught an enticing eyeful of her—of lacy
bloomers and camisole, the creamy tops of lush young
breasts, and a figure as youthfully slim and provocative as a
boy's. Since the day he'd brought Angelique here, Giles had
toyed with the idea of bedding her—by seduction or by force,
whichever proved most expedient. The fact that it would be
incest did not deter him; but at the moment, his screaming
hangover did give him pause.

Yet what ultimately dissuaded Giles from sampling his
niece's charms was her buyer's warning the previous night.
Before he left, Jean Pierre Delacroix had taken Giles aside
and had gripped him by the cravat, just tight enough to con-
strict the air flow. As Giles coughed and sputtered with fear,
the Creole's eyes had been dark and pitiless above his. "The
girl is to be delivered—intact. It is understood, *mon ami*?"

It was understood. Giles had no desire to duel with hotheaded young Delacroix beneath the Oaks. Besides, Jean
Pierre's hefty bank draft was worth far more than a roll with
even the most winsome *demoiselle*. Giles had known when
he brought Angelique here that, sooner or later, he'd find a
way to profit by the girl. And he had done so—quite hand-

somely. Now Delacroix could bed her—for, despite Jean Pierre's noble words about finding Angelique a husband, Giles was certain that the young Creole intended to seduce the girl at first opportunity.

"Uncle Giles!" his niece now stammered.

"Are you ready to leave, my dear?" he asked, eyeing her baldly.

Angelique trembled as she held her wrapper tightly about her. "Uncle Giles, I—"

"There, there, my dear—there's no need for modesty between us," Giles went on huskily, stepping closer and continuing to study her brazenly. "We're blood relations, are we not, my child?"

Angelique felt her heart hammer as Giles edged even closer, the vile smell of his breath, his pungent body odor, wafting over her. "Uncle Giles, please, if you would but give me a moment, I promise I'll be ready."

He smiled, his gaze slipping down her body a less than discreet amount. Slowly, he placed his pudgy fingers on her shoulder, and she fought the urge to cringe from him, knowing that would only infuriate him. His bulbous eyes moved upward, raking her face. "A pity we have to be parted, my dear."

"Uncle Giles, please—I must dress!" Angelique could hear the shrill note of pleading that had crept, unbidden, into her voice.

Reluctantly, Giles backed away. "Very well. But mind you, we'll be leaving within a quarter hour. Wear something feminine and frilly, will you, my dear?" Licking his thick lips, he added, "You're a pretty little thing, you know."

After giving his niece a final once-over, Giles turned and left the room. Angelique drew a sharp, painful breath, rubbing the shoulder her uncle had gripped. She realized that his presence had unnerved her so, she'd forgotten to ask him the identity of the friends she'd be staying with.

CHAPTER
Five

Sunshine sprinkled the Vieux Carre, splattering the shiny black carriage and handsome dappled gray team clattering through the busy streets. Roland Delacroix sank back in the plush interior of his cousin's coach and drank in the passing sights and sounds.

Roland had always enjoyed the closed-in, intimate feel of the New Orleans French Quarter. Though it was just after nine, the streets were already teeming with businessmen, shoppers, and vendors; colorfully dressed black women with baskets on their heads strolled the *banquettes*, calling out to tempt passersby with their pralines, calas, fruits, or vegetables. The air was warm and humid, redolent with a dozen eclectic smells—the nectar of lush flowers spilling from every patio, the smells of hot bread and spicy Creole cooking drifting out from the numerous bakeries and restaurants.

Tall buildings loomed on either side of the street, the brick and stuccoed structures painted mouth-watering shades of pale pink, yellow, or green, adorned by lush flower boxes and iron-lace balconies. As Roland glanced upward, a woman with decidedly dyed red hair opened her window and summarily threw her morning's wash water out on the street.

He smiled to himself grimly, the woman reminding him of his mission this morning. He must have taken leave of his senses to go along with Jean Pierre's mad request that he go to the French Market and fetch home his cousin's new mistress. It was for the young woman's sake, and not Jean Pierre's, that he'd ultimately acquiesced. However questionable the girl's virtue might be, it would have been unpardonably rude to leave her stranded in the market.

Perhaps, too, he was being a bit too hard on his cousin,

he mused. Yet Roland very much feared that Jean Pierre was following the same path of destruction that Roland's older brother, Justin, had chosen. Justin had drunk, gambled, womanized, until the tragic carriage accident claimed his life—and broke the hearts of the innocent wife and son he'd left behind. If only his brother had been sober that one, critical night . . . Roland drew a heavy breath. At least Justin's widow, Emily, had later found true happiness with the honorable Maurice Miro. Roland was looking forward to seeing Maurice, Emily, and young Phillip later this morning.

Roland heard the distant clanging of a steamboat bell coming from the direction of the levee as they swept past the Place d'Armes, which was dominated by the stately St. Louis Cathedral, its tall spires dotted with pigeons. They proceeded down Decateur Street and on into the French Market. A moment later, Roland alighted to a new and dazzling assault on his senses.

Stretching beyond him was a vast, noisy sea of humanity and industry. Everything from rugs and boots to plucked chickens and raw fish hung from the eaves of the stalls. Vendors hawked their wares to the strolling crowd of shoppers—their grating voices raised in several languages. Indians displayed their colorful blankets, while boatmen exhibited exotic caged birds whose squawking added to the general cacophony. An organ grinder's monkey dashed about begging for coins. The air was thick with the mixed smells of fish, fresh fruits and vegetables, coffee, and hot *beignets*.

Glancing about the teeming area, Roland wondered how he would ever locate Giles Fremont—or the young woman who was the object of this adventure—amid the confusion. He needn't have worried, however; for even now he spotted an open barouche coming toward him from the south end of the market. At the front of the carriage sat the driver and a mulatto girl; behind them were seated Giles Fremont and the young woman who was evidently Jean Pierre's new mistress.

The sight of the girl hit Roland like a blow to the midsection, and an eerie silence filled his ears. All the frantic activity around him seemed to recede, and his gaze became riveted upon the approaching carriage. The girl—and, indeed, she was little more than a girl—was exquisite. Dressed all in lacy white, she had a lovely, oval face, dark, dramatic eyes, and lush black hair; an eyelet bonnet graced her head and a dainty parasol was clutched in one delicate, gloved hand. Her bearing was proud, almost regal, and Roland's senses swam with her beauty. As the carriage moved closer, a beam of light shone down on her face, only intensifying the radiance and innocent youthfulness he saw there.

At last Roland remembered to breathe; oxygen stabbed his lungs with painful intensity, and his awe was immediately replaced by rage. So *this* was Jean Pierre's new mistress? Why, this girl was little more than a child, young and lovely beyond words! Clearly, she was no courtesan! Everything about her screamed out that she was an untried innocent. And the very thought of his libertine cousin taking this girl's virtue and then setting her up as his paramour filled Roland with a terrible anger.

And if what Jean Pierre said were true, then Giles Fremont himself may have already abused the girl! That thought was truly unconscionable!

Even as Roland struggled to contain his burgeoning outrage, a grizzled black man approached him with a tray of candied fruits. "What will you have, maître?"

Just to be rid of the man, Roland tossed a coin onto his tray. "I'll take her," he muttered under his breath.

Roland tossed his stovepipe hat to Jean Pierre's astonished coachman. Before the approaching carriage could even halt, he was striding purposefully toward it. "Fremont! Giles Fremont! I'll have a word with you!"

Giles Fremont hastily ordered his driver to halt their conveyance not far from the Delacroix coach. He stared at the approaching, oddly familiar stranger with trepidation. The man was tall, muscular, and moving toward him with lethal menace; he had doffed his hat, almost as if he were expecting an altercation. "Er—good morning, m'sieur," Giles stammered. "I don't believe I've had the pleasure of—"

"Roland Delacroix, cousin to Jean Pierre," Roland snapped, scowling as he came to stand by the side of the carriage. He peered inside, looking past Fremont at the young woman in white. Damn, but she was dazzling, her eyes bright and large, her nose delicately formed, her cheeks rosy and her mouth full and pink, with a heart-shaped indentation on top. She was staring at him with a mixture of curiosity and caution, and when her eyes locked boldly with his, a feeling at once electric and enervating slammed his being. *Mon Dieu*, those eyes—those bright, flaming, radiant eyes . . . Who *was* she, this dark, proud beauty? "Good morning, mam'zelle," he managed to say.

The girl nodded but did not reply. Roland turned back to Giles. "We met at your party last New Years, Fremont, although I'll wager you don't remember the occasion."

Giles colored, extracting a handkerchief to mop his brow. "I—well, it's good to see you again, M'sieur Delacroix."

"Indeed," Roland muttered sarcastically.

"If I may ask, what are you doing—"

"I'm here in my cousin's behalf this morning."

Now Fremont looked extremely flustered, a muscle twitching in his flabby cheek. "Oh, you are? Well, I suppose then we'd best—"

"Have a word in private," Roland drawled. He nodded politely to the young woman. "If you'll excuse us, mam'zelle?"

Saying the words to Angelique, Roland grabbed Giles by the sleeve and half-dragged his dissipated bulk out of the carriage. Pulling the confused man behind a nearby fish stand, Roland nodded toward the barouche in the distance and demanded, "Who is the girl?"

Staring up at Roland Delacroix's pitilessly cold eyes, Giles stammered back, "Why, er—she's my niece—"

"Your niece?" Roland roared. Fury welled in him at Fremont's depravity—especially considering that Jean Pierre was a party to it. "You mean you've sold your very own flesh and blood into whoredom? To my cousin?"

Sweating profusely, Fremont replied, "Please, m'sieur, that's not what really hap—"

"How much did Jean Pierre pay you for her?" Roland demanded.

"M'sieur, you don't understand—"

"How much, damn you!"

"I—er—twenty-five thousand dollars."

"Twenty-five thousand!" Roland hissed back incredulously. "To make an innocent child his concubine?"

Giles became seized by a terrible trembling. "No, m'sieur I assure you that Jean Pierre said he would—"

"Spare me the revolting details of what Jean Pierre said he would do! I can't believe my cousin has sunk himself to these depths! How old is the girl, anyway?"

"Seventeen."

"Seventeen?" Roland repeated, his voice like a snap of thunder. "And my cousin bought her? And you sold her? How did the child come to be in your custody anyway, you miserable miscreant?"

"I—er—her parents died of the fever a month ago—"

"And this is how you perform your familial responsibility?"

"M'sieur, please!" Giles begged pitifully. "I really thought that your cousin had the girl's best interest at heart—"

Roland's hands grabbed the other man's lapels. "Don't insult me by lying, you wretched coward!"

Giles croaked, "I—er—well, I—"

"What does the girl know of her fate?" Roland continued aggressively.

"Sir, please, could you loosen your hold on me?"

With a snort of contempt, Roland released Giles, and the other man tottered, gasping for his breath. With commendable haste, he explained, "Angelique knows nothing, m'sieur, except that she'll be staying with some friends of mine while I'm gone in Mississippi."

"Angelique." Roland's voice had softened perceptibly. "That is the girl's name?"

"*Oui*, m'sieur. Angelique Fremont."

Roland's blue eyes narrowed with anger. "And you would barter away this young angel to the devil himself?"

"Please, m'sieur. As I tried to tell you, I thought Jean Pierre intended—"

"Spare me further lies, and pray hush before you exhaust my patience." Roland's scowl deepened. "I must have a moment to think here."

"Certainly, sir."

While Fremont stood wringing his hands, Roland turned away for a moment, breathing hard, running a hand through his hair and trying to arrange his disordered thoughts. Jean Pierre had really done it this time—buying a virtual child as his mistress! Roland knew he could extricate himself—and his cousin—from this dilemma quickly and simply enough, by sending Giles Fremont and his niece on their way. Yet he didn't trust Fremont; if the scoundrel sold his niece to Jean Pierre, what was to keep him from turning around and selling the girl to the next convenient bidder?

Or bedding the girl himself—if he hadn't already?

This last thought incited such rancor in Roland, he could hear the grinding of his own teeth. He glanced over at the barouche, where the girl sat primly, her eyes focused straight ahead. Seeing again her sweet face, the beauty and soul reflected there, Roland found that these revolting possibilities he simply could not accept. And dash it all, he felt a responsibility to set things right following his cousin's reprehensible act.

At last he turned to Giles and said, "Please tell your niece that there has been a change of plans."

"Oh?"

"Yes. Tell her that she won't be going with your *friends* now, but that the two of you have been invited to their house tonight for dinner." Absorbing Giles's muddled stare, Roland went on, "You and your niece will then come to Jean Pierre's house tonight at seven. This will give me and my illustrious cousin some time to figure out how to extricate all of us from this madness."

"As you wish, m'sieur," Giles said with a heavy sigh, only too glad to be granted a reprieve.

"And don't you dare cross me and not appear," Roland went on.

"Oh, I should not dream of it, m'sieur."

"Good, because if you should . . . Or if you should harm the girl in the meantime . . ." Roland's eyes were mercilessly cold as he took a menacing step toward Giles. "Have you touched her, Fremont?"

Giles had paled to the color of parchment. "M'sieur, I'm sure I don't know what you mean—"

"You know damn well what I mean, you slimy weasel! Have you bedded her?"

Giles looked as miserable as a worm on a hook. "But— m'sieur, she's my niece!"

"Indeed—a fact not likely to deter a reprobate such as yourself," Roland gritted. "Tell me the truth, damn it."

"No—no of course I haven't touched her!" Giles stammered, shaking his head vigorously. "Jean Pierre insisted that—I—we—"

"That you what?"

Giles lowered his gaze. "That I deliver the girl intact."

Roland harrumphed. "Then it seems that you possess a shred of common sense after all. And see that you retain that atom of intelligence until this evening."

"*Certainement*, m'sieur."

As Giles turned to hastily take his leave, Roland called out after him, "Seven o'clock. Mind you, don't be late."

Fremont pivoted to nod stiffly at Roland, then hurried off to the carriage. "Slimy bastard," Roland muttered under his breath. He watched Fremont clamber into the barouche. The man said something to his niece, then she again turned to stare at Roland. A second time, the look in her eyes slammed him right in the gut.

After Fremont's conveyance rattled away from Roland, he started back for his own carriage. He glanced down at his hands, clenched at his sides, and realized he was trembling.

He wondered at the purposeful rage that had consumed him in Angelique Fremont's behalf. One look at her had turned him into a vengeful fanatic. He knew his feelings regarding the girl went deeper than just his desire to right Jean Pierre's wrong—although this was a transgression that he'd see to it Jean Pierre paid for dearly. Jacques, Jean Pierre's father, had indulged the boy shamelessly all his life, and now Roland intended to see that his profligate cousin faced up to the responsibilities of his manhood.

Yet Roland knew the girl had also touched him. For years, he'd been cut off from life, and nothing had affected him—until this morning, when he saw that lovely wisp of a girl and realized how two reprobates were plotting to use her—

Her look alone had practically torn his guts to ribbons. Her eyes had roused in him emotions that had been dead for years, and feelings that, perhaps, he'd never quite felt, not on this level.

Passion. She'd made him feel true passion such as he'd never known before: rage, protectiveness, and a need flame-deep and searing. He realized he hadn't even heard her speak. Yet already, he knew she had the voice of an angel.

* * *

As Giles's carriage rattled back toward the Garden District, Angelique stared confusedly at her flustered uncle. The scene at the market had been nothing like she'd been told to expect. "Uncle Giles, who was that man back there?"

"A member of the family you'll be staying with," he said tersely.

"But, then, why didn't I leave with him?"

"There has been a change of plans," he snapped. "We'll be joining the Delacroix tonight for dinner."

"The Delacroix?"

"That's the name of the family you'll be staying with."

"But—"

"Enough of your chattering, girl!"

Angelique sighed, knowing it was useless to try to prod her uncle further. Yet the entire incident still bemused her. Who was the strange, handsome man back at the market? He'd radiated a power and menace that both frightened and fascinated her. And what of his family? Surely he had a wife and possibly children, else her staying with him would be unutterably scandalous!

Why had the stranger dragged her uncle off behind a shed? And why had he looked at her uncle with such violence in his eyes—and at her with such unnerving intensity? Even now, remembering those bright eyes raking over her, she couldn't repress a shiver.

CHAPTER
Six

Later that morning, Jean Pierre was sitting in his spacious parlor drinking coffee. He was impeccably dressed and shaven, and looked much more at home among the stylish rosewood furnishings, the fabulous rugs, and *objets d'art*.

Setting aside his cup and saucer, he stood and wandered over to the window, drawing aside the Brussels lace panel and inhaling the aroma of honeysuckle and jasmine exuding from the lush, blooming garden. Imagining the shock Roland must have felt when he arrived at the French Market and saw young Angelique, he chuckled aloud and was feeling quite self-satisfied—

Until Roland stormed into the room and knocked him on his heels.

It happened in the twinkling of an eye. Hearing footsteps behind him, Jean Pierre turned to see Roland striding purposefully into the room. Stepping forward eagerly, Jean Pierre said, "Why, Cousin, I hadn't expect you to return so—"

And the next thing Jean Pierre knew, he was lying flat on his back, blinking to clear his senses and rubbing a jaw that felt split in two—no doubt, by the force of Roland's fist.

"Get up, you miserable scum!" Roland hissed. Standing over Jean Pierre, he looked a terrible force to contend with.

"Cousin, I—"

"Get up!"

With commendable haste, Jean Pierre struggled to his feet.

Roland began to pace angrily. "You've really done it this time, Cousin! I knew you led a depraved lifestyle, but this —this!" He finished with a furious gesture.

"This?" Jean Pierre repeated weakly, each syllable he uttered bringing terrible pain to his throbbing jaw.

"This time you've gone entirely too far!" Roland raved. "Why this is little more than child molestation."

"Child molestation?"

"The girl!"

"Girl?"

"Giles Fremont's niece! Angelique! The one you bought to force into your bed!"

"Oh. That girl." Carefully, Jean Pierre asked, "You went to the market then, Cousin?"

Roland glared at the younger man. "Yes, damn it, I went to the market."

"And you didn't bring the girl back?"

"Of course I didn't bring the girl back! Does one cast a lamb to a hungry wolf?" He stepped forward aggressively. "Why did you tell me the girl was Giles Fremont's mistress, when actually she is his niece? And has the man molested her?''

"Well, no, not as far as I—"

"Then why did you lie?"

"Well, actually, Roland, I never said the girl was Giles's mistress—only that she was associated with him. And frankly, I did need your cooperation this morning—"

"So you resorted to misleading me?"

"Roland, please, this is an unusual situation—"

Roland harrumphed loudly. "Pray explain this *unusual situation*."

"Roland, could we sit?" Jean Pierre pleaded. "That's quite a nasty chop on the jaw you just inflicted, and—"

"I should have broken you in two," Roland snarled.

"Perhaps so." Jean Pierre smiled ironically, only to grimace at the pain. "But if you want an explanation, Cousin, you'll have to let me live long enough to answer your questions."

"Pray, sit, then," Roland drawled with elaborate courtesy.

The two men seated themselves in wing chairs flanking a tea table. Jean Pierre fought an urge to shudder as he stared at his cousin. Roland's arms were akimbo, his face set in rigid lines, his blue eyes blazing. Jean Pierre realized he'd gotten precisely the reaction he'd wanted from Roland—in spades, as his own jaw could well testify. Now he'd best proceed cautiously, choose every word with care . . . Tell the truth but not *really* tell the truth.

"Well?" Roland snapped.

Jean Pierre feigned a sigh. "Roland, last night when I was playing cards at Giles Fremont's, we were served by his niece, Angelique, who had lately come to live with him from St. James. It seems the girl is from an humble upbringing, and recently lost her parents to the fever. All her family's possessions were burned, and the sale of their farm barely covered their debts. Now the girl is dependent on Giles for support."

"My sympathies to the young lady—on all counts. Go on, pray."

"Well, Charles Levin and Etienne Broussard were also in attendance. At one point, Etienne dared to—er—pinch the girl—"

"The brute!"

"Indeed, Cousin. Anyway, the young woman slapped his face—"

"As she well should have!"

"I agree, of course. But Broussard became indignant; then, one thing led to another, and before I knew what was happening, Broussard and Levin were bidding against each other to take the girl off Fremont's hands."

"The miscreants!"

"My thinking exactly, Cousin. I decided my only recourse was—"

"Out with it, man!"

"To outbid them."

Roland sprang to his feet. "So you saved the girl from a fate worse than death by buying her as your own personal— concubine?"

Jean Pierre winced. "Roland, please. I wasn't planning to make the girl my mistress right off. I'd thought of sending her to finishing school first."

"We both know exactly what you'd do with her—*first*."

Jean Pierre ground his teeth. While he was actually outraged by Roland's suggestion, he knew his role here was critical. He forced himself to grin ruefully and said, "Doubtless you're right, Cousin."

As Roland took a menacing step toward Jean Pierre, the younger man held up a hand. "Roland, please. We'll not solve this problem through more physical violence. I'm willing to listen to reason, but we must discuss this calmly. Pray, be seated and I'll pour you some coffee."

"No thanks." Nevertheless, Roland grudgingly sat down, grimly watching his cousin pick up his own coffee cup.

Jean Pierre continued tactfully, "So you see, Roland, I did have the girl's best interest in mind last night when I—er— bought her, albeit I assisted her in a roundabout way. I didn't go to Giles Fremont's house looking for a mistress. But what was I to do, man? Giles was obviously intent on selling the girl to the highest bidder, and I couldn't let her become the helpless victim of a man like Charles Levin. You know the man has a reputation as a sadist—"

"I'd kill him if he touched a hair on her head," Roland drawled, shocking Jean Pierre with his vehemence.

"I take it you were impressed by the young lady, then?" Jean Pierre asked.

"I was impressed that she's young and guileless, definitely not mistress material for any man."

"Yes, and she struck me exactly the same way, Roland," Jean Pierre said, leaning forward intently. "That's precisely why I—"

"Bought her?" Roland supplied with a nasty smile.

Jean Pierre glared at Roland. "What can I say? You're obviously determined not to believe me. I would think we might be able to put aside our antagonism for once and think of a solution to this dilemma."

"Now that's the first thing you've said all day that makes any sense," Roland put in dryly.

"Very well then, Roland. Pray make some suggestion regarding Mam'zelle Fremont's welfare. And, by the way, where is she if you decided not to bring her here?"

"I told Fremont to bring her to the house tonight for dinner. That way, we'll have some time to solve this riddle."

"Good thinking, Cousin. So—what do you suggest?"

Roland was obviously already lost in thought regarding their quandary. "I don't trust Fremont," he remarked after a moment, stroking his jaw.

"Neither do I, of course," Jean Pierre concurred. "That's another reason I—"

"Bought the girl."

Jean Pierre was silent, grimly sipping his coffee as he struggled to hang on to his patience.

Leaning forward and lacing his fingers together, Roland said, "The girl should not be anyone's mistress."

Here Jean Pierre wisely nodded. "I agree, Cousin."

"And she won't be safe from that lecherous uncle of hers until she's someone's wife."

"Again, I concur."

Straightening, Roland announced forcefully, "You'll simply have to marry the girl, Jean Pierre."

Jean Pierre choked on his coffee. After he'd recovered sufficiently to speak, he sat down his cup and sputtered, "Pray, see reason, Cousin. Do you really think I'd make a suitable husband for the girl?"

Roland glowered at the younger man for a moment, then laughed cynically. "I see your point. But how else can we protect the girl from Giles Fremont?"

Jean Pierre raised an eyebrow and shook his head, but wisely made no comment.

With a frustrated groan, Roland drew out his pocket watch. "Dash it all, I'm already late for my appointment with Maurice Miro." He stood. "I'll not be back until midafternoon. In the meantime, pray think, Cousin."

Jean Pierre smiled to himself as Roland strode out of the room. The man did not know it yet, but he was clearly hooked.

And Jean Pierre's problem was solved.

Waiters bearing trays heaped with steaming Creole dishes moved fluidly across the stone floors at Antoine's, and the aromas of fish, spicy sauces and hot bread filled the air, along with the half-English, half-French chatter of the customers, the clinking of glasses and utensils.

Roland and the Maurice Miros sat at a linen draped corner table near a sunny window; young Phillip shared a special treat of white wine with the adults as all sampled succulent snails *bourguignon*.

"So, Roland, did you and Maurice get all your business concluded this morning?" Emily asked.

Setting down his wineglass, Roland smiled at his former sister-in-law. Emily Miro was a lovely woman of thirty, tall and slim, with slightly angular features. Her copper-colored hair was heaped into a bun at the back of her head, with a few curls arranged in ringlets about her face. "Yes, Maurice was eminently helpful this morning," he answered her. "It looks like our hogsheads of sugar from Belle Elise will be fetching a good price this season."

"You should stay longer, Roland," Maurice now put in. He was a wiry Creole with a prominent nose, dark, intelligent eyes, and thinning black hair. "You're too much with the business, and then its pouf!—you're off without spending any real time with family here."

Roland chuckled at Maurice's dramatics. For years, the astute Creole had been not only his trusted factor but also a dear friend. Maurice had married Emily a year after Justin's death, and to Roland's immense satisfaction, the marriage had proved an excellent match.

"Well, actually, I had thought of staying on a few days longer," Roland replied to Maurice. Again he found himself thinking of the stunning girl he'd seen at the market this morning.

"Good!" young Phillip chimed in to his uncle. "Now you can take me to the park to launch my new boat, can't you, Uncle Roland?"

"Now Phillip," Emily scolded. "You mustn't impose on Uncle Roland's time too much."

"Not at all," Roland insisted. He grinned at the lad, reaching out to ruffle his hair. To Emily, he added, "After all, I gave your son the boat. So it will be my pleasure to help him launch it."

"I can't wait!" Phillip cried, and Roland felt a tightening in his chest as the boy smiled at him so winsomely. Black-haired and blue-eyed, the eleven-year-old was the very image of Justin.

"So you will be staying on for a time, then, Roland?" Emily pursued.

"Yes, I think I shall," Roland replied, surprising even himself.

"Good!" she replied. Smiling in a flash of pretty dimples, she winked at him and added, "Now I can introduce you to that young lady I've been dying for you to meet for so long—Georgette Dupree."

At this, Maurice laughed and reached out to take Emily's hand. "Emily, *ma petite*, you should know by now that trying to fix up Roland with one of your most eligible young lady friends is pointless."

"Yes, Maman, quick matchmaking," Phillip chimed in.

"It's quite clear that romance is the farthest thing from Roland's mind," Maurice added with rueful humor.

"Oh, you two!" Emily scolded, feigning a pouting look to both husband and son.

Staring at the three of them, listening to their playful banter, Roland found that for the first time, he felt rather jealous of the happiness of this close-knit little family. Again, irresistibly, his thoughts strayed back to young Angelique. He glanced at Phillip and wondered what kind of child he and the girl would have together.

Mon Dieu, had he lost his mind? He was reacting like a lovesick lad, after seeing the girl only once. He must resist this madness of the senses—why she was almost young enough to be his daughter.

Still, he couldn't resist imagining what it would be like to have the young beauty share his life, his bed, to look into those passionate brown eyes and . . . He shook his head ruefully. For all that he'd railed out at Jean Pierre and Giles in sanctimonious fury, was he really any better than the others? Didn't they all, ultimately, want to do the same thing with her? And this the very instant they laid eyes on her?

He scowled. There, perhaps, he was being too hard on himself. For as he and Jean Pierre had agreed, it mattered very much how things were to be done in young Angelique Fremont's behalf. Should the girl be forced into the sinful life of the demimonde, her future would be ruined.

Yet, on the other hand, men had been marrying women from time immemorial, and taking them to bed. Women, after shedding a few initial tears, had reacted admirably. He realized that under the sanctity of marriage, everything he could possibly want from young Angelique Fremont would be right, proper, and only his due—

The thought was such a revelation to him, his hand trembled on his wineglass . . .

Belatedly, Roland realized that all three of the Miros were staring at him with an air of expectation. Tightening his hand on his glass and lifting the goblet to his lips, he murmured, "Oh, I would not presume that romance is that far from my mind."

Now all three Miros stared at Roland with intense curiosity.

Later, at Jean Pierre's house on St. Charles Avenue, Roland barged in on his cousin in his study. "I'll marry the girl," he said tersely. "I'll send her to finishing school and later on we can get an annulment or . . . At any rate, the matter is settled."

"I see," Jean Pierre muttered, looking stunned as he stood

at his desk. "But have you considered, Cousin, that in order to marry the girl, you'll have to secure her cooperation?"

"We'll secure it," Roland said with a grim smile. "We just have to approach her in the right way . . ."

"Indeed?"

"Indeed. I already have a plan. But first . . ."

"Yes?"

Roland fixed Jean Pierre with his chilliest stare. "I want to make it clear that I'll be reimbursing you every penny you spent to force that innocent child into whoredom."

Jean Pierre bristled inwardly. While he'd had no intention of asking Roland to reimburse him the money he'd spent to rescue Angelique, he was also rapidly tiring of his cousin's insufferable insults. Let Roland repay the money, then—it served the sanctimonious braggart right.

Jean Pierre bowed with exaggerated grace and said, "As you wish, Cousin. Now—what is your plan?"

CHAPTER
Seven

That evening, Roland found himself feeling unusually tense and expectant as he dressed for dinner in his bedroom at Jean Pierre's house. He and his cousin had formulated their plan, but Roland knew that the next few hours, when Giles Fremont and Angelique would be present for dinner, were critical.

Roland mulled over his earlier discussion with Jean Pierre. He'd suggested to the younger man that they tell Angelique that when she was still a child, her parents had arranged with Roland's family for the two of them to wed later on. Since Angelique's parents had died before she'd reached adulthood, they'd simply never told her about the *contrat de mariage*.

After Roland had made his suggestion, Jean Pierre had

balked. "What of your first wife, Luisa? Your parents arranged for you to marry her, as you'll recall. Are you going to try to convince this young woman that your family arranged two marriages in your behalf?"

But Roland had held his ground. "Luisa has been dead for seven years. The match with Angelique could have been arranged by my father sometime thereafter. Besides, I see no reason at this point to even burden Mam'zelle Fremont with the knowledge of my first disastrous marriage."

Jean Pierre had looked stunned. "You're not even going to tell her about Luisa?" When Roland had merely shrugged, Jean Pierre had implored, "Roland, do you really think you should attempt to enter into this marriage under such a large-scale deception? Your plan is quite clearly flawed and could easily backfire should Mam'zelle Fremont doubt—"

"Under the circumstances, we'll simply have to take the risk," Roland had cut in. "And I think you'll agree with me that deceiving Mam'zelle Fremont is far preferable to her learning the truth about her uncle—and his planned fate for her."

Jean Pierre had nodded resignedly. "You do have a point there, Roland. By the saints, you're really taken with this girl, aren't you?"

Though Roland hadn't answered his cousin, he privately knew that he was, indeed, quite taken by lovely young Miss Fremont. Since the moment when he'd first seen her at the market, she had consumed his thoughts. Her innocence appealed to him on a very elemental level, as if he could reach out, jaded cynic that he was, and drink of her purity, finding renewal there.

A ripple of excitement coursed through him. He would try to be a good husband to her; hell, if she proved to be biddable, he'd give up his mistress for her. Caroline had kept him satisfied sexually for some years now. Yet his instincts told him that what he could have with Angelique went far beyond satisfaction to something very powerful.

While Roland was dressing, Giles Fremont's carriage was clattering through the Garden District in the balmy dimness. The air was thick with the scent of moist vegetation, the sweetness of honeysuckle. The top of the barouche was raised, with Giles, Angelique, and Coco squeezed onto the single seat in the passenger compartment. Angelique's and Coco's meager possessions were packed in the boot.

Sitting pressed between Coco and her uncle, Angelique felt annoyed that Giles kept insinuating his bulky thigh closer to her skirts. She realized that he was a big man, and that he must be quite uncomfortable in the cramped quarters; yet still, the movements of his leg seemed almost deliberately provocative.

Angelique edged closer to Coco, casually wedging her reticule between her skirts and her uncle's wandering thigh. She felt very uneasy regarding this evening. Finally, this afternoon, she'd been able to wrench from her uncle more details about the people with whom she was to stay while he was gone in Mississippi—

Uncle Giles was leaving her and Coco with two bachelors! At last he'd informed her that she would be staying at the home of Jean Pierre Delacroix—the handsome young man who'd played cards at Giles's house last night—and with Jean Pierre's cousin Roland, the strange man who had met them at the market today.

Mon Dieu, it was a scandal! Both men were unattached and evidently hot-blooded. But when she'd questioned her uncle regarding the propriety of her staying with them, he'd only become furious again. "A child your age should not be insinuating such filth," Giles had rebuked. "Think instead of minding your elders and keeping that impertinent mouth of yours shut. I've made the best arrangements for you that I can under the circumstances. Besides—Coco will be present as your chaperon."

Angelique had been aghast, though she'd wisely said nothing else to her uncle at the time. The idea of Coco—who at fourteen was still a child herself—being a proper *duenna* for anyone was utterly laughable.

Angelique sighed unhappily and stared past Coco at the passing houses—lovely, lacy two-storied phantoms glowing with warm lights in the thick dusk. Nothing made sense to her. Why was her uncle leaving her at the mercy of these two strangers—especially the bad-tempered one who had come to the market this morning? She struggled not to shudder as she recalled the moment when Roland Delacroix had stormed up to their carriage, the odd, intense way he'd stared at her.

Angelique didn't like the sound of any of this—her mother would never have approved of such an arrangement. She had a very real fear that something was going on here, behind the scenes, that her uncle wasn't telling her. But since Giles was her guardian now, she had little choice but to obey him. She thought of asking him if she could accompany him to Mississippi, yet that possibility unsettled her, too.

But what unnerved her most of all was the memory of Roland Delacroix's heated blue gaze raking over her . . .

In due course, they arrived at the Delacroix residence on St. Charles Avenue. As Angelique accepted her uncle's hand out of the carriage, she stared ahead at the stately Greek Revival mansion. The sight of the house was rather daunting to her—it loomed before them in two-storied splendor, narrow across the front but stretching back deeply on the long lot.

Uncle Giles opened the cast-iron gate and Angelique preceded him bravely into the yard. Despite the weakness of her knees, she held her head high as she and Uncle Giles climbed the steep steps to the shadowy front porch. Coco trailed behind them with the bags.

Light spilled through the diamond-shaped, leaded glass panels on the elaborately carved front door. A moment after Giles knocked, Roland Delacroix himself opened the door. Angelique caught a sharp breath; she had expected to be greeted by a servant.

"Please come in," he told them in that deep voice of his.

As they stepped into the central hallway, Roland closed the door and then turned, briefly shaking Giles's hand. "Good evening, Fremont," he said stiffly. He turned to Angelique, his expression softening somewhat as he bowed from the waist. "Mam'zelle Fremont."

Angelique extended her hand, and was shocked when Roland caught it in his and bent over to press his lips against her skin. She wore crocheted gloves tonight, yet the loose webbing did little to mute the sensation of Roland's warm mouth on her flesh, the strength of his fingers clasping hers. Unbidden, a shaft of heat streaked through her at his touch, making her stiffen her spine so as not to betray a shudder. Even as she wondered at the new and devastating emotion this stranger roused in her, he straightened, still holding her hand in his. She felt almost lightheaded as his vibrant blue eyes locked with hers. He was a mysterious man, yet he did look devilishly handsome tonight in his striking black velvet tailcoat and ruffled white shirt. He exuded some delicious male scent—perhaps a mixture of shaving soap and bay rum. Seeing him up close like this, she found his slightly angular face even more handsome than before, his hair even thicker and wavier, dancing with light from the chandelier overhead. *Mon Dieu*, he was so masterful! And so frightening!

At last, he released her hand and the charged moment ended. Roland turned to watch a harried-looking manservant rush up. "Well, Gabriel, about time you arrived on the scene. Will you kindly take our guest's things?"

"*Oui*, maître," the manservant said nervously. He took Angelique's gloves, reticule, and shawl, Giles's hat and walking stick, then hurried off again, ushering Coco with him toward the back of the home.

Within seconds, Roland, Giles, and Angelique were left alone in the hallway. Angelique felt half-undressed without her shawl; she could feel her cheeks burning as Roland's intense gaze again flicked over her. She was wearing the same dress she'd worn this morning, her only nice frock. It was full-skirted and of white eyelet, but rather low-cut and tight through the bodice, since her mother had made it for her first communion three years earlier.

"Follow me, please," Roland murmured after a moment.

He ushered them into a lovely parlor, then said to Angelique, "Your pardon, mam'zelle, but I must have a word with your uncle. My cousin will be joining you shortly to offer you some refreshment."

Even as Giles started to protest, Roland said firmly, "Come along, Fremont."

Giles, knowing better than to protest, quickly fell into step behind Roland and exited the room, leaving Angelique alone.

Before Angelique could even contemplate Roland's odd behavior, she felt compelled to stare at the magnificent room in which she stood. The parlor was long and narrow, filled with rosewood furniture upholstered in tufted silk damask.

A magnificent crystal chandelier hung from a cast plaster medallion at the center of the ceiling, filling the room with the warm glow of gaslight.

Beyond the parlor stretched an equally elegant dining room, with heavily carved chairs and sideboard. At the back of the room, a huge gilt mirror reflected the light of yet another dazzling chandelier! The table was beautifully set, the linen snowy white, the china hand-painted, the goblets of gleaming silver!

Being accustomed to the shabby surroundings at Giles Fremont's, Angelique was stunned at the affluence she saw in this house. And she felt a little less apprehensive about staying here. Obviously, here was a respectable home—with many servants and a degree of propriety and decorum. Even the mercurial Roland Delacroix had acted much more restrained and proper in the dignified surroundings. Yet why had he insisted on speaking with her uncle alone? Before Angelique could contemplate this question, the sound of boots on the floorboards distracted her, and she turned to watch another dark-haired man step into the room. This gentleman was quite familiar—a shorter version of Roland Delacroix with a small, trim mustache. Angelique smiled shyly as she recognized him. "Ah, you are M'sieur Delacroix from last night, are you not?"

"Indeed, I am, Mam'zelle Fremont," Jean Pierre responded with a warm smile, bowing briefly before he stepped forward. He, too, took Angelique's hand and kissed it, but this time no tremor ran the course of her body. She felt much more at home around this younger man, and again she had to wonder at the fearful, unsettling feelings Roland Delacroix had aroused in her—sensations that were, illogically, so very exciting.

Jean Pierre was turning away to the sideboard. "Well, young lady. May I tempt you with some white wine tonight?"

"Oh, *non*, m'sieur," Angelique responded quickly. "Maman and Papa—" she fought a telltale quiver in her voice, then finished—"My parents did not allow me to sip spirits. And I'm certain Uncle Giles would be of a similar mind for someone of my age."

"But my dear, you cannot possibly sample our cook's

fabulous *bouillabaisse* without a suitable wine,'' Jean Pierre said charmingly, already pouring her a glassful. "Even your uncle could not deny that."

Angelique bit her lip, struggling. She did sip wine at communion. "Well, perhaps a small glass, m'sieur." As Jean Pierre approached her with a half-filled crystal wineglass in hand, she added awkwardly, "M'sieur, do you know why your cousin is speaking privately with my uncle?"

Jean Pierre smiled as he handed Angelique her wine, yet she could tell there was much tension behind his polite facade. "All in good time, my dear."

"This is insane, Delacroix! Insane!"

Behind closed doors in the library, Roland and Giles had been conversing for some tense moments. Roland now said tersely, "I tell you, Fremont, it is the only way out of this dilemma."

"You expect me to tell Angelique that it was arranged some years ago for the two of you to wed? Why ever would she believe this, man?"

Roland stepped forward menacingly, his eyes dark with anger. "She'll believe it because you're going to put on a very convincing show, Fremont. Otherwise, I'll call you out and dispatch your misbegotten soul—if you even possess one—straight to the devil."

Stunned, Giles fell back a step. "You'll what?"

"I'll kill you," Roland replied with a ruthless smile. "Any miscreant who would sell his own innocent niece into whoredom—to the highest bidder, no less—deserves to die a slow and agonizing death. I'll plan my aim accordingly, I assure you."

"M'sieur, please—" Giles pleaded, trembling visibly.

"You have but one chance of redemption," Roland went on in a coldly detached voice. "And that is to convince your niece—this very night, at the dinner table—that I am her affianced. As I've already explained, we have two things on our side—Angelique's young enough that her parents might not have told her of the arranged match, and there is the fire, as well, which would have destroyed any written proof of the betrothal."

Giles nodded convulsively. "Very well, m'sieur. I'll try my best to convince my niece that things are just as you say. It may be, though—"

"Yes?"

Giles sighed. "Angelique has a stubborn streak, sir. I may have to be very stern with the child."

Roland nodded. "Be as firm as you need be—verbally." His eyes gleamed with a terrible menace as he added softly, "But should you in any way attempt to intimidate her physically—"

"I should not dream of it, m'sieur."

Roland harrumphed. "And, mind you, don't let anything slip to her regarding the *actual* circumstances of this betrothal."

"Oh, no, m'sieur. Especially not," Giles paused to smile slyly, "if I can count on your continued generosity."

Roland stepped forward violently and grasped the other man by the cravat. Giles's eyes looked ready to pop out of his head as Roland hissed, "Look, you slimy leech, I'd think you'd be satisfied that the girl will be protected by an honorable marriage, especially considering your perfidous plans for her. You've already been compensated quite handsomely for your villainy. Now you dare attempt to blackmail me? Speak one more syllable of this treason, and I assure you, Fremont, it shall be your last!"

"*Oui*, m'sieur," Giles Fremont said, nodding violently as he gasped for his breath.

Roland released him, dusting off his hands as if even touching Fremont's mere clothing were loathsome to him. "Now let's join your niece and Jean Pierre for dinner. And remember when you speak with the girl, Fremont—your life literally hangs in the balance."

CHAPTER
Eight

They dined at the elegant mahogany table, and the cuisine was every bit as fabulous as Jean Pierre had promised—stuffed artichokes, followed by boiled crawfish in red sauce, *bouillabaisse à la Creole*, then a main course of speckled trout *amandine* with green peas *à la française* and creamed whole potatoes.

Jean Pierre and Roland sat at opposite ends of the table, with Angelique and her uncle flanking them. Angelique tried her best to do justice to the succulent fare, and she surreptitiously observed Jean Pierre to make sure she chose the right utensil for each course. Each dish was accompanied by a different wine, and by the time the trout *amandine* arrived, Angelique's cheeks felt warm from indulgence. Thankfully, the liquor did make her feel a bit more relaxed.

Angelique was grateful that the men did most of the talking. The topics were general to begin with—the death of President Taylor and the succession of Millard Filmore, seasonal flooding near the levee. Several times during the meal, Angelique again caught Roland Delacroix staring at her in that intense, unsettling way of his. At least his cousin Jean Pierre was charm personified, and did his best to make her feel at home during a near-interminable repast.

Toward the end of the meal, Giles cleared his throat, laid aside his napkin and said to Angelique, "My dear, there is something I've been meaning to tell you."

Angelique found herself stiffening. "Yes, Uncle Giles?"

He shifted nervously, avoiding her eye. "I'm afraid I've not been completely honest with you, Angelique."

"Concerning what, Uncle?"

Giles Fremont glanced at Roland briefly; then, he hastily

continued with his discourse. "You see, some years ago, your parents and I made an—arrangement in your behalf. We did not want you to know about it until you were old enough to understand."

"What sort of arrangement?" Angelique asked suspiciously.

Giles caught a deep breath, then blurted out, "At my recommendation, they arranged for you to marry—er—one of our hosts this very evening. Roland Delacroix."

There was a moment of near-deafening silence, as Angelique glanced horrified from her uncle to Roland. Shaking her head, she then let out a stream of rapid French that left Roland scowling, Jean Pierre struggling not to grin, and Giles mopping his brow. "*Mon Dieu*!" she finished to her uncle. "This cannot be!"

"I assure you, Angelique, that the contract was made," Giles gritted. "As I just explained, I personally acted as intermediary."

Angelique shook her head proudly. "*Non*. Maman and Papa never would have done such a thing without consulting me."

"Angelique," Giles said impatiently, "how could they have consulted you? You were but—er—eleven years old at the time. A child's opinion is not sought in such important matters."

"I tell you it is not true!" Angelique cried. "And how could you have become involved in this—this presumed arrangement anyway, Uncle Giles? My father never saw you again after he married Maman."

"Ah, but that is not true, my dear," Giles retorted adamantly. "Your father did see me on occasion when he was here in New Orleans conducting business. And on one such visit, I—er—addressed with him the advisability of arranging a suitable marriage for you. You see, I had known the Delacroix family for some years, and was aware that they had a bachelor son. Since I felt at the time that I hadn't been much of an uncle for you, I offered to provide a suitable dowry to secure the match, and your father agreed to this." He coughed nervously. "At any rate, I recently transferred the dowry funds to M'sieur Delacroix's factor here in New Orleans."

Now Angelique paled, swallowing hard as she glanced from Roland, who was still scowling, to her uncle. Holy saints, this was serious. Had her parents lived, she would have expected them to have chosen a husband for her. Such *mariages de convenance* were the rule rather than the exception in the region. And if her parents *had* chosen Roland Delacroix without telling her, if her uncle had already paid the dowry, it could be quite difficult for her to extricate herself from this situation without staining the honor of both her uncle and her family!

Yet still, why hadn't her parents informed her of the match? They were no longer here to speak for themselves, and this made her very skeptical. Facing her uncle bravely, Angelique said, "Uncle Giles, I simply cannot believe that my parents made this arrangement without my knowledge."

"I've already explained that, girl!" Giles snapped back. "You were far too young to be consulted."

"But I still can't—"

Giles drew himself up huffily. "Are you calling me a liar, Niece?"

"Well, no, Uncle, but—"

"Then you have no choice but to believe me."

Angelique bit her lip miserably. She realized that if she didn't accept Uncle Giles's word, she would indeed be calling him a liar. And what reason would he have to lie to her about this?

Truth to tell, Angelique did not completely trust Giles Fremont. She suspected that he was a grasping, selfish man. Yet still, how could he have profitted from this alleged *contrat de marriage*? Hadn't he just informed her that he'd been impelled to supply the dowry himself? She supposed it was conceivable that at some point, Uncle Giles had felt a twinge of conscience regarding his total neglect of his brother Samuel's family, and that he had decided to atone by endowing a suitable marriage for his brother's only child. It was even possible that her parents had decided not to tell her about the match until she was older . . .

Angelique stared at her plate, immersed in tumultuous thought. At last the silence was broken, this time by Roland. "Well, Angelique? Do you find this arrangement so—distasteful?"

His words were gentle, yet Angelique remained hurt and confused. Indeed, at the moment, Roland's use of her Christian name seemed in itself the ultimate insult. Looking up at him with dark eyes blazing, she said, "I do not wish to marry you, m'sieur."

Unexpectedly, Roland laughed, and as much as this maddened Angelique, the transformation of his features also amazed her. She had to admit to herself that he looked ungodly handsome with the laugh-lines framing his sensual mouth, with the sparkle in his eyes—and the direct, bold look he gave her clearly attested that he was not feeling the least bit daunted by her resistance.

This infuriated Angelique most of all.

But she was distracted as her uncle's fist slammed down on the table, rattling dishes. "Angelique!" he bellowed, his expression livid. "Listen to me, child, and listen well. The match is made, and there is no point whatsoever in your fighting it. Indeed, I find it incomprehensible that you would disgrace your parents' memory by defying their wishes and insulting the very man they have chosen for you. Well, my dear? What do you have to say regarding your recalcitrant behavior?"

Now Angelique was fighting tears as her uncle's words regarding her parents hit home with a vengeance. During her seventeen years, nothing had mattered more to her than the love and respect of Samuel and Evangeline Fremont. If this marriage had indeed been her parents' wish, of course she would honor their judgment. Yet still . . . Grasping at a last hope, she asked her uncle, "Tell me, if this match was made between my family and the Delacroix, then where is the proof? Surely my parents possessed some kind of document—"

"The fire, Angelique," her uncle reminded her tersely. "Everything was burned."

A tear trickled down Angelique's face at her uncle's harsh tone, at the painful and bitter memories his callous words brought rushing. Yet pride forbade her to wipe the tear away. "Why did you not tell me of this—betrothal—before tonight, Uncle Giles?"

"Would you have come with me here to dinner?" he asked.

"No," she said, the word barely audible as she lowered

her eyes. Then her head snapped up as a desperate idea occurred to her, and she said to her uncle wildly, "Uncle Giles, I have a solution to all of this! I can return to St. James and live there with Madame Santoni. She said I would always have a home with her and—"

"Ah, but that is not what your parents wished, child," he said.

Angelique stared despondently at her plate, biting her lip in an acknowledgment of defeat.

She heard her uncle expel a relieved sigh. "All right, then, my dear. Don't you have something to say to M'sieur Delacroix?"

Angelique glanced up at Roland with scarcely veiled antagonism. "Very well, m'sieur. I will marry you because my parents wished it, and for no other reason."

Now Roland Delacroix was not so amused, as his dark scowl attested.

"Angelique!" Giles rebuked. "Surely you can do better than that!"

Even as Angelique opened her mouth to issue a retort, Roland intervened. "Fremont, let's not press our luck," he said ironically.

Giles snorted. "The girl should be happy. She'll have everything a woman could want—a home, money, position—"

"Ah, but no one has asked the girl what she wants," Roland put in wisely.

At his words, Angelique turned to stare at him, her expression one of awe mixed with hurt and confusion. Absorbing the vulnerability and pain in her dark gaze, Roland almost smiled back at her, but then the anger flared in her eyes again and she turned her attention to Giles. "Am I still to stay here, Uncle, with these two men? Are you still planning to go off to Mississippi?"

Giles avoided Angelique's eye. "Yes, my dear, I'm afraid I'm leaving later tonight."

"But—then you'll not be here for my—" her voice dropped to a tortured whisper, and she avoided Roland's probing gaze as she finished—"wedding?"

"Afraid not, my dear. It's highly regrettable, of course, but my business is quite pressing . . ."

Now Jean Pierre chimed in with, "Please do not fret, Mam'zelle Fremont. You'll be perfectly safe here."

"I think it would be best," Roland put in, "if my fiancée stays with my former sister-in-law, Emily Miro, until we can be wed. Why throw grist to the local gossips? In fact," he added meaningfully to Giles, "I intend to escort Angelique to the Quarter tonight, myself. So don't let us keep you from your journey."

While a chill streaked down Angelique's spine at Roland's calling her his "fiancée," at his taking charge of her life so quickly and ruthlessly, Giles Fremont appeared more than delighted to receive his exit cue. Thanking Jean Pierre profusely for the repast, he administered a chaste kiss on Angelique's brow. When Jean Pierre offered to see him out, he hastily departed. Within seconds, Angelique was left alone with Roland. She avoided his eye, but could feel his intense stare. She felt unnerved to be alone with him this way, although she was not about to let him know that his presence disconcerted her in the least.

"Well," he said affably after a moment, "would you like me to ring for some dessert before we leave, Angelique?"

Numbly, she shook her head. "No, m'sieur."

"Don't you think that if we're to wed, you should call me Roland?" he asked gently.

She stared up at him, her dark eyes flashing. "M'sieur, a few moments ago, you mentioned that no one has asked me what I want in this. Will you ask me that now?"

An expression of wry amusement gripped his face. "No, I think not," he said after a moment. As Angelique started to protest, he raised a hand and said, "My dear, I'm afraid you're just going to have to bow to my more mature judgment in this matter."

"I'm not a child whose decisions must be made for her!"

"I'm not saying you're a child," he responded patiently. "But had your parents lived, wouldn't you have accepted their judgment in choosing a husband for you?"

"*Oui*, m'sieur," she replied grudgingly.

"Roland," he corrected.

She stared at him defiantly but didn't reply.

He sighed. "Angelique, if things had been different, if your parents hadn't died so suddenly and tragically, there would have been time for you to adjust to this, time for us to get to know each other. We probably would have waited a year or two before marrying. But seeing that your parents did pass away, I have no choice but to see that you are afforded my protection immediately. And the only proper way I can protect you is to marry you—as soon as possible." He leaned forward intently. "Why is it so difficult for you to accept that your parents' decision was made prior to their deaths?"

Again, Angelique didn't reply, although the sensitivity of Roland's remarks did leave her wavering emotionally.

He gestured resignedly. "My dear, I'm sure this has been a long and draining day for you. So I shall now escort you to Emily's for the night. We'll discuss our plans in more detail tomorrow."

As he stood and came to her side to help her out of her chair, she stared up at him resentfully. "Why are you doing this, m'sieur? You can't want to marry me."

He scowled down at her, yet his blue eyes again swept her form with a debilitating intensity. "Who says I don't want to marry you?"

It all happened so quickly. Within just a few minutes, Coco was summoned, then Roland escorted Angelique out to Jean Pierre's waiting coach. Quickly, the three were ensconced inside, then the conveyance rattled off toward the Quarter.

Angelique and Coco sat quite properly across from Roland in the roomy, plush interior. Angelique was still reeling from the drastic turn her life had taken in just a few short minutes. And she was still fighting the finality of what she'd learned at dinner.

Thus, despite Coco's presence, Angelique felt compelled to speak up to Roland again. "M'sieur, there's something I've been wondering about."

"Yes?"

"Why were you so angry with my uncle at the market this morning?"

He was silent for a long moment, and Angelique sorely wished she could read his expression in the deep shadows. At last, he said, "Because Giles was supposed to tell you about our betrothal before he brought you to the market. When

I learned that he hadn't . . . that's when I decided a post-
ponement of our first meeting was in order.''

Angelique shook her head and laughed bitterly. ''You're
very smooth, m'sieur. Are you always so clever with your
explanations?''

''I find the truth usually suffices,'' he said dryly.

''Indeed. Then kindly explain to me why my uncle didn't
inform me of this—betrothal—before he took me to the market?''

Roland shrugged. ''*C'est un mystere*. But perhaps—''

''Yes, m'sieur?''

''Perhaps Giles felt a trifle afraid of you.''

''Afraid?''

''I have observed that you're very forthright, Angelique,''
he remarked ruefully. ''Perhaps your uncle was a bit apprehensive regarding your possible reaction to this—fortuitous
news.''

She gritted her teeth at Roland's calling the news of their
betrothal ''fortuitous.'' ''You're saying that Uncle Giles
waited so that the three of you could—could attack in force
tonight?''

She heard his annoying chuckle. ''Something like that.''

Angelique exhaled a sharp, impatient breath. ''Uncle Giles
is not the least bit afraid of me.''

''Are you so sure? Is it inconceivable to you that your
uncle might have felt a bit intimidated by the thought of
dictating your future to you?''

''Are you intimidated by me, m'sieur?'' she snapped.

Even in the darkness, she could see the flash of his even
white teeth as he replied, ''No, *chérie*.''

Angelique turned away, clenching her jaw. Roland's self-
possessed reply infuriated her. His tone of voice had been
insultingly intimate, vaguely sardonic. And the endearment
''*chérie*'' had rolled off his tongue maddeningly, laced with
the bald stamp of his ownership. Obviously, this man intended to have her and was not in the least daunted by her
resistance.

The drive to Royal Street was mercifully brief, and soon
the coachman halted the carriage before a looming gaslit
archway. He climbed down, rang the bell hanging on the
stucco facade, then assisted his passengers out of the coach.

A grizzled butler creaked open the iron scrollwork gates and bid them enter. They walked down a long stone passageway, then emerged in the largest, most lavish patio Angelique had ever seen.

Roland excused himself and went off with the butler, the two of them climbing a staircase off to one side, leaving Angelique and Coco alone in the courtyard. Angelique glanced around; despite her apprehensions, she couldn't help but feel somewhat soothed by these serene and very private surroundings. The looming walls effectively shut them off from the world. A cast-iron fountain, spurting cascades of gleaming water, predominated the softly lit setting. Ferns and flowers spilled their brilliance from formal beds, and the air was thick with the sweetness of nectar and greenery.

Angelique glanced at Coco, wondering what the slave thought about their being shuttled from place to place tonight. She knew Coco must be very curious regarding her conversation with Roland in the carriage. Angelique was about to broach the subject of tonight's adventures herself; but then she became distracted as Roland and a tall smiling woman descended the corner staircase into the patio.

"My dear, welcome to our home!"

The woman moved forward eagerly, smiling at Angelique. She was dressed in a straight-lined ecru frock with a blue ribbon sash at her waist. She looked to be about thirty, and was pretty and slim, with lush copper-colored hair upswept in a sleek bun.

"Emily, this is my fiancée, Angelique Fremont," Roland said politely. He nodded to Angelique. "My dear, this is Emily Miro."

"How do you do, madame?" Angelique murmured awkwardly.

Emily grasped both of Angelique's hands in hers, squeezing them warmly. "Angelique, I'm so excited about yours and Roland's news. Roland informs me that he can't wait to wed you. And what a pleasant surprise it must have been for you to learn of your parents' wishes only tonight! It's like something out of a fairy tale!"

Though Angelique thought the evening's events were far more characteristic of a nightmare than of a fairy tale, she smiled stiffly at Emily and made no comment.

"And I'm so thrilled that you'll be staying with us until the wedding," Emily went on.

"Are you sure it is not an imposition, madame?" Angelique asked tensely.

Emily waved her off. "No, of course not! I live with two men—my husband and son—and I'll be beside myself to have some feminine companionship for a change."

While Emily and Roland continued to converse casually, the butler reappeared, ushering Coco off with the suitcases. Angelique breathed a sigh of relief. Emily had sounded delighted to have her here, and Angelique instinctively liked and trusted the matron. She did feel much more comfortable about staying here than she would have felt remaining at Jean Pierre's house. Roland had been right to bring her here, she grudgingly admitted to herself.

Soon thereafter, Roland thanked Emily and prepared to take his leave. He turned to Angelique, took her hand and said, "Until tomorrow, my dear." He then kissed her briefly, lightly on the cheek, turned and left. She watched him stride confidently out the archway, his shoulders broad and straight, his boots clicking authoritatively on the stone blocks. She drew an unsteady breath. Just the merest brush of his lips on her cheek had burned her . . .

Emily at once took Angelique in hand. Chatting cheerily, she led her guest to a second-floor bedroom, where Angelique's luggage had already been deposited by the butler. "Roland tells me you're exhausted, my dear, so we'll get acquainted tomorrow. Is there anything you need before retiring? A hot *tisane*, perhaps?"

Angelique glanced at the room, which was long, narrow, and elegantly furnished. She turned to her hostess and shook her head. "No thank you, madame. This is wonderful, but I was wondering—where is Coco?"

"Downstairs in the servants' quarters," Emily replied. "Shall I send her up to help you undress?"

Angelique decided she'd rather explain her new status to Coco tomorrow. "Oh, *non*, madame. I just wanted to check on her. I'd really prefer to go straight on to bed."

"As you wish, my dear." Emily nodded toward a rope pull near the door. "Just ring if you need anything."

Angelique thanked Emily, and after her hostess left, she

collapsed onto the bed with its heavenly soft feather mattress. She found she was, indeed, exhausted—

What a day! The entire course of her life had changed within just a few short hours! Now she was to marry this Roland Delacroix—a handsome, masterful man with a frightening intensity in his eyes. She had judged him to be at least thirty years old—almost old enough to be her father. He'd been polite with her, even patient; but she'd also sensed a darkness, a capacity for violence in him, and she was very unsettled by the thought of submitting to such a man in the marriage bed. The way his bold eyes had raked over her had left no doubt regarding his expectations there.

Truth to tell, Angelique did not find Roland wholly unattractive. While he frightened her, he also kept her senses in an uproar—illogically, a rather exciting uproar. But nothing was as she thought it would be! Everything had been so rushed, so abrupt!

Angelique turned and embraced the pillow. "Oh, Maman!" she wept. "If this is what you and Papa wanted for me, why did you not prepare me for this role I am to assume?"

Because there was no time . . .

The answer hit Angelique forcefully, almost as if it were a message from beyond, and she sat up, blinking at her tears. Of course, her parents would have wanted to prepare her for this marriage, when she came of age. But they hadn't expected to die so suddenly of the fever. And as Roland had said, now there was no time left to wait, no time for courtship.

Roland. Ruefully, she realized that she'd already begun to acknowledge his given name in her mind, and she whispered it as her head again hit the pillow. Yes, she would wed him. She had no choice but to honor her parents' wishes.

Sitting in the dark interior of Jean Pierre's coach as it clattered back toward St. Charles Avenue, Roland was also brooding as he thought over the evening's events. Endlessly he mulled over Angelique's earlier, blunt words: "I will marry you because my parents wished it, and for no other reason."

For no other reason, indeed! Was the girl totally unaffected by all he had to offer her—his home, his protection, his good name? Did she not find him attractive in the least?

Earlier in the evening, when she'd turned to him and had said defiantly, "I do not wish to marry you, m'sieur," he'd actually felt amused by her spirit. But her later remarks had gone too far, chafing his pride. Ah, the girl had a voice all right—and she well knew how to use it to turn the knife!

The hell of it was, he was utterly bewitched by young Angelique. She'd looked so glorious tonight—all in virginal white, with her dark hair gleaming, her young breasts proudly upthrust, her skin as pure and clear as honey. When he'd seen the tears in her eyes—tears of confusion and fear at her plight—it had been all he could do not to grab her and take her in his arms, to tell her not to fear, to kiss her until all her tears were gone. Just the thought of holding her thus made his blood pound—and for reasons that were far from altruistic. While the girl did not know it, she was all innocent seductress. There was such pride in her visage, such fire in those brown, fathomless eyes of hers—

Would that fierce, Cajun heat ever reach out to sear him?

Roland reached into his breast pocket to extract a cheroot, and realized that his hand was trembling, his heart hammering. For all that he had told the girl that she didn't intimidate him, he was daunted more than he cared to admit by her angry resistance.

He lit his smoke and inhaled deeply. He would marry her before she had a chance to think twice, that was for certain. Then she would be his—legally. And wouldn't half the battle be won?

CHAPTER
Nine

The next morning, Emily Miro sat in her sun-drenched courtyard at the wrought-iron table, sipping *café au lait*. Her husband, Maurice, had departed for the Exchange moments earlier, and her young son, Phillip, was still abed.

Emily smiled pensively as she thought of Roland's strange appearance the night before. He'd arrived at their home late; Emily had still been awake, in the parlor reading Mr. Hawthorne's new novel, *The Scarlet Letter*. Roland had quickly and intently requested that Emily provide a temporary home for his fiancée, Angelique Fremont.

When the stunned Emily had asked Roland how he had managed to acquire a fiancée during the scant hours since she'd last seen him, he'd replied gruffly that this marriage had been arranged some years back. When Emily had continued to stare at Roland mystified, he had said passionately, "For the love of heaven, Emily, do pretend you're taking all of this in stride, even if you aren't. The girl is half-petrified as it is, and we must present a confident facade to her or she'll surely bolt. And whatever you do, don't mention Luisa."

At that point Emily had dug in her heels, demanding that Roland explain his bizarre behavior, his arriving late at night with an instant bride-to-be. He'd run a hand through his hair. "Emily, one day I'll tell you the truth of the matter. For now, please know that I must marry the girl immediately— for her own protection. Beyond that, I'd prefer that you know little—so you won't have to lie to Angelique."

There, Emily had finally acquiesced. For she had glimpsed a haunted, desperate quality in Roland's eyes when he spoke of the young, mysterious girl he'd brought to her home. Emily had known then that her former brother-in-law was totally smitten with the girl; and this, more than anything else, had convinced her to cooperate with him. There had been so much tragedy in Roland's life for so long—first he'd lost his brother Justin, who had been Emily's first husband, then he'd lost his first wife, Luisa.

Emily's hand trembled on her coffee cup as she recalled those painful days. She and Roland had shared a special bond during that time and afterward—both widowed within a year of each other.

Emily thought of Angelique, of how frightened and exhausted she had looked the night before. She was a beautiful little thing, hardly more than a child with her huge dark eyes and riotous black curls. She would make an exquisite bride for Roland. She'd worn a lovely dress the night before, yet one of the maids, who had gone to the girl's room earlier this morning while she still slept, had informed Emily that the girl's other garments were highly unsuitable.

That was a matter Emily could remedy, with the greatest of joy. She would also try to help Angelique accept the fact that she was to become Roland's wife; the tension and hesitation in the girl's face last night had not been lost on her. Emily knew that Roland would make the girl a good husband. Indeed, there was a time when Emily might have pursued Roland herself, had Justin not come before him. After Justin's life had come to such a tragic and premature end, there had just been too much shared pain between her and Roland for Emily ever to think of him as anything but a compassionate and beloved brother.

"*Bonjour*, madame."

Startled, Emily set down her coffee cup and glanced behind her; young Angelique stood at the base of the stairway. The girl looked every bit as beautiful as she had the previous night—especially with the bright sunlight illuminating her honeyed complexion and dancing in her thick raven hair. But today, she wore a patched garment that did not do justice to her loveliness.

At once Emily stood, smiling, and hurried over to greet her. "My dear! Good morning. I trust you slept well?"

"*Oui*, Madame," Angelique responded politely, although actually, she'd hardly slept a wink the previous night.

"Please, you must call me Emily," Emily insisted as she took Angelique's arm and led her toward the table. "I'll wager you're starving. Here, do have a seat and I'll see that cook brings you a heaping plate at once."

Angelique dutifully took the seat indicated. "Please, madame, you mustn't go to any troub—"

But Emily was already ringing a porcelain bell. "Nonsense, my dear. You must have a substantial breakfast. We've a very big day ahead of us."

"We do?" Angelique echoed confusedly, accepting the delicate demitasse of *café au lait* that Emily was handing her.

"Indeed, yes. You're aware, of course, that Roland is planning to marry you just as soon as the banns can be read?"

Angelique sighed. "*Oui*, madame."

"Emily," her hostess corrected firmly. Her honey brown eyes danced with happiness as she confided, "I can't tell you how excited I've been since Roland brought you here last night and told me the good news. Why I hardly slept a wink for thinking about it! Don't you think this is all terribly romantic? And don't you find Roland dreadfully handsome?"

Despite herself, Angelique fought a smile at her hostess's effusive comments. Roland Delacroix was indeed, dreadfully handsome—and dreadfully intimidating, as well. To cover her embarrassment, Angelique took a sip of the hot, rich coffee, then said to Emily modestly, "Actually, madame, I haven't had much of a chance to absorb all of this."

"Of course not," Emily concurred sympathetically. "Roland told me how your parents's untimely death made it necessary for the two of you to speed things up somewhat. I'm so sorry you lost your mother and father, my dear."

"Thank you, madame."

"And when are you going to start calling me Emily, pray tell? I'm counting on our becoming the best of friends, you know." Before Angelique could reply, a manservant stepped onto the patio, and Emily turned to address him. "The young lady would like her breakfast now, please, Benjamin."

"*Oui*, madame."

As Emily continued to give instructions to the slave, Angelique found herself again smiling. She liked this pretty, forthright lady with her slightly angular, perpetually smiling face and her lush copper-colored hair. During past weeks, Angelique's world had been turned topsy-turvy again and again. Yet there was a sameness, a stability and warmth, here in the Miro home that drew Angelique like sunshine would a drooping flower.

Once the manservant had departed, Emily asked, "More coffee, my dear?"

"*Oui*, this is excellent." After Emily had refilled her cup, Angelique ventured, "Ma—er—Emily, last night I heard M'sieur Delacroix refer to you as his former sister-in-law. Would you mind telling me just how you and he are related?"

"Of course, dear," Emily replied. A faraway, wistful quality lit her eyes as she explained, "You see, twelve years ago I married Roland's older brother, Justin. I was eighteen at the time, and Justin was barely twenty-one. After our marriage, we went to live at the Delacroix family plantation, Belle Elise. Both Justin and Roland were wild young men at the time—drinking, gambling—they were even involved in a duel or two in the parish, it was rumored. However, I loved Justin desperately, and I foolishly dreamed that my love could reform him. The irony of it is that soon after Justin and I wed, it was Roland, three years younger than Justin, who settled down and began to run the plantation for his aging father and stepmother." Emily sighed. "Justin never did give up his wild ways, I'm afraid, not even when Phillip was born just days after our first anniversary. At any rate, his gambling and drinking increased, and his trips to New Orleans became more frequent. During one such visit, Justin was coming out of a grog shop near the waterfront, late at night. He was drunk, I'm assuming, and wasn't watching where he was going. Anyway, a carriage came by at a high rate of speed, it couldn't stop and . . ."

At this, Emily's voice trailed off and she bit her lip. Even though the matron was now staring down at the table, Angelique could see tears brimming in her eyes. "Oh, Emily." Angelique reached out to touch her hand. "I'm so sorry. I didn't realize my question would cause you such pain."

"Don't apologize, my dear, I was planning to tell you all about Justin, anyway." Emily smiled bravely and wiped a tear with her napkin. "You know, it's been eight years, and you'd think that by now I could relate what happened without falling apart."

"Oh, no," Angelique insisted. "When a loved one is lost, the pain never really goes away."

"You are very sensitive and very perceptive, my dear," Emily said sincerely. "I guess the loss never has completely left me, even though I now have my Maurice, who is my life. Still, every time I look at my beloved Phillip and see those beautiful blue Delacroix eyes . . ." Emily paused, then squeezed Angelique's hand. "One thing you must know, my dear, is that the Delacroix men inspire great passion in their women."

Angelique was again embarrassed, and felt grateful as a maid entered the patio bearing a tray with Angelique's breakfast. The two women fell silent as a plate filled with steaming pancakes and sausages was placed before Angelique. Emily thanked the servant and then said more cheerfully to her guest, "Well, my dear, let's plan our day, then. First we must wrest Phillip out of bed, get him dressed and fed, and then take him to his fencing master. Then you and I are off to the *couturière*. We're going to have you royally outfitted, including the most lavish wedding gown the New Orleans community has seen this season." Emily clapped her hands, beaming at Angelique. "Oh, it shall be such fun!"

Here Angelique felt compelled to protest. "Oh, no, madame, I couldn't dream of allowing you to—"

Emily waved her off with a flourish of a slim hand. "*Non*, Angelique! Maurice and I insist on outfitting you as your wedding present, and Maurice will be giving you away at the mass, as well. This is the very least we can do. Roland is our dearest friend, and Phillip's godfather, as well. I doubt I should have gotten through the first year following Justin's death without Roland's counsel. It is my greatest pleasure to be of some small assistance to him now."

"But madame, I—"

"Now, not another word, you stubborn girl," Emily went on vehemently, "or I swear I shall have to complain to Roland most bitterly that you're spoiling all my fun. He does have a rather formidable temper, my dear."

While Angelique suspected that her hostess's threat was largely bluster, she could not repress a smile. "I am defeated, then, madame."

"*Emily*," her hostess once more corrected.

"Emily," Angelique murmured, her smile widening. Yet inwardly, she was feeling somewhat bemused. Emily and Roland obviously shared a very special relationship, and Angelique had to acknowledge that she was feeling a small spark of jealousy there—

And this regarding a man she barely knew! . . .

Angelique realized that she was having a difficult time accepting the situation at face value—that handsome Roland Delacroix would truly want to marry her, that socially prominent Emily Miro would meet her and instantly become her friend and mentor.

Yet ever since she'd met Roland, her entire life had been taken out of her own hands.

* * *

The morning was every bit as busy and fun as Emily had promised. Angelique was introduced to young Phillip, who was a handsome, polite child whose appearance very much reminded Angelique of Roland. Once they had dropped the child off with his *maître d'armes* on Exchange Alley, Emily took Angelique to see her *couturière* on Esplanade Avenue. Despite Angelique's protestations, she was measured for an elaborate new wardrobe. Emily then treated Angelique to a whirlwind spree through the shops in the quarter to complete her trousseau, buying her delicate lingerie, new stockings, hats and shoes, along with a few ready-made dresses for immediate wear. They lunched at the Napoleon House on Chartres Street, then returned to Emily's townhouse, where Emily directed Angelique to go straight upstairs and have a well-deserved nap.

Yet Angelique was too excited to rest as she perused all the treasures in the quilted boxes laid out on her bed. She realized that the shopping spree had so fascinated her, she'd hardly given Roland a thought all day. For never in her life had Angelique known such luxuries as were now spread out before her—underthings of sheerest silk or lawn, hats of velvet or felt or straw, shoes of soft kid, and slippers of satin. Many of the boxes contained a small gift or praline from the shopkeeper, according to the local custom of *lagniappe*. Angelique couldn't resist dressing up in one of her new frocks—a lovely yellow muslin sprigged with tiny violets. The lace-and-ribbon trimmed boat neckline showed off her firm breasts, and the tight waistline accentuated her slimness.

Angelique brushed her raven hair until it gleamed, drawing it back with a new yellow ribbon. She was admiring her transformed visage in the pier mirror when a knock came at the door. After she called, "Come in," Emily walked in briskly.

"Why, my dear, you look simply divine, and I'm so glad you're not napping. I have the most exciting news!"

"Oh?"

"Roland's here."

Angelique's face fell.

"My dear, what is it?" Emily asked, hurrying to the girl's side.

Angelique bit her lip. "It's just—I don't mean to sound ungrateful, Emily, but I hardly know the man."

"Then it's good that he's come by, don't you agree? You see, Roland promised Phillip that he'd help him launch the toy boat he bought him, and he wants the two of us to accompany them to the park."

"Why don't you go on, Emily? Perhaps I should take a nap."

"My dear, I won't hear of it," Emily said crisply. More seriously, she went on, "Angelique, I know this marriage is sudden for you, but please give Roland a chance. He's a fine man, dear, and I promise you that he'll make you a good husband. Now—won't you come with us to the park?"

Angelique was wise enough to recognize her own defeat. "Of course, Emily," she said.

The park was picturesque and light-drenched, a lofty stand of oaks circling a small pond. Several ducks and a swan glided on the dappled water. Young Phillip's eyes danced with excitement and he whooped with joy as his uncle helped him launch the brightly painted toy boat that had been a recent gift. Emily and Angelique stood close by, watching, each holding a lacy parasol to ward off the sun. Observing the uncle and nephew together, Angelique again thought of how much Roland and Phillip resembled each other.

She recalled the unsettling moment back at the Miro townhouse, when she and Emily had come down the stairs to join Roland and Phillip in the courtyard. Roland's gaze had been riveted on her as she descended the stairs in her new yellow dress. Once she was downstairs, he'd strode quickly to her side, hugging her briefly and kissing her cheek. "You look beautiful," he'd said, staring down at her, and this time there'd been no trace of cynicism in his voice or his eyes. Angelique had been warmed by his sincerity; yet she was also not ready to have him look at her with such burning possessiveness . . .

Beyond them, Phillip now jumped up and down, distracting Angelique from her thoughts. The child clapped his hands as the breeze caught the toy boat's sail, tugging the vessel toward the center of the rippling pond.

"Cheers—a successful launching," Emily called to Roland. She winked at him and added, "Why don't you and Angelique go for a stroll through these lovely trees? I'll watch the boat with Phillip."

Angelique was biting her lip and about to protest, but Roland was already nodding as he strode toward the women. "A splendid idea, Emily—I do need to stretch my legs." He approached Angelique, offering her his arm. "My dear?"

Angelique had no choice but to go along with Roland, else she would appear unpardonably rude. For a few moments, they strolled in silence through the moss-hung trees skirting the pond, their steps accompanied by scattered birdsong and a rustling breeze. Walking this close to Roland, Angelique discovered anew what a big, powerful man he was. He towered head and shoulders above her, his white, planter's-style hat accentuating his aristocratic bearing. His broad shoulders and muscular torso were encased in a dark brown wool frock coat, left open to reveal a gold-brocaded waistcoat, pleated linen shirt, and black cravat. His muscular legs rippled against well-fitting, fawn-colored trousers tucked into shiny black boots. His stride was long and purposeful, causing Angelique to walk briskly just to keep up with him. The man radiated power and virility, and even though Angelique's fingers were perched lightly on his arm, his firm sinew vibrated beneath her touch.

She caught her breath with an effort as they rounded the pond. This was the man she would soon wed, she thought, a stranger whose bed she would share—a man with enough physical strength to crush the life out of her, if he choose to do so. All too soon, she would be his wife, his to do with precisely as he pleased. The helplessness of her fate was driven home today with a vengeance.

After a moment, he asked, "Tell me, Angelique—are you adjusting to the idea of our marriage?"

Angelique looked up at Roland sharply, blushing, feeling almost as if he had read her very thoughts. At last she told him, "As I told you last night, m'sieur, I am accepting my parents' wishes."

The flesh of his arm tightened beneath her fingers and a frown furrowed his brow. "Then I take it the thought of marriage to me still does not fill you with joyous anticipation?"

Angelique did not comment.

Roland sighed and slowed his stride, staring off at a distant passing carriage. At last he said, "Tell me of your life— before."

"Before?"

"When you lived with your parents—if it is not too painful for you."

Angelique gathered her thoughts. "I was very happy at home," she said at last. "Ours was a simple existence—my parents owned a small farm near St. James. There was always work, all week long, to keep food on the table. And on Sundays there was Mass and family fellowship."

"I'll wager you had to do without a great deal," he remarked.

That angered Angelique and she stopped in her tracks, pivoting to face him. "M'sieur," she said hotly, "my parents loved me dearly. They provided me with everything I needed."

"I'm sure they did," Roland responded patiently, also pausing and turning to frown down at her. "My intention is not to cast aspersions on their memory. I'm simply trying to point out that there are many luxuries I can provide for you. I just wish you felt more willing regarding this marriage."

"Willing?" Angelique repeated bitterly. "After I was offered no choice in the matter? Tell me, m'sieur, am I not displaying the proper—" she struggled for a word then snapped, "subservience regarding your generosity?"

Roland whistled under his breath. "I'm not asking you to kiss my boots, Angelique. I would just like to feel you were—well, happier regarding our upcoming nuptials."

"Well, I'm not, m'sieur, and I'll not lie to you on that account," Angelique informed him stoutly. "And what of you? Are you happy in this arranged match? It was not of your choosing either, I might remind you."

At her words, his eyes flashed with anger and his jaw tightened. Then he looked her up and down slowly, in a most insulting manner. "Oh, I think you'll do, *chérie*," he drawled.

His insolent tone made Angelique's blood boil. Drawing herself up with dignity, she said, "Splendid, m'sieur," and started off again, her head held high. Yet her dramatics quickly degenerated into absurdity as she caught her toe in a gopher hole and stumbled, almost tumbling head over heels.

Hard male arms caught her, bringing her upright forcefully against a broad muscular chest. Steely eyes bored down into hers. Roland's scent—a musky mixture of leather, tobacco and shaving soap—assaulted her senses. Absorbing his essence, his murderous scowl, Angelique breathed with an effort; yet there was also a very peculiar weakness slamming her belly, as if she were falling out of a tree or hayloft.

After a moment, he murmured, "You have quite a temper, don't you, little Cajun?"

She tried unsuccessfully to squirm out of his grasp. "Let me go!"

He grinned mockingly, deliberately misinterpreting her remark. "That is impossible, mademoiselle, as we are to wed."

And instead of releasing her, Roland brought his mouth down on hers. Angelique struggled in earnest now, her parasol spinning off to the ground as she flailed out at him. But she was powerless in his crushing embrace. Never before had she been kissed on the mouth by a man, and Roland's kiss was an initiation by fire—carnal, sensual, and voracious. His lips bruised her tender mouth, forcing her lips apart so that his tongue could plunder the sweetness within. A cry of outrage arose in her, only to die, muffled, in her throat. Her senses reeled from his audacious assault and her breasts throbbed from the hard pressure of his chest. To Angelique's horror, she found she did not feel revolted by his boldness —she felt lightheaded, dizzy, strangely aroused. Inevitably, she quit fighting him, clinging to his strength to keep from falling. And as soon as she ceased her struggles, he softened the kiss, his tongue no longer punishing her mouth but moving in slow, seductive rhythms—a motion she somehow knew was depraved, but which drove her crazy, nevertheless.

The kiss ended as abruptly as it had begun. Roland released her and she tottered on her feet, gasping for her breath. She glared at him and he stared back at her cynically. Maddened, she drew back her hand to slap him. "Don't, *chérie*," he warned in a deadly calm voice. "I am your fiancé now, and I have every right to kiss you. I would fight anyone who denied me that—including you, my love." A slow grin spread across his lips as he added, ''Besides, I must say that you did not seem to find my kiss—altogether unpleasant.''

As much as Angelique's cheeks burned at Roland's merciless jibe, as much as she ached to slap his cynically smiling face, she could only let her hand drop to her side as she continued to glower at him, trembling. He had spoken the truth, damn him—on all counts. He did have the right to kiss her—and when he had done so just now, she had largely been putty in his hands, to her own immense shame. He had crushed her resistance with a ruthlessness and dispatch that had made her head spin. And she realized with a shudder that he would likely be just as aggressive in claiming the additional rights he would acquire after their wedding. What was it he'd said earlier? ''You'll do''? The man obviously wanted nothing but a bedmate, and she was to become it— wife in the eyes of the law, but mistress in reality.

Suddenly, young Phillip's voice called out to them, ending the charged moment. ''Uncle! Mam'zelle Angelique! You must come see!''

Roland retrieved Angelique's parasol, handed it to her with exaggerated politeness, then offered her his arm. ''Shall we rejoin the others, my dear?''

Declining to take his arm, Angelique started off proudly, only to once again ruin her show, this time with a telltale limp. She had been so infuriated with Roland, she hadn't even noticed that she had twisted her ankle slightly when she happened into the gopher hole. Now each step she took brought increasing discomfort, despite her efforts not to show it.

Even as she held her head high and hobbled onward, Roland caught her sleeve, then she was swept up into his strong arms, parasol and all.

''Unhand me, m'sieur!'' she snapped.

''I'm afraid that's out of the question, *chérie*,'' he responded with a grin, not even slowing his stride as he carried her easily. ''You obviously twisted your ankle when you stumbled a moment ago, and I can't have you limping up the aisle at our wedding.''

''Would it embarrass you to have a lame bride, m'sieur?''

''Ah, my little Cajun, how you distrust my motives,'' he

lamented. "I would postpone our nuptials rather than cause
you a moment's pain. Unfortunately, though, postponing our
wedding is not something I'm willing to do."

"As you've just amply demonstrated," she retorted.

To her chagrin, Roland only laughed as he carried her back
toward the others.

CHAPTER
Ten

That night, Roland dined with Jean Pierre at the Vieux
Carre Restaurant. They sat on comfortable French side-chairs
at a cozy table, eating broiled redfish smothered in piquant
Creole sauce.

"So you saw the girl again, today, eh, Cousin?" Jean
Pierre remarked as he sipped his wine.

"I did," Roland replied with a frown.

"Things did not go well?"

Roland sighed and set down his fork. "The girl is not
fighting the marriage, if that's what you're asking." Irritably,
he added, "But she has made it crystal clear that she is going
along with the arrangement only because she thinks her parents wished it."

Jean Pierre chuckled. "Then I take it the young lady is
hardly falling at your feet, like all the fair belles of St. Charles
Parish?"

Roland scowled. "What is that remark supposed to mean?"

"Only, *mon ami*, that you have never had to overtax yourself in order to gain the favor of the fairer sex. After all, the
Delacroix family has always been one of the wealthiest and
most esteemed in all the sugar country, their sons much sought
after."

Roland harrumped. "This young lady seems less than impressed by my status. Something else seems to drive her."

"Indeed? What might that be?"

Roland frowned pensively. "I'm not sure."

"Ah—then it seems your child-bride shall be quite an intriguing mystery for you to solve, *n'est-ce pas*?"

When Roland didn't answer, but only continued to scowl, Jean Pierre asked, "You still haven't told her about Luisa?"

Roland's fork clattered onto his plate. "No, and I have no intention of doing so any time soon. The girl is skeptical enough as it is. I'll give her no further cause to question this arrangement."

"But after you're wed, Cousin, surely she'll find out about your first wife then," Jean Pierre argued. "Won't Blanche tell her?"

Roland sighed. He hadn't given much thought to his spinster stepsister, who had also lived at the Delacroix family plantation for many years. "I'm sure I can secure Blanche's cooperation."

"But if Blanche doesn't tell the girl about Luisa, then surely someone else in the parish—"

"By then Angelique and I will be married," Roland pointed out.

"Still, if the girl should ever find out the true circumstances of this match—"

"I do take pity on myself," Roland remarked with a rueful smile. "I suppose it's a good thing, then, that I'm planning to wed the girl as quickly as possible."

"I quite agree, Cousin."

Yet inwardly, Roland remained perturbed as he sipped his white wine, remembering Angelique's less-than-eager attitude toward him in the park today. The girl would become his wife, all right; yet she would be a far from willing bride. Oh, he'd sensed a softening in her, today, when he'd forced his attentions on her. Hell, perhaps she simply couldn't breathe, caught in his crushing embrace that way. He was not particularly proud of himself regarding the incident. But, damn it, the girl had maddened him with her studied indifference—especially since he was anything but indifferent toward her. When she'd scorned all he had to offer, some demon within him had demanded that he kiss her ruthlessly until he broke through that icy veneer to the flame he hoped was buried beneath.

Curse that it was, he wanted the girl with a voracity that was clearly obscene. Just that one taste of her, though forced, had been heaven. Once they were wed, he could hardly envision himself keeping his hands off her. Yet even if he did manage to seduce her, he now felt certain that afterward, she would react with rancor, as she had today. That he could not abide—having Angelique look at him, year after year, with condemnation, with that icy disdain in her eyes. Oh, no. He'd traveled that road once before.

He sighed. T'would be better, perhaps, to continue to seek his ease with his mistress, Caroline, and give his child-bride a chance to grow up. Perhaps an element of her education was still lacking . . .

Yet how would she learn the proper attitude for a wife, left alone with him at Belle Elise? More importantly, how would he trust himself not to claim his husbandly rights at once, his good intentions notwithstanding?

He would think on these matters at length . . .

The next few days passed in a flurry of activity for Emily and her young protégée, and Angelique saw Roland only in passing, when he occasionally dropped by the Miro townhouse to discuss with Emily plans for the upcoming wedding. He invariably greeted Angelique politely; but his cool attitude was not lost on her. She attributed his distance to the incident that had occurred at the park.

Angelique often recalled that afternoon when she and Roland had last been alone. Invariably, she shivered at the memory—of Roland drawing her indecently close and kissing her, of him sweeping her up into his strong arms and carrying her back to the pond. The sensations aroused by his nearness had not been altogether unpleasant, she had to admit. Yet every time she remembered that day, a tremor of fear gripped her as she recalled the anger, the intensity in Roland's gleaming eyes, the implacable strength and purpose in his body. He had made it clear, brutally clear, just what he would expect of her as his wife . . .

Angelique realized that she may have exacerbated Roland's ruthlessness during the incident, through her own show of defiance, through her telling him bluntly that she was not eager to become his bride. Yet the man had exasperated her.

How could he have expected her to fall at his feet, when she had known him barely twenty-four hours, when she had seen him only three brief times in her entire life?

Yet, willing or not, she would wed this stranger in less than two weeks' time. On their way back from the park, Roland had crisply informed her and Emily of his intention to see the wedding performed before month's end, and the steely resolve in his voice and eyes had warned both women that it would be futile to protest. Already, the predominantly Creole Vieux Carre was humming with gossip regarding the rushed nuptials. Emily was doing her best to prepare Angelique and dispatch the invitations in time.

Angelique's days were filled with near-constant fittings at the dressmaker; Emily also took Angelique on a long round of calling about the Quarter. Emily informed Angelique that it was critical she be introduced to the *grande dames* of Creole society, so that when she and Roland visited New Orleans in the future, they would not be lacking for invitations.

In no time at all, or so it seemed, the morning of the wedding arrived. Angelique barely slept the night before, and Emily came to her room at dawn to begin preparation for the day. With the help of Coco, Angelique was bathed, then her rich ebony hair was laboriously curled with a curling iron and piled in ringlets atop her head. She was outfitted from the skin out in new, crisp white: silk pantalets, stockings, and chemise, followed by a tightly tied corset, a lacy camisole, and petticoats. Only then was her wedding dress—a satin and lace vision completed just yesterday—pulled over her head.

"Oh, Angelique—*Que tu es ravissante*!" Emily cried as she pinned the gauzy veil to the young bride's shining curls. Angelique had to smile as she studied herself in the pier mirror. The wedding dress was of white satin, long-sleeved and high-necked, the wrists and bodice gleaming with dozens of tiny seed pearls, the tight waist emphasizing her slim figure. The skirt was full, with a scalloped overskirt of French lace; yards and yards of the delicate filigree trailed behind her in a lovely train. Satin slippers and lovely crocheted gloves completed the ensemble.

Angelique turned to smile at her friend. "You look wonderful yourself," she replied, admiring Emily in her lavender silk gown. "I'm so glad you're going to be my matron of honor."

"My dear, it's strictly my pleasure."

With Emily assisting with her train, Angelique descended into the courtyard, where Maurice Miro and Phillip awaited them, both father and son elegantly dressed in black suits and ruffled linen shirts. "Angelique, you are *magnifique*!" Maurice cried.

"Thank you, Maurice," she replied with a smile.

Spotting his wife, Maurice now added, "Emily, *ma belle*, you take my breath away as always."

"*Oui*, Maman, you look *charmante*. And you, too, Angelique!" young Phillip chimed in. From the table, the boy fetched Angelique's bridal bouquet, bringing it to her proudly. "Now you are ready to walk the aisle, mam'zelle."

Laughing, the four walked through the passageway to the waiting coach just outside the iron gate, both Maurice and Phillip gallantly helping the ladies board. Maurice and Emily chatted about the exciting day as they rattled through the stone streets of the Vieux Carre toward St. Louis Cathedral. Phillip, who was to be the ring bearer, sat proudly with the satin cushion in his lap. Angelique was quiet, staring pensively at the passing sights—two bedraggled chimney sweeps heading for the market with their long straw brushes, a trio of Ursuline nuns examining oranges outside a shop. In her lap was the exquisite bridal bouquet—a white froth of baby's breath and lily-of-the-valley, nestled amid mounds of lace and ribbon streamers. Yet even the delicate scent of the flowers seemed cloying in the morning heat. She smiled ruefully as she recalled young Phillip telling her that now she was ready to "walk the aisle"; she felt more as if she were about to walk the plank.

Angelique felt half-numb, as if she were caught up in a whirlwind or a vibrantly paced dream. In just a few minutes, she would become Mrs. Roland Delacroix and her life would be changed irrevocably. Roland had placed her in this conveyance, she realized. He had taken the reins, indeed, all control of her destiny, out of her hands. She had no recourse but to go through with the wedding, especially with Uncle Giles gone off God knows where in Mississippi. For the dozenth time in recent days, she reflected on how odd her uncle's absence was at this critical time.

Far too soon, the carriage arrived at the Place D'Armes not far from the river. Originally a parade ground and public meeting place, the entire area was now in a state of flux. Emily had told Angelique that the renovation going on was being spearheaded by local society queen Baronness Pontalba, whom Angelique had met at a recent *fête*. For now, the square had been stripped bare, but soon a new formal array of plantings and walkways would be installed. The square was flanked by the Cathedral, the Cibaldo, and the Presbytere; the new red Pontalba Buildings stood nearby.

As the coachman pulled the carriage to a halt, Emily glanced in dismay at the bare ground beyond them, watching dust motes swirl in the slight breeze blowing off the river on this typically hot, humid morning. "Be mindful of the dirt on the walk, Angelique," she scolded as the coachman opened their door.

"*Oui*, Emily," Angelique replied. She did, indeed, take all care as she alighted from the carriage onto the dusty stone *banquette* before the Cathedral. She hiked her pristine satin skirts to the ankle while Phillip followed with her train held high.

Inside the Cathedral, Angelique was whisked away to an anteroom, where Emily put the finishing touches on her appearance. "Oh, my dear, you're the most beautiful bride I've ever seen," she cried, embracing Angelique warmly. "And you're going to be so happy."

"Thank you, Emily. I can't tell you how I appreciate everything you've done." Angelique's smile was brave, if slightly trembling.

In due course, the two women left the anteroom and the small procession started down the aisle of the Cathedral—first Emily as matron of honor, then Phillip carrying the rings, then Angelique on Maurice's arm. White gardenias marked their path, the sweet-smelling blossoms bedecking lush garlands at the end of each pew.

As she moved through the sanctuary, Angelique noted that there had been a good turnout for the wedding—she estimated that at least a hundred stylishly dressed Creoles were seated in the pews. At the moment, every eye in the church seemed riveted on her as she passed. Angelique felt a blush rising in her cheeks, which made her grateful for the covering of her veil.

All too soon the procession ended at the front of the church, before the smiling priest; next to the Father stood Roland.

Angelique's heart hammered as she viewed her husband-to-be. Roland looked incredibly handsome this morning in a black velvet tailcoat, his outfit completed by matching trousers, black satin waistcoat, and ruffled linen shirt with lace jabot. His black hair had never looked thicker, shinier, and his stance was arrestingly male. She realized anew that this man was masculine perfection in feature and in physique. When he viewed Angelique in her bridal gown and veil, his deeply set blue eyes gleamed with an unabashed hunger that made her stomach flutter.

A strange sense of detachment settled over her during the ceremony—as if this could not, indeed, be happening to her. After Maurice smilingly handed her over to Roland, she woodenly repeated her vows, and only half-heard the words the Father intoned during the Mass. A cold golden band was slipped onto her finger, and she felt almost as if she were dreaming as Roland drew back her veil and brushed his lips, for the briefest moment, over hers. Then it was all over; she and Roland emerged into the startling sunshine of the Place d'Armes, scores of happy Creole families rushing forward to congratulate them.

The Miros soon whisked the couple into their carriage and spirited them off to the St. Louis Hotel, where the wedding breakfast was to be held. Within minutes, Angelique was sweeping past the hotel's columned facade on Roland's arm.

Due to the size of the reception, it was held in the St. Louis's rotunda, a circular salon stretching beneath a high airy dome fashioned of thousands of earthenware pots. Today, tables and chairs had been moved into the large salon, which was so often the scene of Creole *bals de société*. Again, Angelique's senses swam with the sweetness of the many lush flowers gracing the tables.

A reception line was formed off to one side. Angelique felt almost numb as she greeted the wedding guests with her new husband; most of the names and faces became a blur to her. Yet she did respond warmly when Jean Pierre came forward; he shook hands with Roland and then kissed her on the cheek.

Once all the guests had been received, everyone was seated for the repast, Roland, Angelique, and the Miros at the head table. Waiters with trays of mouth-watering foods circulated with great efficiency, quickly serving the happy throng. The cuisine and champagne were divine, yet Angelique only nibbled at the luscious meal of Eggs Sardou, jellied crepes, and sherry-baked bananas. She was ever conscious of Roland's presence by her side, of his vibrant gaze so frequently flicking over her. The wide gold band on her hand was a further reminder of the fact that soon, she would be utterly alone with this stranger.

At last, mercifully, the affair ended, and Roland and Angelique accompanied the Miros back to their Royal Street townhome. Roland changed in a guest room while Emily whisked Angelique up to her bedroom, helping her finish packing and change for the riverboat journey to Roland's plantation. Angelique was well aware that there was to be no wedding trip, as Roland had made clear to her that he had pressing duties awaiting him back at Belle Elise. Thus their wedding night would be spent at the family plantation home on the Mississippi.

Emily was helping Angelique place the last few items in her trunk when a knock came at the door. Emily called out, "*Entrez*!" and Coco stepped into the room, her eyes downcast, her stance nervous as she twisted a handkerchief in her hands. "M'sieur, he want to know if madame is ready to leave," Coco told Emily.

"Are you ready, dear?" Emily in turn asked Angelique.

Angelique bit her lip, staring about at the large, sunny room that had been her home, her haven, for the past two weeks. She desperately needed a final moment to prepare herself for this new destiny which had been thrust upon her. "Emily, I would like to check the dresser one more time," she said almost lamely.

Emily was well aware that the dresser was quite empty, yet her woman's intuition understood just what Angelique needed. "Of course, dear. I'll go on downstairs and tell your impatient bridegroom that you'll be joining him shortly. And I'll send Benjamin up to fetch your trunk."

Emily left. While Coco moved about the room straightening up, Angelique eyed her appearance in the pier mirror. Due to the humidity of the afternoon, she wore a light dress of finest, sheerest muslin, pale blue in color, along with a straw bonnet and lawn gloves. She was ready, and protected as best as possible from the sun, which was sure to be brutal aboard the steam packet. How much longer could she delay?

Angelique's reverie was abruptly shattered. Coco, who had been at the dresser rearranging the toiletries, uttered a cry of misery as a cut glass vase full of yellow marigolds came hurtling off the dresser. Angelique whirled about as glass, water, and flowers spewed everywhere on the polished wooden floor.

Coco at once convulsed into hysterics. "Oh, madame, madame! Please forgive me! I am—so clumsy!"

"Nonsense, it's only an accident," Angelique said briskly. Despite Coco's protests, she fetched a small towel from the armoire and helped the girl clean up the mess, depositing the shards of glass and wilted flowers in a wicker basket.

Yet even after order was restored, Coco was still sniffling as she cowered near the dresser. "What is it, Coco?" Angelique demanded.

Coco's frightened dark brown eyes avoided Angelique's. "Oh, madame! Can you not take me with you to m'sieur's plantation?"

Shocked by this request, Angelique replied, "Why, Coco, I'd love to. But you belong to my uncle." She frowned to herself, trying to second-guess the girl's worries. "Tell me, Coco—are you fretting about who will care for you until my uncle returns from Mississippi? Because Madame Miro has already told me you're quite welcome to stay here—"

"No, no, that is not it, madame," Coco interrupted in a small voice, choking on a sob.

"Then what?" Angelique asked. "Coco, I hate to seem impatient, but M'sieur Delacroix and I must leave within a quarter hour or we will miss our river packet. So I implore you to be frank, or there will be nothing I can do in your behalf."

The girl nodded dismally, staring at the floor. In a low, shamed voice, she said, "I am *enciente*, madame."

"*Enciente?*" Angelique repeated. "You mean pregnant?" As the girl nodded, Angelique demanded, "But who is—"

"I cannot say, madame," the girl whispered miserably.

Angelique thought quickly and fiercely. Who could have gotten poor Coco with child? The slave was Giles Fremont's only female servant, and, remembering the way the girl had seemed frightened of "maître," it was not difficult for Angelique to reach the only logical conclusion the circumstances provided. And of course it would violate Coco's every instinct to speak out against a white man. Angelique gritted her teeth at the thought of her uncle victimizing the mulatress, who was still practically a child. "Coco, is maître Giles the father?" she asked. Then, when the girl's only response was to shudder, Angelique took her by the shoulders and implored, "Coco, you must trust me. I swear on the graves of my beloved parents that I will not betray you."

"You won't tell Maître Giles?" Coco asked tentatively.

"Never!" Angelique promised.

"Maître Giles is the father," the girl admitted.

Angelique was so filled with revulsion at this knowledge of her uncle's nefarious behavior, she was tempted to curse him aloud. Again, she concentrated intensely, searching for a solution to Coco's dilemma. She realized at once that there was no cure for it—she would have to secure Roland's help.

Decisively, she told the girl, "Coco, go tell M'sieur Delacroix that he must come up here and have a word with me. Then go pack your belongings as quickly as you can."

"I am going with you, madame?" Coco asked with forlorn hope.

"If I have anything to say about it, you are," Angelique replied. "Now go, Coco! Hurry!"

As Coco rushed from the room, Angelique belatedly wondered if the Miros would be scandalized by her inviting Roland to her room. Then she remembered with a rueful laugh that she and Roland were married now, making his presence in her bedroom eminently proper. *Mon Dieu*, everything seemed unreal, even the ring on her finger.

A rap now sounded at the door, and after Angelique called out, "Come in," Roland stepped inside. He had changed for traveling into a brown frock coat and coordinating, subtly striped trousers. As always, his virile good looks made Angelique's pulses flutter.

"Good afternoon, Mrs. Delacroix," he said as he strode farther into the room. "As much as I am charmed by your desire to converse with me in private, may I remind you that we are about to miss our river packet?"

Angelique felt herself blushing, especially as Roland called her "Mrs. Delacroix." "Roland, a last-minute problem has arisen," she told him breathlessly.

"Indeed?"

"It concerns Coco." Twisting her gloved fingers together, Angelique blurted out, "Uncle Giles—has gotten her pregnant."

Roland was silent, scowling, for a long moment. At last he sighed and said, "Angelique, it is not uncommon for slaveowners to—er—visit among the negresses they consider to be their property."

"Are you speaking from experience?" she snapped.

His gaze darkened. "My dear, that was not fair."

She nodded, realizing that he had her to rights. "I apologize, Roland. You are right, of course. I have no call to blame you for Coco's plight. It's just that I'm so—rattled by all this. Coco is still a child, barely fourteen, and Uncle Giles has—done this horrible thing to her."

Roland nodded. "Reprehensible of him, I'll agree. So what do you wish to do, my dear?"

Angelique stepped forward eagerly. "I want to take Coco with us to your plantation. She can be my maid."

He mulled this over for a moment, then nodded. "If that's what you want, I think it can be arranged."

"What of Uncle Giles? Do you think he'll cooperate?"

To Angelique's surprise, Roland laughed. "Oh, indeed I do. Tell you what, my dear. If you'll come downstairs with me right this minute, I'll draw up a draft and give it to Maurice. I'll ask him to visit Giles as soon as he returns from Mississippi and make the necessary arrangements. Maurice can send us Coco's papers at the plantation."

"Oh, Roland! That will be wonderful!" Without even thinking, Angelique closed the distance between them, embracing Roland warmly. He grinned at her display of affection; but within seconds, she remembered herself and self-consciously pulled away.

That left him frowning. After a moment, he asked, "Tell me, Angelique, did your uncle ever—try anything with you?"

Angelique felt heat rising in her face. "What do you mean?"

He spoke sternly. "You're shy with me, my dear. And I wonder—"

"Yes?"

He drew a long breath. "As your husband, I have every right to know if your uncle ever hit you—or otherwise abused you."

Angelique was not sure just what kind of "abuse" Roland was referring to. Yet she shook her head and replied, "Uncle Giles never hurt me, if that's what you're asking." She was too embarrassed to add that she was shy in Roland's presence because his bold good looks and electrifying masculinity had her senses constantly in an uproar.

Roland did not look completely satisfied with her reply; yet he had no further opportunity to question her as another knock came at the door. He opened it to admit Benjamin, who had come for Angelique's trunk. And when Angelique caught a glimpse of vulnerable young Coco standing out in the corridor, her meager belongings already packed in a threadbare cloth satchel, Angelique felt compelled to rush forward and tell her the good news.

CHAPTER
Eleven

The afternoon heat was oppressive as the threesome—Angelique, Roland, and Coco—journeyed in the Miro coach from the townhouse on Royal Street to the steamboat landing on Canal. The air was odiferous with the waste clogging the open sewers and the toasting commodities clattering by on the various drays—meats and produce, animal hides, coffee, rum, and tobacco.

At last they reached the packet landing. They alighted to view a long line of vessels moored up and down the Mississippi; the river itself was above the level of New Orleans proper, making the city behind them look sunk in upon itself. To the north along the levee were docked large ocean ships, their sails lashed down against giant masts. To the south were smaller flatboats and keelboats, and directly in front of them were the stately steamboats.

At midsummer, the New Orleans docks were not anywhere near as busy as they would be during the coming harvest months. A languid air rolled over the bobbing boats, and on dockside, a handful of stevedores seemed in no hurry to load the barrels and sacks cluttering the levee.

"Which boat will we be taking?" Angelique asked Roland, as they waited for the coachman to unload their baggage.

"The *Bayou Princess*," Roland replied, withdrawing their tickets from his frock coat and pointing toward a medium-size packet that several passengers were boarding just down the levee.

They ascended the ramp to the *Princess*, the coachman following with their luggage. Roland bought an extra ticket for Coco, and a roustabout secured their baggage in the hold.

As the vessel steamed away from the levee, Coco joined the other slaves in the aftercabin; Roland and Angelique enjoyed a cool lemonade in the main cabin. Soon, they followed the lead of other couples and went upstairs to the promenade. They emerged on the upper deck and went to stand at the railing, where a warm, dank breeze wafted over them. They had left the city behind now and were navigating up the immensely wide, silver-gray waterway. Studying the shoreline nearest to her, Angelique viewed a forest thick with towering oak, bald cypress, and tupelo trees. A long canebrake waved at the water's edge. Across a narrow inlet stretched a sandbar, at the edge of which stood giant blue herons and large white egrets, busily digging for crawfish. Overhead, a hawk circled slowly in gleaming cerulean skies.

land, a woman about whom her husband had spoken with pride and protectiveness. Wouldn't this mysterious Blanche resent her as new mistress of the manor?

Half an hour later, Roland pointed at the eastern bank and said, "My dear, there's Belle Elise."

Angelique smiled slightly, feeling rather warmed that Roland had called her "my dear." She glanced at the eastern bank, first seeing the plantation levee, a built-up embankment of dirt, now profuse with blooming wild violets. From the levee jutted a wharf, where a *pirogue* and a keelboat were tied up. Beyond the embankment stretched River Road, where a horse and buggy were now traveling north at a fine clip. As the conveyance rattled past, Angelique's vision settled on a long alley of moss-draped oak trees, similar to other entry vistas she had seen earlier that day. At the end of the avenue stood a home so enchanting it took Angelique's breath away.

The Belle Elise manor house was enormous, yet it somehow managed to maintain a classical delicacy. It combined the best features of all the homes Angelique had seen earlier that day. Raised a few feet off the ground, it was two-storied and fashioned of brick painted white. Across the front stretched eight slender, majestic columns. Railed galleries spanned both stories, with dark green shutters flanking the tall windows. Identical entry doors were centered on each story; three chimneys graced the high, pitched roof, counterbalanced by three dormer windows.

"What an enchanting home," Angelique murmured to Roland.

He smiled. "The first plantation house was closer to the river, and was heavily damaged in flooding some twenty years past. That's when my father built the big house farther from the Mississippi."

The steamboat now blew its whistle as the pilot maneuvered the vessel toward the Belle Elise wharf. It was some ten minutes before the boat was firmly docked with ramp extended; during that time, an open barouche approached them from the long alley of oaks. The conveyance was drawn by a handsome pair of bay horses driven by a liveried black man.

"Ah, *bien*," Roland murmured. "It seems Reuben heard the steamboat bell and has come to fetch us home."

As soon as the ramp was secured, Reuben hurried up the plank to gather their luggage. The handsome young slave greeted "Maître Delacroix," with great respect, and his dark brown eyes betrayed only a brief glimmer of surprise when Roland informed the servant that Angelique was the new Mrs. Delacroix. Reuben bowed to Angelique, then his eyes lingered for a moment on lovely young Coco.

Angelique enjoyed the brisk drive up to the steps of the mansion; the air was cool beneath the oaks. She inhaled the luscious scent of blooming magnolias.

When the conveyance stopped before the house, Roland hopped down to assist Angelique. "Reuben, please see to our luggage," he called to the manservant, adding to the mulatress, "Come along, Coco."

Angelique and Roland climbed the steps, Coco trailing behind them. Even as Roland reached for the door, it was opened by an elderly black man in butler's garb. "Welcome home, maître."

"Good afternoon, Henri," Roland said.

The long, wide hallway they entered was cool and elegant, lined by oriental runners and dominated by a breathtaking spiral staircase about halfway down the passageway on the left. Angelique glanced about in wonder, her vision swirling at the magnificence of the polished tables with marble tops, the elegant hall tree and rosewood side chairs gracing the large corridor. Yet her ears were also delighted by the sound of music—muffled piano music coming from behind the closed double doors to her left, a poignant rendition of Wagner's "Evening Star." The pianist had a touch of such haunting delicacy, it was all Angelique could do not to burst out singing. From what Roland had told her earlier, she was sure the pianist must be his stepsister, Blanche.

"Henri, this is Mrs. Delacroix," Roland was now informing the butler. "We married in New Orleans."

"*Oui*, Maître," Henri replied. Bowing to Angelique, he added, "Welcome, mistress." Angelique noted that this black man, like Reuben, managed to retain his self-possession at Roland's announcement.

"If you'll show my wife into the parlor and see to her maid, I must have a word with Mademoiselle Blanche,"

Roland continued to the butler. "If you'll excuse me, my dear?" he added to Angelique.

"Of course, Roland."

Roland turned toward the double doors on the left, and Henri, murmuring, "Mistress, if you please?" inclined his hand toward an open double portal on the right.

Angelique preceded the servant into a lovely large room filled with carved rosewood furniture upholstered in pastel shades of satin and silk damask. Heavy gold velvet portieres, topped by gilt cornices, draped the tall windows, with airy lace panels fluttering to the floor in the afternoon breeze. The high white ceiling of the room was graced at center by a stunning horsehair and plaster arabesque, from which hung a gleaming chandelier suspended by a striking crystal spray. On the walls were skillful oil paintings, obviously of nearby scenes—a blue heron flying low over a gleaming lagoon, a bayou girl, in sweater, scarf, and plain gray dress, shelling beans in front of a cedar cottage.

Edging farther into the room, Angelique studied the dining room beyond her, which was separated from the parlor by a wide, graceful archway. This room, too, was enormous, its polished wooden floor graced by an Oriental rug of vibrant blue and gold. The table was the largest and most heavily carved Angelique had ever seen.

Feeling awed by the opulence, Angelique was grateful when Henri asked, "Mistress—may I fetch you a refreshment? Perhaps a glass of *eau sucre*?"

There Angelique smiled; the sugared water was a familiar treat from home. "Yes, Henri, that would be lovely," she murmured.

As he left the room, Angelique noted with a frown that the lovely music filtering out from across the hallway had stopped. Her husband must be talking to Blanche now, she thought uneasily.

Across the hallway, Roland had entered the library as quietly as possible so as not to disturb Blanche as she finished her selection on the grand piano. The piano was positioned near a window, and bright afternoon light poured through the lace panels, outlining Blanche's profile—the striking red hair piled on her head, the aristocratic features, the ever-present black clothing she wore, today a high-necked day dress whose severity was relieved only by a cameo brooch at the bodice. Blanche looked almost beautiful this afternoon, Roland mused, with the marred side of her face turned away. Her expression was wistful as her long slim fingers drifted over the ivories. Blanche typically displayed no emotion, except when she was playing the piano.

Then the song ended and Roland cleared his throat.

"Roland!" Blanche exclaimed, getting to her feet, her hand fluttering to her breast.

"Good afternoon, Blanche," he replied, smiling kindly. "I didn't mean to startle you. Your music, as always, is so lovely."

"Thank you Roland." Blanche approached her stepbrother, inclining the left side of her face, with its bright, large port-wine stain, away from the light according to long-standing habit. She smiled as Roland chastely kissed her other cheek. "Well—did you have a good stay in New Orleans, Brother?"

"Ah, yes, quite fine," he replied. Reproachfully, he added, "You know, Blanche, you must end your isolation soon and visit New Orleans. Emily has mentioned many times that she'd be delighted to have you stay with her. You should go to the *couturière* for a new wardrobe. I know you were quite fond of your mother, but five years does seem an over-long time to mourn."

Now Blanche began to look self-conscious, a sheen of perspiration breaking out on her upper lip. Roland well knew that his stepsister chose to wear black not so much to mourn, after all this time, but to keep from drawing attention to herself and her alleged "deformity." Twisting her fingers together, Blanche avoided Roland's eye and said, "Brother, I do so like it here at the plantation. I can always order whatever I need from New Orleans—or even from New York or Paris. There's nothing I'm lacking, truly."

Roland sighed. For years he had tried to convince his stepsister to let go of at least some of her shy ways, to no avail. Perhaps Angelique could be of some help there.

Which brought him to the subject at hand. He realized that he'd been stalling, deliberately avoiding the moment when he must tell his stepsister about his bride. Clearing his throat, he said, "My dear, I have some rather startling news for you—but quite good news, I assure you. Could we sit down a moment?"

"Of course, Roland."

Blanche was frowning as they seated themselves on the small loveseat. "What is this news, Roland?"

He grinned self-consciously. "I'm afraid there's no round-about way to say it. I've taken a bride, my dear."

"A bride?" Blanche repeated in a low, disbelieving voice, her face paling.

"Yes, indeed. While I was in New Orleans. In fact, Angelique is awaiting us right now in the parlor. But I thought you and I should have a word in private first."

"Indeed?" Blanche questioned, her voice rising slightly.

Roland stared at his stepsister intently, leaning toward her. "Blanche, I know you'll like Angelique. She's from St. James Parish, where she was raised simply, on a farm. When her parents succumbed to the fever a few weeks past, her uncle, Giles Fremont, became her guardian and brought her to New Orleans. And—er—that's where I met her."

"I see," Blanche muttered tonelessly.

Roland continued earnestly. "My dear, Angelique was devoutly raised, like you, and I've heard she has a lovely singing voice. I'm sure the two of you will have much in common."

"Will we?" Abruptly, Blanche rose and walked over to the window, her trembling back to Roland.

He sighed, also getting to his feet. "Blanche, she's only seventeen, still a child in many ways. She'll need your guidance and friendship, and I'm counting on you to extend it to her."

Blanche was quiet for a long moment, obviously struggling to gather her emotions. When at last she turned to face Roland, a mask had descended over her features. "Of course, Brother. All you have to do is to ask."

He expelled a relieved breath. "Thanks, Blanche. Now please, come sit down."

Once both were again seated, Blanche asked with a frown, "Tell me, Roland, how did you come to marry this girl so suddenly?"

He ran a hand through his hair. "I'm glad you asked me that, Blanche, because I'm afraid I married the girl under somewhat false pretenses—for her own good, of course. And I must ask—indeed, beg—your cooperation in not revealing the deception to her."

Blanche raised a pale brown brow. "Pray explain, Brother."

"Very well. It came to my attention, through Jean Pierre, that the girl was not safe living with Giles Fremont. In fact, Jean Pierre had witnessed firsthand an attempt by Fremont to sell the girl off into a life of . . ." Roland paused, and finally, for lack of a better word, muttered, "Sin."

"How terrible!" Blanche gasped.

Roland nodded grimly, realizing he was taking the right tack with his deeply religious stepsister. "At any rate, Jean Pierre and I realized that the only way to save the girl from her uncle's infamy was to find her a suitable husband. Jean Pierre was out of the question, for obvious reasons, and that left . . ." With a lame smile, Roland added, "Actually, I was rather taken with the girl . . ."

"I see," Blanche murmured, frowning. "So you married her, just like that? Didn't the young lady have anything to say about this?"

Roland loosened his cravat, looking quite uncomfortable. "I'm afraid that's where the deception came in, sister."

"Oh?"

"We had to move as quickly as possible, for the sake of Angelique's safety, and we knew it was likely she'd balk. Therefore, we decided to tell her that the marriage was arranged between our families some years earlier."

Blanche laughed shortly. "And she believed this?"

"Really, she had no choice, as I prevailed upon her uncle to join in the deception and convince her that the *contrat de mariage* had been effected earlier. You see, after Angelique's parents succumbed to the fever, their belongings were burned, so we argued that the contract perished."

For a long moment, Blanche was silent, her brow deeply furrowed. At last, she drew a long breath and said, "Brother, it seems you must have been very taken with this young lady, to go to such lengths to marry her."

Roland leaned forward, taking both of his stepsister's hands in his. "Sister, may I have your word that you won't tell Angelique of the deception?"

"I don't know, Brother. A marriage entered into under a lie . . ."

He squeezed her hands. "Would it have been better to see Angelique consigned to one of those tawdry little houses on the Ramparts, where the New Orleans Creoles keep their *femmes de couleur*?"

Blanche nodded. "I see your point. Very well, then, Brother. I'll not be the one to tell your bride of the lie."

"Thanks, Blanche," Roland said, releasing her hands.

"But what of Luisa?" Blanche went on. "Didn't your bride think it strange that your parents arranged two marriages in your behalf?"

Roland shifted on the loveseat, avoiding Blanche's eye. "I—er—haven't told Angelique of Luisa yet."

"Roland!"

He glanced at her passionately. "Try to see it from my perspective. I could not afford to do anything that might dissuade Angelique from marrying me. When you see her you'll understand. She's so innocent, so pure . . ."

"But what of Luisa, Brother? Your bride is bound to find out about her sooner or later. When . . . ?"

"Perhaps in a few weeks, you should mention Luisa to her, casually. But please, just give Angelique a chance to get acclimated first, to accept the fact that this marriage is irrevocable."

"This means a great deal to you, doesn't it, Brother?" Blanche asked, unable to contain a small flicker of emotion in her dark brown eyes.

"*Oui*," Roland replied, his voice strangely hoarse.

Blanche squared her shoulders and said bravely, "Very well, then, Brother. Shall we go welcome your bride to Belle Elise?"

CHAPTER
Twelve

Angelique was finishing her *eau sucre* when Roland and a red-haired woman entered the parlor. She set down her glass and stood.

"Well, here she is," Roland was saying to his stepsister as they crossed the carpet together. As soon as Angelique spotted the bright red, large port-wine stain on the woman's cheek, she knew this lady had to be Blanche. Making sure her gaze did not linger on the birthmark, Angelique braved a smile at her.

"Blanche," Roland was now saying, "this is my bride, Angelique." Turning to Angelique, he added, "My dear, meet my stepsister, Blanche Sargeant."

By now, Blanche had extended her hand to Angelique, and the younger woman eagerly accepted the handshake. "How do you do, Mademoiselle Sargeant?"

"Please, call me Blanche," the other woman said, though her tone lacked warmth. "Welcome to Belle Elise, my dear."

"Thank you, mad—I mean, Blanche," Angelique responded shyly.

"Well." Roland clapped his hands together. "Blanche, if you'll be kind enough to show Angelique to her room, I'm sure she'd like to rest and freshen up from our journey. The heat was quite oppressive coming upriver this afternoon."

"Certainly, Brother," Blanche replied. "Which room would you like me to put Angelique in?"

Roland didn't bat an eyelash. "The east bedroom next to mine will do nicely, I think."

"As you wish, Brother," Blanche said tonelessly.

"Well, then, ladies, I think I'll go have a word with the overseer, and see what has happened during my absence."

Roland excused himself and left the room. Angelique

wasn't too thrilled that her bridegroom had deserted her mere minutes after their arrival, but she managed to maintain an unruffled facade.

With Blanche leading the way, the two women proceeded upstairs. Blanche spoke not a word as they ascended the wide spiral staircase. Angelique sighed to herself, not really knowing what to make of Roland's stepsister. Blanche was polite, but, obviously, very reserved. Her features betrayed no hint of her feelings, and her black clothing lent her a rather intimidating air.

As they stepped into a wide upstairs corridor quite similar to the central hallway downstairs, Angelique smiled at the older woman and ventured, "Was it you I heard playing the piano when Roland and I came in? The music was so very lovely."

Looking taken aback, Blanche paused and turned to Angelique. "Yes, it was I."

" 'Evening Star,' " Angelique murmured. "I do so love the music from *Tannhauser*, even though some may call Mr. Wagner a radical."

Blanche raised a pale brow. "You're familiar with the opera?"

"A little," Angelique demurred.

"My dear, we must become better acquainted," Blanche said with a smile, yet her tone lacked enthusiasm.

Blanche showed Angelique into a large, airy room done in shades of pale rose and mint green. The enormous canopied bed with ruffled taffeta spread and matching canopy-cover practically took her breath away. "What a lovely room!" she cried.

Blanche nodded. "I'll leave you to it, then. I'm sure you do need to rest. Shall I send up a maid to attend you?"

"That won't be necessary. You see, I've brought my own maid, Coco. I'm not sure where she is at the moment, however."

"I see. No doubt, Henri dispatched her to the kitchen for some refreshment upon your arrival. I'll see that she's sent up, along with your luggage."

"Thank you, Blanche."

"You're quite welcome. Dinner will be served promptly at six." With a half-smile, the older woman turned and left.

Watching Blanche leave, Angelique frowned. Her reception by Roland's stepsister had been polite, but cool. Not that she could really blame Blanche. She was sure that Blanche Sargeant was used to presiding over Belle Elise, and Angelique's appearance would naturally threaten the older woman's position. Angelique knew it was critical that she assert herself as new mistress of the manor; but some tact would also be in order, of course. Perhaps with care, she might be able to win Blanche over to her side.

Angelique removed her straw hat, and carefully laid it and her reticule on a carved desk with satinwood inlays. She studied the room in more detail—the flocked pale rose wallpaper, the lovely green velvet drapes bracketing the French doors, the carved mahogany armoire and matching dresser and dressing table. Obviously, her husband was a wealthy man, to own a home so large and lavishly furnished. What would he say if he knew she'd prefer her austere yet well-beloved surroundings back in St. James?

Ah, but she was spinning wool today. Like it or not, Belle Elise was now her home, and she'd best learn to accept this.

Angelique ventured toward the south side of the room, where the double French doors led to a charming sun porch. The porch was long and narrow, flanking the entire bedroom; it was graced by lovely ferns and wicker furniture, edged by wall-to-wall, tall windows where wispy curtains billowed in the warm breeze. Glancing through a corner window, she viewed another double line of oaks, which extended for several hundred yards behind the house. Angelique at once fell in love with the porch and the view, and knew she would spend many hours here. It had been kind of Roland to give her a room with this lovely solarium, she mused.

Leaving the sun porch, she explored an anteroom on the east side of her bedroom, a ladies dressing room with racks for clothing and a single bed near one narrow window. This would be a perfect place for Coco to sleep, she decided. Then she crossed the lush wool rug and opened a door on the western wall. It led to a man's dressing room, filled with suits, hats and boots. These were Roland's things, she knew. She breathed in the familiar masculine scent of him—shaving soap, bay rum, leather, and tobacco. An open door on the far side of the anteroom revealed another large bedroom, this one with a dark brown rug and handsome cherry furniture.

That was Roland's room, she thought. Feeling like an intruder, she returned to her room and sat down on her bed, the crisp taffeta counterpane rustling as she arranged her skirts.

It was strange that her bridegroom wasn't expecting her to share his sleeping quarters, she mused with a frown. Her mother and father had always shared the same room, the same bed, at their home near St. James. Their cedar cottage had been small, and sometimes late at night, Angelique had heard their laughter drifting through the thin walls, and occasionally, even low moans of pleasure. As a child, she had wondered about the significance of these sounds; then when she had turned thirteen, an older girlfriend from church had explained to her how babies were made. Angelique felt herself blushing slightly at the remembered specifics, especially as her mind irresistibly transposed the particulars to Roland and herself. *Mon Dieu*—that image was enough to make her cheeks burn, her heart pound. At any rate, she could hardly envision herself and Roland accomplishing the physical aspect of marriage in separate bedrooms—

Of course, the *haute monde* of Louisiana might do things slightly differently. Blanche had certainly seemed to take entirely in stride the fact that Roland wanted his wife to have her own room. But then, she was a strange one, this Blanche Sargeant.

Angelique's ramblings were interrupted by a knock at her door. She called out, "*Entrez!*" and Henri came in with her luggage, followed by Coco. Angelique found she did feel rather tired, and after Henri left, she napped on the magnificent bed, inhaling the aroma of honeysuckle drifting in from the porch as Coco quietly unpacked her things . . .

At dinnertime, Coco attended Angelique's coiffure, piling her elegant black curls into a fashionable knot on top of her head. The sophisticated style made her look older, and she welcomed an infusion of maturity to her countenance. Then the slave helped her don a frock of the finest, ivory-colored muslin; it had a rounded neckline, tight waist, full skirt, and colorful red ribbon trim.

As a finishing touch, Coco rubbed Angelique's cheeks lightly with rouge, then applied a small amount to her mouth. Then she dusted the girl's face with rice powder. Only a few weeks past, Angelique would have objected to Coco's using any artificial enhancements on her complexion; yet Emily had already schooled Angelique in the light usage of makeup by many Creole women.

A moment later, Angelique went downstairs, hiking her skirts above her satin slippers as she descended the spiral staircase. She found Roland and Blanche seated in the parlor. Roland stood when she entered the room and smiled as his eyes swept over her. "You look lovely this evening, Angelique."

"Thank you, Roland," she replied. She noted that he, too, had dressed for dinner. He looked quite dashing in his chocolate brown velvet frock coat, tan trousers and white ruffled shirt. Her heart fluttered at his masterful presence, especially as his bright blue gaze again raked over her, seeming to sear her flesh.

In the dining room, Roland seated both ladies, Angelique at the farthest end of the table, and Blanche on its eastern side. Roland sat down in the host's chair opposite his bride and nodded to his stepsister. Angelique dutifully crossed herself as Blanche returned thanks. In a far corner of the room, a black child dressed in a blue cottonade dress stood demurely in the shadows as she pulled the cord attached to the giant polished Punkah fan, which swept to and fro over the table, stirring the heavy air.

What followed was a long meal of many courses, each accompanied by a different wine. A hearty, succulent turtle soup was followed by steaming plates of crawfish, then shrimp with a spicy horseradish sauce. Angelique's stomach was already screaming a violent protest when the main course arrived, stuffed redfish and eggplant souffle. She couldn't believe her eyes when a final course of chicken in a delicate white sauce was placed before her.

Of course, none of the three finished or even half-ate all of the rich courses, and the waste of the fabulous cuisine bothered Angelique. She knew she would make some adjustments when she took over as mistress; she'd been poor too long to tolerate such wanton excess. She wondered if Blanche wasn't trying a bit too hard to please Roland.

The meal passed mostly in silence, though Roland did make a few remarks regarding plantation business. Occasionally, Angelique caught him staring at her in that familiarly intense, unnerving way of his, his blue eyes glittering as he thoughtfully fingered his crystal wineglass. She felt relieved when dessert arrived, a thick rice pudding flavored with sweet fruits and wine. Yet the *pièce de résistance* remained, as Henri set aflame an entire bowlful of coffee liberally laced with brandy and spices. At this point, Blanche suggested they retire to the parlor to drink their *café brûlot*.

Angelique felt rather ill at ease as she sat near the window drinking the strong brew—Roland settled across from her in a matching French armchair, while Blanche sat on the settee. Angelique felt she'd handled herself well during dinner—yet she longed for simpler days when she'd taken meals at home with her parents.

"Blanche," Roland remarked after a moment, "tomorrow morning, would you be kind enough to show Angelique around the house?"

Blanche's coffee cup clattered into its saucer, but otherwise she betrayed no emotion. Everyone in the room knew that Roland's unspoken message to Blanche was that he expected her to turn over the reins of the household to Angelique.

"Of course, Brother," Blanche muttered after a moment.

"Splendid," Roland said. "And tomorrow afternoon," he added to Angelique, "I'll take you for a drive around the estate, if you'd like that, my dear."

"Yes, Roland. I'd like that very much."

Little else of consequence was said, and after everyone had finished coffee, Roland offered to escort his wife upstairs. Angelique's heart hammered as they went up the staircase together; she wondered if *the moment* was about to arrive. Her flesh seemed to burn where Roland's strong fingers gripped her arm, and she dared not meet his eye as they continued upward.

Yet at her door, he merely smiled at her stiffly, chastely kissed her forehead and said, "Goodnight, Angelique."

And he turned and left her.

Angelique frowned as she entered her room. Would Roland be joining her later? His distance and formality since they had wed were becoming nerve-fraying.

Coco rushed forward to greet her. "How was dinner, madame?"

"It was fine, Coco. But I fear all the wine has made me sleepy. I think I'd like to go to bed now."

Angelique was grateful for the maid's assistance as she prepared to retire. Once Angelique had washed, donned a handkerchief linen nightgown, and climbed into her huge bed, Coco drew the mosquito *baire* about the bed, then retreated to the anteroom and closed the door.

Angelique smiled ruefully in the darkness. Obviously Coco expected her mistress to be joined by maître tonight. Yet as the long moments passed, Angelique realized that her husband would not be joining her on their wedding night.

The featherbed was heavenly soft, and the sound of the breeze rustling the curtains was very soothing. Yet Angelique's mind was enmeshed in turmoil concerning Roland. Was he planning to assert his husbandly rights at all? Since they had wed, he'd become even more of a stranger than before. Was his shunning her bed his way of telling her how he, too, resented this arranged marriage?

Actually, Angelique was well aware that she was better off married to Roland than she would have been remaining with Giles Fremont. And, realizing that this marriage was irrevocably her destiny, she really did want to make it a success.

Yet Roland was obviously of a different mind; so far, their union was fulfilling none of her girlish dreams. Angelique had always envisioned herself one day falling in love, marrying, and having children, many children. She did so love being around little ones. Yet the way things were proceeding, she'd be having no babies with her aloof, mysterious husband.

Angelique also knew that this was not the real reason a tear now trickled down her cheek and splashed onto the starched, embroidered pillowcase . . .

Long after the house was quiet, Roland sat at his desk in his study downstairs, staring grimly at an account book as he sipped his absinthe. At last he slammed the ledger shut.

He knew that by all rights, he should go upstairs and climb into his wife's bed—no, take her into his room, the master's room, and consummate their marriage there. Angelique had looked so lovely tonight, with her luxuriant hair piled on her head. Her cheeks had been beautifully flushed, her mouth red and ripe for kisses. The ivory-colored frock she'd worn had been the perfect showcase for her slim form—its red trim teasing him with a promise of passion, its neckline just low enough to provide him an alluring glimpse of her lush breasts.

His hand tightened on his glass. Emily had done an excellent job of outfitting the girl, her clothing a taunting enough mix of angel and temptress to drive a man insane. Why then, wasn't he plucking the rosé, taking what was his?

He muttered a curse under his breath. He well knew that it was the girl's earlier comment about duty that impelled him to sit here brooding, instead of claiming his husbandly rights as any other fool would have done. As much as he hungered to make love to Angelique, he simply couldn't stand the thought of having another cold, passionless body "submitting" beneath him in his bed. On, no—he'd had his fill of such "duty" with his first wife, Luisa.

In fairness to Angelique, Roland knew that she had promise—her spirit, her forthrightness, even her temper were both admirable and enticing. Sometimes when she looked at him with such mettle, with such bright defiance in those dark eyes, it was all he could do not to grab her and kiss her until she melted.

Yet not once had the girl done or said anything to indicate that she really wanted this marriage, that she was anything more than his unwilling captive. And, damn it all, he refused to accept her body as some sort of grand virgin sacrifice to her parents' memory and her sense of Christian duty. And thus he knew that he would not take this child-woman until he was sure she would welcome his advances—nay, demand them.

And duty be damned.

CHAPTER
Thirteen

The next morning, Angelique arose a bit later than usual, feeling in a much better frame of mind. She said her morning prayers, as always requesting a special blessing for the souls of her dear parents. After she had her breakfast, she went downstairs for the appointed meeting with Blanche to tour the house.

Blanche stood as Angelique entered the parlor. "Good morning, my dear. I trust your sleeping accommodations were comfortable?"

"Yes, very," Angelique replied. Glancing about, she asked, "Where is Roland this morning?" Then, realizing that she may have made a blunder in admitting her ignorance of his whereabouts, she added, "My husband appears to be an early riser. I haven't seen him so far this morning."

Blanche typically displayed no reaction. "Roland is inspecting the cane fields with our overseer, Mr. Jurgen. I imagine he'll return in time for luncheon. And he also mentioned to me again that he wishes to drive you around the plantation this afternoon."

"I'll look forward to that," Angelique murmured.

"Fine. Would you like to see the house, then?"

"Very much."

Blanche efficiently took Angelique through the rooms. Downstairs, the parlor and dining rooms flanked one side of the wide central corridor, while four smaller, more narrow rooms occupied the other side—a library, Roland's study, and offices for the housekeeping and overseeing functions of the plantation.

As the two women approached the library, Angelique glanced at an oil painting on the wall near the door. "I've

been noticing these lovely oil paintings all over the house,"
she remarked to Blanche. "Who is the artist?"

Blanche glanced at the vivid painting of a swamp scene,
of a lagoon ablaze with light, an alligator sunning himself at
water's edge. "My mother was the artist," Blanche murmured evenly. "She's been dead five years now."

"Ah—your mother." Angelique glanced at Blanche sympathetically. "Why, she was a wonderful artist. And, of
course, her daughter has continued the tradition by becoming
a talented musician."

"Thank you, my dear." Blanche smiled at Angelique, but
it was one of those fleeting smiles that lacked true conviction.
Angelique sighed to herself as they entered the library; she
was increasingly coming to recognize that winning Blanche
over would not be easy.

Angelique was fascinated by the cozy room lined by floor-to-ceiling bookshelves. She couldn't wait to dive into the
many, gilt-edged volumes. At home, she and her family had
owned but a few treasured volumes of Shakespeare and Dickens, along with some theological writings her father had enjoyed.

She lingered in the small room for a moment, studying the
grand piano, which looked decidedly cramped wedged in a
corner. The instrument was magnificent, of gleaming red
mahogany, with a scrollwork music stand, shining ivory keys,
and heavily carved legs. The sheet music for "Evening Star"
was laid out as if in welcome. Angelique couldn't resist
walking over to the instrument and lightly running her fingers
over the ivories.

"Do you play?" Blanche asked from behind her.

Angelique turned to Blanche, blushing slightly. "Very little, actually. My music teacher at home taught me a few
scales and chords so that I could practice my singing. My
family did not own a piano, but the priest in our village let
me practice at the church."

Blanche eyed Angelique curiously for a moment. She
started to say something, then clamped her mouth shut. "I
see. Well, would you like to see the upstairs, now?"

"Blanche, I was wondering something," Angelique murmured.

"Yes?"

She gestured at the small room. "Why do you keep the piano in here? It's so beautiful—why not move it out into the parlor, where everyone can appreciate it, and enjoy your lovely playing?"

Blanche drew herself up stiffly. "I like privacy for my music. Roland has never objected to that."

Angelique bit her lip and decided not to pursue the subject at the moment. But she did intend to see that the piano was moved—it seemed a sacrilege to have it closeted away in these cramped quarters. Obviously, though, she would have to proceed with care where Blanche's feelings were concerned.

After the tour of the main house was completed, Blanche took Angelique out back to the kitchen, which was separated from the main house by a long covered walkway. Inside the large flagstone building, a sea of activity greeted them. At a large wooden table, several black women were chopping squash, husking corn, shelling peas, and kneading bread; the loaves baking in the room's huge stone ovens filled the air with a mouth-watering aroma and a near-debilitating heat. Angelique wondered how the black women could endure working in this inferno. Yet all seemed to take the heat in stride: the "grannies" who sat carding cotton, looming, or spinning, even the young girl who was minding the spicy pot of gumbo hanging on the open hearth. The black women gave Angelique and Blanche brief, curious glances, but mostly kept their gazes respectfully lowered.

The kitchen, like everything in the main house, was scrupulously clean. "I must compliment you, Blanche," Angelique said, glancing from the scrubbed stone floor to the various spices hung up to dry on a rack overhead. "Everything at Belle Elise is in beautiful order."

"Thank you, Angelique," Blanche replied, and for once the spinster smiled with obvious sincerity.

On the breezeway heading back for the house, Blanche paused and turned to Angelique. Awkwardly, she extracted a ring of keys from her pocket. "I suppose you'll be wanting these now," she said. "These are the keys to the house and all the cabinets, as well as those to the safes for coffee, tea, and sugar out in the kitchen."

Angelique stared at the older woman levelly, knowing that

here was a critical moment. Though Blanche had spoken casually and her features betrayed no hint of her feelings, Angelique realized that in effect, the transference of the keys meant the transference of the reins of mistress of the manor. She was wise enough to accept the keys at once. "Thank you, Blanche," she murmured, placing the jangling ring in her pocket. "But I must tell you that I'm counting on your help in getting acclimated to my duties as mistress here at Belle Elise."

"Oh?" the other woman replied stiffly.

Angelique nodded. Taking a step forward, she added firmly, "This is a very large house, and there are the servants to think of, as well. I can't conceive of ever not needing— or counting on—your assistance. I trust I may depend on your continued generosity there?"

For a moment, a half-smile pulled at the older woman's tight mouth, then the familiar mask returned. "Of course, Angelique. Roland would want me to assist you in any way I can."

Just inside the back door, Angelique thanked Blanche for the tour, then the two women parted company. Angelique watched Blanche walk upstairs, her black skirts sweeping sedately. She sighed. Blanche Sargeant was an enigma— aloofly formal, impossible to figure out. And this, she had to concede, bothered her no small amount.

Upstairs, Blanche retreated to the safety of her room on the west side of the house. She leaned against the closed door, trembling. It was done now, she thought grimly. The girl had taken her place—and this just a few short hours after Angelique Delacroix had come to Belle Elise.

Blanche hadn't fought the transfer of reins—but then, what good would it have done? Roland was obviously smitten with her.

And besides, Blanche had no intention of revealing her hand that way. Not yet.

Blanche walked over to her dressing table, studying her reflection in the mirror. She touched the hated, bright red, spidery mark on the left side of her face, then her hand fell away, in recoil.

She unhappily reviewed the last twenty-four hours. She

had been stunned yesterday when Roland had appeared with his child-bride. He had left for New Orleans weeks earlier strictly on business, then had returned suddenly married, without directing so much as a "by your leave" toward his stepsister.

Roland's bride was beautiful, charming, young—indeed, she was everything Blanche was not. The young woman was wise, too, telling Blanche this morning that her services would still be needed now that this slip of a girl had come to usurp her.

Had the girl spoken the truth? Or had she lied, as Luisa always had? Blanche's mouth tightened at the thought.

Seven years had passed since Roland's first wife had died, but Blanche's emotional pain remained real and raw. Luisa had been crafty, lying to Blanche, accepting her outwardly while cruelly plotting her downfall and undermining her with Roland. Surely this girl was different, she thought. Angelique seemed guileless, kind, and giving.

Yet Blanche well knew that appearances could be deceiving, just as she knew that she must proceed with caution where Angelique was concerned. For there'd be the devil to pay before Blanche Sargeant would allow another woman to try to ruin her at Belle Elise.

As Blanche had predicted, Roland returned to share the noonday meal with his wife and stepsister. After they ate, he asked Angelique to meet him on the front veranda in ten minutes. She hurried upstairs, touched up her appearance, and grabbed her parasol and gloves. She joined Roland on the front gallery just as Reuben was pulling up in the barouche.

Reuben helped them board, then drove them off briskly. The rear seat was narrow, and of necessity Angelique sat close to her husband, his warmth seeping into her side. She found Roland's nearness both unnerving and provocative. Her lungs kept filling with the masculine scent of him, her eyes kept straying to his magnificent physique—the long muscular legs pulling against well-fitting trousers, the broad shoulders straining at the elegant lines of his frock coat, the handsome male features jutting beneath the wide brim of his hat.

Studying her husband's rather remote expression as he

stared ahead, the firm set of his jaw, Angelique again wondered why he hadn't come to her bed last night. She was his wife now, and claiming her body would have been every bit his conjugal due. But some sixth sense warned her that now was not the time to bring up the subject. After all, they'd only been at Belle Elise for one day—perhaps Roland was just being considerate, giving her a chance to rest and get acclimated before he asserted his husbandly rights.

They were now passing down the grassy avenue of trees behind the house, and Angelique smiled as she watched birds flit about beneath the canopy of a huge oak. The afternoon was uncharacteristically mild, an even breeze caressing Angelique's face and cooling her skin. Peeking through the trees flanking either side of them, she spotted the *garçonnières*, hexagonally shaped guest houses that stood on either side of the wide avenue. Next to each *garçonnière* was a smaller, octagonal *pigeonnier*, or pigeon house.

Unexpectedly, Angelique heard her husband's voice. "Well, Angelique, are you getting settled in?"

She turned to him and braved a smile, wishing she could read his eyes beneath the brim of his hat. "Yes, thank you."

"Is your room comfortable?" he continued politely.

"Indeed."

"Is there anything you're lacking?"

A husband in every sense of the word.

The unspoken reply flitted into Angelique's brain without conscious volition, bringing hot color to her cheeks in its wake. And her sudden blush was evidently not lost on Roland, who turned, abruptly, to stare at her. *Mon Dieu* she thought, she was shameless, to have his most innocent question set her senses reeling with the traitorous attraction she felt for him—an attraction he obviously did not feel in anywhere near equal measure. She glanced away and whispered unsteadily, "No. There's nothing I'm lacking."

Roland turned away with a shrug, and mercifully, Angelique again became distracted by the landscape they were passing through. They had now left the alley of trees and were trotting down the perpendicular "street," a string of brick quarters for the slaves. The neat, cozy cabins were largely deserted, and Angelique presumed the hands were occupied elsewhere with their duties. She did hear the loud

sounds of children laughing and babies crying coming from
the direction of one of the larger cottages; Roland explained
that this building was the nursery.

Behind the street was an endless row of neat, private gardens belonging to the slaves, and beyond that stretched the
main garden of the plantation—waving corn, wheat,
sorghum, watermelons, squash, and other vegetables. Half a
dozen slaves were weeding, hoeing, or plucking harvest, and
the smell of the moist black earth and ripe vegetation was
heavy in the air.

Flanking the plantation garden to the south were three large
greenhouses. Roland explained that two were filled with various fruit trees, while the third housed flowers and spices.
Angelique could see the lush greenery stretching toward the
ceiling in each house. "When my grandfather established
Belle Elise," Roland told her, "he wanted the plantation to
be as self-sufficient as possible. That's why he imported the
fruit trees, and that's also the reason we have one field planted
in cotton. Actually, what cotton we gather here is used mostly
for slave clothing. Our main cash crop is cane."

In due course, they moved past that narrow field planted
in cotton, the snow white tips just beginning to emerge across
the sea of dark green. A small cotton gin separated this field
from the rest of the deep, narrow plantation—which was
comprised of a vast, shimmering ocean of cane plants, six
feet tall, their stalks approaching the purple hue of maturity,
their tips waving gaily in the breeze. Only a handful of slaves
attended the field today. "At this point in the season, the
cane crop is laid by," Roland informed Angelique, "meaning
that it largely takes care of itself. We allow the crop to mature
as late into the fall as possible. Then it's cutting time—and
Belle Elise is busier than a beehive for the rest of the season."

The road cut through the large cane field then curved past
the brick sugar mill, where, Roland explained, the cut cane
would be pressed into juice that would then be boiled down
in huge outdoor kettles. He pointed to a collection of enormous, cast-iron pots lined up against one outside wall of the
mill, and he also directed his wife's attention toward the front
of the building, where two field hands were busy hammering
together the huge "hogshead" barrels which would carry the
brown sugar crystals to market.

Beyond the mill, Roland pointed to a deep, swampy forest which separated the plantation from Lake Ponchartrain. The path made a loop here, and they proceeded for home along a stretch of road forming the southern boundary of the manor.

Soon, they passed a cozy, dog-run cottage. Smoke curled from its flagstone chimney, and on the deep front porch, a blond man in a black suit sat on a rocker, waving to them as they passed.

Waving back, Roland ordered Reuben to halt the barouche. The blond man set down his pipe then hurried down the steps to join them.

"My dear, this is our overseer, Mr. Jurgen," Roland told Angelique as the stocky man drew close. Nodding to the overseer, he added, "Mr. Jurgen, may I present my wife, Mrs. Delacroix."

"Pleased to make your acquaintance, m'sieur," Angelique said politely, extending her right hand toward Jurgen.

The man grinned broadly as he firmly accepted her handshake. "I'm honored to meet you, Frau Delacroix," he said in a heavily accented voice. "As I told your husband yesterday, 'tis a happy day we're having with a new bride here at Belle Elise."

"Thank you, m'sieur," Angelique replied. Jurgen had a ruddy, sincere face and clear blue eyes, and she immediately liked him.

"I hope you haven't been in need of me, sir," Jurgen went on to Roland. "I was just enjoying my pipe after having a bit of dinner with the family."

"No, not at all," Roland assured him. "Although I do have some figures I'd like to go over with you in my office later this afternoon."

"Of course, sir."

While the two men continued talking, Angelique glanced off toward the back yard of the cottage. There, a slim blond woman was hanging clothes on the line while at her feet two towheaded toddlers were rolling a bright red ball between them, laughing and waving their plump little arms. The tender, loving scene caught at Angelique's heartstrings, reminding her of how much she wanted a child of her own. And the simple warmth of the cabin, its similarity to her parents' home, washed her in poignant memory.

"How are Brigette and the twins?" she heard Roland ask Jurgen.

"Splendid," he replied heartily, clapping his sun-browned hands together. "Little Ernst and Elsa are getting fatter each day, and making *Mutter* step lively to keep them fed and clothed."

"As I can see," Roland commented with a chuckle. "Next thing I know, you'll be demanding an increase."

"Indeed, sir," Jurgen replied, also grinning.

The two men said goodbye, and the barouche rattled off. Staring back at the scene, Angelique murmured, "Their children are beautiful."

"Are they?"

She turned around and her gaze slammed into Roland's. He'd tipped back his hat and was staring straight at her, that well-remembered, debilitating gleam in his blue eyes. Merciful saints, he was so handsome, his eyes as searing as a blue fire! "Surely you—you noticed," she stammered, her heart hammering.

He tugged down the brim of his hat. "Actually, when the twins were born, I established a small trust fund in the name of each child. Those monies are quietly gathering interest in New Orleans."

"You—did that for Mr. Jurgen's children?" she asked rather disbelievingly.

That left him frowning. "Jurgen has proven himself to be quite an indispensable overseer—a fact well-known to every other planter in the parish, I might add. Therefore, I have no intention of making it convenient for him to seek employment elsewhere."

"Oh," she muttered irritably. "Then you established the trust funds in order to hang onto an efficient overseer, not due to concern for the children?"

"Who says I don't care about the children?" he snapped.

Angelique turned away, annoyed by her husband's less-than-gracious response. He was playing verbal games with her, and acting churlish, to boot. Why was he reluctant to admit that there might be a tender spot in his heart for another man's children?

And why had he brought her on this drive, anyway, if it was his intention to frustrate her efforts to get to know him better? She ground her teeth and vowed not to say another word to him.

Yet as they headed back for the manor house, curiosity got the better of her. Staring at a looming, vine-tangled forest to the south of her, she asked, "What's beyond those trees?"

He sighed. "The swamp stretches on both sides of Belle Elise beyond the trees." Sternly, he added, "And you must never venture into it alone, my dear."

"Oh?"

"The lagoons have their beauty," he conceded. "I fished there as a boy, but one must take care to avoid the snakes and alligators, and stay clear of the water, as it tends to be stagnant, infused with the breeding spores of a dozen life-threatening maladies. The fall is the time to see the lagoons if you must—when the mosquitoes have subsided. I'll take you there then, if you'd like."

"Yes, I'd like that, Roland," she replied evenly. Though his offer to take her to the swamp had hardly been brimming with enthusiasm, he had sounded sincere, and she welcomed a lightening of the tension between them.

They were almost back to the house when Angelique spied a cemetery off to the south, neatly enclosed in a wrought iron fence. "Is that where your father and stepmother are buried?"

He hesitated a long moment, then said, "Yes. My real mother is buried there, as well."

"Oh?" Angelique asked. "How did she die? I mean, if you don't mind telling me."

"She died in childbirth, when I was but twelve," he replied grimly. "The babe was also lost."

"How terrible," Angelique murmured.

Roland was still staring back at the cemetery. After a moment, he turned to Angelique and said bitterly, "My step-mother used to go sit in the swamp and paint with her oils —against my father's wishes. Then she succumbed to the cholera and so did he."

"Oh, Roland, I'm so sorry." She thought of the lovely paintings she'd seen all over the house, and realized the terrible price Roland's father and stepmother had paid for them. No wonder he had warned her not to venture into the swamp. Indeed, under the circumstances, his concern was endearing. Instinctively, she reached out and touched his arm;

he glanced at her briefly and didn't pull away, but his flesh was tense beneath her fingers.

Sighing, she released his arm and turned away. It was obvious that in large measure, Roland blamed his father's second wife, Blanche's mother, for his father's death. This made his brotherly attitude and affection toward Blanche even harder to figure out.

CHAPTER
Fourteen

During the next week, Angelique saw Roland mainly at meals, and he did not join her in her bed. The warning he'd issued the day they'd driven around the plantation, that she should stay away from the swamp, was the only real indication he'd given that he was the least bit concerned about her. He was occupied with plantation business during the day, and often in the evenings, he went out, with no explanation given. Blanche did tactfully tell Angelique that Roland often indulged in evenings of cards or political discussion with planter friends in the parish. Yet it irritated Angelique to have her new husband ignore her this way. It was as if he'd washed his hands of her, his unspoken message clearly: "Here is the plantation. Here are your duties. Now you're on your own."

The attraction she continued to feel for Roland only intensified her frustration both with herself and with him. Every time she passed him in the hallway or saw him at a meal, her heart increased its tempo. His blatant masculinity, his powerful presence, continued to frighten and fascinate her. Even his maddening distance drew her to him, intensifying the poignance of her yearning. She realized that a part of her hungered to be touched by him, to explore that dark, sweet mystery known as wedded bliss, to move beyond the brief, chaste kisses he occasionally planted on her cheek or fore-head. Often as she lay in her lonely bed at night, she'd be consumed by the memory of the day they went to the park together in New Orleans, when he'd grabbed her and had kissed her so hungrily. She realized that experience had awak-ened something carnal in her, an elemental need that refused to be stilled. Even though Roland's passion had been near-violent, her body traitorously longed for a repetition of his assault—anything but this cool, killing indifference.

When Sunday came, Roland did escort Angelique and Blanche to Mass at the small Catholic church his grandfather had built. Angelique enjoyed the Mass and meeting the priest, as well as several families from neighboring plantations. Yet back at Belle Elise, right after the midday meal, Roland rode off. This time, he really piqued Angelique's temper. When she'd lived with her parents, Sunday after Mass had been a hallowed time for them to be together as a family. To have Roland rush through his luncheon then dash off afterward seemed the ultimate insult.

Thus her days passed, in loneliness and frustration. She did busy herself with Blanche, becoming better acquainted with the running of the household. Angelique volunteered to write the menus and was pleasantly surprised when Blanche politely acquiesced. Blanche was invariably helpful toward her, though she persisted in acting stiffly formal and distant.

All of that changed one August morning. Feeling bored, Angelique had wandered into the library, sitting down at the piano. She wasn't very advanced as a pianist, but she could accompany herself on a few of her favorite selections. She pulled out a collection of sacred music. Her fingers drifted to the ivories, and her voice rose in the poignant strains of "Panis Angelicus," which was a favorite of hers, one she often sang at church back in St. James. This morning she delivered the sacred melody with powerful emotion, her voice searing and clear; her heartfelt rendition made her feel closer to God and to her dear, departed parents.

Angelique was nearing the climax of the piece when abruptly Blanche burst into the room, looking stunned. Ange-lique at once quit singing as Blanche gasped, "*Mon Dieu! Was that you singing?*"

Self-consciously, Angelique glanced at the older woman.

There was so much tension etched across the Blanche's face, that Angelique's initial reaction was that she had angered her with her singing. "I'm sorry, Blanche. I did not mean to disturb you—"

"Disturb me?" Blanche repeated with an amazed laugh, further confusing Angelique. "Disturb me? Oh, my dear!" She rushed toward Angelique, her eyes gleaming zealously as she added, "You shouldn't have stopped. Oh, I do apologize for interrupting you!" She reached out, gently taking Angelique's arm and nudging her to her feet. "Here, I'll play and you just sing. Yes, you must sing!"

To Angelique's continuing astonishment, Blanche sat down at the piano and began the opening strains of the selection, nodding a cue to her. Deciding not to question further, Angelique sang. Blanche's accompaniment was wonderfully skillful, never detracting from her glorious execution of the song.

When Angelique finished, she was stunned to see tears in Blanche's brown eyes. "Oh, my dear," Blanche whispered, dabbing at her eyes with a handkerchief. "You'll have to excuse me."

And without another word, Blanche fled the room. Angelique shook her head, not knowing whether she had pleased Blanche with her singing, or had upset her terribly.

Mercifully, that afternoon, Blanche took Angelique aside in the parlor. Once they were seated on the settee, Blanche said glowingly, "Angelique I must tell you that when you sang this morning . . . I've never heard anything so wondrous in my life. Your voice is the most marvelous gift, like a celestial fire—indeed, an angel flame. But how did you develop your talents to such an advanced degree? Who taught you to sing so brilliantly?"

At once Angelique warmed to the subject. "It was Madame Santoni Rivaldi back at home in St. James."

Blanche gasped. "You can't mean *the* Bella Santoni—the Italian prima donna? *She* taught you to sing?"

Angelique nodded. "Yes, but how did you know about . . . ?"

Blanche waved her off. "Oh, my dear, I've always taken an avid interest in the opera, and of course I've followed the careers of all the great singers of the European stage—Jenny

Lind, Giuseppina Strepponi, and certainly Madame Santoni." Blanche clapped her hands. "Oh, this is so exciting.
I was aware that Madame Santoni had mysteriously disap-
peared from the Italian stage twelve years ago, but I had no
idea she was living in this country! Why haven't I heard more
about her?"

"Because Madame has refused to make any public appearances since she left Italy and settled in Louisiana." Angelique hesitated a moment then went on carefully, "I do
remember when I was still a small child and some representatives of the New Orleans opera came to our parish to
invite her down to sing. But she declined."

"But why? I realize that some among the *haute monde*
look poorly upon a gentlewoman's choosing the stage, but
Madame had already established herself in Italy. Why didn't
she return to the opera?"

Angelique bit her lip. "Madame told me her reasons, but
I'm not sure I should repeat them—"

Blanche leaned forward and grasped the girl's arm, her
expression one of intense fascination. "Oh, please, Angelique, do tell me! I give you my word I'll never repeat what
you say."

Angelique was torn between her loyalty to her teacher and
her desire to please and befriend Blanche. She knew that
Madame Santoni had never actually asked her to keep secret
the story of her past. "Well," she said at last, "Madame
had quite a tragic personal life in Italy. You see, when she
was only a baby, her parents promised her in marriage to the
son of another prominent family. By the time Madame was
eighteen, her gift was apparent, but both her family and her
fiancé's family were opposed to her going on the stage. At
any rate, Madame's talent could not be denied and she
yearned to join the opera. Finally, she and her young man
reached a compromise—that Madame could sing at the opera
for four years, but that thereafter she'd give up the stage
permanently and marry him."

Blanche was listening raptly. "Oh, do tell me the rest!"

"Everything went according to plan for several years, and
Madame was the toast of Rome. Then during Madame's final
season on stage, tragedy struck. A young man in the audience
fell in love with her on sight, and even though the date for

Madame's wedding had been set, this second young man
began to court her. Madame tried to resist Antonio's charms,
but she fell in love with him, nevertheless. Madame's fiancé
found out and challenged Antonio to a duel. Afterward . . .''
Angelique sighed, shaking her head. ''Antonio won, but I'm
afraid Madame's fiancé died a slow and agonizing death.''

''How terrible! What happened to Madame and her sweetheart?''

''They ran off and were married, then fled to this country
in disgrace. That was twelve years ago. But ever since, Madame has remained a torn and haunted woman. She truly
loves Antonio, but she is afraid her fiancé back in Italy was
killed as God's punishment for her own sin of pride, when
she insisted on singing at the opera. She has always blamed
herself for her former fiancé's death, and many times she has
said to me that if only she hadn't insisted on a career on the
stage, that poor young man in Italy would still be alive. She
told me that soon after the young man's death, she vowed
before God that she would never again sing in public—except
at church.''

''My—that's such an intriguing story—and so very
tragic,'' Blanche said. ''So you've been taught by the very
best, my dear.''

Angelique nodded. ''Madame started with me when I was
just five. Soon after she and Antonio settled in St. James,
she heard me singing at church. From then on she had me
in to her home three times a week. I'll never forget the endless
scales she prescribed, the practicing of my trills and cadenzas.
Mostly, she taught me sacred music, but occasionally she
could not resist pulling out some of her arias for me to try.
I think, in a way, Madame continued her music through me.
Anyway, my parents were so proud that Madame had taken
me on. And she never would accept any recompense for my
training.''

''What a fascinating account, Angelique! And of course I
quite understand why Madame took you on. You're a natural,
my dear. You know with your talent, you could become an
opera singer.''

''Oh no,'' Angelique returned solemnly, her brown eyes
gleaming. ''I'm in total agreement with Madame as to why
I sing. I have no desire to use my voice for material gain. I

sing in church to praise God—as Madame does. That is the way my parents wished it, as well, and that is the way it will always be with me."

"I see you were devoutly raised," Blanche commented, and Angelique was warmed to see a glint of admiration in her eyes. Suddenly, Blanche clapped her hands. "Then you must sing at our church here. Your talents must be shared." She leaned forward intently. "Angelique, we must practice in the afternoons. It would mean so much to me to hear you sing and to help you continue your art. You see, I don't go to New Orleans to the opera—"

"But why not, if you're so interested in it?" Angelique asked. Then she could have kicked herself as Blanche nervously lowered her gaze and inclined her face away from the light, favoring her birthmark. Angelique frowned to herself. Since she had gotten to know Blanche, she hardly ever thought of the mar on the spinster's cheek that was obviously such an abiding trial to the older woman. It occurred to Angelique now that if only Blanche would act as if the birthmark didn't exist, then the rest of the world would follow suit. To cover the awkwardness, she patted Blanche's hand and said brightly, "Thank you, Blanche. I would be most honored to practice with you in the afternoons."

Blanche beamed back at her, and for the first time since Angelique had been at Belle Elise, she knew a moment of sheer happiness.

Thereafter, music filled Belle Elise in the afternoons. Blanche dug up reams of sheet music, and wanted Angelique to sing all of it, everything from Franck's sacred music to Stephen Foster to Mozart and Rossini. "But we mustn't overtax that lovely voice," Blanche would always warn. "An hour each afternoon should suffice."

Angelique would inevitably smile to herself when Blanche scolded. She had a powerful voice, and she'd always been able to sing all day if she wanted to, without straining her vocal chords in the least. But Blanche's protectiveness was endearing. Angelique knew she was fulfilling a need in the spinster's life—allowing her to hear operatic selections she had always yearned to hear but had never gotten to, due to her own reclusive nature—and it warmed the girl's heart to know she was doing something so gratifying for this lonely, troubled woman. Though Blanche still acted reserved outside the library, when the two women practiced their music she became a different person—animated, alert, and sometimes even filled with joyous laughter. Angelique began to look forward to their practice sessions.

A few days after they had started their music hours, Angelique was concluding an aria from the opera *Lucia* when she heard the sound of applause coming from behind her. She turned to see Roland standing at the portal. Like Blanche when she'd first heard Angelique singing, Roland looked stunned. He was staring at his bride as if he'd never seen her before—and he looked so devilishly handsome standing there, his muscular body outlined by the sunlight streaming in from the hallway, his gleaming gaze riveted on her. Angelique's heart did a funny little lurch at his intense scrutiny, and her cheeks bloomed with high color. After a moment, he cleared his throat and said to her rather unsteadily, "My dear. I had no idea of the scope of your vocal talent."

Before Angelique could respond, Blanche burst up and hurried toward him. "Oh, yes, Roland. Isn't she divine? You must come hear her!"

Roland was actually laughing as Blanche pulled him into the room. At her direction, he sat down on the love seat and listened as Angelique sang several more selections. After she had finished, he stared at her again, making her blush even more profusely. At last he glanced at Blanche and said, "Sister, we must move the piano out into the parlor. I'd enjoy listening to the two of you in the evenings."

After Roland made his proposal, Angelique glanced tensely at Blanche, knowing that she might view his suggestion as a threat. But to Angelique's surprise, Blanche clapped her hands and smiled. "Oh yes, Brother. Let's do move the piano into the parlor."

As Roland and Blanche discussed details, Angelique shook her head in amazement. Thus the music Blanche Sargeant had practiced in exile for so many long years was brought out of the darkness, out into the bright parlor of Belle Elise for all to enjoy.

* * *

For several nights thereafter, Roland remained in the parlor after dinner to enjoy his wife's singing. Sometimes he would leave after the women finished their selections, but on a couple of nights, he stayed home all evening. Always when Angelique sang, she would catch him gazing at her with searing intensity.

Then came the night when Angelique sang, "The Last Rose of Summer," from the opera *Martha*. She and Blanche had practiced the soleful selection for several days. That evening, Angelique wore a soft red cotton dress with a low, eyelet-trimmed bodice; her ebony hair fell in rich waves about her face and shoulders, and she had even threaded a small spray of miniature red roses behind one ear. Roland stared at her throughout dinner, unnerving her, and by the time the two of them and Blanche retired to the parlor for the evening's music, Angelique felt lightheaded.

Yet her voice, as always, was perfect, strong and clear, a world of poignant feeling in every silvery note. The music was exquisitely sad and Angelique executed the song with great feeling, although there was an underlying sensuality in the aria that left her avoiding her husband's burning eyes. Only when she finished did she dare to glance over at him, and what she saw sent fire racing through her veins. He sat on the settee with his long legs crossed, a glass of absinthe in his hands, his tanned fingers idly stroking the crystal stem. His gaze was meeting hers, holding it boldly; his eyes were filled with emotion. After a moment, he rose and came to her side, saying hoarsely, "Please. Sing it again." In her ear, he whispered, "Look at me this time."

Angelique's heart skidded crazily as Roland turned and walked back to the settee. *Look at me this time*, he'd said, the words intimate, commanding, like those words of a lover lost in passion's heat. Unsteadily, Angelique nodded to Blanche. Then she repeated her song, this time bravely meeting her husband's glowing blue eyes. She found his gaze was so vibrant, so alive with feeling that her stomach did a slow, agonizing somersault the entire time she sang. She realized that this man, who had been so distant since they had wed, was now seducing her with his eyes. And she was revealing herself back to him with each glorious note.

When Angelique finished, there was a long charged silence,

the electricity thick in the room. Then Roland stood and came to her side, still staring at her in that frightening, captivating way. "I think it's time for me to escort you upstairs, my dear."

Angelique felt herself blushing in sudden anticipation and some fear as her husband added to Blanche, "Goodnight, Sister."

"Goodnight, Roland," Angelique heard Blanche reply tightly.

Angelique held onto Roland's arm as they climbed the stairs together. At her door he paused, his eyes again raking over her, lingering on the firm swell of her breasts. Smiling at her, he murmured, "Angelique, when you sing . . ."

"Yes?" she whispered breathlessly, her heart hammering at his nearness. His voice had been like the smoothest caress.

"Do you have any idea what it does to me?" Before she could reply, he stroked her hair where the flowers were and murmured, "The last rose of summer. I wonder—is it ripe to be plucked as yet?"

Angelique was drowning in his bright, heated gaze as he hooked an arm about her neck, pulled her close, and kissed her. From the instant his lips touched hers, she was reeling, seared by his heat—and needy, so very needy. Ravenous. She knew she'd been wanting him to do this for weeks—and now, at last, he was hers. At first his mouth was tender and warm on hers, experimenting, and then his kiss deepened, becoming feral, demanding. He tasted heavily of alcohol and fierce male need, the heady essences deepening her excitement. Small, incoherent cries rose muffled in her throat as she clung to him, opening her mouth wider to his probing tongue. He responded with a satisfied groan, crushing her fragrant softness closer, flattening her tender young breasts against his hard chest. Darts of flaming arousal streaked down her body, invading the very core of her with hurtful intensity. She wanted to beg, *Please . . . please . . .* but she couldn't, his mouth was too deeply locked on hers. Yet when his hands sought her hips, tilting her into the hard, frightening length of his manhood, she automatically stiffened.

She was gasping with both fear and need when he abruptly released her, leaving her lips bruised and bereft. She stared up at him in trembling anticipation, only to find him scowling darkly.

"Perhaps not yet . . ." he murmured ironically.

He was turning to leave when she touched his sleeve. "Roland?"

He turned to her. "Yes?"

Angelique bit her lip, floundering beneath his heated gaze, the impatient quirk of his mouth. She had been raised to be forthright and she could no longer go on with such distance between them, with such a critical matter left unaddressed. Tonight Roland had at last taken a small step in her direction, giving her a taste of an aspect of their marriage she was eager to explore. They had begun to communicate through her music, and now she yearned to deepen that communication. She was frightened, yes, but also so hungry for his touch, so ready to make this marriage something more than an empty shell. Tilting her chin, she asked, "Roland, I must know. Are you going to expect me to—to fulfill my wifely duties?"

To her deepening dismay, Roland cursed under his breath, then laughed sardonically. "Angelique, I don't want your *duty*," he gritted with bitter sarcasm. "But tell me, my dear—is there anything you want from me?"

Staring up at his cynical visage, stung by his words, Angelique found pride dictating her answer. "No, m'sieur," she snapped.

Ten minutes later, Roland was downstairs pacing his study, drinking absinthe and brooding.

Had he totally taken leave of his senses? Mere minutes ago, his beautiful young bride had offered herself to him and like an idiot, he had refused to take his rightful place in her bed.

He uttered a string of oaths as his boots continued to pummel the carpet. For weeks Angelique had haunted his senses, consumed him like a fever. Yet he knew she didn't return his feelings, that only her devotion to duty and her parents' memory had kept her here. He'd tried to escape her, by playing cards with friends almost every night. He'd lost heavily each time because—damn her eyes!—all he could think about was his child-bride. He'd even gone to see his mistress, Caroline, promising himself the night of sexual abandon he so desperately needed. Yet from their first kiss, something inside him had turned to ice. She wasn't Angelique. He'd been forced to leave Caroline, apologizing like a bumbling schoolboy, feeling eminently humiliated and frustrated.

And the rest of the time, all day and far too often at night, he had an ache in his loins that newly defined the fires of hell! All he had to do was to look at her, his seductive little bride, to imagine stripping those enticing clothes off her slim body, pulling her beneath him in his bed and burying himself inside her, so deeply inside her . . . Then he'd feel great guilt because she was so very young and he lusted after her so shamelessly—and then the very thought of her youthful guilelessness would make him lust after her all the more. Innocent maiden, fiery temptress. She was his obsession.

And all that insanity had come before she'd started singing. *Mon Dieu*, when she sang! The girl had the voice of an angel, her name the perfect appellation. He'd been captivated, mesmerized, by every diamond-bright, searing note. And aroused . . . aroused to the excruciating degree that on several recent nights, he'd had to take long rides in the moonlight just to cool off. And he no longer slept—not unless he drank himself into insensibility first.

He had to face it. The girl was making him demented. That promise of passion which filled her singing, her eyes—

Luisa had promised passion, too, had teased him remorselessly. But there'd been nothing but coldness beneath that seductive veneer.

And what of Angelique? Why hadn't he taken what was rightfully his tonight, whether it was in the girl to respond or not?

Because he just couldn't. Her slight stiffening when he had kissed her tonight had warned him that she wasn't responding with abandon; then her new remark about duty had put him off completely. He just couldn't be sure about her. Was her withdrawal a case of maidenly jitters, or was she another coy little tease? What truly lay behind that passionate veneer—fire or ice?

Now he was in a fine fix. He couldn't live without making love to her, he couldn't live *with* making love to her, and no other woman would do.

Roland hurled his empty glass across the room, where it crashed against the fireplace in a thousand tinkling fragments. Then he continued to pace and, for the hundredth time that night, he damned himself a fool and cursed duty.

Upstairs, Angelique found herself fighting tears as she lay in her lonely bed, listening to the low, mournful breeze. She didn't understand this strange man who was her husband. During the past few days, she and Roland had at last begun to draw closer. She knew that they both had felt the attraction steadily building between them. Tonight, that spark had erupted into flames. Roland had kissed her passionately, sweeping her up in a vortex of need, of desire . . . . And then at the last moment, he'd cruelly withdrawn, withholding himself from her. Now she lay here alone and bereft, burning with unfulfilled longing, wishing his powerful arms would hold her, aching to hear him say, *Yes, I want you, chérie . . . I want you here with me . . .*

She'd really laid her pride on the line tonight by asking him whether he would expect her to join him in his bed. Yet his reaction had been cold, bitter, and cynical. Perhaps she'd put him off with her words about duty. To her, duty in a marriage represented a joyous mandate from God. Perhaps he didn't see it that way.

She sighed, clutching the sheet with trembling fingers and staring at the shifting shadows on the dark ceiling. Maybe he simply found some other woman more exciting.

And maybe it was time she accepted the fact that theirs was a hollow marriage. After all, neither of them had asked for this arranged match. She had tried to meet Roland halfway, but he had scorned her efforts. Perhaps she should just give up—

She couldn't somehow, not completely. Yet one thing was for certain, she thought as the tears won out, stinging her throat with aching sobs: She wouldn't ask him again.

CHAPTER
Fifteen

After the night Roland had kissed Angelique at her door and then left her there, he did not remain at home in the evenings. Sometimes he left Belle Elise by horseback, late in the afternoons, and did not return for the evening meal at all. Angelique tried not to show how devastated she felt by her bridegroom's rejection, but it was hard. As much as she hated to admit it, Roland had deepened her longing for him that night when he kissed her—and the fact that she obviously did not stir an answering response in him seemed the ultimate insult.

Late one afternoon, Angelique ventured out onto the front gallery to watch Roland ride off down the long, sun-drenched avenue of oaks, his coattails flying behind him. Damn him for treating her this way! As his wife, she deserved much more respect than this.

"So Roland's gone for the evening again," she heard a feminine voice murmur at her side.

Angelique turned to see Blanche standing beside her, wearing the inevitable black. "Blanche, what ails your stepbrother?" she asked bluntly. "Why does he act this way?"

Blanche slanted Angelique a sympathetic glance. "I think we should talk, my dear."

The two women seated themselves in porch rockers. Blanche was silent for a long moment as the rockers creaked. At last she said, "I think Roland's behavior may have its roots in his first marriage."

Angelique was stunned. "Roland has been married before?"

Blanche nodded. "Yes. But it's been some time. Luisa died seven years ago."

Angelique shook her head, still dumbfounded. "I had no idea Roland was a widower when he met me."

"I'm not surprised," Blanche said. "Indeed, Roland asked me not to tell you about Luisa right away. You see, his first marriage was hardly a source of pride to him. He and Luisa were both quite young, and theirs was an arranged match that neither wanted—"

"Wait a minute!" Angelique interrupted. By now her skin was beginning to crawl. "Are you telling me that Roland's marriage to his first wife was also arranged? Then how could his parents have contracted for him to marry me?"

Blanche looked uneasy for a moment, avoiding Angelique's eye. "You're forgetting, dear, that Luisa died seven years ago. I'm sure your marriage to Roland was arranged some time after that."

Angelique was too flabbergasted to comment.

"At any rate, Roland and Luisa were not happy together. There were some very public scenes, and my stepbrother began staying away from the house . . ." Blanche's voice trailed off meaningfully.

"As he does now?" Angelique supplied.

Blanche reached out to squeeze Angelique's hand. "I'm sorry, dear. You know, you're nothing like Luisa. She was flighty and shallow, and while I hate to speak ill of the dead, I must confess that she could be cruel. I would think that Roland would see that you have much more substance and worth as a person than she did."

"Ah, but perhaps he would also feel that he'd been forced into yet another marriage he did not want—*n'est-ce pas*?" Angelique put in despondently, suddenly understanding much more than she wanted to.

Blanche did not comment.

After a moment, Angelique asked, "How did Luisa die?"

Blanche hesitated a moment, then said, "It was an accident."

Angelique's brow tightened. "What sort of accident?"

Another moment of silence, then Blanche said, "Why don't you ask Roland? He was there."

Without another word, Blanche got up and went back into the house, leaving Angelique to mull over the spinster's startling, confusing revelations.

* * *

Inside the house, Blanche went up to her room, lost in troubled thought. She wondered why she'd told Angelique about Luisa, so bluntly and unfeelingly. Truth to tell, Blanche really liked Angelique. Her world had been much fuller since Roland had brought her to the plantation. Angelique's company was quite pleasant and her singing was wonderful.

Yet deep inside Blanche, scars were still buried from the past. Her more suspicious nature couldn't quite believe that this beautiful young woman would actually want to be the friend of a freak. For that's how she'd always thought of herself—as a monster, an aberration. In her less secure moments, Blanche suspected that Angelique had befriended her only to increase her own esteem with Roland.

Ah, but her emotions were always at war where the girl was concerned! Blanche was a devout Catholic, and she felt great guilt for saying things to cause Angelique doubt or pain. Yet some demon inside her seemed determined, at times, to undermine the young bride; and while Blanche recognized that the reasons for her own pain went way beyond Angelique, at times those reasons did prevail.

"I must speak with you, m'sieur—at once!"

It was early the following morning, and Angelique had just burst in on Roland and Mr. Jurgen in her husband's office. The men stood near Roland's desk going over some papers. At the banging open of the door, Roland quirked a dark brow at his bride. "Good morning, Angelique," he said rather irritably. Setting down his work, he added to the other man, "Mr. Jurgen, if you'll kindly excuse my wife and myself for a moment . . . ?"

"Certainly, sir." Looking quite ill at ease, Jurgen deposited his own papers on Roland's desk and hurriedly took his leave.

Roland followed Jurgen, closing the door behind him. He turned to give Angelique a look of reproach. "My dear, I would have thought you'd have better manners than to interrupt my business this way."

"Manners!" she scoffed, gesturing her contempt. "You're hardly one to speak of manners!"

His jaw tightened. "What's on your mind, Angelique?"

"Why didn't you tell me you were married before?"

For a moment there was dead silence in the room, and Angelique noted to her satisfaction that Roland had actually paled beneath his tan. Good! she thought fiercely. It was about time the insensitive cad experienced some discomfort! She had hardly slept the previous night, endlessly mulling over the startling revelations Blanche had made regarding the first wife Roland had never even bothered to tell her about. And the fact that her husband had evidently stayed out to the wee hours—and looked no worse for wear this morning— only exacerbated her fury.

"I said, why didn't you tell me you were married before?" she repeated, her eyes gleaming with fierce challenge.

Roland drew a hand through his hair, then walked off toward the window, his profile turned to her as he stared grimly through the lace panels. Oh, he was a handsome devil, she thought, especially with the sunlight outlining his chiseled features and gleaming in his dark, wavy hair. But at the moment, she was angry enough to strangle that tanned male neck of his. What hurt the most was knowing how much she wanted him—even at this moment—and that he was heartless, utterly heartless.

"Well?" she prodded.

"Who told you?" he asked.

"Blanche. And I ask you again—why didn't you tell me about your first wife before we were wed?"

He turned to her and said, "It didn't seem important at the time."

"Not important?" She laughed incredulously. "To tell me that you were a widower?"

He sighed. "Angelique, my first marriage was not happy—"

"And neither is your second!" she cut in, her bosom heaving.

That comment gained his full, immediate attention, and he stared at her in intense curiosity, only increasing her wrath. Feeling the humiliating sting of tears, she whirled for the door, but he hurried after her, catching her arm.

"Angelique—"

"Let me go!" she cried, shaking off his touch. "You don't want to be married! You don't even want me here—"

"Are you quite sure that's true?" he asked with sudden anger.

"Yes! Quite sure!" Tears threatened to spill over, but she forged on. "This entire business is bizarre, anyway—two arranged marriages and you didn't want either of them. Why did you marry me, Roland? Why go through with it?"

There, he had no answer, beyond the storm clouds in his eyes.

"You're never here," she went on accusingly. "I may as well be—a peg on the wall for all you take note of having a wife—"

He grasped her by the shoulders. "And if I were here?" he asked meaningfully, searing her with his challenging gaze.

Angelique's cheeks burned and she swallowed hard, not knowing how to answer the bold question in his eyes. He edged closer, one arm reaching downward to hook about her waist, yet she was far too hurt and angry to allow such intimacy. Pushing him away, she demanded, "How did Luisa die? Blanche told me you were there."

He scowled. "It's not something I discuss."

"Certainly not with a stranger like your wife!"

He gestured in supplication. "Angelique, perhaps in time, when we know each other better—"

Yet Angelique was not in a mood to be appeased. "The way things are proceeding, sir, that will never occur in this century!" Her rage would not be contained and words she would soon regret continued to spill out, unheeded. "You must have neglected to warn your first wife about the swamp. Indeed, perhaps I should take a stroll there sometime soon and see if I can't manage to wander into some—some quicksand or something! I'm sure that would suit your purposes just—just admirably—"

He again grabbed her shoulders, and had she not been so furious, she would have been cautioned by the murderous intent now gleaming in his eyes. "You even try that, you little fool, and I'll have you over my knee—"

"Oh, but you can't!" she pointed out spitefully. "How could you possibly dream of disciplining me, when you're never here?"

She turned on her heel and walked out on him.

Roland walked back to his desk and collapsed into his chair, a stunned expression on his face.

He rode off late that afternoon and didn't come home for supper. Angelique begged off sharing the meal with Blanche, claiming she had a headache. Blanche sent a tray up to her room.

After nibbling at the repast, Angelique ventured out onto the upstairs gallery and watched the distant sunset over the wide Mississippi. She leaned on the gallery railing and inhaled deep breaths of the sweet, nectared breeze. Yet all the beauty of nature was powerless to soothe the ache in her throat, her heart—

She remained flabbergasted by her behavior toward Roland. Whether she had possessed good cause or not, she had behaved like a cruel shrew of a wife. No wonder he had left.

Angelique had always been a warm and giving person. But the maddening things Roland Delacroix had done to her . . . He definitely managed to bring out the worst in her. She remembered when she was but a child of four, one of her first memories of home. She had been so eager to eat her mother's gumbo, just ladled from the iron pot, that she'd badly scalded her tongue. In her childish rage, she'd thrown her soup bowl down on the floor, only to feel immediate remorse for having behaved so badly. Her father hadn't punished her but had wisely talked it over with her. "You've got your mother's Cajun temper, child," he'd told her. "It's good to have spirit, but it needs to be tempered with good judgment."

Roland Delacroix sent all of Angelique's good judgment spinning off into the netherworld. True, the man had provoked her terribly with his callousness, but that still did not excuse her unfeeling behavior toward him today. To taunt him about his first wife's death, when the woman may have died under tragic circumstances that were still painful to him! That could well be the reason he hadn't spoken of his first wife before—and had refused to today.

Angelique's sense of justice did demand that a wrong be righted, even if she were the perpetrator. Blow that it would be to her pride, she knew that she would now have to apologize to him.

He obviously would be little affected either way. It was
clear that he didn't want her, hadn't wanted his first wife,
either, if he'd stayed away from her, too, as Blanche had
claimed.

Or perhaps—cruel thought that it was—he had wanted his
first wife all too much.

When Angelique went to bed, Roland still hadn't returned.
She couldn't sleep, her senses acutely attuned to the night-
sounds drifting in her window—bullfrogs, cicadas, crickets,
and owls. Well past midnight, she heard sounds coming from
downstairs, and realized that Roland must have returned. She
wavered for a long moment, wondering whether she should
go down and speak with him.

At last she got out of bed and donned her wrapper. She'd
never rest until she got this matter off her conscience. Even
if Roland had no conscience, she still had her own values to
contend with. She would go down, apologize briefly, then
return to bed.

Since her eyes were already accustomed to the darkness,
she didn't light a taper. The downstairs was also dark, and
at first she thought he had already gone upstairs to bed. Yet
his study door was open, and something compelled her to
enter the shadowy room.

She spotted Roland sitting slumped on the loveseat in his
shirtsleeves and trousers, his body outlined in quicksilver
light. His shirt was partially unbuttoned, revealing the dense,
dark hair on his chest, and his sleeves were rolled up, baring
his muscular forearms. He was asleep. A crisp breeze wafted
through the window beyond, billowing the curtains, and she
reasoned that the wind must have blown out the lamp.

She approached him, and found there was something quite
endearing about his countenance as he slept, his breathing
deep and regular.

Leaning over him, she whispered his name.

He didn't respond and she said it again, louder.

Her husband's eyes opened and he stared up at her.

"Roland, I'm sorry," she whispered achingly.

When he still didn't respond, and she added breathlessly,
"I mean—about the things I said today. They were cruel
and—it's not like me to be cruel."

Still, he said nothing, just staring up at her with his beautiful, deepset eyes, hypnotizing her. He looked sad and oddly vulnerable. After a moment, for a reason she couldn't fathom, she leaned over and pressed her mouth gently on his—

The next thing she knew, she was dragged down into Roland's lap, his arms like bands of steel about her as he crushed her lips with his own. His mouth was hot, devouring, tasting heavily of absinthe. Her senses swam in his male scent. His tongue stole into her mouth, drinking boldly of every texture and recess. She felt electrified, terrified, aroused . . . And she couldn't have been more conscious of the fact that she was half-clothed, totally vulnerable to this powerful, violent stranger.

Within seconds, she was pressed beneath him on the loveseat, his dark gaze burning down into hers. And then he spoke—hoarse, agonized words. "Do you know why I've been staying away, little Cajun? Haven't you any idea how you've haunted me? Oh, I want you, *ma chére*. I do want you so!"

His words were frighteningly harsh, the animal gleam in his eyes making her heart race, and even as he spoke, his strong thighs were forcing hers apart, a bold hand raking up her bare thigh.

"By God, tonight you'll find out," he said, lowering his lips to hers.

His arousal now pressed painfully into her pelvis even as his hand moved to hike up her nightgown. All at once Angelique knew that this was all wrong. Roland was drunk and out of control, and this was no way to begin their marriage —in a few brutal, uncaring moments here on this settee. Pushing against him, she said in a half-hysterical whisper, "No, Roland! No!"

At once he grew limp and then rolled off her. She heard him curse as he stumbled out of the room.

The next morning, when Angelique came down to breakfast, Roland was there. He was usually gone before she came down in the morning, and she inwardly cursed her ill luck as she stepped into the dining room. She knew she couldn't be so rude as to turn and leave. She'd have to face him sooner or later, anyway.

"Good morning, Angelique," he said. He stood and crossed around to her side of the table to pull out her chair, that familiar ironic smile tugging at his mouth, as if nothing had happened between them the previous night. Indeed, as always, he showed no effects of his own indulgence—he was clean-shaven, dressed in crisp black and a fresh shirt, his eyes as clear and bright as sapphires.

As he seated her, the scent of his shaving soap wafted over her, and she felt rather lightheaded as blatant memories slammed her senses. But she managed to hold onto her composure as they sat quietly across from each other, eating their eggs and rice fritters.

After a long moment of electric silence, Roland set down his coffee cup and murmured, "Last night, a child came into my office and kissed me."

Despite her embarrassment at his forthright words, Angelique's reaction was immediate. Her fork clattered onto her plate, and her head shot up. "I'm not a child!"

He gave her an openhanded gesture. "Angelique, last night you came down to my study to apologize for some imagined sin, I presume. And now, I, in my blundering way, am trying to apologize, as well. I guess I haven't been much of a husband to you."

"That's eminently true," she said tersely.

"I suppose there are aspects of our marriage—that just aren't meant to be—"

"I disagree," she cut in.

"You do?" He stared at her boldly, for once looking fascinated.

"This is not a marriage," she told him in a low, bitter voice. "A marriage means trust, and sharing, and children—"

"And duty?" he supplied cynically.

"Yes—and duty!"

His jaw clenched into a rigid line. "I commend your devotion to your wifely responsibilities, my dear. But may I point out that I wasn't the one who stopped things last night?"

She lowered her gaze miserably. "Roland, you frightened me."

There was a long moment of silence, then he said tightly,

"I tend to see things in a different light. I'm a man, my dear. And you're not ready for a man's passion."

"That . . ." She started to say that wasn't true, but found the words stuck in her throat. She could only stare at her plate.

"Quit trying so hard," he said after a moment.

"I beg your pardon?" She dared to meet his gaze.

"You don't have to try so hard," he said. "I'm not going to force on you something you obviously don't want."

She started to hurl at him, "You're the one who doesn't want this marriage!" but found again that she couldn't force the words out. Damn him—he made nothing easy on her. Did he expect her to declare openly, here across the breakfast table, that she hungered for his touch? Especially when it was so obvious that he was indifferent to her presence. To her horror, she felt new tears welling, and though her meal was largely untouched, she tossed down her napkin and stood. "Excuse me."

Roland also stood as she started out of the room. Yet at the portal, she couldn't resist turning to challenge him one final time. "You give up rather easily, don't you, Roland? Before we were wed, I would have sworn it would be impossible to put you off. But then, one must want something in order to be put off. Isn't it so?"

Her words made their impact on Roland, a glower replacing his cynical facade. He started toward her aggressively, only to stop as Blanche strolled into the room.

"Good morning, Brother, Angelique," the spinster said pleasantly, as if oblivious to the thick tension in the room. "I trust that both of you slept well last night?"

That day, Angelique brooded over her argument with Roland at breakfast, as well as their electrifying encounter the previous night. She realized that last night when he grabbed her, she could have been anyone, just a convenient outlet for his lust. For all that he'd drunkenly insisted that she haunted him, his callous behavior over past weeks screamed out another message—that it mattered little to him whether she was at Belle Elise or not.

Then this morning, when Roland had cynically informed

her that she wasn't ready for a man's passion, his real message had come through clearly—that he didn't desire her, not beyond the animal hunger he'd displayed last night. And he'd seemed indifferent to the fact that he'd actually frightened her with his drunken advances. Obviously, her innocence put him off, and he preferred a woman of experience.

She felt frustrated, and hurt. Remembering the richness, warmth, and love of her parents' marriage, her own seemed the cruelest joke. She didn't know how much more of this she could stand.

Roland, too, was brooding, as he rode through the waving fields of "Big Grass" in the mugginess of the August morning. He pondered over Angelique's surprising visit to his study last night, the electric moment when she'd pressed her exquisite young mouth on his.

Obviously, some misguided Christian ethic had compelled his bride to come down to his study last night and apologize for the things she'd said about Luisa. He drew a heavy breath. Angelique knew about Luisa now, and the house of cards they were living in might collapse about them at any moment. He had, of course, wanted Blanche to tell Angelique about his first wife eventually—yet obviously, things had gone horribly awry.

He remembered how he'd felt just a few weeks ago, his obsession to marry Angelique, to make her his wife in every way. Then he'd brought her here, and had mostly ignored her ever since. It was still the girl's commitment to duty that stood between them like a stalwart barrièr. He simply refused to accept her virginity as some pious offering on the altar of their marriage. Last night when he pulled her into his arms, half-crazed from wanting her, it couldn't have been more obvious that it wasn't in her to respond.

Just like Luisa! And he had hoped for so much more between them, had seen such a promise of passion in her eyes.

He sighed. He would have to talk with the girl again, convince her to go off to Paris to school. They couldn't go on hurting each other this way, or there'd be no hope for them ever. By the time Angelique graduated from finishing school, perhaps her attitude would change. If not, he'd grant her an annulment then.

But one thing was for certain, he thought, his hands tightening on the reins. He couldn't keep her here in this house with him, or surely before many days passed, he'd take from her what she'd never willingly give. And even if she lay there, coldly submissive as Luisa had, in his mind it would be no better than rape.

Far better to send her away than to destroy himself forever in her eyes. He rode on briskly, trying to ignore the sudden tightening in his chest and the stinging of his eyes.

At midafternoon, Roland was in his office reading some correspondence when Henri knocked. "Maître, Mademoiselle Caroline Bentley is here to see you."

Roland groaned. This was all he needed today, for his mistress to come calling. But courtesy dictated that he at least speak with her. "Thanks, Henri. Please offer Mademoiselle Bentley some refreshment and tell her I'll join her shortly."

A moment later, Roland stepped into the parlor. Caroline was sitting in a rosewood chair near the window, twirling her half-open lace parasol on the floor. She looked quite delicious today in a full dress of crisp rose organza, her lush blond hair in a smooth chignon, a small feathered hat on her head.

"Good afternoon, Caroline," he said stiffly.

A smile lit Caroline's pretty, rounded face as she turned to him, dimpling becomingly. "Good afternoon, Roland."

Unsmiling, he took a seat across from her. "What brings you to Belle Elise today?"

Caroline slanted her lovely amber gaze on Roland. "Why curiosity, of course, darling."

"Curiosity?"

"Yes—concerning the surely enchanting young thing that you have married."

Roland sighed. "Caroline, as I tried to explain to you last week, I really had no choice in marrying Angelique—"

"Ah, but darling, one always has a choice." The words, though evenly spoken, were laced with an underlying heartache. "In the eight years that you've known me, you've never felt compelled to sweep me off to the altar."

He gestured resignedly. "I don't know what to say, Caro."

"I think your behavior speaks for itself, my love." An uneasy silence settled between them, then she leaned toward him and continued earnestly. "But darling, it's all right. I do forgive you. I'm a fool, I'm sure. I've never had any self-control where you're concerned. But I'll take whatever part of you that you're willing to give. You know I've never made any real demands on you. It's just that—it's so difficult when you ignore me this way . . ." Her voice trailed off and she sniffed pathetically, waving a hand as if drowning.

Roland was scowling, feeling highly uncomfortable and hellishly guilty. He and Caroline Bentley had had an "understanding" for many years—one he'd abruptly and crudely severed by marrying Angelique. He was sure that Caroline hadn't believed his lame explanation that he'd married the girl due to a familial obligation. Notwithstanding this, Caro had been patience and understanding itself since he had returned to Belle Elise with his bride—a fact that made him feel even more of a bastard now. And, considering the current impasse in his marriage, his baser nature was far from immune to what Caro had obviously come to offer. Certainly if he were sending Angelique off for a year or more, he could resume sexual relations with his mistress. He was not a monk, after all. Bearing this in mind, he said to her carefully, "Caroline, my marriage with Angelique—well, it's just not working out. It's truly a marriage in name only." He ventured a smile at her—one of those bold, intimate smiles she found so devastating. "I think that if you'll just be patient, in a few weeks, I can get this entire business settled, and you and I—"

"Can be together again, darling?" Caroline asked, her voice rapt with renewed hope. "Oh, love, you can't know how I've ached to hear those words from you!"

Roland was grinning back at her, feeling quite smug and self-satisfied, when abruptly Angelique walked into the room. He shot to his feet, eyeing his wife in genuine panic. How much of his conversation with Caroline had she overheard?

Enough, he realized, for Angelique's brown eyes were blazing with a hatred that made him flinch as she glared accusingly first at Caroline, then at him.

He stepped forward awkwardly. "Well, good afternoon, dear," he said. "Angelique, I want you to meet a neighbor of ours, Caroline Bentley." Sheepishly, he added, "Caro, this is my child-bride, Angelique."

As Caroline stood and came forward to greet Roland's bride, Angelique turned to him with all the vengeance of hell burning in her eyes. "Get her out of here," she hissed.

And Angelique turned on her heel and walked out of the room.

There was a moment of stunned silence as Roland watched his wife proudly exit the room. Then Caroline came forward. "Well, now I know what I came here to find out."

"I beg your pardon?" Distractedly, he turned to her.

Ironically, Caroline said, "I know why you did not stay with me the other night, *chéri*. Your wife is exquisite. Why did you not simply tell me you are in love?"

"In love?" he repeated woodenly.

Caroline laughed ruefully. "Ah, but if you could see yourself staring at her." She shook her head, a deep regret glazing her eyes. "How lucky that young thing is."

He frowned. "Caro, it's not that simple—"

"But darling, it is." She stepped forward and embraced him fondly. There was a telltale catch in her voice as she whispered, "Don't worry, Roland, I won't intrude on your marital bliss again. I just had to find out how things stood between us. Now that I know it's hopeless"—she tried to shrug offhandedly, but the gesture came out as merely sad—"what's the point, my love?"

Roland was still scowling as she released him. "Caroline, things between Angelique and me—"

She pressed her fingers to his mouth, and there were tears brimming in her eyes as she beseeched, "Darling, don't lie to protect my feelings. Please, let it be, before I disgrace myself by falling apart at your feet. Go apologize to that very lovely—and very jealous—young wife of yours."

"Jealous?" he repeated, forlorn hope raw in his voice.

Caroline laughed again, yet it was a broken, hollow sound. "Roland, are you blind?"

"Apparently so," he replied.

After he'd escorted Caroline to her carriage, Roland sat in his study, staring into space, feeling stunned.

And strangely euphoric. Angelique was jealous! Ah, yes, Caroline had been exactly right about it. No other emotion could have accounted for the rage he'd seen in her eyes when she'd spotted him with his mistress. Never had Roland seen his bride looking more beautiful than she had when she proudly tossed her head, turned on her heel and walked out of the room.

She was jealous—why hadn't he seen it in her angry behavior over past days? Had he been too blinded by his own fear that she would never truly want him?

Too in love to see the truth? For yes, he did love the girl, had probably loved her from the instant he'd laid eyes on her in the French market. He loved her strength of character, her beauty, and her spirit. And it had taken an outsider to make him see this undeniable fact, as well.

His love, his need for her, had made him crazed, terrified that she would never return his feelings. Yet obviously she did care for him, at least on some level. He smiled wonderingly as he recalled Angelique hissing, "Get her out of here."

Caroline was definitely gone from this house for good. As for his young wife . . . it was high time for him to end this nonsense, to take her to his bed and watch that Cajun anger flare into Cajun passion. Her seeming to recoil from him before was obviously a simple matter of maidenly modesty. That particular problem would resolve itself in time, once the barriers were down.

His mind was made up. He would love her before this night was out. The mere thought made his heart pound and brought an excruciating tightness to his loins.

Roland frowned and extracted his pocket watch. He had an afternoon appointment with a planter friend, Louis Junot. Should he attend the meeting or stay here?

Best that he go and give his hotheaded little bride a chance to cool down. Tonight, he'd bring her roses from the greenhouse, a sincere apology and a heartfelt declaration of his devotion . . .

Upstairs, the object of Roland's newfound affection was blessing him out in rapid French as she packed her suitcase. Roland's bringing his mistress to their home was the final blow for Angelique.

She'd come downstairs just in time to watch Roland grin lewdly at Caroline, to hear him telling her that his marriage wasn't working out and that soon he would "settle" things with his bride. *Mon Dieu*—now she was mere business for him to settle! How dare the cad plot to get rid of her, sitting right there in the parlor of their home with his doxie. Well, she'd save Roland some trouble, by leaving this very day! Ogling his mistress in their parlor, indeed! The reprobate! No wife should have to tolerate such treason!

Angelique was thankful that right before she'd left New Orleans with Roland, Emily had insisted she accept some money. The matron had also told her, "Remember, whenever you're in New Orleans, this is your home, dear." Doubtless, Emily wasn't expecting her back this soon, but she would have a houseguest before nightfall.

Angelique was aware that river packets regularly passed the Belle Elise landing. She'd simply walk down to the wharf and hail the next passing steamboat. Once she was in New Orleans, she would write to Madame Santoni. She was sure that Madame and Antonio would come to New Orleans at once to escort her back to St. James. There she would some-how rebuild her life.

Angelique was almost through packing when a knock came at her door. Oh, holy saints, surely it would not be Roland. "Who is it?" she called out irritably.

"Blanche," came the reply.

Angelique sighed heavily. "Come in."

The older woman entered the room, gasping as she saw the portmanteau opened on the bed. "Angelique, you're not . . . ?"

"I'm leaving."

"Oh, no." Blanche stepped forward. "Angelique, I was just coming in from cutting some flowers in the greenhouse when I saw Roland escorting Caroline to her carriage. What happened?"

Not answering Blanche's question, Angelique snapped the now-filled portmanteau shut and turned to face the spinster. "Caroline is Roland's mistress, isn't she?"

Blanche hesitated a moment. "Well, yes, but—"

"My husband has made his regard for our marriage—or should I say, his lack of regard for our marriage—crystal clear to me. I can no longer live this sham, this lie. I'm returning to New Orleans to stay with Emily Miro."

Blanche looked highly dismayed. "Angelique—don't you think you're being a bit rash?"

"Do you, Blanche?"

Blanche's silence spoke for itself as Angelique hefted her portmanteau and headed for the door. "Tell Roland that I hope he and Caroline will be very happy together," she called over her shoulder, humiliated to hear her own voice breaking. She managed not to succumb to her tears until she was safely outside in the hallway.

CHAPTER
Sixteen

A long wait was in store for Angelique down at the muggy landing.

She sat primly on a crude bench at the end of the wharf, her portmanteau at her feet. Her gingham dress clung to her, and she itched where her stiff undergarments abraded her sensitive flesh. Her lacy parasol afforded her little protection from the merciless sun, and even the silk roses on her hat seemed to be wilting.

Beyond her, the river gleamed silver-gray, and a hot haze hung above it. Angelique wiped sweat with her handkerchief and swatted at the fat mosquitoes that buzzed at her, even out here in the full light of the wharf. The only sound was the monotonous slapping of water against the jetty.

Often in the afternoons, she had stood on the upper veranda of Belle Elise and watched a seemingly endless parade of vessels float downriver. Why was it, then, that there was not a steamer in sight this oppressive afternoon, when she was so desperate to get away?

A miserable hour passed, and then, to Angelique's delight, a huge three-decked sidewheeler steamed into view, its tall twin smokestacks billowing black clouds into the bright sky. The name *Natchez* was emblazoned on its side, and its yards of railings resembled delicate lace filigree. Jaunty bric-a-brac edged its high gleaming wheelhouse. Elegantly dressed ladies and gentlemen were strolling on the promenade, visiting gaily and perusing the sights.

As the steamer moved closer, Angelique rose, waving her parasol. Mercifully, a deckhand spotted her and signaled back, calling up an order to the wheelhouse.

Escape, at last! she thought. Thank *le bon Dieu*!

Roland was just returning from the Junot plantation, galloping down River Road, when he saw an alarming sight ahead of him—

The steamboat *Natchez* was moored at the Belle Elise landing, and his bride was climbing the ramp, her head held high. A deck hand was following her with her portmanteau.

Mon Dieu! She was leaving him!

Roland laid crop to his mount, and the huge black stallion thundered on toward the landing. Quickly Roland dismounted and hurried up the ramp. He boarded the steamer just as Angelique was handing some coins to the captain. He rushed to her side and grabbed her arm. "Angelique, what is the meaning of this?"

She turned to him angrily. "I'm returning to New Orleans."

"Like hell you are," he gritted, tugging on her arm.

She struggled against his steely fingers. "Unhand me!"

A small crowd of fashionably dressed passengers had gathered about them on deck, shocked whisperings filtering through their ranks. The heavyset, bearded captain stepped up to Roland. "Sir, may I help you?" Then, watching Roland turn to glower at him, the captain grinned sheepishly. "Why, M'sieur Delacroix. What a pleasure to see you again."

Roland did not return the captain's smile. "Captain Leathers," he acknowledged grimly.

"Is there, er—" Leathers cleared his throat awkwardly— "some way in which I can assist you and the lady?"

"*Sir*, this lady is my wife," Roland stated tersely.

"Oh, I see." The captain tactfully retreated.

Yet Angelique was still trying to break away from her husband's tenacious grip. "Wife?" she hissed to Roland incredulously, furious that he'd come after her. "You have no idea what to do with a wife, m'sieur! You're a heartless reprobate! A lecher!"

At that, mortified gasps coursed through the crowd, and Angelique heard one woman wail, "Oh, Virgil, I shall swoon!"

In the meantime, Roland's features had turned bloodred, and his hand was now so tight on Angelique's arm, her flesh throbbed. "My dear, if you're quite through assassinating my character, shall we go?"

Angelique turned wildly to the captain. "M'sieur, this man brought his mistress to our home—"

Now the crowd issued a collective cry of horror, even as the woman down deck screamed, "Oh, Virgil!" and fell over with a thud. A deckhand ran off for smelling salts, while passengers looked on, wringing their hands. Captain Leathers glanced askance at the scene, then turned to Angelique, awkwardly replacing the coins back in her hand. "I'm sorry, ma'am. But since you *are* M'sieur Delacroix's wife . . ."

"Well put, Captain," Roland concurred sarcastically. He grabbed the money in his wife's hand, opened her reticule, and dropped the coins inside. Nodding curtly to Leathers, he drawled, "Now if you'll excuse us . . . ?"

Still, Angelique struggled with Roland. He cursed vividly, and the next thing she knew, she was hefted over his shoulder like a sack of grain, her hat flying off, blood rushing to her face. The fringe of her petticoats flapped indecently as her feet flailed the summer air. Mortified, she beat on his back with her parasol, screaming out her outrage. But he seemed oblivious as he strode down the plank with her easily dangling over one shoulder. She noticed that a red-faced deckhand was following close behind them, holding her hat in one hand and her portmanteau in the other. The men on deck—damn their eyes—were cheering Roland on, while the women continued to exclaim to one another in scandalized voices.

Angelique fought Roland every inch of the way. At his horse, he summarily dumped her to her feet and pushed her up against the animal's hard flank. He grabbed the offending parasol and sent it scuttling off. In a dangerously soft voice, he said, "Stop it, Angelique, or I swear, I'll take you to yonder bench and put an end to your obstinacy—before God and everyone.''

Looking up into her husband's murderously gleaming eyes, Angelique was wise enough to abandon further resistance. He released her and mounted his horse, extending his hand. When she grudgingly accepted his assist, he hauled her to a sidesaddle position behind him. The deckhand handed Roland the portmanteau, then sheepishly gave Angelique her hat. She placed it askew on her disheveled coiffure and tried to maintain a dignified mien as they trotted off, to the humiliating cheers of the men on the steamboat. Angelique didn't dare look back; she was forced to cling to Roland's waist to keep from falling, her breasts pressed against his muscular back.

Back at Belle Elise, the second they were inside the door, Angelique turned to him in her fury. ''I hate you!'' she hissed.

But he was grinning as he watched her storm off up the stairs.

Angelique had thrown herself across the bed and was sobbing disconsolately. She did not even hear the door click open. But she did hear her husband's voice as he whispered, ''*Chérie*, don't cry.''

She immediately sat up, turning to face him. ''Go away!''

Yet he continued to approach her, undaunted, a riveting sensual gleam in his blue eyes. ''There—it can't be that bad.''

''Go away!'' she screamed. ''Go see Caroline!''

He scowled. ''Angelique, I didn't invite Caroline here—''

She sprang to her feet, waving a fist at him. ''No, you only undressed her with your eyes—right in front of me—''

''Then forgive the momentary weakness of a desperate man. You see, since we wed, I haven't . . . I mean, it was you I truly wanted, *mon amour*, you I have always wanted—''

''The devil it was!'' A crystal vase came sailing off Angelique's night table—flower and all—and crashed against the door, narrowly missing Roland.

Roland shook his head, a crooked grin pulling at his mouth. ''I do so love it when you're jealous, little one.''

"Ooooh!" His brutally accurate words made her cheeks flame.

Gently he said, "I'm sorry about the tears—"

"Go away!" To her horror, new sobs wracked her.

"But you made an erroneous statement down at the landing—"

"Oh?" Intrigued, despite herself, she hiccoughed, wiping her eyes with her sleeve and eyeing him warily.

"And now I must correct it." He was standing directly before her now, his eyes blazing down at her, his male essence filling her senses. "You see, I do know what to do with a wife, *chérie*. Now it appears I must demonstrate."

And Roland grabbed her and kissed her until she couldn't breathe. She fought him at first, but it was useless. His mouth was everywhere—on her mouth, on her cheek, on her neck. His hands gripped her breasts through her dress, kneading roughly, and as much as she hated him, it felt glorious! Angelique was sobbing, moaning, "No, no, no . . ." and clinging to him with all her being.

"Has it occurred to you, my lovely one, that it's been killing me to keep my hands off you?" he asked roughly. One arm hooked beneath her and her toes left the floor as he rocked her against his arousal. His eyes smoldered into hers. "Feel my need—feel it!"

Totally mortified and equally consumed with desire, Angelique could only kiss him back to cover her own shame. She was tangled about him like a ripe vine, dizzy and mindlessly aroused, when he swept her up into his strong arms and carried her through the dressing room to his own bedroom. Then she remembered his treason and struggled in earnest again. "No, I don't want this! I don't want you! You're heartless and cruel and—and I'm angry at you."

He smiled tenderly at her flash of spirit, yet his hold on her didn't slacken one bit as he carried her to his bed. "Don't fight me, love," he advised as he set her on her feet. "You'll lose."

Angelique stared up at him, swallowing hard and realizing that he was absolutely determined to bed her—as was every bit his right. Furious and hurt though she was, she knew that she couldn't deny him his husbandly due. "Now? In the afternoon?" she managed to murmur.

"We've waiting long enough, *n'est-ce pas*, my love?" he whispered, reaching for her hair. She caught a sharp breath as he pulled at pins. Her heavy locks tumbled about her shoulders, and he kissed the silken tresses, murmuring, "Ah—*bien*."

His strong hands gripped her slim waist, easily lifting her onto his bed. He doffed his coat, then his hard body followed hers. Boldly he hiked up her skirts and drew her knees up, settling himself between her spread thighs. She gasped, for even through the remaining layers of their clothing, the intimacy was searing, blatant, the hunger in his beautiful blue eyes electrifying. At once he was everywhere on her flesh— strong, hard, sleek, and aroused—ravishing her mouth with deep kisses, ripping aside her clothing, scolding, "No," when she would have clung to the shreds of her modesty. When her bodice was revealed before him, he seemed to lose all control. "Such breasts," he whispered, his hands kneading their fullness. A cataclysm of pleasure and fear sizzled down her body as his lips attacked the firm globes, the cutting edge of his teeth arousing the nipples to an excruciating tautness.

"Oh, God, I must have you, sweet."

Her back arched at his bold words, his hot mouth at her breast. Wildly she tangled her fingers in his thick hair, drawing his lips deeper, harder, into her breast. She was drowning, bursting with her need of him, yet still afraid of the inexorable intent gripping his huge, powerful body. He yanked his shirt open, pressing his hard, hair-roughened chest against her tender breasts, and she moaned feverishly, panting beneath him. Her chemise was still half-on, half-off her body, her bloomers ripped aside, when he eased her thighs farther apart and stroked her wetness with bold fingers.

"No," she said weakly, but then his mouth took hers again. His fingers grew insistent, probing painfully, but also bringing pleasure.

"*Pauvre petite*," he murmured after a moment. "You demanded a woman's due, and now you must shed a woman's tears."

And she did, as his fingers were replaced by the huge tip of his manhood. He kissed her lips gently, his expression filled with an apology for what must follow as he stared down into her beautiful eyes—eyes so dilated, so huge with passion and alarm. His entering her slowly only seemed to intensify rather than lessen her pain as he pierced her maidenhead. Tears spilled from her eyes as he invaded her tight passage, splitting her apart. She bucked, tossing her head and biting her lip until she drew blood. He comforted her as best he could, but refused to let her squirm away, placing a hand beneath her and holding her fast while he pressed hard, forcing the small vessel which seemed destined never to accommodate him to accept his vast unyielding length in full. She sobbed, her flesh seared, throbbing about him as he settled in deep and tight.

"Relax, love," he whispered. "You're taut as a bowstring."

She softened just slightly and he rewarded her with a deep, satisfied growl and a passionate kiss. The pain lessened as he began to move inside her, trying his best to be gentle, but soon losing control in her sweetness. With one deep, stabbing thrust it was over, his mouth smothering her low cry.

Soon afterward, he rolled off her. She sat up, wincing, avoiding his eyes as she quickly gathered her clothes.

"*Chérie?*" he questioned, frowning.

But she was already heading for the door. At the portal she turned and said vehemently, "*That woman* never sets foot in our house again."

Unwittingly, he smiled. Then she was gone, leaving him to frown at the proof of her shattered virginity on the sheets . . .

It was hard for Angelique to meet Roland's eye at dinner that night. She was still sore from their afternoon encounter, and her condition was not helped by the hard bottom of the chair on which she sat. She felt mortified by the memory of giving herself over to him, so wildly and completely. Now, her husband's gaze kept raking over her, leaving her awash in hot memories.

Blanche was evidently aware of the tension between the newlyweds. She made no comment regarding the events earlier that day, but tried to lighten the mood with small talk. Roland answered his stepsister's inquiries mostly in monosyllables, and Angelique found it difficult to say anything to either of them.

Her mind kept mulling over the strange events of the afternoon—Caroline's visit, her own flight to the landing, Roland's bizarre appearance to take her home, and his consummating their marriage so quickly and forcefully afterward.

Lovemaking was nothing like Angelique had expected. At first she had felt so aroused, and then the pain had come. It was as if she'd been reaching for sweet honey at the hive, only to get badly stung by the bees. In a primal way, she felt she belonged to Roland now. She no longer felt in total possession of her own person, and this was highly unsettling. Especially since she'd learned that her husband had a mistress—a mistress he may well have visited since they had wed—his denial this afternoon notwithstanding.

She sighed to herself. If she wanted this marriage to be a true marriage, she'd have to take the bitter with the sweet. If she wanted to have children with her husband—and she did—she would have to endure the confusing pain-pleasure of lying beneath him in his bed. And while she hardly blamed herself for Caroline's appearance in their home earlier that day, in a way she could understand Roland's feeling tempted, considering the impasse their marriage had been in. She knew that as his wife, it was her mandate to see that he had no cause to feel tempted again.

Only, she hoped he wouldn't expect her to join him in his bed again tonight. She still felt overwhelmed, physically and emotionally, and needed time to recover herself.

Roland, too, was brooding as he stared at his wife across from him at the dinner table. How he hated having to hurt her when he took her virginity upstairs this afternoon. She'd responded with passion until those final moments. She'd been so small, so tight—but ah, so heavenly. Her innocence had delighted him; her tears had touched him deeply. If only she could have known one small iota of the pleasure she'd given him.

He realized, too, that his impatience to bed Angelique this afternoon hadn't helped matters. After she'd almost succeeded in leaving him, he'd been in a mood to devour his bride, not to woo her gently. Following the scene at the landing, he'd felt compelled to make a very immediate—and very physical—statement regarding the future dynamics of their marriage. And he'd done so. He hadn't forced the girl; he hadn't been brutal. But his actions had been more those of a crazed, passionate lover than a patient husband's first, tender seduction.

Alas, the deed was done now, his irrevocable claim to her established, and more gentle wooing and lovemaking could follow. He did feel relieved to have learned conclusively that his wife had come a virgin to his bed. God, if he'd discovered that Giles Fremont had abused her before . . . ! Now, could he make Angelique understand that true pleasure would follow? Was she capable of knowing that ecstasy with him?

He couldn't endure it if she recoiled from his touch again.

Later, Roland escorted his bride upstairs. Both of them were tensely silent. When she started past his door, he caught her arm, pulled her close, and kissed her. His tongue, snaking into her mouth, bespoke blatantly of his desire, and his arms clamped about her like a steely vise. The fierce male need in his body frightened her.

Almost at once, he felt her stiffening, and released her, cursing under his breath.

Angelique was trembling as she stared up into her husband's handsome, angry face. She knew that what she said here was critical. She had to let Roland know that she wouldn't deny him in the future. She was determined to make this marriage work. Touching his arm, she said carefully, "Roland, after this afternoon, I—I need some time to recover."

At his wife's miserably self-conscious words, Roland went limp, damning himself an unfeeling idiot. Of course the girl would need time to heal after losing her virginity, and he deserved to be horsewhipped for his callousness. "Are you all right, my dear?"

She lowered her eyes. "Yes, I'm fine. I just need—"

"I understand." He embraced her tenderly. After a moment, he kissed her cheek and asked gently, "When?"

She blushed, and never had she looked more beautiful to him. He ached to kiss her again, but resisted, for her sake.

"In a few days," she said shyly.

"In a few days, then." He drew his index finger across her wet mouth, smiling as she trembled slightly. In a husky tone, he went on, "I want all of your things moved into my room, and I want *you* moved into my bed. It is understood?"

"Yes, Roland," she said breathlessly.

He pressed his lips against her fragrant hair. "Goodnight, my angel."

CHAPTER
Seventeen

For several days thereafter, Angelique avoided another romantic encounter with Roland. She kept busy with her duties, and read and practiced her music with Blanche.

Unhappily, Angelique soon surmised that the showdown between herself and Roland at the Belle Elise landing had hardly passed unnoticed in St. Charles Parish. When Angelique, Roland, and Blanche went to Mass on Sunday, she heard the unmistakable sound of tittering as they passed down the aisle. And the next day, dowagers began dropping by Belle Elise, ostensibly to welcome the new bride to the community. The scandalous scene was not, of course, mentioned directly; but Angelique felt unsettled to have the matriarchs look her over with such sly, amused curiosity.

Blanche was obviously perplexed by the sudden onslaught of visitors, and finally Angelique felt duty-bound to explain to her, as tactfully as possible, what had transpired at the landing. She of course left out the fact that Roland had consummated their marriage afterward.

Blanche typically displayed little emotion. "Thank you for telling me what happened," she said afterward. "I've been wondering what transpired that day you headed off for New Orleans, then returned to the house. I must apologize for my stepbrother's rather excessive behavior at the landing—but then, Roland has always had a formidable temper."

"So I've noticed," Angelique said ruefully.

"Did you and Roland—er—get the matter of Caroline resolved?"

Angelique frowned, as Caroline was still a sore subject with her. While she realized that Blanche might well be able to shed some light on her husband's relationship with his mistress, she wasn't about to let Blanche know that she was staying on at Belle Elise without having fully disposed of the matter of Caroline. Besides, this was a problem to be addressed between husband and wife; Blanche had no place in it.

"I—um—do believe Roland and I have managed to resolve the matter of Caroline," she told Blanche, meeting the other woman's gaze unflinchingly.

Following that emotion-charged day when Roland dragged his wife off the steamboat *Natchez*, then bedded her so passionately, he began staying around in the evenings, and again requested that Angelique and Blanche entertain him with music. Angelique graciously complied; but immediately after each music hour, she would claim to be overtired or to have a headache, and would dash off upstairs, hoping to forestall a repetition of the afternoon when Roland had made her truly his wife. Roland would be left in the parlor to scowl at her departure.

Angelique was well aware that she had no just cause to deny her husband; indeed, she had already resolved not to do so in the future. Yet she found herself continuing to hold him off as the days passed. It wasn't just fear of the pain that she was avoiding, for she instinctively knew that this would resolve itself in time. But that day when she and Roland had first made love—she lying naked and open beneath him with the sun streaming down—something had been changed in her irrevocably. Roland had left no part of her untouched, had branded her his in every way. It was the giving over of herself, of control to him, that bothered her most of all, she decided. The man attracted and compelled her, it was true; yet the act had also bonded her to him, had made her vulnerable to a man who was still in so many ways a stranger, a man whom she couldn't really trust. After all, hadn't his very own mistress sat in their parlor? Hadn't she caught him gawking at the woman? She wondered if Roland had been using Caroline's services during the first weeks of their marriage, and if he would seek her out again now. And what of this mysterious Luisa, his first wife? What of the accident that had caused her death—a tragedy Roland refused to discuss?

Despite all these fears and misgivings, Angelique increasingly recognized that Roland held some power over her. Even during her busiest moments, he consumed her thoughts, and she found herself longing for a repetition of their first encounter. The lovemaking had seemed to soothe something in him, and now she could see the storm clouds gathering in his eyes as she continued to avoid him. She wanted her marriage to work, and she kept thinking that perhaps if they did make love again, it might be a beginning on which they could build a relationship and learn to trust.

Still, doubts about Caroline and Luisa held her back.

On a sunny August afternoon a week later, Angelique and Blanche were practicing at the piano in the parlor when Henri announced two visitors. The two women ceased their music as Henri ushered the guests in.

Angelique received the women graciously. She had already met Annette Junot and her daughter, Clara, at Mass, and she knew that the Junot plantation bordered Belle Elise on the north. But she hadn't had a chance to get fully acquainted with her neighbors.

"My dears, who was singing that fabulous song as we came in?" Mrs. Junot asked once she and Clara were seated on the settee. Annette was fortyish with graying brown hair; her daughter was about sixteen, a younger version of her mother. Both women were slender and pretty, with creamy skin and large hazel eyes complemented by their lime green, flowered frocks and coordinating bonnets.

"Ah, that was Angelique," Blanche replied, her black taffeta skirts rustling as she sat down on a rosewood chair. "Doesn't she sing divinely?"

"Indeed," Mrs. Junot concurred. "My dear, you must sing for us at Mass."

"She's planning on it—we've been practicing quite a bit," Blanche said.

Sitting across from Blanche in another rosewood chair, Angelique was happy to observe her visiting so comfortably with Annette Junot. While Blanche never ventured far beyond Belle Elise, she did seem reasonably at home around the people of the parish, with whom she'd attended church for many years, and who had surely long since grown accustomed to her birthmark.

"Tell me, my dear, are you getting settled in?" Annette Junot asked Angelique. "Clara and I would have come sooner, but one doesn't want to disturb a new bride right off."

"I'm doing quite nicely, thank you." Angelique glanced up as Henri entered the room with a gleaming sterling silver tea service. After he placed the tray on a pedestal table near her, she offered her guests the repast. As she poured steaming cupfuls of the strong brew, she noted that Clara was staring at her rather pointedly. After Blanche and Annette had been served, Angelique turned to the girl and smiled. "Clara, would you like some tea and rice cakes?" Charmingly, she added, "I hope you don't mind if I call you Clara—and that you'll call me Angelique."

The girl was silent for a moment, then said curtly, "No thank you, Madame Delacroix."

Clara's terse words were followed by a moment of uncomfortable silence. Then, Mrs. Junot patted her daughter's hand. "Now, Clara." She glanced apologetically at the other women. "I'm afraid my daughter is a bit out of sorts today. We've had a family tiff about her schooling. But next week she's going to return to New Orleans like a dutiful daughter and finish her studies at Ursuline Convent, just as Papa wants. Isn't that right, Clara?"

"What choice do I have?" the girl asked sullenly.

Mrs. Junot gave the other two women a shrug and a forbearing smile. "Well, my dear," she said to Angelique. "Do tell us a little about yourself."

"There's not too much to tell," Angelique said awkwardly, knowing that her background would seem quite humble to their aristocratic guests. She told Mrs. Junot about her upbringing in St. James and her parents' deaths, then added,

"Afterward, my uncle, Giles Fremont, took me to live with him in New Orleans, and that's where I married Roland— as had been arranged previously between our families."

Mrs. Junot was frowning, about to make a comment, when a deep masculine voice murmured, "Good afternoon, ladies."

With a collective "Ah," the four women turned to see the master of Belle Elise standing in the archway. Angelique's heart fluttered at the sight of her tall, masterfully handsome husband. Roland had obviously just come in from riding— his dark hair was ruffled, his riding crop still in his hand. She wanted to go over and rake some order through his thick, tangled hair—a thought that filled her heart with an odd tenderness toward him.

"Oh, good afternoon, Roland," Annette Junot called out brightly.

He stepped into the room. "How pretty you look, Annette." He gallantly kissed the hand Annette extended, then repeated the ritual with Clara. "And you, too, Clara. You're blossoming into quite a lovely young woman."

"Thank you, m'sieur," Clara breathed, staring at him, captivated.

"And how is Louis?" Roland asked Annette.

"He's fine. He's told me we must have all of you over to dinner soon, to welcome your bride properly to the parish."

Roland glanced smilingly at Angelique. "Ah, we'd love that, wouldn't we, my dear?"

"Yes, Roland," she replied, smiling back shyly. "Will you join us for tea?"

"Oh, no thank you," he said amiably. "I do have business to attend to. If you'll excuse me, then, ladies?"

Roland left the room, and Annette beamed at Angelique. "What a handsome man you've married, my dear. You know, you're the envy of all the belles in the parish."

"Thank you," Angelique murmured. After observing Clara's rapt response to her husband, she knew of at least one belle who was *very* envious of her. Clara's features were still flushed as she stared mesmerized at the hand Roland had kissed.

That hand would not be washed for many a day, Angelique was sure. How many young women in St. Charles Parish

were in love with her husband? Just knowing of this one was
enough to send a hot needle of jealousy shooting through her.

Meanwhile, Annette was clapping her hands. "And now,
my dears, you simply must enchant us with that divine song
we interrupted upon our arrival. Wasn't it 'Old Robin Gray'?
I do insist, now, or I swear, I shall sit here for the rest of
the summer."

Laughing, Angelique and Blanche dutifully went off to the
piano.

Down the hallway in his office, Roland could hear his
young wife's lovely singing as he paced about, and it seemed
the most potent and cruel aphrodisiac to his ravenous senses.

This last week had been purest agony for him, with Angelique avoiding him again and again. Every time he saw his
proud, beautiful young wife, his hunger for her built until it
threatened to become a voracious fire eating up his entrails.
Just now, she'd looked so adorable, sitting in his parlor with
her summer skirts about her, her lush black hair curling riot-
ously about her captivating face and lovely neck as she served
tea to their guests. His wife. His mistress—the queen of his
home, his heart.

He must have her again! He couldn't endure being apart
from her any longer. Loving her had been the sheerest heaven
he'd ever known, and being deprived of her was a hell he
could no longer endure.

Had he scared her off for good with his aggressiveness last
week? Was the situation beyond salvage? Was she able to
feel the passion he felt, or was she frigid, as Luisa had been?
He groaned, turning sharply on his heel. By the saints, he
would not give her up without a good fight. And the first
thing he would do would be to get her back into his bed—
and keep her there for quite a spell.

He knew he'd have to coax this time, not demand. He'd
been wild with desire last week, and this time he'd fight to
hold on to his control.

He now heard her voice rising in a magnificent, silvery
crescendo, and then the lovely song ended and he heard
Annette clapping and uttering exclamations in the parlor. He
frowned, recalling the words he'd overheard as he stood at
the archway—when Angelique had told Annette that their

marriage had been arranged. Annette had frowned confusedly. This came as no surprise to Roland, since details of *mariages de convenance* were generally common knowledge in a parish as closely knit as St. Charles. However, the specifics of this particular *contrat de mariage*—since it did not exist—would not have been known to anyone. And Angelique's telling people about it now would naturally arouse suspicions.

Hmmmmmmm. Perhaps he should return to the parlor and claim his bride before she heard something that might generate additional doubts in her mind.

And he knew just what he wanted to do to keep her occupied . . .

"My dear, you're wonderful!" Mrs. Junot was saying glowingly to Angelique. "I've never heard such a glorious voice as yours! And Blanche—your playing was divine, as always! Now I must hear another selection! Tell me, do you know, 'Home, Sweet Home'?"

Angelique was about to reply, when Roland again stepped into the room. "Ladies," he said to the guests, "would you mind if I steal my wife away for a moment?" He turned to Angelique. "My dear, I hate to disturb you while you're entertaining, but I'm afraid a matter has arisen that we must attend to at once."

Angelique felt herself blushing at her husband's direct stare, while in the background, Annette Junot said, "Well, of course we understand, Roland. Really, Clara and I must be leaving, anyway . . ."

"Please give my regards to Louis," Roland said to Annette. He extended his arm to Angelique. "My dear?"

She had no choice but to apologize to her guests and leave. She exited the room on Roland's arm—albeit her legs were trembling.

Just outside the parlor, Angelique asked him, "Shall we go to your office?"

"No," he said firmly. "Upstairs."

Blanche followed along soon after Roland and Angelique, escorting the two Junot women to the front door. The threesome arrived in the hallway just in time to watch the master of Belle Elise escort his bride up the stairs. Young Clara observed this occurrence in trembling outrage, while her mother looked extremely ill at ease, her fingers twisting the tie of her reticule. "Well, Blanche, it's been so lovely and we must repeat this again soon—"

"Of course," Blanche muttered. After she had seen the two women out, she remained in the hallway, staring at the now-empty stairs and feeling a startlingly strong wave of jealousy roll over her. She knew that Roland and Angelique had gone upstairs to make love. She'd seen the change in them ever since that fateful day when her stepbrother had hauled his wife home from the landing.

She wasn't jealous because of Roland—although at one time, many years past, she had fashioned herself in love with him. Oh, no, Blanche had long since discovered that she truly loved another. Yet his world was forbidden to her, forever. Most of the time, Blanche managed to live with the reality of her loss, to push her pain to the farthest reaches of her mind; yet today, the tragedy of her plight was brought home to her, cruelly and poignantly.

Now, Blanche was seething with envy because Roland and Angelique shared something so very special, something she could never have. The trembling way Angelique looked at her stepbrother—the burning intensity in his eyes when he gazed back at her. Every longing glance the two exchanged screamed that they were off in their own little world now, totally consumed with each other—

Blanche's fingertips brushed across her hated birthmark, then recoiled. It was their happiness that was so hard to forgive.

Upstairs, Angelique was trembling as Roland led her down the hallway. When she started toward her own room, he grasped her arm and said, "No, in my bedroom."

Oh, by the saints! she thought. Her heart lurched as he led her firmly into his room and shut the door. She moved away from him, eyeing him cautiously as his gaze swept her up and down boldly, as if he owned her—didn't he?

"Don't be frightened," he said soothingly.

She bit her lip, not reassured in the least. "Roland—did

you have to drag me off upstairs in front of our guests? Now they're bound to think—''

"Let them think it," he cut in fiercely. With a half-smile, he added, "It will be the truth, after all.''

Roland's remark brought an electrifying silence in its wake, and Angelique could barely breathe over the pounding of her heart. The way he was staring at her—oh, *mon Dieu*, she would be lost, devoured by this man. He looked so strong, so powerful standing across from her, his blue eyes gleaming with such a frightening hunger. Suddenly, she felt very small.

After a moment, he drew a long breath and said, "*Chérie*, I want to know why you've been avoiding me.''

"Avoiding you?''

He stepped closer and drew her into his arms ever so slowly. His scent—all man and leather and tobacco—filled her senses like an aphrodisiac. She knew she was dying as he lowered his mouth onto hers. His kiss was a long, tender seduction, filled with a devastating sweetness. Despite her fears, she moaned and clung to him.

Afterward he stared down at her flushed face and ran a finger over her wet mouth. "Why are you avoiding—this?''

Angelique twisted out of his arms and walked over to the window.

She heard his voice, coming sternly this time. "Angelique, you must know that I'll not tolerate your withholding the truth from me. Tell me—does my touch revolt you?''

"No,'' she whispered.

"Then what?''

Miserably she turned to him. "Last week, I just didn't know what to expect. That it would—be that way.''

He gave her an openhanded gesture. "Angelique, there is some pain involved for every woman the first time. But the pleasure will come, I promise.'' Moving close to her, he placed his hands on her shoulders. "Forgive me if I was a somewhat impatient bridegroom. But I was very badly in need of you, *chérie*. After you went down to the landing and almost succeeded in leaving me—''

Angelique bravely tilted her chin, fighting the treacherous softening his words stirred. "You never asked me if I was content to stay here with you after that—''

He cut in darkly, "Indeed, that is something I shall never ask you, *petite*, because it's not an avenue open to you."

She lowered her eyes, her jaw clenched.

"By the saints, what is it?" he asked impatiently, flinging his hands outward. "Last week, you told me you but needed a few days to recover yourself. Then you agreed you'd move in with me. Now this . . ."

She dared to look up at him. "There's Caroline . . ."

He scowled at her. "Angelique, last week you told me that woman never sets foot in this house again, and I have every intention of honoring your wishes. Yes, she was my mistress before, but you are my wife now. Only you must uphold your end of the bargain."

Her heart skipped a beat. "I beg your pardon?"

He pulled her close, and she felt as if drowning in his nearness as he whispered, "*Chérie*, last week you started something, and you can't just slam the door. You have obsessed my thoughts every minute since. Don't you have any idea how I've hungered for you? Now I must have you— every day."

His lips sought hers again, and this time she shuddered violently then opened her mouth to him, kissing him back with a consuming need to match his own. After a moment, when his mouth moved to torture the fevered flesh of her neck, she whispered, "Now?"

"You'll only make things worse by postponing this," he said, his hot mouth sending shivers down her body. "Let me love you," he coaxed. "Let me show you that you can know true pleasure in my arms."

She was reeling by the time his mouth moved tenderly to her ear. Huskily he asked, "May I undress you now, sweetheart?"

She nodded, too weak to speak. He turned her about and began unfastening her gown. Once her gown, petticoats, and slippers were removed, he went to sit on the bed. "Come hear, my angel," he said with arms extended wide, his heated gaze everywhere on her flesh.

She walked over to him unsteadily, surprised her legs supported her. He reached out and pulled her to him forcefully, settling her between his knees. When his mouth nudged aside her chemise and fastened on the tip of one breast, she bucked in ecstasy, but he held her fast. "Does that please you, my darling?" he whispered as his tongue flicked over her taut nipple.

"Oh, yes, yes!" she cried, shamelessly tangling her fingers in his hair and clinging to him.

"Open my shirt," he suggested, and she brazenly ripped aside buttons, her fingers seeking the warm expanse covered with coarse hair.

He pulled her close then, her tender breasts pressed hard against his rough chest. He stared into her eyes for a long moment, watching passion dilate the irises. "Kiss me," he whispered.

She fastened her mouth on his, groaning as his tongue slipped inside. It seemed so natural when he rolled her over onto the bed with him. He covered her with kisses as he lovingly removed her undergarments. He stared at her naked beauty for a long time, caressing her with his bold fingertips, convulsing her body with shivers. An intense ripple of anticipation coursed through her when he left her momentarily to shuck his own clothes. When he returned, she stared frankly at his body—it was beautifully muscled and strong, but the sight of his swollen manhood did make her eyes widen.

At once he caught on to her unease. "Not till you're ready, *chérie*," he promised, kissing her gently.

He continued to seduce her with his mouth and eyes. Angelique felt stripped of all defense as she lay beneath him, the center of her throbbing, yearning for his filling heat. His mouth on her breasts was exquisite torture, and when his skilled lips moved to her stomach and lower, her senses soared. But she protested when his mouth moved to the mound where her legs were joined, and he made no move to force her, returning his lips to her own. When one finger insinuated itself between her thighs, just grazing the bud of her desire, she went wild, rolling her head from side to side.

"Please . . ." she found herself begging. "Please . . ."

Only then did he position his strong body on top of hers. She winced slightly as he began pushing into her; the pressure was intense, but there was no terrible pain like before. She could feel her own tight resistance as he pressed deeper, determined to bury himself inside her. When at last he pressed against the core of her, she was throbbing and achy, bursting with the depth and breadth of his heat. Yet it felt wondrous!

"*Chérie*," he groaned, "you are exquisite." He stared down into her passionate eyes. "Am I hurting you?"

"No! No!" she cried. Even if he were this time, she was so transported by his kisses and caresses that she wouldn't have cared.

Roland began to move, driving her crazy with slow, searing thrusts, and the wonderful friction of his possession made her passions soar. She dug her fingernails into his back and urged him on, opening to him more and more, wanting him to know her deeper. Her breath came in gasps and she felt herself nearing some magic breakthrough, a moment when she became a part of him and he a part of her.

She tilted her hips slightly toward him and he went wild, pressing his hands beneath her as he drove into her with deep, pounding strokes that brought tears to her eyes. Yet the pain seemed only a flimsy barrier soon shredded by the hot beam of pleasure now exploding inside her with a force that rocked her world and left her crying out, reeling—

They seemed galvanized in that final hard thrust when he poured himself into her, then collapsed, panting, on top of her. The moment was so moving that Angelique burst into tears.

At once her husband rolled off her. "*Chérie*, what is it? Damn me to eternal hell if I've hurt you again—"

"No, no you didn't," she whispered between shudders.

"Then what is it?"

Unable to face the stark question in his eyes, she turned away. He cradled her back against his chest, moving her hair aside to kiss the sensitive back of her neck and gently caressing her back and buttocks. "*Chérie*?"

She couldn't tell him what she was feeling. All of this was too new, she felt too raw, too exposed from the intimacies that they had shared. She couldn't tell him that she no longer belonged to herself, she belonged to him—

And he was a taskmaster she didn't really know.

His lips were at her ear now, his hands moving down her body again. She didn't turn, but her hand reached out, experimentally, to caress his strong male thigh.

Abruptly she was pulled over and brought astride her husband. His eyes were blazing with desire, his knees firmly bracing her back. Her eyes grew huge as he slowly lowered her onto his manhood until she was so full of his passion that she was left gasping from the taut depth and hardness of him. She thought surely she was dying as she slid lower still, and yet she couldn't wait for the moment to overtake her—

"Angelique, do you want this?" he demanded.

"Oh, yes!" she cried, leaning forward to press her aching mouth on his.

CHAPTER
Eighteen

It was soon all over St. Charles Parish how the master of Belle Elise spent his afternoons.

Lazy days followed. Days of September, days of passion. Nights of indescribable ecstasy.

Angelique bloomed. Her cheeks grew beautifully flushed and her breathing quickened every time she saw Roland. She was falling in love. Every minute of every day, he consumed her thoughts. She would sit staring at him over the breakfast table, and her mind would irresistibly stray to their lovemaking an hour earlier—his strong hands everywhere on her flesh, the sweet agony in his eyes as he thrust slowly into her, the pounding ecstasy of their shared climax.

Her thoughts were indecent, carnal, and from his answering smile, he knew, and his thoughts were the same—

And neither cared.

She got to know him better in little ways. He was a considerate lover and an ever-solicitous husband—brushing her hair for her, reading to her a favorite story or poem, bringing her *café au lait* in the mornings. With occasional reports of yellow fever still occurring in the parish, he was ever watchful

over her health. He refused to allow her to arise with him in
the morning, when he first got up in the pre-dawn to inspect
the fields with Mr. Jurgen. After being carried back to bed
for the third time, Angelique got the message and slept in,
joining her husband for breakfast later—on the days when
he didn't return to their bedroom to surprise her with a tray,
and more sweet kisses.

In some ways, she still didn't know him. But she loved
him. Yet her doubts kept her from telling him of her feelings.
After all, theirs was an arranged marriage; Roland was obviously trying to make the best of things, and she was sat-
isfying his needs on a physical level. He certainly seemed to
want her as a wife—

But did he want her as his only lover, as a full partner in
the marriage, a soulmate he cherished above all others? He'd
never really told her that she was more than a convenience
to him—

He'd never told her that he loved her.

And nagging doubts about those who had come before
her—Luisa and Caroline—continued to plague her. Thus,
even when she and Roland were in the heaviest throes of
passion, when she was dying to cry out her feelings to him,
something held her back.

Blanche had grown cooler toward her since she had moved
into her husband's bedroom, and this bothered Angelique, as
well. She and Blanche still spent time together practicing
their music; yet, the spinster's withdrawal was obvious, when
she answered a question in a monosyllable, or cut short one
of their practice sessions.

One afternoon, as the two women had tea before their music
hour, Angelique decided to take the bull by the horns and
find out what was troubling the woman. "Blanche," she
began carefully, "I must know—have I done something to
offend you?"

Blanche looked startled and embarrassed as she set down
her teacup. "My dear—why ever would you offend me?"

"It's just that you seem preoccupied lately."

"Oh?" Blanche inquired stiffly. "I wasn't aware that I'd
acted that way toward you."

"Blanche, I'm just concerned," Angelique said sincerely.

"Well, I suppose I've been concerned about some things myself."

"Oh? Please tell me, then."

"Well, I've noticed that you and Roland seem much happier, and I'm pleased about that, of course. However—I'm afraid there are some things about my stepbrother that trouble me—things you may not know."

"Indeed?"

"Are you aware, for instance, that Roland declined the Junots' recent invitation for dinner?"

Angelique frowned. "No. I wasn't even aware that we'd been invited."

Blanche swept a wisp of red hair from her brow. "I wouldn't have known about it, either, except that I happened to be around when Roland received their servant with the invitation."

"But—why would Roland not accept?" Angelique asked. "Does he usually decline social invitations?"

"Not usually," Blanche replied. "And of course, there's the annual Delacroix Harvest Ball, which has been a tradition in St. Charles Parish for over fifty years. I'm sure we'll be holding that here at Belle Elise soon after the cane is cut, as we do each year."

Angelique's frown deepened. "So Roland does socialize with the parish. Then his turning down the Junots' invitation makes no sense—unless, of course, he dislikes their company."

"That's not the case. He and Louis have been friends for years."

Angelique shook her head slowly. "How do you account for my husband's behavior, then?"

Blanche bit her lip, then said, "Well, dear, I mean this as no slight. But I feel the reasons have to do with you."

"With me?"

"You see, Roland has quite a possessive streak. It showed up in his first marriage. And I fear he doesn't want you to become too friendly with the parish because he's afraid you'll hear things—well, about Luisa."

Angelique felt the skin prickling on the back of her neck. "What about Luisa?"

"You mean my stepbrother still hasn't told you about her?"

Angelique shook her head. "But I really would like to know."

"Very well, then." Blanche gathered her thoughts. "Luisa Rillieux hailed from a prominent New Orleans family. She was convent-educated, and quite the toast of the city when she made her debut. Roland married her nine years ago and brought her here. She was only eighteen at the time. I'm afraid she adjusted poorly to married life and plantation living, and missed her family in New Orleans. She was a frail creature, and a little . . ."

"Yes?" Angelique prodded.

"Somewhat on the unhinged side, I fear. Anyway, my stepbrother was not patient with Luisa's outbursts or her childishness—and truth to tell, Roland, at twenty-one, was hardly mature himself. Theirs was a troubled marriage, and there were some very public scenes. Luisa—well, she flirted with other men, right here in this home beneath Roland's eyes. It enraged my stepbrother—and he retaliated in kind."

"I see," Angelique murmured, trying to imagine the turbulence of her husband's first marriage. "How did Luisa die?"

"Well, there I must backtrack a bit, dear. You're aware that Roland had a brother, Justin, who was killed in a carriage accident?"

"Yes. In New Orleans, I stayed with Emily Miro, who was Justin's wife."

"Of course. At any rate, prior to his death, Justin and Emily lived here at Belle Elise. When Justin was killed eight years ago, Roland did his best to help Emily and young Phillip make the adjustment. And I'm afraid Roland's spending time with his brother's widow drove Luisa over the edge. One rainy night, right after a party held here at Belle Elise, there was an argument between Luisa and Roland in his study. Evidently, there was a struggle over a pistol and—Luisa was killed."

"Oh, my God!" Angelique murmured. "Then . . ." She drew herself upright in her chair and stared at Blanche proudly. "I'm sure Luisa's death must have been strictly an accident."

"Of course." Blanche avoided Angelique's eye as she added, "But Luisa did torment my stepbrother so."

Angelique regarded Blanche suspiciously. "Just what are you implying?"

"Oh, nothing, dear." Carefully, she added, "Tell me, did you ever ask Roland about Luisa?"

"I did—but it wasn't a convenient time for my husband to discuss her with me," Angelique replied stiffly. "I shall, of course, bring the subject up again now that you've—er—told me these things. I'm sure there is some perfectly logical explanation for what happened the night Luisa died."

Blanche was skeptically silent, then murmured, "You might want to wait a while to ask him, my dear."

"Why should I wait?" Angelique asked.

"Well, Roland does have quite a temper . . ."

"Indeed?" Angelique inquired. "Then why ever did you advise me to ask him about Luisa in the first place, a few weeks back?"

"That was remiss of me, wasn't it?" Blanche replied evenly, looking totally unruffled as she lifted her teacup. "However, in thinking it over, I feel it might be best if you give your marriage more time before you question Roland about Luisa."

"Thanks for the advice, Blanche," Angelique said coolly.

For the balance of the day, Angelique felt deeply troubled. The very idea that Luisa had been killed during a struggle over a gun with Roland! It was appalling! Had Blanche lied to her?

She again thought of Blanche's coolness toward her ever since she and Roland had begun living together as husband and wife. She supposed that with Blanche's background and her painful feelings regarding her supposed "deformity," the spinster might well consider marriage to be out of the question for herself. She might be jealous of Roland's and Angelique's happiness—

She might be jealous because of Roland. As much as Angelique hated to admit it, she now had to acknowledge the possibility that Blanche could be in love with Roland. After all, he was the only man she had been exposed to much of the time, and they weren't actually related by blood; it made sense that she might fall in love with a man who protected her from the world and behaved so chivalrously toward her. If this were true, Blanche might have made her statements about Luisa just to stir trouble between the newlyweds.

On the other hand, Angelique knew it was likely that there was at least some truth in what Blanche had told her, for the woman could easily have gotten caught in outright lies. As to precisely how Luisa had died, only Roland could tell her that. She remembered Blanche's warning about Roland's temper. Yes, she had caught quite a glimpse of it at the landing ten days past, when he'd so forcefully dragged her home, and there had been a near-violent passion in his consummation of their marriage—

But would he have killed his wife in a fit of temper, as Blanche seemed to be hinting?

That she refused to believe!

That evening, after dinner and the customary music hour, Mr. Jurgen stopped in to see Roland. Roland excused himself, and since the two men were sequestered in the office for some time, Angelique went on up to the room she now shared with her husband. She settled herself in a chair near the window and read. She found it hard to concentrate on the print in front of her, for she'd decided late this afternoon that she would confront Roland regarding Luisa. She wished his meeting with the overseer wasn't taking so long, for her nerves grew tauter with each passing moment. When at last the bedroom door opened, she half-jumped.

Roland came into the room and shut the door. His wife, sitting in the chair near the window, was a vision tonight. *Dieu merci*, he thought, how lucky he was that she was his. She wore her soft gown of muted red; its rounded neckline revealed an enticing glimpse of her breasts and its puffed sleeves accentuated her youthful loveliness. Her thick raven hair was piled on top of her head, with vibrant red camellias interlaced in the thick curls. The blooms couldn't compete with the lush color on her cheeks. Yet her mouth was puckered tonight, a small frown surrounding her eyes, as if she were preoccupied. He wanted to grab her and kiss her until he banished all worries that dared to plague her beautiful mind.

"I hope I didn't startle you, darling," he said.

She was still frowning as she stared back at him. "You were a long time with Mr. Jurgen. I hope there is nothing wrong?"

Roland sighed, then crossed the room toward her, unbuttoning his frock coat. "Well, actually, a rather unpleasant business has arisen. It seems that one of the field hands forced himself on one of the black girls—"

"How awful!"

"Well, the man claims the girl enticed him, but still, I suppose we'll have to sell him. Several plantations in the vicinity are always in need of good working hands, and it would doubtless be best to get the man away from the girl."

"Yes, I suppose that would be wise, Roland."

Roland studied Angelique carefully as he removed his coat. Still, she was frowning. Dare he hope it was impatience for his company? He sat down across from her on the edge of the bed, laying his coat across the footboard and loosening his cravat. He smiled at her kindly. "How is the novel?"

"Oh, fine."

Silence fell between them, then he asked, "My dear, are you happy here?"

A blush spread across her exquisite young face. "Well, yes . . ."

Yet she lowered her eyes and avoided his gaze, and he felt bemused. "Have I done something to trouble you?"

"No."

"Would you look at me then, please?"

She looked up and he noted with dismay that her young mouth was trembling, her beautiful dark eyes turbulent. She looked so vulnerable, like an exquisite bird perched for flight. Things had been wonderful between them lately, but now— he could sense her pulling away, and a wave of stark fear washed over him.

"Roland," she said after a moment, "why did you decline the Junots' invitation to dinner?"

He sighed in relief. "Oh, is that it? I suppose Blanche told you."

"Yes."

He smiled at her tenderly. "Is it so much of a crime that I desire you all to myself for a while, before we begin socializing with the entire parish?"

"No, that's not a crime." She wet her lower lip, an un-
consciously sensual gesture that made Roland mentally wince
as his loins tightened painfully. Self-consciously, she went
on, "You say you desire me for yourself, but in many ways,
I still don't know you."

"In what ways?" he asked patiently.

"Well . . . There's still the matter of Luisa."

He sighed heavily. "Angelique, I simply wish to go forward with you, with our marriage. The past should be left
where it belongs—dead and buried."

"Unless it has an impact on the present," she said carefully.

"Why ever would Luisa have any impact on our marriage?"

She almost blurted out, *Because Blanche said you killed
her*, but thought better of the idea.

Roland came to her side, took the book from her lap and
set it on the table. Helping her to her feet, he whispered,
"Come here."

Angelique felt as if drowning as Roland pulled her gently
into his embrace, tucking her head beneath his chin. His arms
were so comforting, the masculine smell of him so
soothing—and she loved him so, despite all the torment of
her doubts.

He pressed his lips against her hair and whispered, "Surely
you can't think I still love her?" He drew back slightly,
touching the very center of each camellia in her hair, the
gesture blatantly erotic. "I never did, you know."

Do you love me, Roland? her heart demanded.

Too late. He was already kissing her and as always, she
was drowning in his taste, his touch. Long, sensuous moments later, he undid her hair, plucking away both the flowers
and the pins. Holding a camellia blossom in his hand, he
kissed her heavy, silken locks, then he rubbed the fragrant
flower slowly, seductively over her smooth neck, her bodice.
She shuddered violently, her heart pounding, her senses thundering as she looked up at her husband with passionate surrender in her eyes.

He groaned and pulled her to him roughly, and in that
moment, he knew he would die if he ever lost her. Someday,
she would learn the truth—about their marriage, about every-

thing. Knowing this, he was consumed by an obsession to bond himself with her. He backed away toward the bed and just stared at her, so beautiful with her breasts falling and rising, with the need in her eyes—

Need for *him*, for his heat deeply inside her. "Come to me, little Cajun," he said raggedly, and she hurried to him, flinging herself into his arms and pressing her eager mouth on his . . .

Much later, Roland lay awake, watching Angelique sleep and aching just to look at her beauty—her flushed cheeks, her passion-bright mouth, her long lashes resting peacefully against her face.

How long, he wondered, before she found out everything about his past—and the lies he'd told her? How long before she turned from him, the passionate glow in her eyes becoming hurt and mistrust?

CHAPTER
Nineteen

The lazy days of September stretched on into October. Then November brought the first crisp autumn winds twisting through the bayous; relief, at long last, from long months of oppressive heat.

As soon as the weather cooled and the mosquitoes subsided, Roland took Angelique on the promised tour of the swamp. She was enchanted by the beauty of the lagoons, seen firsthand from their pirogue. It was a lovely afternoon Angelique would long remember, especially as autumn deepened and Belle Elise approached its busiest time—the cutting of the cane. The crop had ripened perfectly in the cool, dry weather, and with the arrival of late November, Angelique got to see a plantation running at a continuous and backbreaking peak. The timing of the cutting was critical—the

"Big Grass" had to be harvested late enough in the season to ensure a ripened crop, but not too late, else the efforts of many months would be destroyed by the first frost.

Roland put in long, tireless days, helping Mr. Jurgen supervise the harvesting. Angelique was deprived of her husband's company much of the time, but she well understood the reasons. Roland drove her through the fields so that she could observe the process firsthand—the negroes working in shifts from dawn to dusk, hacking at the twelve-foot-high cane with machete-like knives, while others loaded the stalks onto wagons. The harvested cane was taken to the sugar mill, where it was pressed into juice. Outside the mill, the black women manned the huge kettles—the juice was boiled down until the syrup crystallized, the process filling the entire atmosphere with a cloying sweetness. Back at the house, Angelique often heard the huge wagons rattling by, carrying giant hogsheads of brown sugar to the landing for shipment to New Orleans.

One night, Roland brought Angelique a bowl of *cuite*—a thick syrup not quite ready to granulate—and showed her how to dip pecans into the delicious goo to make a luscious treat. They sat on the bed sampling the delicacy. Angelique went wild over the thick, fresh syrup, especially when the tasty pecans were dipped in. Roland chuckled, scolding his wife that she'd make herself fat. She made a face at him and he drew her close, licking the nectar from her lips—

In his arms, she discovered a much sweeter feast . . .

They got along very well, even though they weren't together that much. Angelique missed their afternoons alone, but at night, they were the most passionate of lovers. In many ways they were also becoming friends, if not true soulmates.

At the back of Angelique's mind, she still harbored doubts about Luisa and Caroline. She still wondered how Luisa had died, and whether her husband had continued to see his mistress during the first weeks of their marriage. Yet she didn't approach Roland again regarding either woman, knowing that he'd have to become willing to trust her, to share his past and his feelings with her.

Angelique was quite busy with Blanche during this period, as the two women began planning the traditional Delacroix Harvest Ball. Exotic foods and liquors had been ordered from

New Orleans, and the entire house had to be given a thorough fall cleaning.

Despite the tensions of the preparation, Angelique was excited regarding the forthcoming *soirée*, and eager to become better acquainted with the people of the parish. Roland had mentioned that Jean Pierre would be coming out from New Orleans to join in the festivities, and she was looking forward to seeing him again, too.

Then something rather unsettling happened for Angelique, one day while she and Blanche were discussing plans for the ball. They were in the library, and Blanche was at the desk completing an invitation list.

"I'm so glad you're preparing the guest list, Blanche," Angelique said from the loveseat. "Most of these people attend the ball every year, I take it?"

"Oh, yes," Blanche replied, setting aside her pen. Smiling, she added, "It's really the social event of the season here in St. Charles Parish."

Angelique glanced at Blanche thoughtfully. "I'm glad to see you filled with such anticipation regarding this *soirée*. You know, Blanche, you should get out more."

The spinster's expression grew guarded. "Get out more?"

"Yes—do some traveling, go to New Orleans, perhaps. I know Emily Miro would be delighted to have you stay with her. You could shop for new clothes—and just think, you could attend the opera!"

Blanche lowered her eyes. "Thank you for your kind suggestion," she said stiffly. "But I have no desire to go to New Orleans."

With these cool words, Blanche turned back to her work. Angelique sighed to herself. She felt that Blanche was missing out on so much by staying sequestered here at Belle Elise, and she resolved not to give up trying to get her to expand her horizons.

"There—that should do it," Blanche said. She blew on the wet ink, then brought the list over and handed it to Angelique, sitting down beside the girl. "I presume you'll want to write the invitations yourself?"

"Yes, I will, thank you," Angelique murmured. Yet as she glanced over the list, she suddenly frowned. "Wait a minute! Caroline Bentley's name is on this list."

"Is that a problem?" Blanche inquired blandly.

"Well—of course it is!" Angelique bristled. "You're well aware of Roland's relationship with Caroline prior to our marriage."

"Yes, but . . ." Blanche bit her lip and avoided Angelique's eye.

"What is it, Blanche?"

She sighed. "I'm afraid it was Roland who instructed me to invite Caroline in the first place."

Angelique's temper flared. "By the saints—that simply cannot be true! My husband is well aware of my feelings!" She squared her jaw. "I'll ask Roland about this immediately—I'm sure there is some misunderstanding."

Blanche frowned. "You can do that, of course, my dear. But considering my stepbrother's temper . . ."

Vehemently, Angelique continued, "At any rate, that woman is off the list and that's final."

"Do you think that's wise, Angelique?"

"I think it's eminently wise!"

Blanche went on calmly, "You see, dear, the problem is that Caroline's related to a number of people in the parish. Thus, if we cut her from the party, we'll also have to exclude her brother, George, and numerous others." With a sagacious smile, Blanche added, "Besides—why send out a message to the entire community that this woman is a threat to you?"

Angelique was broodingly silent. After a moment, she thrust the list back at Blanche. "Very well, you decide. Send Caroline an invitation if you must. But as for me, I shall never invite that—that woman to this house."

In a rustle of skirts, Angelique stood and proudly left the room. Blanche remained behind, feeling consumed by guilt as she stared at Caroline Bentley's name on the list—a name she herself had added, with no prompting from Roland. Why had she deliberately tried to come between her stepbrother and his wife?

Blanche swallowed painfully. She knew the reason all too well. Sheer panic. When Angelique had suggested that she leave Belle Elise, a choking, sick fear had consumed her. That's just the way it had all begun with Luisa—insidiously. "Why don't you leave, Blanche? Go to New Orleans . . .

See the world . . ." The suggestions had rapidly become
threats and finally, cruel action—

Now, the very idea of being cast out of her home again,
out alone into the world, where all could see her hideous
face—

Trembling, wiping tears, Blanche went back to the desk
and wrote out an invitation to Caroline Bentley and her
brother, George. She had to do something. It was a matter
of self-preservation. She had to knock Angelique off balance,
force the girl to become concerned enough about her marriage
that she wouldn't have the time or the inclination to threaten
a lonely, frightened woman who wanted nothing more than
to stay here—secluded and safe—at Belle Elise.

Blanche sealed the envelope with trembling fingers, blinking back tears. She wouldn't go to confession this week.

Angelique didn't see Roland for the remainder of the day.
She felt very hurt, infuriated by the thought that he might
have asked Blanche to invite Caroline. But she was not about
to let her husband know of her feelings—after all, hadn't he
demonstrated that he had no real regard for her sentiments?

Roland didn't come to bed until late that night, when the
bedroom was dark. Angelique didn't usually care when he
joined her—when he whispered her name, she rolled over
eagerly, entwining her arms around his neck, kissing him
and asking him about his day.

Yet tonight when he said her name, she didn't answer,
even though she lay awake for a long time—her eyes burning,
her throat tight—until she heard the deep, regular sound of
his breathing.

She felt so betrayed.

CHAPTER
Twenty

"Well, Cousin, I must say married life seems to agree with you," Jean Pierre said to Roland.

It was the eve of the Delacroix Harvest Ball, and Roland and Jean Pierre were enjoying a brandy in the library. Jean Pierre had driven out from New Orleans yesterday to join in the festivities. Tonight, both men posed striking figures, standing near the fire, dressed in black tailcoats and matching trousers, their shirtfronts, vests, and cravats tailored of finest white linen, silk, and satin.

"Yes, I must say that Angelique has been a delight to have around," Roland replied. "She's a good wife, and having her here has demonstrated to me," he paused to smile thoughtfully, "how empty my life was before."

Jean Pierre studied Roland with mingled delight and astonishment. Such words of honesty and humility coming from Roland Delacroix's lips. It was a small miracle! From the moment Jean Pierre had arrived, it had been apparent to him that Roland's disposition had been vastly improved by the addition of his bride. "So, Cousin, I take it Angelique has shown no further suspicion regarding the circumstances of your nuptials?"

"No," Roland replied, but a frown was also pulling at his handsome mouth. "Still, I must say that something seems to be troubling her of late."

"Oh?"

"Of course, she's been most solicitous and devoted. But on some level—" he scowled for a moment, swirling his brandy "—she seems to have withdrawn into herself."

Jean Pierre also frowned, mulling over Roland's words. Then he snapped his fingers and said, "Ah, Cousin, you have been quite preoccupied with the harvest, *n'est-ce pas*?" He stepped closer and elbowed Roland slyly. "A young wife like your Angelique would naturally want her husband's fullest attentions."

Roland grinned. "You may have a point there."

"Or perhaps *le bon Dieu* has already chosen to bless the two of you with a little bundle from heaven. Women tend to become a bit out of sorts then—or so I've been told."

Roland's brow was furrowed again. "Angelique is too young to be bearing children."

Jean Pierre coughed self-consciously. "I do not mean to speak indelicately, Cousin, but seeing that the girl is your wife—and being aware of your rather hot-blooded nature—"

Now Roland drew himself up and shot Jean Pierre his steeliest glare. "You're right, Cousin. You are speaking indelicately."

"I humbly apologize, then," Jean Pierre replied evenly.

Roland continued to glower at Jean Pierre for a moment, then he downed the rest of his brandy and set his snifter on the fireplace mantle. "Well, with our guests due to arrive any moment, I'd best go upstairs and fetch down my bride. Perhaps you'd be more comfortable waiting for us in the parlor?"

"*Bien*, Cousin."

Roland and Jean Pierre left the library just as Blanche came down the stairway. Roland smiled to himself as he studied his stepsister. For the first time in many years, Blanche was wearing a color other than black—tonight, a lovely silk gown of shimmering lilac. He was sure Angelique was behind Blanche's shift in wardrobe, and the thought deepened his expression of pleasure.

"Good evening, Sister—how lovely you look," Roland told her.

As Jean Pierre added a sincere compliment of his own, Blanche nodded self-consciously to the men. "Well—I do believe everything is just about ready."

"You and Angelique have done a marvelous job on the house," Jean Pierre told Blanche, glancing at the cut flowers in crystal bowls, at the garlands gracing the stairway banister.

"Thank you, Jean Pierre," Blanche said, unable to repress a smile.

"You know, Blanche, I've been meaning to tell you something ever since I arrived," Jean Pierre continued.

"Oh?"

"My father should be returning to New Orleans from Copenhagen any day now. In fact, I was hoping he would be able to attend tonight's *soirée*—but alas, luck has not been with us there. But I did want you to know that Papa has spoken so fondly of you in his letters. He has mentioned several times how he looks forward to seeing you again."

"Oh—how kind of Jacques," Blanche muttered awkwardly, lowering her eyes. She'd begun to look increasingly ill at ease as Jean Pierre had spoken. "Well, gentlemen, if you'll excuse me, I still have some last minute details to attend to . . ."

Blanche's voice trailed off as she swept away. Roland shook his head. "She turned white when you mentioned Jacques," he murmured to Jean Pierre.

Jean Pierre nodded ruefully. "So I noticed. Do you suppose there's any hope for my father and Blanche? Papa has been so lonely these last years since Maman passed on."

Roland glanced toward the parlor, watching Blanche converse with the conductor from the small orchestra they'd hired out of New Orleans. Resignedly, he informed Jean Pierre, "Like you, I'd love to see your father and Blanche get together. Every time Jacques visits us, it's apparent that he and my stepsister are attracted to each other. But, alas, the two of them are so different—Jacques traveling the world much of the time, and Blanche a veritable recluse here at Belle Elise. I feel we'd be foolish to hold out too much hope." He clapped Jean Pierre across the shoulders and forced a more pleasant expression. "But do tell Uncle Jacques to come visit us as soon as he returns to New Orleans. God knows, Blanche won't go down there to see him."

Jean Pierre nodded. "I'll be sure to relay your invitation."

"*Bien*. Now if you'll excuse me, I must check on my bride."

Roland headed upstairs, his thoughts turning to his beloved Angelique. A troubled frown drifted in as he recalled Jean Pierre's suggestion that she might be expecting. His wife was still so young, at seventeen, and so small, her figure girlishly slim. He'd heard of far too many women who'd died in childbirth. Of course, the idea of having a child with his bride was appealing, and he did want heirs for his plantation. Yet he was also selfish enough to want Angelique all to himself for a time.

He sighed. None of his misgivings about getting his wife pregnant were sufficient to make him keep his hands off her. Perhaps it would be best if he did for a time; yet dying would be easier. Angelique continued to be his obsession—during the long weeks of harvest, she was never out of his thoughts. He could never wait to come to her side, to hear her laughter, gaze into her beautiful eyes and hold all of heaven in his arms.

He did look forward to the coming weeks, knowing they would get to be together more. Just the idea put a spring in his step as he entered the upstairs hallway. Then he opened the door to their bedroom and saw her—the vision filling his eyes took his breath away. He stood there with heart hammering, staring at her with so much love he thought he would burst.

His bride was standing near the window, her exquisite profile turned to him as Coco put the finishing touches on her coiffure. Her hair was piled high on her head, with a few corkscrew curls trailing down at the back. Her ball gown was wonderful—of a deep red velvet, its tight waist and full skirt showing off her figure to perfection, its scalloped hem revealing a lace underskirt. The décolletage was lined with white lace interwoven with narrow red ribbon, outlining the firm swell of her bosom and revealing the enticing cleft between her breasts. The half-sleeves were gathered at the shoulder to puff out fully, with a generous edging of lace trailing down at the elbows. Altogether, his wife looked a totally enchanting mix of angel and siren. He couldn't take his eyes off her.

"How lovely you look," he murmured to her in a choked voice.

Angelique turned to see her husband standing just inside the door. She hadn't even heard Roland come in. Tonight he looked quite dashing in his formal black. His blue eyes gleamed as they raked over her with a lover's possessiveness. Staring at his handsome, chiseled face, she felt her heart flutter with the excitement his presence always aroused. She smiled at him. "Good evening, Roland." Turning to Coco, she added, "Are we finished?"

"*Oui*, madame," Coco said.

"You did a splendid job on madame's coiffure," Roland told the girl kindly.

"Thank you, maître," the girl replied to Roland, keeping her gaze respectfully lowered as she left the room, her movements awkward due to her obviously advancing pregnancy.

Angelique noted that Roland was scowling as he watched the pregnant girl slip out the door. "Coco will be having her child in the early spring," she murmured.

Roland turned to her, and there was a raw intensity gleaming in his blue eyes. "Thanks to your Uncle Giles. Lord, I'm glad you're not living with that man any more, *chérie*."

Roland came to her side and drew her into his arms for a long, passionate kiss. Afterward, she was floating in sensation as he whispered, "You're so incredibly beautiful, Mrs. Delacroix. I'm not at all convinced that I should turn you loose tonight. I have a feeling I'll be fighting every man in the parish for your attentions."

Now the romantic mood abruptly ended for Angelique, as Roland's words reminded her that he was not the only one who might feel jealousy tonight. She was very aware that Caroline Bentley would be attending this *soirée*—ostensibly, at her husband's request. Staring up at Roland, she asked, "And what of you, my husband? Won't there be other women present to turn your head tonight?"

"Never," he said, startling her with the vehemence of his denial as he swooped down for another hungry kiss.

After a moment, Roland released her and walked over to the tallboy. He opened a drawer and extracted a small, handsomely carved chest. He brought the box to her side and placed it on the table near the window. "I've been meaning to tell you that all of these are yours now," he said casually as he flipped open the box.

Angelique gasped as she stared at the jewelry: emerald and ruby necklaces, silver and gold bracelets dotted with tiny sapphires, diamond tiaras and chains. "Roland, I can't accept all of this."

"Nonsense," he replied. "These jewels have been in the

Delacroix family for many generations, and belonged of late to my mother. Of course they're yours, now.''

Angelique bit her lip. "Did they ever belong to Luisa?"

A shadow crossed his eyes, then he said stiffly, "Luisa had her own jewels. Upon her death, I returned them to her family." He took a step closer, his male scent filling her senses as he reached into the chest. "I think the pearls tonight, my pet—and the matching earbobs, of course."

"If it makes you happy, Roland."

"It does. Most happy. Now turn around."

Angelique turned around, and Roland fastened the heavy double chain about her neck, then attached the earrings to her earlobes. The contact of his warm hands on her skin was electric, and she caught a sharp little breath. She heard him whisper an endearment, then his hand caressed her bare throat, moving to her front to slip inside her bodice. She shuddered as his fingertips caressed her taut nipple. Her knees felt weak and she tottered slightly. He slipped an arm about her slim waist and nestled her against his strength as he continued the slow sensual torture with his fingers.

"Tell me something, my angel," he whispered, pressing his hot mouth against her throat.

"Yes?" she whispered tremulously.

"Is there any chance that you're expecting?"

She stiffened and he turned her in his arms, his hand moving from her breast to caress her flushed cheek. "Don't be shy, darling."

Angelique bit her lip. "Not yet, Roland. Are you terribly disappointed?"

He laughed huskily and drew her close. "Not at all."

"Don't you . . . ?" Breathlessly, she inquired, "Don't you want children?"

"Of course I do. But I really don't mind if we're not blessed right away." Thoughtfully, he continued, "You know, my dear, I've yet to take you on a proper honeymoon. How would you like to go to New Orleans for a few weeks now that the harvest is over?"

"Oh, I'd love that, Roland!" Angelique responded eagerly. "It would be so good to see Emily again, and—"

"Don't count on seeing too much of Emily," Roland

scolded. "I'm taking you to New Orleans mainly because I want us to be alone. Such is only a bridegroom's due. I want to spoil you and pamper you. But mainly, I just want to enjoy you. Damn, if only our guests weren't coming so soon . . ."

"We do need to be getting downstairs, Roland," Angelique whispered.

"After the party, then." Her husband smiled, offering her his arm.

The visitor arriving at Belle Elise an hour later found the plantation house gaily lit and as filled with music and laughter as the most elegant steamboat on the Mississippi. Lamps were aglow in all the windows, colorful lanterns strung between the pillars. The tall front columns were festooned with greenery and camellia blossoms. The November night was lovely, clear, and starry, with just a hint of bracing coolness in the air.

A mood of great excitement consumed the arriving guests—fashionably dressed planters, their wives, and older children—who were assisted from their stylish carriages by liveried slaves. Eagerly they headed for the open portal to Belle Elise—for the Delacroix Harvest Ball was the event of the social season in St. Charles Parish. No one dared to miss it. The cuisine was fabulous, the liquor excellent, the music and conversation lively.

Inside the front door, the visitors were met by a feast for the senses—a lilting Strauss waltz spilled out from the large parlor on their right, where dashing gentlemen swirled ladies dressed in mouth-watering ball gowns. From the dining room beyond drifted the tantalizing aromas of two dozen succulent Creole dishes, everything from crawfish on ice, to *bouillabaisse*, braised duck, vegetables in vinaigrette, and rich desserts of every variety.

Inside the parlor, the guests were greeted by the master of Belle Elise and his bride, Angelique. Many had already met M'sieur Delacroix's lovely young wife at the parish church. Many had already heard her sing, had dabbed at tears at her moving rendition of the *Magnificat* or *Agnus Dei*.

Yet M'sieur Delacroix's bride looked especially ravishing tonight in her fabulous red gown, wearing the double strand of pearls at her throat; her matching, luminescent earrings contrasted vibrantly with her beautifully unswept raven hair. And the master of Belle Elise had never looked prouder or more handsome as he stood at his bride's side, smilingly greeting his guests.

Standing next to Roland, Angelique found herself caught up in the gaiety of the occasion. The arriving guests were quite gracious, and the evening so far was a smashing success. Earlier, Angelique had tried to get Blanche to join them in the receiving line, yet the spinster had demurred. Glancing across the room, Angelique noted with a relieved smile that Blanche did look relatively at ease as she sat in a corner visiting with Annette Junot. Blanche's skirts of lavender silk created a delicious splash of color next to Annette's swath of mint green. Earlier, Angelique had enjoyed meeting Annette's dashing, dark-haired husband, Louis, although Clara Junot had acted cool toward Angelique again tonight.

"Well, Caroline, this is a surprise," Angelique heard Roland remark.

Angelique turned, her dark eyes gleaming with suspicion as she watched Caroline Bentley and a fair-haired gentleman walk past. Both were elegantly dressed—Caroline in an ice blue taffeta gown graced by yards of white lace, her companion in formal black garb similar to Roland's. Angelique had previously seen the man with Caroline at church; Blanche had told her he was Caroline's brother.

"Good evening, Roland," he was now saying, extending his hand to his host. "Why, we wouldn't have missed the annual Delacroix *soirée* for all the cane in the parish. Right, Caro?"

"Of course," Caroline murmured as Roland dutifully shook hands with her brother. She turned to Angelique. "My dear, you look lovely tonight. It's no wonder your bridegroom is so obviously smitten with you."

Angelique found her cheeks flaming at Caroline's unexpected, bold compliment. "Thank you, Mademoiselle Bentley," she replied stiffly. "I do hope you'll enjoy your evening at Belle Elise."

"Oh, I intend to," Caroline said. She nodded toward her brother. "Have you met George, my dear?" When Angelique shook her head, she added, "Madame Delacroix, meet my brother, Mr. Bentley."

George Bentley came forward eagerly to take the hand Angelique politely extended. He was a handsome man, she noted, if almost femininely slim and pale. His hair was white-blond, his features thin but pleasing, his eyes a light blue. His pale eyelashes fluttered as he took her hand and said, "Mrs. Delacroix, it's such a pleasure to meet you, at last! How I've admired your singing at church."

"Thank you, m'sieur. I'm pleased to meet you, as well." Angelique felt embarrassed as George leaned over to brush his lips against her hand. Through the corner of her eye, she caught Roland frowning at them fiercely. Well, he was one to act affronted—after he'd again brought his former mistress into their home!

"You'll find that George has quite a passion for music," Caroline was saying. "Well, then, George, shall we go sample that delectable-smelling buffet?"

"Yes, do make yourselves quite at home," Roland said stiffly.

As Caroline took her brother's arm and nudged him toward the dining room, George glanced over his shoulder at Angelique. "Mrs. Delacroix—we must talk later!"

The newlyweds stood in tense silence as the Bentleys headed off. Roland was about to say something, when Jean Pierre came up, looking quite animated. Angelique wondered how much he'd had to drink as he grinned at her and said, "Enough of this receiving line nonsense, *chérie*. It's time for you to join in the festivities. Come dance with me—that is, if your bridegroom has no objection?"

"Be my guest," Roland drawled.

Angelique barely had a chance to glance at her glowering husband before Jean Pierre caught her arm, pulling her out into the throng of dancers and sweeping her about to a charming waltz. "You look enchanting tonight, *ma belle*," he whispered.

Angelique stared up at Jean Pierre's handsome face, the thin mustache, the dark Creole eyes. In many ways, he reminded her of Roland—yet he didn't quite have her husband's substance, his intensity. "Are you flirting with me, Jean Pierre?"

"Indeed, I am," he replied with a laugh.

"You're aware that I'm a married woman now?"

"Eminently married, from what I've seen of the way you two lovebirds keep staring at each other. I'd say my formerly irascible cousin is quite hopelessly in love with you."

All at once, everything seemed to stop for Angelique, and she looked up at Jean Pierre raptly. "Would you?"

"Indeed, *chérie*," he replied. "But it never hurts to have a little—shall we say—insurance, to keep one's husband's attentions from straying?" Deliberately he pulled her closer.

Angelique giggled. "Why, Jean Pierre—that's wicked!"

"It's the Creole way," he told her devilishly.

Across from them, Roland was indeed burning with jealousy as he observed his bride dancing with Jean Pierre. Rationally, he knew he had no reason to object. Yet a moment ago, he'd glimpsed Angelique staring up at Jean Pierre with a look of fascination—a look he'd foolishly assumed was reserved only for himself. Then Jean Pierre had pulled her indecently close. Now she was laughing, obviously flirting with Jean Pierre and—

Enough, he decided. He would go break up this little ballroom tryst and show the girl her true master.

Roland was just about to dive into the sea of dancers when he felt a tug at his sleeve. He turned, annoyed, to see Clara Junot standing by his side, looking very girlish in a coral silk dress with puffed sleeves. "Good evening, M'sieur Delacroix," she said breathlessly, staring up at him with devoted eyes.

"Good evening, Clara," he replied, struggling to disguise his impatience. The music had stopped now, and there was no telling what Angelique was doing with Jean Pierre.

"Maman and Papa let me come home from convent school just for your *soirée*," Clara was continuing, a plaintive quality in her voice. "I was hoping that later, perhaps you and I, I mean we—"

Roland was hardly listening to the girl. "It's good to have you here, dear," he muttered as he searched the crowded room for his bride. "See that you get plenty to eat from the buffet."

And Roland walked off, unwittingly leaving Clara to tremble in the humiliation of rejection.

The orchestra had started up another tune, and by the time Roland located Angelique, she was swirling about in the arms of another man—this time, George Bentley. He glowered to himself. It was beyond him why Caroline and George were here tonight, anyway—he certainly hadn't expected his wife to invite them.

But then, many aspects of Angelique's behavior were startling and dismaying him tonight. Obviously she enjoyed playing the coquette—indeed, every man in the room was ogling her as she dipped and swayed about with George. Clenching his jaw, he started toward her.

Yet this time, it was Blanche who caught his arm.

Irritably, Roland turned to his stepsister, as she said brightly, "Well, the evening is quite a success, isn't it Roland?"

"It is," he replied, struggling to hold onto his patience. "Are you enjoying yourself, Sister?"

"Ah, yes." She inclined her head toward the dancers. "And Angelique seems to be having a marvelous time, as well."

"So it appears," he said dryly. "Well, then, Blanche, if you'll excuse me . . ."

"Oh, Roland," Blanche went on, "Louis Junot has been looking for you. I believe it's quite important."

Roland sighed, looking longingly at his wife out on the dance floor. He'd have to wait a few minutes before claiming her for his own. "Very well, Blanche. I'll go find Louis."

Roland found Louis in the dining room and the two men went off to Roland's study. They ended up having a lengthy discussion regarding some new vacuum pots Louis was planning to order to boil down next year's crop of cane. Yet the conversation abruptly ended as Roland heard a voice raised in song out in the parlor—the sweet strains of "Rocked in the Cradle of the Deep."

"That's my wife singing," he told his friend in astonishment, snuffing out his cigar.

The two men returned to the parlor to find Angelique at the center of a circle of spellbound admirers; she was singing at the piano, and George Bentley was accompanying her. Roland was far from pleased that his wife had chosen to perform in public this way. He was glowering at the scene as Caroline edged over to him and whispered, "A few moments ago, your stepsister actually got up before everyone and insisted that Angelique sing and George accompany her. Will wonders ever cease?'' Nodding toward Angelique, she added ruefully, ''I must admit that she's wonderful, Roland. Such a voice I've never heard before—not even at the opera.''

A hearty round of applause marked the end of Angelique's selection, and the guests were already calling out the names of additional requests. Scowling, Roland edged away from Caroline. He'd been pleased that his former mistress had kept her distance tonight. After all, there were Angelique's feelings to consider.

Yet what consideration was Angelique showing for her husband's feelings? At the moment, none. As his wife launched into the old riverboat song, ''Shenandoah,'' it couldn't have been more obvious that every male in the room was captivated by her. George Bentley's hands might be on the piano, but his eyes were riveted on the lovely girl as she sang. Roland's blood boiled. Why, she was just like—

Luisa, he thought, as old, bitter memories brought a haze of rage to his eyes. His first wife had been a shameless flirt, humiliating him so many times. Just like Angelique was doing now. And he could have sworn she was different.

Obviously, she had never truly wanted this marriage. Her brazen behavior tonight demonstrated that she was far from satisfied with his attentions alone. Well, to hell with what she felt, then. She was his wife, and he wouldn't tolerate such treason.

She had finished her song now, and in the moments that followed, the audience demanded encore after encore. Even the musicians, who had taken a break, had joined the others and were listening to his bride, enraptured. When at last the singing ended and the orchestra resumed playing, Angelique was at once claimed for a dance by the eldest son of the Beaufort family.

This time, the hounds of hell couldn't have stopped Roland as he strode forcefully toward his wife. Tapping Angelique's partner on the shoulder, he said, ''By your leave, m'sieur.''

Roland's tone of voice was so bloodchilling that the boy at once bowed out. Roland practically yanked Angelique into his arms.

''Why, Roland! I was beginning to think you were going to ignore me all night,'' she informed him, smiling up at him so sweetly that he could have loved her to insensibility if he didn't kill her first. When his reply was inarticulate, she added, "Roland—why ever are you growling so?"

"Because my wife has been making a spectacle of herself—and flirting with half the parish!"

Her mouth fell open. "Roland! What a rude thing to say. And I haven't been flirting with anyone—"

"You've been flirting with everything in pants!"

"I have not!" she insisted in a hoarse whisper, glancing around, mortified. "What an indelicate thing to say with our guests present!"

He dragged her closer, and his senses swam with her. God, he loved her so, and she was bewitching him—and obviously every man present!—with her innocent eyes and temptress body. "We'll discuss this later," he growled into her ear.

The second the dance was over, Angelique was taken aside by an elderly matron who praised her lavishly for her singing and invited her to sing at the next meeting of the Ladies Beneficent Society. Angelique accepted, and by the time she looked around for Roland, he'd been taken aside by another of his planter friends. She brooded silently. She'd been shocked when her husband had accused her of making a spectacle of herself—and flirting. Obviously, he hadn't been pleased when she had sung in front of his guests. This galled her. Wasn't the entire purpose of this evening to entertain his friends? Could she help it if Blanche had insisted she sing?

And could she help it if several male guests had insisted that she dance with them? Of course, she would have preferred to dance with Roland, but they both had their obligations as host and hostess. Did he truly want her to rudely refuse his guests?

He was one to talk, anyway, after he'd invited Caroline here tonight! Of course, she had to concede that Roland had kept his distance from his former mistress all evening. Perhaps, as Blanche had hinted, Roland had wanted the woman here simply for the sake of appearances, as Caroline's absence would have called attention to the fact that she and Roland had once been lovers.

Angelique drifted out into the central hallway to catch some of the breeze blowing in the front door. She was also hoping to avoid another dance invitation from a man who wasn't her husband. Yet the muffled sound of sobbing drew her toward the library. She entered the room to see young Clara Junot standing by the far window, her thin shoulders heaving. "Clara? Are you all right?"

The girl whirled on Angelique, her face pinched with grief and her eyes blazing with hatred. "You! Why did you have to marry him!"

Angelique frowned at this confirmation that Clara was in love with her husband. The girl was only a year younger than she, but somehow Clara seemed far removed from her in maturity. "Clara, you're distraught," Angelique said evenly. "You mustn't say things you'll later regret. Let me take you upstairs—"

"I hate you!" Clara cut in heedlessly. Her fists were clenched at her sides, her chest heaving. "I've loved him all my life and then you stole him from me. He leaves for just a week then comes back with the likes of you! What did you do to trap him? It must have been something pretty tawdry, because everyone knows that otherwise, no Delacroix would marry a trashy little Cajun like you—"

"Clara, I think you'd best stop," Angelique put in with strained patience.

"I don't want to stop, and I shan't!" she cried, stamping her foot. "I can't believe that Roland's parents arranged for him to marry you. Such a marriage contract has never been heard of in this parish. And it's been known for years that sooner or later Roland would choose to merge Belle Elise with my father's estate. He and Papa have been best friends all their lives—"

"Clara," Angelique cut in firmly. "Did my husband ever make any promises to you?"

"No! Because you stole him away before he could!"

With these angry words, Clara fled the room. Angelique sighed. She knew better than to take the girl's hysterics too seriously. It was unfortunate that the girl was smitten with Roland, but obviously, her husband had done nothing to encourage her. It was unsettling for Angelique to learn that no one in the parish had ever heard of her and Roland's marriage contract. But then, would such a private covenant become public knowledge, anyway? Angelique knew little about Creole traditions regarding such matters.

She drew a deep, steadying breath. Time to go find her jealous husband. In a way, Roland's possessiveness had pleased her. Could he really be "smitten" with her, as Jean Pierre had insisted?

At the portal to the parlor, Angelique paused, looking for him. He was nowhere in sight, but Jean Pierre sauntered up. "Another dance, *chérie*?"

Scanning the room, Angelique caught sight of young Clara sitting along one wall, her face downcast. "Not for me, thanks, Jean Pierre. But I would appreciate it if you would dance with Clara Junot."

Jean Pierre glanced across the room, frowning. "That one? Why, she has the complexion of a persimmon, and doubtless, the disposition to match."

Angelique's brown eyes blazed. "Jean Pierre, either you'll dance with her or I swear I shall not speak with you the rest of the evening!"

He feigned amazement. "Well, you don't have to resort to threats, *chérie*," he grumbled, starting off toward Clara.

A moment later, Angelique watched the two dance, Clara staring up at Jean Pierre shyly, Jean Pierre trying his best to be charming.

"A dance, Mrs. Delacroix?"

Angelique turned just as Roland caught her arm and led her out onto the floor. "I thought you'd never ask again," she murmured with a smile as he caught her close.

"You're mine for the rest of the evening," he whispered tensely, "or I swear, I shall make a very public scene."

It was two in the morning by the time all the guests had either left or had gone to their rooms. Upstairs, Angelique dismissed Coco as soon as her ballgown was safely in the armoire. Roland sat on the bed, still dressed, watching his wife don her nightgown, then sit down at the dressing table to take down her hair.

After a moment, he got up, removed his boots, took off his coat and went to hang it in the armoire. Returning to the bed, he sat against the headboard and watched Angelique work with her heavy tress. "So many pins," he grumbled. "Why must it take so long?"

"That's the last of them," she said smoothly, her heavy hair tumbling down about her shoulders as she reached for her hairbrush.

She heard Roland groan, caught his intense gaze in the mirror, watching her. "Bring the hairbrush and come here," he said.

She came to his side, setting the hairbrush next to him on the bed. She started to crawl onto the mattress, but he grabbed her about the waist and pulled her to him, nestling her between his spread legs. He leaned over and fastened his mouth on hers for a long, deep kiss. Then he sighed and said, "Sit up."

She did as he bid and he gently began brushing out her long hair, until it shone like silk. "Now let's discuss your flirting with all our male guests," he said grimly.

She turned in his arms. "For the last time, Roland, I didn't flirt. It's not my fault if all your friends wanted to dance with me. Did you expect me to tell them all to go jump off the wharf?"

A hint of wry amusement pulled at his forbidding mouth. "That would have done quite nicely."

"Well, I could never be so rude!" she replied indignantly. "Furthermore, I'm well aware of my obligations as your wife—and as hostess for your guests."

He was scowling darkly. "Ah, yes, you always have managed to do your duty by me, haven't you, my dear?" Turning her chin so that she met his smoldering gaze, he added, "So tell me, my fine little flirt, would you have married me had our parents not arranged it?"

Later, Angelique would decide it was his calling her a flirt again that had made her so righteously angry, that had prompted her to stare up at him defiantly and say, "No."

She only heard that growling sound again, coming from deep within his throat, before she was abruptly rolled and pressed beneath him, her nightgown raised. She felt his hand between their bodies, at his trousers. "Roland, what—"

Yet his searing presence deep inside her was answer

enough, and it took her breath away. He felt hot, huge, and so hard, her senses were in tumult. His hands pinned hers into the mattress, and his angry face hovered close to hers as he demanded, "Have I your complete attention now, little Cajun?"

"Oh, *oui*," she whimpered, her mouth soft beneath his plundering kiss.

Roland took her with fierce, near-violent need, and she did not flinch from the intensity of it, even when he rose to his knees and wrapped her slim legs around his waist. She began to cry out and dragged a pillow to her face, but he flung it aside, her whimpers and the mindless surrender in her eyes driving him crazy. Together they rode the crest of a long, riveting climax, then he cuddled her trembling, satiated body close, whispering endearments in her ear.

CHAPTER
Twenty-one

By the time Angelique awakened the next morning, the room was flooded with sunshine. She stretched dreamily, inhaling the sweetness of honeysuckle.

Roland was gone, of course. She remembered him reaching for her in the dimness right before dawn, pulling her into his arms and making love to her for the third time since the party ended. Her breasts were slightly sore, abraded by his rough, whiskered face, and her entire body felt tender from their shared, insatiable passion. She smiled at the memory.

Last night right after the party, she'd been angered, righteously resenting Roland's accusation that she had flirted with all the men at the *soirée*. Yet this morning, in retrospect, she could better understand his feelings. Her husband was wildly jealous, she realized. His intense lovemaking last night had more than demonstrated this to her. And even while they'd slept, he'd held her close all night, one muscled arm hooked possessively about her waist. While she had never meant to provoke such dark passion in him, the result, she had to admit, had been terribly exciting. A little frightening, but quite wonderful.

She truly loved him, she realized. He was a fascinating man, dynamic and charming, even a little mysterious. And sensitive, too, else he wouldn't have gone on such a tear regarding her supposed sins. He had pricked her pride last night with his accusations, but now she could see that she might have well hurt him when she'd hotly denied that she would have wed him had their parents not arranged it. Now she could see that he had doubtless put a lot on the line in asking her that question; and instead of meeting him halfway, she had dashed any hopes he might have had. She didn't like the idea that she might have hurt him; indeed, she didn't want to hurt him.

And she had lied—and the fact that she may have had good cause did not alter this reality. She realized now that, although her circumstances in meeting Roland had confused her emotions, she had nevertheless felt drawn to him from the moment she laid eyes on him. Even then, there had been some dark pain, some need in him that was so compelling, evoking an answering response in herself. She too, had been needy at the time, reeling with grief and confusion and loneliness. Their time together, especially since they'd started living together as man and wife, had been so healing. Looking back, she could see a radical change in Roland, just as she could observe a wondrous transformation in herself.

Of course, she'd had doubts, about Luisa and Caroline. But as Roland himself had pointed out recently, it was time to go forward. Last night, when Roland asked his question, he'd needed reassurance that she truly wanted to be his wife, and she, full of pride, had denied him. That had been wrong, and now it was time to be honest with him, to tell him how very happy she was to be his wife. If she let him know her feelings, this could be a real beginning for them, opening the door to deeper communication between them.

Thus with a spring in her step, Angelique hopped out of bed and rang for Coco to bring her breakfast tray.

* * *

While Angelique was breakfasting and dressing, Roland and Jean Pierre were visiting over a cup of coffee in the parlor.

"Are you sure you must go back to New Orleans so soon, Cousin?" Roland asked.

Jean Pierre grinned. "Yes, I think I'd best be on my way this morning. As I mentioned last night, I'm expecting my father back from Europe at any moment. And besides, there are far too few temptations for a libertine such as myself here in St. Charles Parish. In fact, I fear that if I linger here overlong, you'll put me to work loading the last of your hogsheads onto a river packet."

Roland laughed dryly. "Not a bad idea." Without a trace of humor he added, "And perhaps it is best that you return to New Orleans. It seems that last night, you had some difficulty keeping your eyes off my bride."

"As did every man in the parish."

"True. But you were the only man there who at one time bought the girl as his mistress."

Jean Pierre glanced about the parlor, looking ill at ease. At last, he sighed and said sheepishly, "Cousin, there's something I've been meaning to tell you about that entire incident."

"Indeed?"

Nodding, Jean Pierre set down his coffee cup. "You must know that it was never my intention to make Angelique my mistress."

Roland looked highly skeptical. "It wasn't?"

Jean Pierre shook his head. "On the night I played cards at Giles Fremont's house, it was obvious that the reprobate was determined to sell his innocent niece to the highest bidder. I couldn't watch Angelique become the helpless pawn of a lecher such as Charles Levin or Etienne Broussard. Nor did I want her to be left at the mercies of—" he smiled ruefully "—a lost soul such as myself. I realized that the girl needed a proper husband, and when I bid on her, it was always my intention to see that she was delivered into your hands as your future wife."

Roland looked stunned. "Then why did you lie to me— telling me you bought the girl as your own mistress?"

Jean Pierre's dark eyes sparkled with devilment. "Well, Cousin, I had to give you some incentive to appoint yourself the girl's protector. After all, time was of the essence."

"And doubtless, you decided you couldn't count on my nobler instincts," Roland put in cynically.

Jean Pierre shrugged. "What can I say, *mon ami*? You were a different man then, so locked up in your own darkness. I realized at once that the girl was perfect for you, but at the time, I couldn't count on her arousing your immediate and passionate protectiveness . . . Which, it turns out, she did arouse—and quite thoroughly."

While Roland sat in thoughtful silence, Jean Pierre stood and crossed the room to his side. From his breast pocket, he extracted a bank draft, thrusting it toward Roland. "Here. I want you to take this back."

Roland scowled at the slip of paper. "What is it?"

"It's the bank draft you gave me to reimburse me the money I paid Giles Fremont for Angelique. I've never deposited it, and I only accepted it at the time because—well, frankly, Cousin, I was growing rather tired of your insults."

Roland waved off Jean Pierre. "Keep it."

Yet Jean Pierre adamantly shook his head, drawing himself up with dignity. "It was never my intention to accept reimbursement for my role in this drama. No gentleman worth his salt would have done any less for Angelique under the circumstances. And for once, dear cousin, I would like to think of myself as a gentleman."

Studying Jean Pierre, Roland felt moved by his sincerity. Realizing that the money represented a matter of honor to the younger man, he nodded. "Very well, then, I accept—with my humble thanks for your assistance in this matter." Taking the draft and tucking it in the breast pocket of his frock coat, he added ruefully, "Actually—while I still haven't completely forgiven you for ogling my wife last night—I am beginning to realize that I owe you quite a lot."

"You do, indeed." Jean Pierre was grinning as he returned to his chair. "By the way, Cousin, are you ever going to tell the girl that your marriage to her was never arranged by your families?"

Roland stroked his jaw with tanned fingers. "I'm not sure. Angelique is very trusting and idealistic, and I rather hate the thought of diminishing myself in her eyes. She also remains quite devoted to her parents' memory, and I do dread her reaction if she ever finds out they never countenanced our marriage.''

''Then it's a good thing the girl never questioned the veracity of your claim.''

Roland nodded soberly. ''Ah, yes. It's a good thing . . .''

The two men continued to talk, not knowing that Angelique stood just outside in the hallway, trembling in outrage as she listened.

She had been about to enter the parlor when she had heard Jean Pierre say, *You must know that it was never my intention to make Angelique my mistress.*

These words had frozen her in her tracks. She'd stood there listening in helpless rage and horror as the men continued, shattering all her dreams and illusions in the course of a few cruel minutes.

She learned that on the night Jean Pierre came to her uncle's home to play cards, her uncle had put her on the auction block, selling her to the highest bidder—who turned out to be Jean Pierre! Jean Pierre had then turned around and sold her to Roland! And, worst treason of all, her marriage to Roland had never been agreed to, never sanctioned, by her parents!

It was all a lie! All a sham! These enraged thoughts consumed her as she hurried back upstairs, retreating to her bedroom. She shut the bedroom door and leaned against it for support, tears burning her eyes, her throat so tight she could barely swallow. She had been used, lied to, bartered over like some street creature! Her entire marriage to Roland was based on dishonesty! His fabrication had robbed her of all choice, had forced her into marriage with him, had scoffed the memory of her dear departed parents! She had tried to forgive and forget the other women in his life—but this monstrous lie she could never forgive!

And here, she'd been on the verge of baring her soul to him—the heartless deceiver!

What an idiot she had been, so naive and trusting, actually believing that Roland Delacroix's parents had arranged two marriages for him. All along, the telltale signs of Roland's deceit had been there, but she had ignored them in her intoxification with her betrayer. Now, too late, the obvious questions bombarded her mind. Questions such as, why would a wealthy, powerful planter marry an impoverished girl from a Cajun farm? Why had the presumed marriage contract been such a well-guarded secret in St. Charles Parish? Why had Roland kept her away from the other families for so long?

Tears trickled down her cheeks, tears of terrible anger and hurt and betrayal. She had trusted this man with her heart, and he had broken it with his perfidy. A marriage based on a lie was no marriage at all—

How much else had Roland lied to her about?

The question was too tormenting to be borne. Instead, Angelique rushed to the armoire, grabbed a tapestry bag and began packing.

An hour later, Angelique stood in a small grove of trees near the swamp, watching Jean Pierre board his stylish carriage at the side of Belle Elise. She was dressed for an arduous journey, wearing a straight-lined muslin dress, a thin shawl, and only one petticoat; the carpetbag clutched in her hand held but a few hastily packed garments.

She felt relieved that Roland wasn't seeing off Jean Pierre. Half an hour earlier, looking out her window, she had spotted her husband riding off toward River Road. She had bitterly rejoiced at the thought of never seeing him again—and then that same reality had made her illogically collapse on the floor in tears.

Now, with Jean Pierre safely inside his coach and the driver heading for the front of the conveyance, Angelique knew her moment had arrived. On tiptoe, she hurried toward the back of the vehicle. Luckily, Jean Pierre's carriage was a big custom coach with an overlarge boot—and with only Jean Pierre's one small bag inside, there would be just enough room for herself and her small cache of belongings. She tossed in her bag then gingerly climbed into the boot, squeezing into the tight quarters—and immediately regretted her decision as the carriage jolted off, rattling her very bones.

Just as the conveyance departed, Blanche came out on the porch, and saw, to her bewilderment, Angelique's bonneted head bobbing out of the boot. At first she thought her eyes were deceiving her—but no, it was the girl, stuffed in the luggage compartment of Jean Pierre's coach.

Why was Angelique hiding in Jean Pierre's carriage? Why was she running away? Blanche considered calling out to the girl, but then realized she'd never be heard in the din of flying hooves.

Oh, dear. Should she tell Roland? No, she couldn't, could she? He'd gone to see Louis Junot and wouldn't be home for hours.

She'd just have to wait till he returned. What a pity.

An hour later, Angelique had had as much jolting as she could endure as Jean Pierre's carriage bounced down River Road toward New Orleans. Her head felt as if it might snap off at any moment, and her sides felt raw from being rubbed against the unyielding walls of the compartment.

"Stop!" she at last cried out. "Please stop!"

At first her protests seemed to have no impact, but finally, after she'd beaten on the back of the carriage several times, the conveyance clattered to a bumpy halt. Seconds later, she was facing a flabbergasted Jean Pierre.

"*Mon Dieu!* What are you doing in there, *chérie*?" he gasped.

"Don't call me *chérie*!" she snapped back. "And get me out of this—torture chamber."

"Of course." Jean Pierre caught the girl under the arms and lifted her out of the boot.

Though Angelique's feet were wobbly as they hit the ground, she at once turned on Jean Pierre. "I want you to take me to New Orleans, to Emily Miro's house."

Jean Pierre continued to look stunned. "Why ever for?"

"Because I'm leaving Roland."

"By the saints!" Jean Pierre cried, his eyes wild. "Do you mind telling me the reason for this—sudden change of heart?"

"Certainly! Roland is a liar and a thief! He violated my trust, and—" All at once, to Angelique's horror, she burst into tears.

"There, there, *chérie*," Jean Pierre said, hugging Angelique, awkwardly trying to comfort the distraught girl.

She thrust him away, blinking at hot, angry tears. "Don't you touch me, you—you swine! You're worse than he is! And—don't you dare ever again call me *chérie*."

Jean Pierre stared at the girl in bewilderment for a moment; then realization dawned and he snapped his fingers. "Oh, *mon Dieu*! You must have overheard Roland and me this morning!"

"Indeed I did! Now I want you to take me—"

"Angelique, please, you must allow me to explain—"

"I want to hear nothing from you!" she cried, her words edged in hysteria. "You said quite enough this morning—you and my liar of a husband. Now I want you to take me to Emily Miro's. If you don't—I swear I shall walk every step of the way."

Jean Pierre sighed. "Very well, dear. I'll take you to Emily's. But this will not go over well with your husband—"

"I couldn't give a damn how it goes over with my husband!"

"Don't you think we should at least notify Roland of your whereabouts, show some respect for his feelings—"

"Like he respected my feelings when he forced me to wed him?"

There, Jean Pierre had no answer. Resignedly, he escorted Angelique to the carriage door.

CHAPTER
Twenty-two

Two hours later, Roland was in a reflective mood as he rode his black stallion down River Road; he was returning home after meeting with Louis Junot. The late autumn breeze felt crisp and cool against his face; the leaves of the large trees stretching over the roadway had turned a deep russet.

His thoughts turned to Angelique. She was never out of

his mind for long. Last night had demonstrated to him that his young wife was the envy of every man in the parish. It had been exquisite torture for him to watch her lovely smiles, her easy laughter, directed at so many—to see her waltzing in the arms of every man there. Was his bride truly just trying to fulfill her role as mistress of the manor, or was she a flirt at heart? It was so hard to know whether her behavior had been motivated by guile or wickedness.

Then, when he'd asked her whether she would have married him had their parents not arranged it, she'd said no, and that had been the crowning blow. He'd bedded her passionately, held her close all night, even as he'd wondered if his love was really touching her, bonding her to him.

The girl was so elusive, like glorious quicksilver, ever mesmerizing him, then slipping from his grasp. He would have to take her off, it was the only answer. He'd take her to New Orleans for a month—yes, a month would do quite nicely. The harvest was over and Jurgen could handle things now. He'd take her to the St. Louis Hotel, and, if he had his way, they wouldn't even leave their room for a week. He knew that if he made love to her every second they were there, he still couldn't get enough of her. He never would.

But it would be a beginning. After their time alone, he'd take her shopping, to the opera, and maybe they'd ride the train out to the lake for a day. He'd woo her and spoil her, get to know her better, and perhaps, break down some barriers between them.

Yet a ragged pain caught in his throat as he faced one central, heartbreaking question: could he make her love him?

Once he was back home at Belle Elise, Roland's expression was resolute as he took the stairs two at a time. He would get Angelique packed and they'd be off to New Orleans this very afternoon. Yet upstairs, just inside his bedroom door, he froze.

The room looked as if ransacked. The wardrobe and dresser were askew, and clothing was everywhere—on the bed, hanging out of drawers. It looked as if someone had been packing in an extreme hurry—

His eyes wild, Roland hurried out of the room and raced

downstairs. He found Blanche in the parlor knitting an afghan. "Sister, where is Angelique?"

Blanche put down her knitting and stared tensely at him. He grabbed her by the shoulders. "Where is she?"

Blanche bit her lip. "I'm afraid Angelique left—with Jean Pierre."

Roland uttered a string of oaths in rapid French, his eyes crazed. "She left? But why? Did she say anything to you?"

"No, Brother."

"Did she seemed unhappy? Angry?"

"No, brother. Neither of them seemed . . ." Blanche lowered her eyes. "Unhappy."

The truth hit Roland with blinding clarity. "When did they leave?" He shook Blanche slightly. "When?"

She stared up at him. "Two hours ago."

"And you didn't send word to me?"

"Brother, I'm sorry, but I just couldn't—embarrass you that way, in front of the Junots—"

Without another word, Roland tore out of the room.

Twenty minutes later, Roland was flying down River Road on a fresh horse, a hastily packed bag hanging from his saddle.

Just as he suspected, the girl was trying to cuckold him. She'd never wanted this marriage, had never cared for him, and now she'd run off with the first convenient man. What a fool he'd been to let her dance with Jean Pierre last night. What an idiot he'd been to believe Jean Pierre when he had claimed he'd never wanted the girl as a mistress.

Well, he'd be damned if he'd let the two of them make a laughingstock of him. Angelique was his wife, and it was high time she was taught to behave accordingly. As for Jean Pierre—he sighed heavily. It was a matter of honor now. He hated the thought of issuing a challenge to a blood relative, but the blackguard had given him no choice. And here he'd almost been convinced that his cousin might one day be redeemed. He'd been a dolt to believe Jean Pierre could think with anything but his loins.

He gritted his teeth in murderous resolve at the thought of confronting his bride. Theirs would be a reckoning he'd see she never forgot!

* * *

"Angelique, please, you mustn't rush off to Emily's."

Jean Pierre's coach was now pulling up to his house on St. Charles Avenue, and he was feeling desperate. During the journey from St. Charles Parish, he had tried endlessly to make Angelique see reason, but the girl had turned a deaf ear to his every plea.

"I want to go to Emily's now," she replied stubbornly.

"But *chérie*," he persisted, beseeching her with dark, panic-stricken eyes. "You're rather—shall we say, rumpled from your time in the boot. Won't you please take a few moments to freshen up? Otherwise, you may well alarm the Miros when you arrive."

Angelique scowled at Jean Pierre. Though she didn't really trust him, his argument did make sense. She glanced past him at his home, which did look beckoning, neatly tucked away beneath a blaze of autumn colors. Actually, she welcomed the thought of having a few minutes to relax and freshen up before they journeyed on to the Quarter. "Very well—I'll change my frock," she informed him ungraciously. "But you must give me your word that afterward, we'll leave at once for the Quarter—and that you'll not send word to Roland of my whereabouts."

Jean Pierre sighed. "Very well, Angelique. You have my word as a gentleman."

She harrumphed. "I'm quite reassured."

Moments later, as Jean Pierre escorted the rather disheveled young woman into the ornate central hallway of his home, he was pleasantly surprised to hear a familiar male voice boom out from the parlor. "Jean Pierre! How good it is to see you, son!"

"Father!" Jean Pierre cried. He watched Jacques Delacroix hurry out into the hallway. The elder Delacroix cut a striking figure in his European-style clothing—a black tailcoat, white shirt, and vest of silver moire, along with buff-colored knee breeches and shiny black boots.

The two men embraced. "Father, I didn't expect you home quite so soon," Jean Pierre said with a broad grin. "How was Copenhagen?"

"Always lovely this time of year, with the chestnut trees changing colors." As the two men moved apart, Jacques glanced with frank admiration at Angelique. "And who is this vision of loveliness gracing you with her company this afternoon?"

Jean Pierre nodded awkwardly toward Angelique. "Father, this is Roland's bride, Angelique Delacroix." To the girl, he added, "My dear, meet my father, Jacques Delacroix."

While Angelique nodded at Jacques, the latter was scowling at his son. "Whatever are you doing with Roland's bride? Not that I was even aware that my nephew had one."

Jean Pierre coughed. "Actually, Roland and his bride are—"

That's when Angelique interrupted, facing Jean Pierre's father squarely. "Actually, m'sieur, Roland doesn't have a bride anymore."

Jacques raised a bushy eyebrow at the lovely young woman who had spoken out so forthrightly. "Indeed? A most lamentable situation for Roland, I would think." He stepped closer to Angelique and smiled at her warmly, bowing from the waist. "Nevertheless, madame, I am most pleased to make your acquaintance."

"Thank you, m'sieur." Angelique extended her hand to Jacques, who in turn gallantly kissed it. She noted that he was a very handsome, older version of Jean Pierre. But his eyes were dark and shrewd, and he radiated much more presence and self-confidence than did his son.

Realizing she was staring at Jacques, Angelique turned to Jean Pierre. "I don't mean to be rude, Jean Pierre, but if you'll excuse me, I do need to change so that you may take me on to Emily's. Besides—" she smiled at Jacques "—I'm sure that you and your father need some time to become reacquainted."

"Of course, dear," Jean Pierre said politely.

Once Angelique had been spirited upstairs by a hastily summoned maid, Jacques and Jean Pierre settled themselves into the parlor with glasses of absinthe.

Jacques slanted an admonishing glance at his son. "Now, Jean Pierre, would you kindly explain to me what you are doing with Roland's exquisitely beautiful bride? I rather pity you when he comes after her—and after seeing the girl, I'm quite sure the man will come after her."

Jean Pierre nodded dismally, taking a bracing sip of the liquor. "Actually, Father, it's quite a long story."

"Then by all means, begin, as I got the distinct impression from the young lady that she'll be rejoining us shortly."

Jean Pierre dove in, telling his father the whole, unvarnished truth—beginning with the events which had transpired at Giles Fremont's fateful poker game and ending with Angelique's flight from Belle Elise earlier that day.

When Jean Pierre finished, Jacques whistled low under his breath and then chuckled. "It seems that you and my nephew have stirred up a fine witches' brew here. And it does make me wonder which of the two of you is the more in love with the girl."

"I'm not in love with her," Jean Pierre replied with absolute sincerity, "although I would truly cherish being her friend. On the night when I rescued her from her uncle's clutches, I did so because for once, I wanted to do something . . ." Jean Pierre hesitated a long moment, then grimaced and said, "Noble."

His father roared with laughter. "Why, my dear son, there may be hope for you, after all."

"Indeed," Jean Pierre concurred dryly, neatly emptying his glass. "That is, if Roland doesn't cut me to mincemeat first." Setting down his glass, he leaned forward intently, lacing his fingers together. "What are we to do about the girl, Father?"

Jacques stroked his mustache. "Let's see if we can't detain her a bit. Tempt her with dinner in the Quarter, ply her with wine, and get her calmed down somewhat. By the time we return, Roland will doubtless be here."

Jean Pierre looked thunderstruck, falling back in his chair. "He will? How can you be so sure of that?"

"Because while the girl is dressing, you're going to dispatch him a message."

"But Father! I promised the girl I wouldn't—"

Jacques held up a hand. "There are promises, and there is the matter of what is right. What do you think is right here, son?"

At once Jean Pierre nodded, speaking with painful resignation. "I'll dispatch my manservant at once for Belle Elise."

* * *

"My dear, you simply must sup with us at Antoine's," Jacques said gallantly to Angelique.

It was an hour later. Angelique, Jean Pierre and Jacques were heading down the front steps of the house. Angelique had changed to a becoming rose-colored wool frock and a matching pink taffeta bonnet. Beyond them in the street waited Jean Pierre's carriage, the liveried coachman standing by its open door.

Angelique turned to Jacques, answering him firmly. "Thank you for your kind invitation, m'sieur, but I must decline. Really, I must go straight on to Emily Miro's."

Jacques and Jean Pierre exchanged a distressed glance over the girl's head. Then, summoning his most unruffled facade, Jacques drew an ornate pocket watch from his vest, flipped it open, then shook his head at Angelique. "My dear, it is the dinner hour. While I'm certain Emily will be delighted to see you, it could be embarrassing if she hadn't planned on a guest for the evening meal."

"Oh," Angelique muttered, paling. "I hadn't thought—"

"Don't worry," Jacques went on with fatherly concern, taking her arm and leading her into the yard, "we'll make it a quick repast, and then you won't have to worry about arriving at the Miros at an inopportune time."

"Well, I do suppose that would be the best course," Angelique conceded, biting her lip.

Jean Pierre opened the wrought-iron gate for Angelique, and the three filed through. Yet even as Jacques escorted Angelique on toward the carriage, she heard the sound of angry hoofbeats approaching. She whirled, her heart pounding. A glance down the street confirmed her worst fears. Oh, *mon Dieu*, it was Roland, riding toward them hell-bent-for-leather, his horse lathered, his coattails flapping in the breeze. He either hadn't worn a hat or had lost it during his ride, and his wildly ruffled hair and fierce features lent him a demonic light.

Oh, merciful saints! How on earth had he discovered where she'd gone so soon? He would surely kill her now!

Wildly, Angelique turned to Jean Pierre. "Jean Pierre—please! You must help me!"

* * *

As Roland rode toward Jean Pierre's house, the scene ahead of him consumed him with both relief and rage. Relief that Angelique was there. Rage that there she was, haughty, untouchable, and beautifully dressed, all set to leave with not just one man but two! She had the body of an angel and the heart of a whore! Did she intend to betray him with everything in pants?

He would kill her, he thought angrily.

No, he would kill himself if he lost her, he realized, his feelings of hurt and frustration sinking in on him with a vengeance. As much as Angelique's betrayal wounded him, the sight of his beautiful young wife also filled him with such crazed need that he knew now that he would do anything—*anything* to get her back.

He couldn't lose her. He just couldn't lose her.

For Angelique, watching her husband ride up, then dismount, was like a nightmare in slow-motion—a thousand times worse than the day he'd come after her at the Belle Elise landing. As he strode up to join them, grinding gravel beneath his boots, she noticed anew how long and powerful his legs were. Indeed, every inch of his body radiated a lethal menace. Her heart was hammering so fast she could barely hear him as he pierced her with his steely stare and said cynically, "Good evening, *chérie.*"

Angelique's voice was frozen in her throat and she could only stare at him, terrified. Fortunately, Jacques stepped up, trying to lighten the deadly tension. "Well, hello, Roland. Jean Pierre and I have so enjoyed visiting with your lovely bride. We were just going to take her out to sup, then straightaway to Emily Miro's to await your arrival—"

"Hello, Jacques," Roland cut in tersely, not even taking his eyes off his wife. "You say you and Jean Pierre were leaving?"

"Why, yes, but—"

"Then by all means, leave!" Turning angrily to Jean Pierre, he added, "I'll settle with you later, Cousin."

Jacques and his son exchanged an alarmed glance, then Jacques wisely said, "Of course, Roland. We'll all visit another time."

Yet Angelique turned desperately to Jean Pierre as the two men started to board the carriage. "No! You can't leave me alone with him like this."

Jean Pierre shook his head resignedly. "Sorry, Angelique. He is your husband."

Within seconds, the two men had driven off, and Angelique was left alone with Roland in the charged silence as the dust settled about them. She trembled as she finally dared to face him in his rage.

The look in his eyes made her blood run cold.

With a cry of fear, Angelique whirled about and raced back into the house, rushing up the stairs to the room where she had changed. Inside, she locked the door. She backed away, trembling, desperately hoping he wouldn't follow her—

He did. Within seconds, the door flew open with an ear-splitting violence and Roland was inside, shaking a fist at her. "Don't you ever—*ever* try to lock me out again!"

"Go away!" she cried, backing away against the dressing table, picking up a porcelain cachepot. "Go away or I'll throw this at you."

His laughed cynically as he steadily stalked her. "Throw away, my dear. For I'm not going away. You seem to have conveniently forgotten that you're my wife."

"I'm not you're wife!" she ranted. "I want an annulment."

Now his laughter was cruelly derisive. "I'm afraid it's a bit late for that, my darling innocent. If you'd wanted an annulment, then you never should have given yourself to me. As for what you've given Jean Pierre—and perhaps others —that will never again be tolerated, even if I have to keep you in chains."

"What I've given Jean Pierre?" she repeated incredulously. "You're one to talk—you cheating reprobate—after you brought your mistress into our home—twice!" Furious, she threw the cachepot at him.

He ducked, and it shattered on the floor with a nerve-fraying crash. "Keep throwing, *chérie*," he said with a frightening smile. "For I shall keep coming. You will never escape me—never!"

She kept throwing—the hand mirror, a perfume bottle, anything she could find—and maddeningly, Roland dodged them all and just kept coming at her, so steadily and remorselessly, the sound of his boots, grinding broken glass, awful to her ears.

But when she took the silver-plated hairbrush in hand, ready to hurl it, he held up his hand. "Enough, Angelique. I warn you that I'll not tolerate such wanton destructiveness—"

She let the hairbrush fly, and there was a horrid cracking sound as it glanced Roland across the jaw. Angelique gasped, for despite her anger, she was appalled by the sight of the thin cut she'd inflicted on him. Roland didn't move for a long moment, just staring at her in the awful silence, not even touching his jaw, which had to smart fiercely, she knew. Then he picked up the hairbrush and started toward her. "Why you cheating little—must it come to violence, then? So be it!"

"No!" she screamed. But it was too late. There was nothing left to throw, and within seconds he had grabbed her, pulling her down with him onto the dressing table stool. She was thrown across his knees, her skirts raised and the brush smartly applied to her bottom.

When at last he let her up, she attacked him with fists flailing, sobbing furiously as he tried to contain her on his lap. "Let me go, you bastard! I hate you!"

"Why? You must tell me why!" he demanded.

She managed to spring out of his lap. "Because you lied to me! You—you and Jean Pierre! You bartered me about like some whore!"

"Oh, Christ," he whispered incredulously, turning white as he struggled to his feet. "You overheard this morning."

"Yes, I heard, you liar! Now get out of here! I was never your wife—it was all a lie! And I never, ever want to see you again!"

Roland's eyes were crazed, bright with tears as he started toward her, shaking his head like a man in shock. "Chérie, please, don't say that."

"Get out! Ours has not been a marriage but just one big lie—"

"Don't say that, I beg you!"

"You bought me, you bastard!"

"I love you!" he cried.

He hauled her resisting form into his arms, crushed her close and kissed her.

She fought him desperately, his words not penetrating her crazed mind. "No! No!" she sobbed. "I won't let you do this to me! I won't!"

"*Chérie*, please, I love you and I can't lose you like this."

"No! No! Let me go!"

But he just went on kissing her—wild, desperate kisses—ignoring the blows of her fists and the resistance in her out-of-control body. After a moment, she went limp and began to sob heartbrokenly. "No, no, I can't let you—I just can't!"

"Then I'm afraid you're doomed, my love, because I can't let you go."

Yet she was cleaving to him as he picked her up and carried her to the bed. At once he was her tormentor and yet her sole salvation. They fell across the mattress together, and Roland kissed her with such raw hunger that she threw her arms around his neck and kissed him back, sobbing and calling his name brokenly. Passion consumed them both and they ripped at each others' clothes. They were still half-dressed when Roland sat up and brought her into his lap. He tangled a hand roughly in her hair and stared down into her eyes. She gasped as he thrust high into her womanhood, filling her until she thought she would explode. His strokes were hard, rough, consuming, his teeth moving to her breast. It was the deepest, most shattering possession she had ever known. "Yes! Yes!" she cried, panting as she ricocheted from one exquisite climax to another. Then Roland brought her down forcefully and held her fast as he moved convulsively toward his climax. They dissolved in a conflagration of healing pain and pleasure, his mouth swallowing her mindless cry.

When it was over, when they collapsed on the mattress together, every inch of her felt stamped with his imprint, and she knew she could never escape him. The power he held over her made her fearful, and she turned away, curling up in a ball.

He stroked her back gently. "Darling—we must talk, you know."

She nodded but didn't turn.

"I'm sorry I hit you," he whispered, and she could hear the raw pain in his voice. "I thought you had betrayed me

with Jean Pierre, and then you just stood there, telling me
you hated me and you wanted an annulment, as if to flaunt
everything you'd done right in my face. If only I'd known
that you overhead Jean Pierre and me, I never would have
raised a hand against you. I should have figured it out, but
I was too blinded by jealousy. Had I known, I would have
let you hit me till all your rage was gone, my love.''

She turned to him, tears in her eyes, and almost fell apart
when she saw the dark, ugly bruise rising on his jaw, the
long, wickedly thin cut where the hairbrush had glanced him.
''I hurt you more.'' Her voice catching on a sob, she tenderly
kissed the bruise. ''I'm so sorry, Roland.''

He drew her closer, breathing raggedly. ''I always wanted
to tell you about the true circumstances of our marriage. I
hated keeping the truth from you, but—well, Jean Pierre and
I ultimately decided it would be best if you didn't learn what
your uncle did. We felt that would have hurt you so much
more.''

She swallowed hard. ''Uncle Giles really tried—to sell
me?''

''Yes, darling, and I'm so sorry. And the two men who
wanted to buy you were reprobates who would have used you
up and then cast you aside.''

Angelique nodded soberly. She'd been so angry when she
had heard that Roland had lied to her, she hadn't really
thought things through. Now, at last, her rage were clearing
enough that she could realize that Uncle Giles was the true
villain in this piece—not Roland or Jean Pierre. Looking up
at her husband, she asked tremulously, ''Then you and Jean
Pierre—only wanted to help me?''

''Oh, yes, my darling. At the time, we had to lie to you,
had to tell you your parents arranged the marriage in order
to make sure you'd cooperate. You see, time was critical,
since we were half-afraid your uncle might—''

Angelique's shudder stopped him, and she buried her face
against his neck. ''You don't have to say it. Considering what
happened to Coco, I think I know.''

''Will you forgive me?'' Roland asked.

''Yes,'' she whispered achingly. ''If you'll forgive me.''

''There's nothing to forgive, *ma chére*.'' He sighed heavily, stroking her hair with loving fingers. ''And you must

know something, my dearest heart. It is true that our marriage was never arranged by your parents, and for that very necessary deception, I do apologize. But from the moment I laid eyes on you in the French Market, I wanted you. God, I wanted you so.'' His voice was breaking as he added, ''But I never knew if you wanted me.''

Angelique began to sob, his last words tearing her apart. ''I want you, Roland,'' she said, pressing her mouth on his. ''I do want you so!''

CHAPTER
Twenty-three

''There's something you must know,'' Roland said.

It was an hour later, and they'd just finished making love again—slowly, thoroughly, passionately. ''Yes?'' Angelique murmured, kissing his throat.

''When we were first married, I did not betray you with Caroline. Since we wed, I've slept with no woman but you.''

Angelique looked up at her husband in awe, stunned and warmed by his honesty; his vibrant blue gaze, meeting hers so boldly, left no doubt as to his sincerity. ''Thank you for telling me that, Roland.''

''I had thought that—perhaps you wondered about it.''

''I did. But—where did you go all those nights when we were first wed—and you left Belle Elise again and again?''

He laughed ruefully. ''Mostly I played cards with Louis Junot, until Annette grew weary of being denied her husband's company. Then I idled away the hours with Jules Beaufort and other planters I know.''

''But why, Roland? Was it so terrible being with me?''

He grinned. ''Indeed, terrible—because frankly, my angel, I couldn't trust myself to keep my hands off you.''

Angelique giggled, shaking her head. "If only you'd known—"

"Known what?"

She blushed. "That actually, I was dying for you to put your hands on me."

His lips twitched. "Indeed? Then why all the sanctimonious talk about your wifely duties?"

A frown framed her lovely dark eyes. "Because, of course I took my duties quite seriously. And a young woman simply isn't trained to tell her husband—"

"That she wants him to make love to her?"

She nodded shyly.

He chuckled, shaking his head. "Then it seems we were at cross-purposes all along."

"Yes it does."

"But no longer, my angel?"

She snuggled closer to him. "No longer."

He laughed again. "So you wanted me to make love to you."

"Yes," she said in a small voice.

"When did you decide this?"

She felt her cheeks burning. "Really, Roland, must I—"

"Yes. You must tell me." He rolled her beneath him and pinned her hands into the mattress, forcing her to meet his tenderly amused gaze. "I'll tolerate no further secrets between us, my angel. Tell me when you reached this—most interesting conclusion."

She looked up into his eyes and whispered, "Almost from the moment I met you. You were so handsome, so exciting, and—"

"Yes?"

She drew a shaky breath as she felt his loins tighten provocatively against her. "Mysterious and—a little frightening."

His hands now released hers, moving boldly down her spine, caressing her hips then nudging her thighs apart. "And do I frighten you now, *ma chére*?"

"A little."

"And why is that?"

She shuddered with pleasure. "Because the things you

make me feel—are so powerful. I seem not to belong to myself anymore—''

"That is true. You belong to me, *chére*, and I to you. That is how it should be."

"It does feel—right."

"But still a little frightening?"

"Yes."

"Then let's work on assuaging some of your fears," he whispered, kissing her . . .

Later, they awakened to the sound of voices out in the hallway. Roland sat up tensely, his expression grim.

"What is it, Roland?" she asked.

"Evidently Jean Pierre and Jacques have returned from dinner in the Quarter. It's high time I settled up with my illustrious cousin."

At once, she sat up. "Settled up? Over what?"

"Over his taking you away with him, *chére*. Certainly, you had reason to be upset, but Jean Pierre should never have interfered between husband and wife. He should never have aided you in your plan to leave me."

"But Roland! He didn't know!"

Roland frowned murderously. "How could he not have known?"

She smiled guiltily. "Because I hid in the boot of his carriage."

Roland was incredulous. "You didn't! Why, you little minx, I should take you over my knee again." He scowled. "Blanche didn't tell me this."

Angelique raised an eyebrow. "Blanche told you I left with Jean Pierre?"

"She saw the two of you drive off. It's odd she didn't mention that you were in the boot—but then, I didn't give her much of a chance to explain things. I was far too wild to go chasing after you."

"So I noticed."

He chuckled. "Well, then, my pet, it seems our business here is concluded. That is good. I did not particularly like the idea of challenging Jean Pierre."

"Challenging Jean Pierre? Oh, Roland! Surely you wouldn't have—"

"Shhhhh," he admonished, placing a finger over her poised lips. "They might hear you. Besides, as I just said, the matter is settled." His hand moved to toy with a lock of her hair. "Now I can take you off."

She giggled. "Take me off?"

"To the St. Louis Hotel for a proper honeymoon. I intend not to let you out of my sight—or my bed—for quite a number of days."

Her eyes grew enormous. "Roland, it occurs to me that you are—"

"Yes?" he prompted with a broad devilish grin.

"Insatiable."

He chuckled huskily and pulled her into his lap. She gasped as his dark head moved down the front of her body. His teeth caught the tip of her breast as his hand slipped boldly between her thighs. "My love, you have yet to learn the meaning of the word."

True to his word, Roland took Angelique off to the opulent St. Louis Hotel, and they did not leave their room for three days.

Their room was large and airy, fronted by an iron-lace gallery that overlooked the Vieux Carre. They spent many a delightful fall morning on their balcony, eating a leisurely breakfast and watching the bustling streets below.

Angelique gloried in the long days with Roland, making love or just talking, lying close to him on the bed. Often, she recalled the emotion-wrenching day when she'd run away from him and he'd come charging after her, how they'd flailed out at each other until the very act of flailing had galvanized them. And every time she remembered his crying out, "I love you!" and then crushing her desperately to his breast, it brought a tear to her eye.

He hadn't said he loved her again, and she hadn't as yet affirmed her love for him, either. Sometimes she wondered if he'd truly meant the words, or if they'd been spoken in the despair of the moment. She deeply regretted not expressing her own feelings to him that day; now that the opportunity had passed, no moment seemed quite right for telling her husband what was in her heart.

But what her voice could not yet express, her body said

eloquently, as she gave herself to him again and again. Roland would give her that special, sexy smile of his, and whisper, "Come here, my angel," and she would fly into his arms, so eager, covering his rough male face with kisses. Sometimes in the moments of intense rapture, she would say a silent prayer that their lovemaking would bring a child. She so wanted a baby now—a son with Roland's deep voice and proud bearing, or a daughter with his ready laughter and shining blue eyes. A child would make their happiness complete.

On the third day of their self-imposed seclusion, they received a message from the Miros, inviting them to go with the small family on an excursion to the lake the next day. When Roland asked Angelique if she wanted to go, she eagerly said yes. He promptly took her shopping for a new dress to wear.

Their jaunt the next day was marvelous, the weather dry and bracingly cool as Roland, Angelique, and the three Miros went out to the lake on "Smoky Mary," the local train line that ran from St. John's Bayou out to the area known as Milneburg along the lakefront. They had a marvelous day strolling through the park and gardens, and lunching at a fabulous seafood restaurant overlooking the water. Beyond the pavilion where they ate, the lake was glorious, tranquil and blue, and seemed to stretch on forever.

After all had eaten their fill of crab gumbo and crawfish *étouffée*, the men left with Phillip. They strolled beneath bald cypress trees near the edge of the water, Maurice and Roland smoking while Phillip skimmed stones on the lake. Emily and Angelique remained behind to visit on the restaurant's veranda.

"My dear, you're radiant," Emily said to Angelique, as the two women shared a second cup of *café au lait*.

"Oh, Emily, I'm so happy with Roland," Angelique replied.

"I must admit that I was rather concerned when I ran into Jean Pierre in the Market the other day," Emily went on. "I don't mean to speak indelicately, dear, but the poor man was distraught. He confided in me that both he and his father were quite worried after you and Roland had something of a row at his house."

Angelique nodded, smiling ruefully. "Ah, yes, we did."
She leaned forward and confided, "What happened is that I
found out Roland married me under, shall we say, less than
honest circumstances." Watching Emily go pale, she added,
"You knew, didn't you?"

Emily bit her lip. "Well, yes, dear, I surmised that something strange was going on. But I really didn't know any
details."

Briefly, Angelique explained to Emily how Roland had
lied to her when they first met, manipulating her into marriage
with him.

When she finished her account, Emily was agog. "My
dear, that is quite an astounding story. And it looks like
Roland married you in the nick of time, as well. You're not
still angry with him?"

Angelique shook her head. "Oh, I was furious when I first
discovered he had lied. But he finally got across to me that
the deception was necessary, for my own protection." She
felt herself blushing slightly. "Really, it's all rather romantic
when you think about it—the lengths he went to to wed me."

Emily laughed, clapping her slim hands. "Oh, my dear—
indeed it is romantic. You realize, of course, that Roland is
totally in love with you?"

Angelique's blush deepened. "Well, I do hope I have
pleased him."

"Pleased him?" Emily repeated with a disbelieving laugh.
"My dear, you are the answer to all of our prayers. Haven't
you any idea what he was like before?"

Slowly, Angelique shook her head.

"Why the man never laughed, never smiled. He was just
a walking bomb, full of tension and surliness. But since he's
met you—why he must have loved you from the moment he
laid eyes on you."

Angelique smiled radiantly. "Oh, I hope so, Emily. I do
know that I—"

"Loved him from the moment you laid eyes on him?"

"Yes."

Emily leaned forward, grasping Angelique's hand. "Have
you told him, dear? You know he worships the ground you
walk on."

"Well—actually, I've been waiting for the right moment."

Emily released Angelique's hand, and her expression was wistful as she turned to study Roland, Maurice and Phillip, who were now striding back toward them. "Take care, my dear. That right moment may just forever elude you, and then it could be too late."

Angelique also turned to look at the approaching three-some. Roland and Phillip were walking along, hand in hand, both laughing. A chill gripped her heart as she again thought of how much the uncle and nephew resembled each other. And why was Emily staring at the two of them with such longing? Was she remembering her own bittersweet time with Justin—or suffering some other private torment?

The small group returned home from the lake late that afternoon. Roland politely declined Emily's invitation for supper at the Miro townhome. Angelique felt relieved that they weren't staying, as the excursion had been a long one; yet she couldn't contain a small stab of jealousy as she watched Roland kiss Emily and Phillip goodbye. She felt guilty for her feelings of possessiveness, especially since she was quite fond of Emily and Phillip; yet she remained be-mused regarding the poignant look she had seen in Emily's eyes as she watched Roland and Phillip today.

Roland took Angelique off for supper at Antoine's in the Quarter, where they dined on *Pompano en papillote*. Angelique felt more relaxed now that she was alone with Roland, and, indeed, her husband did not take his eyes off her through-out the meal. He seemed to be reading her mind when he reached across the table, took her hand gently in his and said, "*Chérie*, only a few hours with others, and I become mad to have you to myself again." His thumb, sensuously stroking her warm palm, drove her wild, and when she dared to look up into his eyes, the vibrant intensity there left no doubt as to how their night would be spent. She could hardly contain her trembling hands as they finished their meal.

Yet the magic was abruptly shattered as they were leaving the restaurant. Roland was escorting Angelique toward the door when he stopped in his tracks, staring ahead at an elderly couple in evening clothes who stood waiting to be seated.

She heard him curse under his breath, and his gaze was stony as he led her toward the strangers. The couple, spotting Roland and Angelique approach, also looked tense.

When Roland and Angelique paused by the couple, the gentleman spoke first. Nodding to Roland, he said coldly, "Well, hello Roland. This is—a surprise."

"Hello, Bernard," Roland said stiffly, not offering the older man his hand. He nodded toward the woman. "Lenore."

"Hello, Roland," the woman said imperiously. She fixed cold gray eyes on Angelique. "And who is this—young woman you are with?"

Roland drew himself up with dignity. "Lenore, Bernard, may I present my bride, Angelique Delacroix." As the two older people exchanged glances of astonishment, Roland added to Angelique, "My dear, meet Bernard and Lenore Rillieux."

The woman now fixed a gaze of icy hostility on Angelique as she said, "Why, Roland, this is a shock. I would have thought that you—"

"Lenore, if you'll excuse us," Roland cut in firmly, "our carriage is waiting. And we certainly don't want to keep you and Bernard from your dinner."

Without another word, Roland pulled Angelique past the scowling couple and out the front door into the coolness of the night. Their rented carriage awaited them at curbside, awash in the yellow glow of a gas light. As the coachman helped them board, Angelique heard Roland telling the man to drive them along the levee before returning them to the St. Louis.

Roland was grimly silent as the coach clattered off. After a moment, he lit a thin cigar, and the light of the match, wavering over his face, illuminated his handsome, troubled features. Angelique reached out and took his hand. "Roland, who were those people we passed at Antoine's? Why did they upset you so?"

He didn't answer, but she could feel his fingers stiffening.

"Roland?" she nudged. "Won't you please tell me who they were?"

He sighed fiercely. "They were Luisa's parents."

For a long moment, neither said a word. Then Angelique

murmured, "Don't you think it's time for you to tell me about her?"

Roland's cheroot glowed as he drew on it savagely. The scent of smoke wafted over her. "Perhaps you're right, *chérie*. Perhaps it is time for me to tell you about my first wife—and her family." He gathered his thoughts for a moment. "You see, when I was but a child, my parents arranged for me to marry Luisa Rillieux. At the time, her family owned the plantation just south of Belle Elise. Later, she and I married. I was twenty-one at the time, she was eighteen. And things just—didn't work out."

"What do you mean?"

"Luisa hated . . ." Angelique could hear him grinding his teeth as he finished, "the sexual aspect of marriage. Hell, she hated being married to me, period. Evidently others gave her what I couldn't, for she sought it from them often enough."

Angelique gasped. "Oh, Roland, how terrible for you!" Carefully, she added, "There must have been something wrong with Luisa. Why, she would have had to be a fool not to—love being with you."

He shrugged. "I was no saint either. You see, Luisa was not the only one who didn't want the marriage, who felt trapped and resentful."

"I see," Angelique murmured.

"Luisa seemed to be made of quite fragile stuff—she did not have your substance, my dear. She was not equal to the task of being mistress of Belle Elise—or anyone's wife, for that matter. And I'm afraid I was neither sympathetic nor helpful. At any rate, we were on a collision course and it's a miracle our marriage lasted two years."

"How did Luisa—die?" Angelique asked slowly.

He drew a long drag on his cigar. "As I mentioned, Luisa betrayed me with other men. And toward the end, she became—irrational. Blanche thinks she was a bit unhinged all along. Any time I looked at another woman, Luisa went wild. I think she even imagined there was something going on between Blanche and me. But things really started building toward a head after Justin was killed."

"That's right—Justin, Emily, and Phillip were living at Belle Elise when he died, weren't they?"

"They were." Roland's voice was tight as he continued, "Justin went into New Orleans one night, got drunk in the canal district and was run over by a carriage. That was it— no warning whatsoever, and Emily was a widow. Of course the poor girl practically lost her mind, left all alone with a tiny son to raise. I did everything in my power to help her afterward—but I'm afraid it was my efforts to help Emily that ultimately drove Luisa over the edge."

"How was that?" Angelique asked.

"Somehow Luisa had gotten the demented idea that I was sleeping with Emily. She even thought we'd been committing adultery while Emily and Justin were married, and that Phillip was my son."

Angelique had been listening with a deepening sense of dread. "How did you find out Luisa—thought these things?"

"I found out the night she—died. You see, we had given a party at Belle Elise that night, and I'm afraid . . ." He cleared his throat. "Luisa flirted with every man there, and I'm afraid I retaliated in kind. At one point, she told me that if I dared to dance with Emily that night, she would kill me. So, just to spite her, I danced every remaining dance with Justin's widow." His fist slammed the seat. "Oh, Christ, I should have listened to her! I just didn't realize that she'd gone over the edge by then!"

"What happened?" Angelique whispered.

"Later that night, once the guests had left, Luisa confronted me in my study with a loaded pistol. That's when she accused me of sleeping with Emily and fathering Phillip. I tried to convince her that none of it was true—and of course, it wasn't. But she was beyond hearing me. There was a struggle, and ultimately it was Luisa who pulled the trigger even as I was trying to deflect the gun. The next thing I knew, she was on the floor, staring up at me with eyes wide open, and there was blood everywhere. The authorities called it an accident, but I've felt great guilt ever since, nevertheless."

"Oh, Roland." Angelique's heart twisted with pain for him, and her hand clutched his tightly.

At last he turned to her in the darkness and said ironically, "Well, my dear, how does it feel to be married to a man who killed his first wife?"

CHAPTER
Twenty-four

"Roland," Angelique cried, hugging him, "do you truly think I'd blame you for Luisa's death? There's no way you could have known—"

"I should have tried harder."

"But it doesn't look as if Luisa would have met you half-way."

He sighed. "We'll never know, will we?"

She snuggled closer to him in the cold darkness of the carriage. "Oh, Roland." Inwardly, she felt troubled. While she was glad Roland had shared his past with her, it was disconcerting to discover that his first wife had experienced exactly the same fears about Roland and Emily that she had.

"Are you content to stay with me, my angel, now that you know the dark secrets of my first marriage?"

Roland's question was filled with so much emotion that Angelique hastened to reassure him. "Of course I am. And I just want you to know that your second marriage will be so much happier."

"It already is, *chérie*."

Roland kissed her then, holding her close all the way back to the hotel. Yet back in their room, in bed, his lovemaking was more demanding than usual—not violent, but lacking the sweet tenderness of recent days. Afterward, he still seemed tense as he clutched her close to him all night.

This made Angelique wonder if talking about Luisa had unleashed a demon in Roland which their sharing had not completely exorcised.

* * *

The next morning as Roland and Angelique shared break-fast in their room, he was scowling over a letter brought to them by the bellhop.

"What is it, Roland?" she asked.

He set aside the correspondence and glanced up at her. "Jacques and Jean Pierre have invited us to dine with them tonight."

"Oh, Roland, let's go!" Angelique urged.

Roland frowned at her. "I'm still not feeling too kindly disposed toward Jean Pierre after the events of last week."

"But Roland—I've already explained that it wasn't his fault. And you and I created such a scene at his house, not to mention my breaking all those things. From what Emily told me yesterday, Jean Pierre has been distraught regarding our argument. Don't you think we owe him and Jacques an amend? I do think you should let Jean Pierre know that there are no hard feelings between you."

Roland harrumphed.

Angelique stood and went over to embrace her husband. "Please?"

He pulled her down into his lap, suddenly grinning. "How can I resist when you plead so prettily?"

They spent much of the day shopping in the Quarter. Ange-lique insisted that they replace the toiletry items she had broken during their fight at Jean Pierre's. With a rueful grin, Roland agreed.

Angelique took special pains with her appearance that night, dressing in a full-skirted, low-cut gown of emerald velvet. Ro-land, elegantly dressed in formal black, stood watching her as she tied back her hair with a matching satin ribbon. Studying the reflection of her bare neck in the dressing table mirror, he frowned. "A pity I didn't bring along your jewels from Belle Elise. But then you always do shine, *chérie*. Indeed, you look far too lovely tonight for me to share you with two other men."

Angelique quickly stood and went over to hug her husband. He looked so handsome, and his worried scowl was endear-ing. "Oh, Roland. Don't you know by now that I have eyes only for you?"

"That may be, Angel, but what of Jean Pierre and Jacques? Who do you think they will have eyes for tonight?"

She stiffened. "Roland, they both respect you too much to try to steal your wife."

His response was a deprecating growl.

They were both silent in the coach on the way to Jean Pierre's house. It was becoming obvious to Angelique that Roland felt quite touchy about their spending the evening with two other men. While his possessiveness was exciting on one level, his lack of trust was starting to rankle.

At Jean Pierre's home on St. Charles Avenue, he and Jacques laughed over the gifts Roland and Angelique presented: a porcelain cochepot, a matching hair jar, a crystal perfume bottle, and a hand mirror. "Really, these weren't necessary," Jean Pierre said. "If you two want to throw things at each other, just be my guests, any time."

Catching Roland's scowl through the corner of her eye, Angelique quickly said, "I was the one who threw things, not Roland," and to her pleasure, all three men laughed.

The four had a long, leisurely meal in the dining room, and both Jean Pierre and his father seemed relieved that there was no noticeable tension between the newlyweds. Jacques made a toast to them and afterward, said to Roland, "It's good to see you and your bride getting along so famously tonight, nephew."

In return, Roland stared straight at his uncle and replied, "Indeed, Uncle. It's interesting how three days spent alone with one's bride at the St. Louis can work wonders in a marriage."

Jacques, far too worldly to become flustered, chuckled at Roland's daring remark, winking at Angelique, while Jean Pierre dabbed at his mouth with his napkin to conceal his own mirth. Angelique felt mortified.

Luckily, at this point, Jacques launched into a fascinating discourse on his recent travels to Denmark, and Angelique was afforded ample opportunity to regain her composure. Later, over *café brûlot* in the parlor, Jacques asked Roland, "Are you and Angelique staying on for the Jenny Lind concert after the first of the year?"

Angelique glanced expectantly at her husband. On the way back from the lake yesterday, Emily had mentioned the famous Swedish opera singer's scheduled performance in New Orleans. Roland now nodded to Jacques and replied, "I read about the concert in the *Crescent*. But isn't it already sold out?"

"Indeed," Jacques replied. "However, my friend André Bienville of the opera has reserved my traditional box, and I would truly be honored if you and Angelique, as well as the Miros, would be my guests for the evening."

"That's quite generous of you, Uncle." Roland turned to Angelique. "Would you like to hear Miss Lind sing?"

"Oh, yes, Roland!" she said with eyes glowing.

"Of course then, Angel." Saying the words in an intimate whisper, Roland reached out and brushed a wisp of hair from Angelique's brow. His words and touch comprised another brazen message—hardly lost on the other two men. As before, Angelique found her face flaming at her husband's bold demonstration.

"Actually," Jacques was continuing, "I've known Miss Lind's sponsor, P. T. Barnum, for many years."

"Ah, yes, I believe I've heard you refer to Mr. Barnum before," Roland replied politely.

"I've been a guest at Iranistan, the Barnum home, on many occasions. In fact, last year, Phineas asked me to help back the Lind tour, and fool that I was, I declined. Soon afterward, I heard *La Lind* sing in London and realized my folly. But by then, it was too late for me to join in Barnum's venture."

"You heard Miss Lind sing?" Angelique asked excitedly.

Jacques smiled at Roland's captivating young bride. "Indeed I did, my dear. And the woman truly has a gift. I'll never forget hearing her in London. They say the elderly Duke of Wellington was utterly smitten with her that night. Chopin was there, sitting just a few rows ahead of me. The poor chap was in wretched health, but nevertheless glowing just to hear her. Miss Lind sang Mendelssohn's songs for the first time since his death, and ah! 'Twas so moving! They say she took his passing very hard."

Angelique noticed a tear in Jacques's dark eyes as he finished his account. "I can't wait to hear Miss Lind sing," she told him sincerely.

"Neither can I, my dear." Almost too casually, Jacques added to Roland, "And we must, of course, bring Blanche down from the plantation for the performance. I trust she's doing well?"

"She is," Roland replied. "And we can certainly try to bring her down to New Orleans. But you know how it is with her, Uncle."

"Roland, she does so love the opera," Angelique put in.

Roland nodded to her. "That's true, *chérie*. But I wager we'll not be able to budge her, nevertheless."

"Perhaps I should drive out to the plantation myself and prevail upon her to come," Jacques said.

"That might help," Roland concurred. "She does seem to set quite a bit of store by what you think, Jacques."

"Does she now?" Jacques murmured, grinning.

Jean Pierre, who had been silently drinking wine through much of the evening, now piped up in a slurred voice to Angelique. "My dear, I've been telling my father what a marvelous voice you have. Won't you honor us with some after-dinner music?"

"Ah, yes, Angelique, you must!" Jacques seconded.

But before Angelique could reply, Roland cut in with, "I beg your forgiveness, Cousin, Uncle, but Angelique and I must be going along now." Reaching over to touch the curve of his wife's face, he winked at her and added, "You know how it is with us newlyweds."

Angelique was seethingly silent in the coach going back to the hotel, embarrassed over Roland's possessive behavior at dinner.

Back in their room, he helped her remove her cloak, then shed his greatcoat. He turned to her with a forbearing frown. "Very well, Angel. Are you going to tell me why your feathers are ruffled?"

"You don't know?" she asked angrily.

He shrugged. "Pray, illuminate me."

"You embarrassed me tonight!"

"Indeed? How did I accomplish that?"

"By . . . first of all, by telling Jean Pierre and Uncle Jacques that we spent three days alone here!"

Feigning innocence, he raised an eyebrow. "Was that a lie?"

"That's not the point. Heaven knows what they imagined—"

"Good." His voice was hoarse, his eyes gleaming. "Let

there be no doubts in their minds as to the inviolability of this marriage. Let them know what we have—and what they cannot have.''

Angelique flung her hands wide. "Roland! By the saints! You're talking about your own uncle and cousin. Do you really think that they'd—''

Yet his cynical laughter stopped her. "You really are a starry-eyed innocent, my pet. Don't you know that you turn men's heads every place we go? Do you know how crazy that makes me?''

"Roland, you don't understand. I'm not interested in those other men.'' She paused for a moment, catching her breath, staring at him in anger and anguish. "You think I'm like Luisa, don't you? That I'm just looking for an opportunity to betray you?''

"No,'' he denied, coming quickly to her side, his expression impassioned. "You're nothing like Luisa. But I do think you're young and guileless, and could easily be seduced into—''

"*Seduced*?'' she repeated furiously, backing away. "Just how naive do you think I am? Why I would never—''

"You didn't recognize the danger your uncle posed,'' he cut in ruthlessly. "And, Angel—in a few more days, that man would have sold you or molested you—most likely, both.''

Angelique lowered her eyes. She had no answer for him there.

"No more arguing now, *petite*,'' he cajoled. "Come here, and I'll help you out of your frock.''

She stared up at him defiantly. "No.''

"No?'' he repeated, his voice filled with soft menace. "I don't have to accept that, you know.''

She faced him proudly. "You will or I'll hate you for it.''

He gestured resignedly. "Suit yourself, then.''

Her hand slashed the air. "You treat me like a child, Roland! Tonight when Jean Pierre asked me to sing, you answered for me.''

He smiled cynically. "Ah, but there, I was only being merciful, my darling. For if your singing did for them what it does for me, letting you perform would have been cruel, *n'est-ce pas*?''

Despite the high color flaming in her cheeks at his provocative words, she held her ground. "Not letting me answer
for myself was cruel."

He sighed. "No more fighting. Come here and let's make
up."

Angelique struggled to hold onto her resolve. Roland
looked very sexy and masterful standing across from her, his
male implacability tugging like a magnet at her softer feminine nature. Yet what would be resolved if she gave in?
Sadly, she shook her head. "No. I'm sleeping on the
daybed."

"As you wish," he conceded wearily. "But, Angel—do
ask yourself who you're punishing."

In the sleepless hours that followed, Angelique knew who
she was punishing, and as far as she could determine, it wasn't
her husband. The daybed was hard and uncomfortable, and
she shivered with more than the cold beneath her single wool
blanket. Finally, she sat up in the darkness and whispered,
"Roland?"

"Yes, dear," came his deep voice.

"Are you sleeping?"

"Not at the moment. Actually, I've been wondering . . ."

"Yes?" she asked tremulously.

"Whether you're coming over here or I'm going over
there."

Angelique climbed off the daybed and went over to stand
before her husband. Her voice shook as she said, "I'm sorry
we fought."

He pulled her into bed with him, kissing her hard, and she
gloried in his nearness, his warm, protective embrace.

"I'm sorry, too, *chére*," he whispered.

"No you're not," she said, nibbling on his bare shoulder.

"I'm not?" he repeated with a laugh.

"You'd do it all again—eagerly."

His hand slid up her leg. "Ah, Angel, you know me so
well—"

"And you're utterly impossible!"

"Utterly!" he solemnly agreed.

Then he was raising her gown, bonding her body with his.
Tears filled her eyes at the sweet torment of loving him, and
she didn't care.

CHAPTER
Twenty-five

The next few weeks passed quickly. Roland and Angelique spent much time alone, shopping, or going to plays or operas. They attended a couple of *bals de société* given by prominent Creoles from the Quarter. Though they occasionally spent time with family, Roland made no repeat performance of his possessive behavior that night they had dined at Jean Pierre's house. Evidently Roland felt he'd gotten his message across, Angelique decided; he seemed content to have her to himself much of the time. His need of her never abated—nor did hers for him—and their nights of intense passion often impelled them to sleep late into the mornings.

Christmas came, and they observed it in the quiet Creole fashion, attending Mass with family. New Year's Day was the Creole holiday of note, and they accepted the Miros' invitation to spend the day at their townhome in the Quarter. Jacques and Jean Pierre were also invited, and the family enjoyed the traditional day of celebrating and feasting, exchanging presents and visiting around the New Year's tree. Angelique gave Roland a new dressing gown, and she was touched when he gave her a stunning ruby drop, along with matching earrings.

Late that afternoon, as the gathering broke up, Jacques reminded one and all that they were to be his guests at the Jenny Lind performance the following week. As Roland and Angelique were leaving, Jacques took his nephew aside and added, "With your permission, Roland, I'm going up to Belle Elise soon to prevail upon Blanche to come down for the concert. Emily has said she would be delighted to have her stay here."

Roland nodded. "By all means, Uncle, use all your per-suasive powers. Good luck."

Once they were traveling back to the hotel in their coach, Angelique remarked to Roland, "Jacques seems quite inter-ested in Blanche. Has he known her for long?"

Roland nodded. "Jacques has been a visitor at Belle Elise for many years, and he and Blanche have become close friends. I've often seen them out on the veranda together—Jacques fascinating her with tales of his world travels. I sus-pect that he's in love with her—and she with him."

"Then why . . . ?"

Roland squeezed her hand. "They're simply from different worlds, my dear. You know Blanche refuses to leave St. Charles Parish. And Jacques would never be content to give up his travels and secrete himself off from the world at Belle Elise."

She frowned sadly. "But perhaps if Jacques can convince her to come to New Orleans for the Lind performance, that might be a beginning for them. Oh, Roland, Blanche does so love the opera."

"And you are the soul of kindness to be thinking of her." He wrapped an arm around her shoulders, pulling her closer. "Now enough about them. I can't wait to get you alone, Mrs. Delacroix."

"You never can," she said with a laugh.

Before dawn the next morning, Angelique awakened to the discovery that she would not be bearing Roland's child. After seeing to her needs, she returned to bed, tears trickling down her face.

He heard her sniffling and pulled her close. "*Chére*, what is it?"

"It's just that—I want a baby so," she sobbed, "and I don't think I'm ever going to have one."

He chuckled softly, stroking her hair. "Angel, don't you think you're being a bit impatient? We haven't been married that long, and you're still so young—"

"If I'm old enough to be your wife, I'm old enough to be a mother," she put in heatedly.

"Well, that is a point well-taken," he agreed with a smile.

"My mother had a difficult time conceiving," she went

on, sniffing. "Maman and Papa tried and tried for years, but they were blessed only with me—"

"That was ample blessing, my love."

Unheeding, she continued, "Now I'll probably never get pregnant."

"Now, Angel, don't assume there's no hope. Perhaps you're just feeling sad right now due to your—ah—indisposition."

"But I really do want a child—"

"I know, love, and so do I," he whispered, hugging her tightly. "Perhaps we'll simply have to work harder at it."

"Work harder at it?" she asked indignantly. "However could we do that?"

He chuckled. "Wait and see, Angel." He kissed her brow. "Now rest. It isn't even light yet, and as I recall, some passionate creature keep me awake into the wee hours last night."

Angelique nestled close to her husband and slept. Watching her, Roland felt his heart welling with love. Her weeping because she wasn't to bear his child had touched him deeply. And what he had told her was true. He did want a child with her—he wanted it as badly as she did now. A baby would be an ultimate expression of their love, growing deep within the very place where they were joined each night.

And knowing how badly they both wanted it scared him. It would happen soon—he knew that somehow. And he wondered if she were ready. She was woman, yes, but part of her was still child. Was she prepared to bear the pain of childbirth, the responsibilities of motherhood?

He smoothed a wisp of hair from her brow and kissed her sweet mouth. He loved everything about her, and he would grieve if the coming of their child made any part of her lost to him. Or to herself.

Two days later, Jacques Delacroix drove up to Belle Elise in his son's coach. A brisk, cold wind tugged at his greatcoat as he hurried up the steps. Henri admitted him, and he waited for Blanche in the parlor, rubbing his hands near the blazing fire.

When she stepped into the room, his heart soared. She

looked so lovely standing near the portal, with her red hair in a becoming chignon, her brown eyes glowing at the sight of him. She wore a becoming lavender wool gown and a white shawl—it was the first time in many years that he'd seen her wear anything but black.

Her color deepened as she stared at him, and she smiled shyly. "Why Jacques! What an unexpected—and pleasant —surprise!"

"Hello, my dear. You look lovely today." Jacques approached her eagerly, and when she politely extended her hand, he gave her an admonishing look. "None of that, now!"

Jacques pulled Blanche into his arms for a warm kiss. She was stiff in his embrace, but didn't resist him. Afterward, she stared at him, trembling. She found he looked handsome as ever in his black wool tailcoat, pleated shirt and dark knee breeches; his brown eyes gleamed with the zest for life that she had come to love so much, and every feature of his chiseled face was well-remembered and beautiful to her. Being in his arms again, if only for a brief greeting, was heavenly, and she could barely contain her tears of joy.

She cleared her throat self-consciously. "Well, won't you have a seat? I've sent Henri for tea."

Jacques led Blanche over to the settee, sitting down close to her. "Have you been well, my dear?"

"Oh, yes. And you?"

"Getting along quite famously, thank you."

She smiled tremulously. "How were your travels this time?"

"Copenhagen was splendid, as always, and I stopped off in Paris and London before beginning the voyage home." Grinning, he reached into his breast pocket, extracting a small black box. "For you, my dear. A New Year's remembrance."

Blushing, Blanche took the box and opened it. She gasped as she stared at a fabulous topaz ring. The stone was huge and brilliant, the setting solid gold filigree. Her eyes were enormous as she stared up at him. "Oh, Jacques! I can't accept this."

"Of course you can," he said in a tone that brooked no

nonsense. He reached out, took the ring, then slipped it on her finger. "I saw it in the window at Bond Street Jewelers in London—couldn't resist. See—it's perfect for you."

Blanche would have protested further, but she knew Jacques would hear none of it. And she couldn't help but glow with pride as she stared down at the dazzling stone. "I—well, thank you, Jacques. You're always so thoughtful."

Henri brought in the tea service then, and once Blanche had served them both, she asked, "So you're staying in New Orleans for the time being?"

"Yes."

"Then you must have seen Roland—and his bride."

"Indeed, yes. My nephew is a veritable picture of wedded bliss, and Angelique is a darling, of course." Setting down his tea, he added, "My dear, I've come here today to insist that you join the rest of the family for the Jenny Lind performance at the St. Charles Theater two days hence."

"Oh, Jacques!" At first, Blanche's eyes glowed with excitement, then a shadow crossed her gaze and she averted her marked cheek away from the light. "Why I'd love to hear Miss Lind—I've read all about her tour in the papers. But surely it's too late to get a ticket—"

Jacques held up a hand. "My traditional box has been reserved for me at the St. Charles, and there's plenty of room for you and quite a few others. Roland and Angelique will be joining me, as well as the Miros. You simply must attend, my dear."

"Well, I—"

He squeezed her hand and continued earnestly. "I haven't even told you the best news, my dear. Phineas Barnum answered my recent telegram saying he and Miss Lind will be delighted to attend the reception Jean Pierre and I are hosting after the concert."

"Oh, my!" Blanche's cheeks lit with high color. "That's right—you're a friend of Mr. Barnum's, aren't you?"

"Indeed, I am. It's truly a once in a lifetime opportunity, my dear. Knowing how you love the opera, I don't see how you can refuse."

Blanche lowered her gaze, taking a sip of tea to hide her discomfiture. "Well, actually, Jacques, I know Roland is counting on me to watch over the plantation while he and Angelique are away—''

"Stuff and nonsense," Jacques cut in stoutly. "Roland told me he would have fetched you to New Orleans himself, except that he knew you wouldn't budge. That overseer of his, Mr. Johnson—''

"Mr. Jurgen," Blanche put in with a smile.

"Well, whatever. That fellow is perfectly capable of taking charge of things here—particularly with the cane already harvested."

Yet Blanche was biting her lip. "I'm sorry, Jacques. It's just—impossible."

With a low curse, he stood and began to pace. "It's the nonsense about your face again, isn't it?"

Her teacup clattered onto the coffee table. "Jacques, please—''

He turned to her sharply and spoke passionately. "My dear, no one gives a thought to it except you."

"I—that's not true."

"It is true! When are you going to quit crippling yourself with this presumed deformity and start realizing what a beautiful and sensitive woman you truly are?"

She shook her head helplessly. "I—I'm none of those things."

He strode to her side and pulled her to her feet. "You are all of those things—and furthermore, you're coming with me to New Orleans. Now go upstairs and start packing, woman."

She stared downward miserably. "I can't, Jacques."

"Then in that case, I'm staying."

"I—beg your pardon?" Blanche stammered.

As she watched, alarmed, Jacques seated himself on the settee and casually crossed his long legs, a wicked glint in his eyes. "I said I'm staying. Just think of it, dear—the two of us here, alone, unmarried, with no suitable chaperon."

"But why—''

"I'm staying here with you until the entire parish considers your virtue suitably compromised. Then you'll have to marry me—and obey my every command thereafter."

Blanche was flabbergasted. "Jacques—surely you jest—''

"Indeed not." Stroking his mustache, he added with relish,

"Emily Miro is expecting you in time for dinner tonight. 'Twill cause quite a scandal if you don't appear at her town-home by then, don't you think?"

Blanche shook a finger at him. "Jacques, that's blackmail—"

"Indeed it is. Now choose. Pack—or be compromised."

Blanche frowned a moment, then sighed. "I'll pack." Watching a satisfied grin light his face, she couldn't resist a smile. "You rogue!"

"What can I say? I'm Creole, my dear."

But as she started to leave the room, he followed her and took her arm. "I mean to have you as my wife, Blanche."

Her eyes were suddenly filled with anguish. "Jacques, we've been over this before—"

"And one of these days you'll stop fighting me." He reached out and lovingly caressed the birthmark on her cheek.

"No!" she cried, trying to pull away.

"Don't cringe from me, Blanche," he ground out angrily.

Jacques pulled her close and kissed her again, more passionately this time, and she surrendered with a sobbing moan, wrapping her arms about his neck. When he pressed his lips against her birthmark, he tasted the wetness of her tears. He felt an aching shudder rack her slim body, but she didn't pull away this time. "Go pack, *ma chére*," he said more gently. "We'll talk in New Orleans—we'll talk quite a lot."

Upstairs packing, Blanche felt both excited and terrified. She had been shocked and delighted to see Jacques earlier, but his insistence that she accompany him to New Orleans had caught her off guard.

Oh, how she wished Roland and Angelique were still here, and that Jacques was staying for another of his visits. For years, she had lived vicariously through Roland's dashing uncle, traveling all over the world through his descriptions of the places he had visited.

Now, with Roland and Angelique off in New Orleans, she would have to join them, or risk looking unpardonably indiscreet in the eyes of the parish. She smiled. Despite her trepidations, she did admire Jacques's cleverness in forcing her hand, and of course she was dying to hear Jenny Lind sing.

But to go out in public with Jacques in New Orleans! People in the parish were used to her, but in New Orleans, Jacques would soon discover how revolting strangers found her.

Blanche knew she loved Jacques, had loved him for many years. In the depths of her soul, she wanted to please him, to do his bidding. When he had mentioned marriage downstairs, her heart had fluttered with intense longing. Yet she knew that, despite his ardent declarations, what he really felt for her was pity. He just didn't acknowledge this consciously. When Jacques saw what a freak she was in the eyes of the rest of the world, he would surely come to grips with his true feelings and realize, once and for all, that they were doomed—

And yet . . . being with him was so heavenly, it was almost worth the hell of ridicule and exposure. She would love him always, even when he no longer looked at her with such fond regard.

CHAPTER
Twenty-six

On a cold January night two days later, Angelique felt filled with excitement as she and Roland drove up to the fashionable new St. Charles Theater for the Jenny Lind performance.

Angelique had been reading newspaper accounts of the Swedish Nightingale and her sensational tour of the United States. Her manager, Mr. Barnum, had ostensibly paid Lind the astounding sum of $187,500 in advance to bring her to this country. She'd been a smashing success ever since she'd made her debut at Castle Garden in New York.

And Lind's arrival in New Orleans yesterday had stirred a tremendous furor. Vendors had made a fortune selling shirts and cravats to mark the occasion. And from the moment

Lind's ship, the *Falcon*, had docked at the levee, an enormous
throng of admirers had followed her everywhere. Even when
Lind was finally sequestered in her suite at the Pontalba Buildings, a fireman's parade, complete with torches and bands,
had come up to serenade her.

Roland had insisted they stay away from the mob scenes
yesterday, fearing Angelique could be hurt. He'd reminded
her that they would be meeting Lind and Barnum at the
reception Jacques and Jean Pierre were hosting after tonight's
performance. Although yesterday, Angelique had felt disappointed that Roland wouldn't take her to catch a glimpse
of Lind, this morning, after reading how some citizens had
been injured in the mass hysteria, she'd realized he was right.

The carriage now clattered to a halt beneath a gaslight, and
the coachman helped them disembark. Roland gripped Angelique's arm as they climbed the steps to the stately, pillared
building. Inside the elegant lobby, they glanced around at the
arriving Creole families. A sense of rising expectation consumed the scene.

"Jacques said we should wait for him here," Roland murmured to Angelique.

She nodded, as an attendant came forward to take their
outer clothing. Roland helped Angelique out of her cloak,
then removed his own greatcoat and silk top hat, handing all
to the negro. Angelique noted how dashing her husband
looked in his formal black, with his ruffled white shirt and
white silk cravat. She wore a full-skirted, tight waisted gown
of gold velvet, deeply cut off the shoulders. The vibrant,
shimmery fabric was complemented by the ruby jewelry Roland had given her for New Year's. Her hair was pinned in
lush curls on top of her head; she wore no hat, but had
intertwined a few white camellias through her dark locks, in
the tradition of Creole women at the opera.

Roland's gaze flicked over her approvingly. "I suppose
we're early," he remarked. "Although I assume Jacques and
Jean Pierre must go to the Quarter to fetch Blanche and the
Miros."

"Isn't it wonderful that Jacques was able to persuade
Blanche to come to New Orleans?"

"Ah, yes, I was so pleased when I ran into him at the
Exchange yesterday and he told me of his success."

"I was stunned that he managed to get her to leave the plantation," Angelique confessed. "I've tried for ages to convince Blanche to come here on an excursion—but no luck."

He chuckled. "We Delacroix men do have our persuasive powers."

She smiled back at him radiantly. "Indeed, you do."

All at once, Angelique turned as a familiar voice rang out. "Angelique! Oh, *Dio mio*, do my eyes deceive me?"

Angelique's dark eyes lit with joy and surprise as a tall, slender, regally beautiful woman hurried toward her. She recognized every feature of that classical, beloved face. "Madame Santoni!"

The middle-aged woman, in glittering dark shawl and gray silk dress, embraced Angelique warmly. "Oh, Angelique!" she cried, tears in her eyes as she stared at the girl, who was her former pupil and the darling of her heart. "This is such a wonderful surprise! You look so lovely and so happy, my dear." She glanced warmly at Roland. "And this must be the husband you wrote me about?"

"Yes, Madame." Smiling, she continued, "Madame Bella Santoni Rivaldi, this is my husband, Roland Delacroix."

"Enchanted, madame," Roland told the Italian woman, gallantly kissing the gloved hand she extended.

"It is my pleasure, M'sieur Delacroix. Oh, where is Antonio?" she continued with excitement and some impatience. "He must see this!" As a graying gentlemen in evening clothes strode toward them, she called out, "Antonio, look who I've found! Our darling Angelique and her new husband."

The tall, handsome Italian came forward and graciously greeted the younger couple. Once the introductions were made, Angelique told her teacher brightly, "Why, Madame, it is such a pleasant surprise to see you here in New Orleans."

"This is one performance Antonio and I wouldn't have missed for the world. We bought our tickets weeks ago—and a good thing, too, since we heard the concert sold out almost immediately."

"My wife has spoken so fondly of your great talent as a singer and vocal coach," Roland put in.

Madame chuckled to Angelique. "He is a great charmer, this husband of yours, eh, *cara*? And so handsome!"

Angelique blushed, smiling at Roland. "He is that." Excitedly, she added, "Have you heard Miss Lind sing before?"

"Indeed, I have. Many years ago, I saw Jenny Lind play Lucia at the Royal Theater in Stockholm. This was long before Garcia trained her in Paris. It should be interesting to see how she has progressed." Madame turned to Roland. "This one," she added, nodding toward Angelique, "is the one with a truly world-class voice."

Roland smiled proudly. "Angelique's singing is quite remarkable," he told Madame. "However, I shall never be selfless enough to share her with the world."

Madame waved Roland off with a slim, gloved hand. "You Creoles. So passionate and possessive."

At that, Antonio stepped closer to his wife and fondly wrapped an arm about her slim waist. "And we Italians are not?"

Everyone laughed, but inwardly Angelique felt a bit unsettled. She'd known all her life that she had a concert-quality voice, yet she'd never desired to use if for material gain; indeed, Madame Santoni had always reinforced this belief, urging her to sing only in church, as was considered fitting for young ladies of breeding. Yet Angelique was also aware that Roland had never really asked her if she'd ever desired to sing in public, and this rankled, somehow. It was another example of his speaking for her instead of soliciting her own feelings.

And she had to acknowledge, too, that she'd taken a certain vicarious pleasure in reading about Jenny Lind's career. Just to think of singing all over Europe, of being entertained by princes and kings, being loved by Hans Christian Anderson and befriended by composers like Mendelssohn and Chopin . . . These were heady temptations Angelique had never even considered before. Now, just to look around the lobby, packed with animated operagoers, to think that all were waiting in breathless anticipation to hear but one shining voice—

What if that voice were her own?

Then her thoughts became scattered as a deep masculine voice called out, "There they are!"

Angelique turned to watch Jacques approach with Blanche on his arm. Blanche looked lovely in a dress of deep purple velvet, although the black hat she wore, with its heavy veil, did look out of place. Angelique knew Blanche had worn the veil to cover her birthmark, and she wished the spinster had dared just to be herself tonight. Angelique was sure no one would have stared at her or acted put off. She sighed. At least Blanche had come.

Behind Blanche and Jacques walked Jean Pierre and a lovely blond woman in gold satin; the Miro family, all elegantly dressed, completed the entourage. Both Roland and Angelique embraced Blanche and expressed their joy at seeing her. Jean Pierre introduced his companion as Georgette Dupree, a friend of Emily's; then Angelique introduced one and all to the Rivaldis.

Jacques was beside himself when Angelique introduced Madame. "You're not *the* Bella Santoni of the Rome opera?"

"*Si*, m'sieur," Madame replied with a modest smile.

"Why I heard you sing Donna Anna in Rome many years ago. You captivated me. I had no idea you were living in this country."

"Madame was my singing teacher in St. James," Angelique put in.

"Well, I'm not surprised at all," Jacques told Madame. Inclining his head toward Angelique, he added, "I've not heard this one sing as yet, but Jean Pierre tells me she's a marvel."

"She is, indeed," Madame said proudly.

"You will, of course, join us in our box tonight, as well as at the reception my son and I are hosting for Miss Lind and Mr. Barnum after tonight's performance?" Jacques asked.

Madame glanced awkwardly at her husband. "Well, actually, Antonio and I already have tickets, and we wouldn't want to impose—"

Jacques waved her off. "I insist. We have ample room left."

Madame looked beseechingly at her husband, and Antonio nodded to Jacques. "We'd be honored, *signor*."

The group filed upstairs to Jacques's impressive private box overlooking the main floor of the theater. Angelique was delighted to be seated with Madame on her left and Roland on her right.

"I still can't believe that we're all here together," Angelique told her teacher brightly. She glanced with rising expectation at their surroundings. Everything about the St. Charles was plush and elegant, from the velvet-upholstered seats to the huge crystal chandelier hanging above the main floor, its hundreds of gas mantles aglow. The theater had four levels and numerous sprawling galleries. Downstairs, practically every seat was already taken. The orchestra members were tuning up in their box beneath the stage.

"And I can't believe my good fortune in getting to see you again, *cara*," Madame replied. "It was all such a nightmare last summer—your beloved parents dying so suddenly, then your uncle coming and taking you off. Tell me, do you still see your Uncle Giles?"

Angelique shook her head. "Not since my marriage. My husband—" she paused, and seeing that Roland was involved in a conversation with Jacques, she added—"Roland does not like my uncle."

Madame nodded wisely. "Neither did Antonio and I. We would have loved to have you stay on with us—but what could we do when your uncle refused? He was family—we were not."

Angelique nodded. "Please, Madame, I understand completely."

"And you're happy now?"

"Oh, yes."

Madame smiled, squeezing the girl's hand. "That is what matters. Tell me, will you come back and visit us soon at St. James?"

"I would love to. I'll ask Roland to bring me—perhaps in the spring. I have so wanted to visit my parents' graves."

"Of course, dear. And do not worry—on All Saints Day, I draped your parents' graves and brought candles and flowers, just as you requested in your letter. I would have done it anyway, *cara*—I hope you know that."

Angelique smiled through tears of gratitude. "I do, Madame."

An expectant hush now fell over the audience as members of the chorus trooped onstage to take their seats. "*La Lind* should make her appearance soon," Madame murmured. She glanced off toward the wings, watching a wiry, balding man with a baton walk onstage. After bowing to the applauding audience, he descended into the orchestra pit. "There's her conductor now, Jules Benedict."

As Benedict began tuning the orchestra, Angelique asked, "Is Jenny Lind really as good as everyone says?"

Madame frowned. "They say she really bloomed after Manuel Garcia, the European singing master, trained her in Paris. But you must realize that Fraulein Lind came from a humble background, and she was forced to act at the Swedish opera for many years before she could afford formal lessons. They say by the time she got to Paris for her training, she was well past twenty, and it was feared that she had permanently damaged her voice through improper use."

"And you've not heard her sing since then?"

"No. But tonight should be quite a test for *La Lind*. As I'm sure you're aware, Creoles are true epicures of the opera."

"Yes, I'm aware," Angelique replied ruefully. "Roland and I attended a poorly done opera last week, and the Creoles in the audience actually booed the baritone off the stage."

Madame laughed. "I think they'll respond more warmly to *La Lind*."

"I should hope so. You know, I was rather shocked to read of how much Mr. Barnum had to pay to bring her to this country."

"Ah, but the newspapers neglect to print figures on how many charities Jenny Lind contributes to. She's devoutly religious and quite philanthropic, I've been told."

Angelique nodded, then turned to her husband. He smiled at her and took her hand, as the orchestra launched into the dramatic, energetic overture from *The Marriage of Figaro*. Angelique delighted to the sound of the lovely, trilling violins. After the overture was concluded and the applause died down, the audience issued a collective "Ah!" as a tall blond woman dressed in a full-skirted white dress came onstage.

"That's Jenny Lind?" Angelique whispered to Madame Santoni over the new wave of applause rippling through the theater.

"Indeed, yes."

"But she seems so—"

"Ordinary?"

"Yes."

"They say she looks quite ordinary until she sings."

Angelique turned to study the Swedish singer. Jenny Lind had a plain but pleasant face; her braided blond hair was wrapped about her head. She stood statuesquely, her countenance nearly expressionless as she waited for the applause to die down. Then she nodded to the conductor. As Benedict led the musicians in the lilting opening strains of "Casta Diva" from Norma, Angelique turned to Roland with eyes aglow, and he winked back at her.

From the moment Jenny Lind sang the powerful opening notes of the grand aria, she had the Creole audience captivated. Angelique thought she had never heard a voice more flawless—its power sent a shiver down her spine. *La Lind's* range was truly remarkable, well over three octaves; and there was also an inner fire, an exultant emotion, in her shining soprano strains. Just as Madame had hinted, when Lind sang, she became transformed. She became beautiful. During the entire aria, even when the chorus joined in, no one in the audience seemed to move; all were mesmerized by her voice, her radiant smile, her sweeping, graceful gestures. When Lind concluded her selection, she was rewarded with deafening applause and a standing ovation. Lush bouquets were tossed on the stage.

As Angelique and her former teacher stood with the others, Madame murmured, "All this, and only on her first aria? It seems that Jenny Lind has conquered New Orleans."

Watching Lind smile glowingly as she bowed and gathered the bouquets, Angelique asked, "What do you think of her voice now?"

"Quite brilliant, I must say," Madame replied. "There's still some fuzziness in her middle register, which indicates that Garcia wasn't able to undo all the damage of her earlier, untrained performances. But her shakes and cadenzas—ah, *magnifico!*"

"I agree," Angelique said.

As they seated themselves with the others, Madame eyed her former pupil sagely. "You're every bit as good as her, *cara.*"

"Oh, Madame! I can't agree—"

"In fact, my dear, I think you're better."

Angelique would have replied, but the orchestra was already beginning the opening strains of Mendelssohn's "On Wings of Song." For the remainder of her performance, the Swedish Nightingale held the audience in the palm of her hand.

CHAPTER
Twenty-seven

It was close to eleven o'clock by the time Angelique and Roland arrived at Jean Pierre's home for the reception. When they climbed the steps, they found lights and laughter spilling out everywhere. They entered the house through the central hallway, weaving their way through the throng of humanity in the parlor and proceeding on into the dining room, which was also packed with people gaily visiting, sampling the elaborate buffet and drinking champagne.

A reception line had formed on one side of the room, and Angelique could spot P. T. Barnum's smiling face towering over the Creoles. He was a large, pleasant-looking man with blunt features; even from a distance, she could see the sparkle in his fine eyes.

"Well, Roland!"

Angelique turned to watch Jacques approach. "Come meet Miss Lind and Mr. Barnum," he said.

As they navigated through the crowd, Angelique asked Jacques, "Where is Blanche?"

He sighed. "Upstairs resting. I'm afraid she begged off with a headache after the concert."

Angelique frowned. "Shall I go up and check on her?"

Jacques shook his head. "She made it through the concert

and enjoyed it tremendously. Perhaps we should not push her unduly.''

Angelique nodded, realizing the wisdom of Jacques's words. "Well, Phineas," he was now saying as they finally broke through the reception line, "I've some people here you must meet.''

Angelique found herself face-to-face with Phineas T. Barnum. He was dressed in an elegantly tailored black suit with a silver brocaded vest and a black cravat. His rough features broke into a smile as Jacques introduced her, and his handshake was firm and friendly. "I'm enchanted, Madame Delacroix," he said, bowing. "Jacques is so fortunate to have you gracing his family. The ladies of Louisiana are truly exceptional beauties.''

"Thank you, m'sieur. And I think it is so wonderful that you've brought Miss Lind to our country.''

"My pleasure, madame.''

As Barnum turned to shake hands with Roland, Angelique moved on to Jenny Lind. She looked radiant, her gray-blue eyes glowing. But she also looked tired—telltale lines etched her fine, intelligent eyes. Angelique felt awed in the famous soprano's presence, but managed to murmur, "Fraulein Lind, you were brilliant tonight.''

"Thank you, my dear," Lind replied, shaking Angelique's hand. She spoke English in a broken, heavily accented voice, but her tone was warm and sincere. "I do so love New Orleans. These Creoles are so full of the—how shall we say?—the *joie de vivre*?''

"Yes, Fraulein. But you . . .'' Words failed Angelique, and she could only add, "Tonight you were so very inspiring.''

Lind again thanked Angelique, then turned to greet Roland, who also lavishly complimented her on the performance. Once Lind and Roland had exchanged polite small talk, Jacques smoothly maneuvered Angelique and Roland forward to meet others in the reception line.

Afterward, Angelique and Roland drank champagne and sampled the buffet while visiting with the three Miros, Jean Pierre and his companion. Angelique was pleased to observe Madame Santoni across the room, immersed in a lengthy and

animated conversation with Lind. She knew that the two
prima donnas would have much in common.

An hour later, only about twenty guests remained; the
Miros had long since departed to take young Phillip home to
bed. Jean Pierre invited everyone into the parlor for *café
brûlot*. Madame Santoni and her husband sat down next to
Roland and Angelique on one of the settees, while Barnum
and his daughter, Miss Lind and Jacques sat down across
from them.

"Fraulein Lind is fascinating," Madame Santoni whispered excitedly to Angelique. "Would you believe she re-
members seeing me play Amina in Paris?"

"I'm not at all surprised, Madame," Angelique replied.
"Who could ever forget hearing you sing?"

They now turned to listen to Mr. Barnum, who was regaling
the guests with a tale of how he had hoodwinked the overly
enthusiastic crowd at the New Orleans docks yesterday. "The
throng was demanding a glimpse of Jenny Lind, so I threw
a shawl over my daughter and led her off the ship. The ruse
worked, and in the meantime, Fraulein Lind slipped off quietly to her suite at the Pontalba Building."

Everyone laughed at this tale of Barnum's typical inven-
tiveness. Once the chuckles died down, the inevitable request
was made to Lind by an elderly Creole. "Fraulein Lind, won't
you sing for us again?"

Jenny Lind turned to the gentleman. "Actually, sir, I think
you've heard quite enough from me tonight." She turned her
dazzling smile on Madame Santoni. "However, it has come
to my attention that there is a brilliant Italian prima donna
among us tonight. I should love to hear an aria from Madame
Santoni. And I also must hear the beautiful young protégée
she has spoken of so glowingly." Lind shifted her gaze to
Angelique.

Angelique felt her face warming at the unexpected request,
and she glanced confusedly from Roland, who was scowling,
to Madame, who had lost not a trace of her composure.
"Fraulein Lind," Madame replied, "we are truly touched
beyond words by your kind request. However, Angelique and
I should not dream of singing unless you honor us first."

Now Lind glanced at her manager. "Ladies," Barnum

began diplomatically, "I'm afraid it's out of the question for Miss Lind to sing again tonight. One of our cardinal rules is that she does not risk overstraining her voice following performances." He fixed his warm smile first on Madame, then on Angelique. "However, I would be forever in your debt if you two lovely ladies would grant Miss Lind's request and favor us with a song."

Madame glanced questioningly at Angelique, and she in turn fixed Roland with a beseeching look. Angelique knew her husband would not be pleased by her singing publicly this way, yet she also realized that being asked to sing by Jenny Lind was the thrill of a lifetime for Madame. Thus she was greatly relieved when Roland nodded to her stiffly. She turned to smile at Madame.

"Do you remember the duet from *Figaro, cara*?" she asked.

"Oh, yes," Angelique replied.

Jules Benedict volunteered to accompany the two women on the piano, and Madame and Angelique proceeded to dazzle the audience with their rendition of the Mozart duet. They sang the sweet, poignant aria in turns, and then their lovely voices intermingled in soaring crescendoes and purest harmonies. They concluded to warm applause. Jenny Lind herself clapped gaily and called out, "Bravo!"

Madame thanked Jules Benedict for his skillful accompaniment, and after the conductor had returned to his seat, she took his place at the piano. "Now *cara*," she directed to Angelique, "sing the aria from *Semiramide*."

Angelique had no chance to protest as Madame played the opening strains. She faced her audience and sang the Rossini aria with great power and beauty, her voice, as always, bright and searing as a flame.

As Angelique continued to captivate her listeners, André Bienville came forward to tap his friend Jacques Delacroix on the shoulder. The two men slipped off toward the back of the room.

"What didn't you tell me about the girl?" Bienville whispered, nodding toward Angelique. "I've known about Santoni for years, but there's been no persuading her to return to the opera. But this one . . ." Bienville paused, shutting his eyes in ecstasy as he listened to Angelique's powerful cadenza. "If only I could get my hands on her for our forthcoming season."

Jacques nodded. He too, looked stunned and moved. "André, I had no idea of her talent. My son told me she was good, but when I recently dined with the girl and my nephew, he wouldn't let her sing."

André glanced toward the seating circle. "The girl's husband is your nephew, Roland Delacroix?"

"Indeed."

André stroked his jaw thoughtfully. "That will be a problem, then. No self-respecting Creole would allow his wife to appear on stage. I know I should take a strap to my Hélène before I should allow her to do so." He paused again, as Angelique's crystal-pure voice executed a brilliant trill. "Still, she's so damned good."

"I agree," Jacques replied. He elbowed his friend. "A pity we can't take her on tour as Barnum has *La Lind*—eh, *mon ami*?"

André chuckled. "Is it true that Barnum asked you to be one of his backers, and you declined?"

"Must you remind me?" Jacques grumbled, his brow deeply furrowed. Observing Angelique as she concluded her aria and bowed to effusive applause, he mused, "Perhaps there's a way we can have our own little nightingale, André."

"A Cajun nightingale?" he inquired with an ironic smile.

"A Cajun angel," Jacques replied reverently.

Back at the hotel with Roland, Angelique felt as if she were floating on air. Endlessly she relived the moment after she had sung for the guests at Jean Pierre's house. P. T. Barnum had strode toward her with face aglow, soundly shaking her hand, telling her that she was sublime and stuffing his card in her hand. Then Jenny Lind herself had come forward, embracing Angelique with tears in her eyes. "My dear, you have a gift. It must be shared with the world."

These were words Angelique would never forget.

Now, sitting at the dressing table, she turned to watch Roland sit down on the bed across from her. He looked very handsome and appealing in his burgandy brocade dressing gown. Yet his expression was abstracted, as it had been much of the evening. "Did you enjoy the Lind performance?" she asked.

Surprisingly, he smiled at her. "Yes. But her voice does not compare with yours."

Angelique felt touched by his words, yet his voice held an undercurrent that troubled her. "Still, you did not approve when I sang for the guests tonight?"

He was quiet for a moment. "Most of those people were strangers. It seemed—very public."

"Jenny Lind sings in public—as did Madame Santoni," Angelique pointed out, tilting her chin slightly.

"They come from cultures vastly different from our own." He scowled. "Do you truly want to sing on stage—like Miss Lind?"

"I'd never even thought about it until tonight," she answered honestly. "The idea does have a certain allure, I suppose."

"I won't share you, Angel," he said bluntly.

A proud frown furrowed her brow and they stared at each other in tense challenge. Then Roland got up and came to stand behind her. He reached down and grasped her breasts through her thin gown, kneading the firm globes with skilled fingers. She shuddered, and a satisfied smiled sculpted his lips. As she stared up at him expectantly, he whispered, "Now, Angel—is it not time for us to begin working on that child you want so badly?"

She blushed, but resisted the impulse to tear her gaze away from his heated, emotional perusal.

When she didn't answer, he frowned. "Having second thoughts?"

"No," she replied tremulously.

He pulled her up into his arms, turned her and kissed her hungrily. With a groan, he drew off her gown and tossed it aside. Bracing his knee on the dressing table stool, he leaned over to capture the taut tip of her breast with his teeth. His hands reached boldly for her bare, rounded bottom. He kneaded her buttocks and pressed his mouth deeper into her breast, his lungs filling with the lingering sweetness the camellias had left in her hair. She whimpered and clawed at his back; yet she remained stiff in his embrace. When he straightened and looked down at her face, he found her eyes lacked the familiar heat of surrender. Remembering the evening, the adulation of those who had listened to her, he felt a stab of fear. For the first time, he questioned whether her talent might one day take her away from him.

The thought was unbearable, and as painful to him as the resistance he still felt in her lovely body. That barrier must be shattered, he knew, for he would tolerate nothing coming between them. Determinedly, he lifted her into his arms and carried her to the bed, laying her down then quickly shedding his dressing gown. His eyes blazed down at her as he covered her with his hard, aroused body. He kissed first her hair, then his fiery lips trailed down her body. She tugged at his hair as his teeth nipped playfully at her belly. When his voracious lips didn't stop at her stomach, she bucked. But he held her fast, his hands firmly spreading her thighs.

"Don't fight me, Angel," he said hoarsely. "I want this night to be so special."

He buried his lips in her sweetness, and she moaned as a seizure of pleasure ripped through her. She knew she should be scandalized by his brazenness, yet she was powerless to resist the hot flames of rapture flicking her most intimate parts. She tossed her head helplessly, clawing at the sheet with desperate fingers. He tortured her with his mouth and probing fingers until she could stand no more, writhing and crying out at the powerful, painful ecstasy. She was begging for release by the time he finally thrust himself into her, and when he did, her hot tightness drove him wild. She arched at the intensity of their coupling, her sensitized flesh clenching about his arousal. It was almost more than she could bear, but he held her fast, whispering, "Surrender, love . . . just surrender. It will feel so good, you'll see."

She surrendered. The tears in her eyes were as sweet and hot as the melting deep inside her as she threw her arms around his neck and clung to him, wildly kissing his rough male face and opening herself to the depth and power of his possession.

He whispered raggedly at her ear, words of love and fierce need. "My angel . . . my love. Every man there tonight must have wanted to do with you what I'm doing now."

"But only you can," she gasped achingly.

"Say that again, Angel," he whispered back. "Say that again."

Much later, he said, "I want to take you home tomorrow."

Angelique glanced up into her husband's eyes. She lay beneath him, and he was still sheathed inside her. "So soon?"

Gently, he brushed a wisp of hair from her eyes. "Don't you want to go home with me?"

She felt touched by his tender, revealing question. "Of course—but I was hoping I could visit more with Madame Santoni—"

"A compromise, then. We'll see if we can take the Rivaldis to lunch tomorrow, then we'll take a packet home in the afternoon."

"That's thoughtful of you Roland."

"I mean to keep you happy, Angel."

"You do." Smiling up at him, she had to admit to herself that she'd never felt happier than she did at this moment. Thinking of tomorrow, she added, "I wonder—"

"Yes?"

"Do you suppose Blanche will want to go home with us?"

He sighed. "I presume she will. I wish she would stay on a while and give herself and Jacques a chance. But I suppose we'll need to check on her in the morning, and see what she wants to do."

"Perhaps I can prevail upon her to stay."

"I hope you will," he said, kissing her. "And now, Angel . . ."

While Roland was again making passionate love to Angelique, Jacques was seeing Blanche home in Jean Pierre's carriage. "I never should have sent the maid to awaken you after the party," he grumbled to her in the darkness of the plush interior. "I should have let you sleep out the night at Jean Pierre's, so you would have been forced to marry me in the morning." When she didn't reply, he squeezed her cold, gloved hand and added, "My dear, I so wanted you to meet Phineas and Miss Lind."

"I did have a terrible headache, Jacques," she said lamely.

"And that's why you hung on every note Miss Lind sang at the theater?"

Blanche sighed. "I can't fool you."

"Indeed you can't." He wrapped an arm about her stiff, resisting shoulders. "But you made it through the concert, my dear—a real breakthrough for you. Now you must stay on in New Orleans with the Miros. We'll be together every day and we'll take it slowly—a few visits with friends at first, then perhaps a ball or another concert. You'll see, in time—"

"No, I can't stay. I'm going home with Roland and Angelique."

He sighed explosively. "And right back into your shell."

"Jacques, it's the life I'm meant for—"

"And that's the biggest bunch of balderdash I've ever heard!"

Blanche automatically slid away from him as the carriage rattled to a halt before the Miro townhome. Actually, Blanche hungered to stay on in New Orleans to be with Jacques, but she knew it would never work. She'd seen the pitying glances people had cast her way tonight, even though she'd worn the heavy veil.

As Jacques climbed out of the carriage, the gaslight illuminated his haggard, defeated expression. Blanche accepted his hand, averting her face so he wouldn't see her tears.

CHAPTER
Twenty-eight

In the days following their return from New Orleans, Angelique spent much time remembering her weeks alone with Roland. She'd discovered how passionate he was, and how possessive. She'd discovered that he did not quite trust her, especially not around other men.

And she'd discovered what she felt was the reason for his mistrust—his disastrous first marriage to Luisa. She knew that there was a capacity for violence in him, a capacity Luisa had pushed to its brink. The implications for their own marriage were disquieting. Yet Roland had also shared his terrible past with her, and it so endeared him to her that he'd bared his soul that way, making himself vulnerable. And he'd told her he loved her—just once, that emotional day when he'd come chasing after her. But he'd told her.

Why hadn't she told him? She thought long and hard on this. She did love Roland—there was absolutely no doubt in her mind now. Even when she was angry at him, all he had to do was to touch her, and she was lost. She'd felt resentful toward him that last night in New Orleans, after he'd criticized her for singing at the party. Yet he'd so easily shattered her resistance. Now, she felt awed and humbled at the memory of their emotional lovemaking—of her total surrender to him, and how good it had felt to give in.

Yet pride was no doubt at the root of her reluctance to express her love to him. Pride because in so many ways, he still spoke for her, he still thought of her as a child. Pride because he did not even trust her to sing in front of a roomful of people.

And in that pride, she had to concede, there was a touch of vanity. Vanity because she had discovered in New Orleans a world of music and grandeur that, under other circumstances, might have been her own. The captivating world of Jenny Lind and P. T. Barnum, of travels throughout Europe and a triumphant tour of the United States.

It was not a world she truly wanted—this she honestly recognized. Yet some voice inside her, whether perverse or vain, cried out that Roland should be selfless enough to offer her a choice. Since the day he had met her, he had offered her no choices at all.

She knew that pride was the most destructive of all sins —her mother and father had often told her this. Yet her sense of justice still demanded that Roland accept her as a trusted partner in this marriage; and thus, both her feelings and her intellect conspired to make her keep from him the one thing she most desired to say.

Blanche had been quite morose since they'd returned. Back in New Orleans, both Roland and Angelique had argued that she should stay on in the city, but predictably, she had insisted on returning to Belle Elise with them. Angelique tried to cheer her up each day, with little success.

On the Saturday following their return, as the two women sat in the parlor quietly knitting, Angelique studied Blanche's tragic countenance and decided it was time to frankly address the matter of her unhappiness. She set aside her knitting and spoke candidly. "Blanche, why don't you return to New Orleans?"

Blanche at once stopped knitting, glancing up at Angelique. She looked both disconcerted and suspicious. "I beg your pardon?"

"I said, why don't you go back to New Orleans and spend some more time with Jacques before he leaves on his travels again?"

"Are you so anxious to be rid of me?" Blanche inquired.

Angelique mentally shored up her patience in the face of Blanche's touchiness. "Well, of course not. But I can't help but have noticed—you're in love with Jacques, aren't you?"

Blanche colored, nervously lowering her gaze. Her knitting needles began to click again. "I really can't know what you mean."

"Oh, I think you do," Angelique said wisely. "And I think he loves you, as well."

"Nonsense," Blanche retorted, yet there was a telltale quiver in her voice.

"Why shouldn't Jacques love you?" Angelique went on. "Why, the two of you have so much in common—"

"We have nothing in common," Blanche cut in bitterly, looking at Angelique with eyes filled with angry turmoil. "I'd never fit in his world."

Angelique was growing exasperated in her attempt to get through to Blanche. She leaned forward, gesturing as she spoke intently. "Blanche, that's strictly a limitation you've imposed in your own mind. If you'd just allow yourself to get out, sample Jacques's world with him a bit—"

"That would suit you just fine, wouldn't it?"

Angelique fell back in her chair, expelling a bewildered sigh at Blanche's hostile tone. "Blanche, I'm speaking only out of concern for you—"

"Concern that I transfer my whereabouts elsewhere?"

Angelique bit her lip. Blanche had erected such barriers

against the world that she obviously refused to believe anyone could act solely out of concern for her welfare. "I just—it would mean so much to me if you could find what Roland and I have—"

"And do you think that what you and my stepbrother have is so very special?" Blanche continued caustically.

Angelique's brows moved closer together. "Just what do you mean?"

Blanche drew herself up in her chair. "Just that my stepbrother seems destined, like me, for tragedy."

Angelique at once picked up on Blanche's subtle reference to Luisa. "Blanche, Roland told me all about his marriage to Luisa—and how she died."

"Then he told you he killed her," she said bluntly.

"*Accidentally*," Angelique added, the tremor in her voice bespeaking her growing vexation.

"I see. Then I don't suppose he told you of the rumors?"

"What rumors?"

Without batting an eyelash, Blanche continued, "That Phillip was Roland's son, and that Luisa's death was—not quite an accident."

At once Angelique was on her feet, her patience snapping. "Blanche—how dare you say such hateful things. And about your own stepbrother!"

"I just didn't want you to hear the rumors from someone else," she said defensively.

"Indeed?" Angelique's resentment soared at Blanche's trying to justify her disloyal and mean-spirited remarks. "Actually, Blanche, you're the only person I know who would say anything so cruel. Tell me, if you think so little of Roland, then why do you stay here with him?"

Blanche didn't answer, staring coldly at Angelique.

Angelique swung about to leave the room, but turned at the portal. "If you're regretting your decision to leave New Orleans, Blanche, I think you know what the remedy is. And if you're jealous of Roland's and my happiness, I would again suggest that you look to yourself for the answer."

Angelique swept angrily from the room. Blanche started to go after her, then stopped. Angelique had spoken the truth just now—for ever since Blanche had returned from New Orleans, she'd found she did feel intensely jealous of Angelique and Roland's happiness. Theirs was a closeness that made her feel like an intruder—

And hadn't the girl suggested, twice now, that she leave? How long before she insisted, as Luisa had?

Obviously, Angelique could not understand her own dilemma. The girl was a stunning beauty, and had no idea what it was like to venture forth in the world, terrified, to have everyone look at her in pity and revulsion. Blanche loved Jacques, but she had to live with the never-ending torment of knowing that she could never find happiness with him, that she could bring him only pain.

Thus, her lot was hurt and confusion, and while she knew it was wrong, sometimes she couldn't help but rail out at Angelique for having everything she would always lack.

The next morning, as Roland, Angelique and Blanche were finishing breakfast, all three were astonished when Henri ushered Jacques into the dining room. He looked very handsome in a black wool suit, a gold watch fob glittering on his brown satin vest.

"Good morning, nephew," Jacques said, shaking hands with Roland, as if his bizarre, sudden appearance were entirely ordinary. He flashed his charming smile first on Blanche, then Angelique. "I thought of joining all of you for services today, if you don't mind."

"Not at all, Uncle. This is a most pleasant surprise," Roland said. "By all means, join us at Mass—and for the midday meal."

Jacques declined the breakfast Angelique offered, although he did accept a cup of *café au lait*, and sat drinking it while the others finished eating. He made small talk with Roland and Angelique, but mostly stared at Blanche, who sat directly across from him. Observing the spinster, Angelique found she looked flustered, excited, and quite radiant in Jacques's presence. Angelique crossed her fingers under the table, silently praying that when Jacques left later today, Blanche would be with him.

Later, in the small village church, Jacques sat next to Blanche, and Angelique was pleased to observe the two exchanging shy smiles throughout the service. After Mass, while Roland was introducing Jacques to some of his friends in the churchyard, George Bentley came up to Angelique, looking quite debonair in a black silk tophat and wool great-coat. His breath formed white puffs on the cold air as he began excitedly, "Oh, my dear Mrs. Delacroix! Did you get to attend the Lind performance in New Orleans?"

Angelique smiled at George. "Yes, it was wonderful. Didn't you and Caroline attend?"

He shook his head. "Unfortunately, no. Miss Lind's performance conflicted with our first cousin's wedding in Mississippi."

"Oh—I'm so sorry you had to miss it."

"If I come calling this week, will you tell me all about *La Lind*?"

Angelique stared at him a moment. George looked so wistfully expectant that ultimately, she couldn't refuse him. "Of course, Mr. Bentley. Please do drop by for tea some time this week."

He grinned. "Splendid." Glancing off at Blanche, who was visiting with Annette Junot beneath a tree, he added, "I've been meaning to come by Belle Elise, anyway. Many of our flowers and vines froze while Caro and I were in Mississippi, and I was wondering if your greenhouses could spare us some cuttings and bulbs. We've made similar exchanges with Blanche in the past."

"How practical of you. I'm sure you're welcome to anything you need from our greenhouses."

He nodded, smiling. "Thank you. Caro will be delighted."

Angelique glanced about the churchyard. "By the way, where is your sister today?"

He sighed. "Down with one of those seasonal agues, I'm afraid."

"How unfortunate," Angelique murmured, finding herself incapable of adding that she hoped Caroline would recover soon.

George looked uncomfortable, shifting from foot to foot. Watching Roland approach them, he tipped his hat and cleared his throat. "Well, my dear, I'll see you some time this week, then."

As George hastily strode off toward his carriage, Roland arrived at Angelique's side, glowering. "What did Bentley want?"

Angelique stared at her husband steadily. She didn't like

his distrustful tone or the challenging look in his eyes. "He asked if he could come calling this week to hear details of the Jenny Lind performance, which he had to miss."

"And what did you tell him?"

She tilted her chin. "I told him he's welcome at Belle Elise."

"You didn't," he snapped.

"I most certainly did," she snapped back.

"Then you can just go untell him," he continued obdurately.

Angelique nodded toward George's departing carriage. "I can't. He's already left."

"In that case, you'll dispatch him a note this afternoon, informing him that it's most inconvenient for him to drop by. Do I make myself perfectly clear?"

By now, Roland's voice was chillier than the frigid air hanging between them, and Angelique's jaw hurt from clenching it. Before she could grind out a retort, he grabbed her arm and led her resisting body toward their carriage.

Riding home, Angelique was seething about Roland's high-handed directive following Mass. She couldn't believe he had actually forbidden her to entertain George Bentley in their home. Here, she had never tried to intrude on her husband's very special relationship with Emily Miro—and she surely had much greater cause for jealousy there. She had never done anything to merit Roland's lack of faith, and thus his unjust dictate inspired in her only defiance. Ruefully, she mused that it was almost inevitable that they come to a clash about this. Roland's possessiveness had really begun to escalate while they were in New Orleans.

During luncheon, Jacques proved, as always, marvelously diverting as he entertained them with tales of meeting Queen Victoria and the Prince Consort in England, of hearing Franz Liszt perform in Paris. Blanche, in particular, hung on every word he said. His discourse shifted to Jenny Lind's visit to New Orleans, and he regaled them with an account of how Phineas T. Barnum had delivered a lecture on temperance before leaving the "sinful" city with Miss Lind. "If Phineas wasn't carrying coals to Newcastle!" he concluded with a hearty laugh.

Jacques explained how Barnum and Lind would be traveling upriver for performances in Natchez and St. Louis. "New Orleans shall be desolate without *La Lind*." He winked at Angelique, then added casually to Roland, "Although my friend André Bienville would doubtless give his right arm to bring this one to New Orleans and have her perform."

That's when Roland's water glass slammed down on the table. Looking straight at Jacques, he gritted, "Then evidently your friend shall retain his arm, since *my wife* is not going anywhere, nor performing for anyone."

Infuriated by Roland's rudeness, Angelique shot him a scathing look, which he conspicuously ignored. The rest of the meal passed awkwardly, bits of desultory conversation sprinkled between long, strained silences. Finally Jacques excused himself, asking Blanche to accompany him for a stroll outside. Once Angelique and Roland were alone, she stared at him rebelliously, finding that his relentless facade hadn't wavered a bit. He looked devastatingly handsome sitting across from her—and a tyrant to his intractable soul!

"Haven't you some correspondence to do, my dear?" he asked in an ominously soft voice.

Not trusting herself to speak, she tossed down her napkin and stormed from the room. In the study, she wrote the note to George. She scanned it quickly, and then, muttering something very unlady-like, she ripped the parchment into several dozen small pieces.

Outside in the bracing coolness, Jacques and Blanche were walking near the house, the brown winter turf snapping beneath their feet. "It was such a pleasant surprise to see you again," she murmured with a shy smile.

He paused, placing his hands on her shoulders. He looked down at her intently, the cold sunshine outlining his tall form. "My dear, I've come to beg you to relent." As she looked up at him in fear and expectation, he added, "I'm leaving to spend the spring with some friends in New York. Won't you come with me?"

She shook her head, staring at the ground. "Jacques, we've been over this again and again. You know I can't go with you."

"And you know I can't wait forever."

"Jacques, have I ever tried to hold you?" she asked passionately.

"Whether you've intended it or not, you have, my dear," he whispered. As she bit her lip in silent frustration, he added, "I must tell you that later this year, I'm leaving for an extended tour of Europe. I'll be gone for several years. And I must know—before I go—whether there is hope for us."

As she started to reply, he pressed a gloved finger on her mouth and spoke with great pain and yearning. "There's so much I want to share with you—the charm of Vienna, the great galleries of Munich and Dresden, the splendor of Rome."

She tried to speak, but he shook his head. "Don't answer now. Tell me when I return from New York. If you do not leave for Europe with me then—as my wife—I shan't ask you, ever again."

Blanche nodded dismally. "But you'll come back first—later this year?"

"Yes. For your answer."

Silence descended, as a mournful wind played its haunting cadence. Blanche already knew that when Jacques returned, her answer would be no. But she didn't have the heart to tell him not to come back. She lived for her brief, fleeting moments with him.

He glanced about awkwardly. "Well, then, my dear, I suppose I must be going. But first . . ."

Jacques pulled Blanche close for a searing kiss that took her breath away. She clung to him, shuddering with emotion as she realized that everything she wanted in life was here in her arms—yet just beyond her reach. And she felt the answering trembling in Jacques's body, his own frustrated need and anguish. As he gently released her and walked away, his shoulders were slumped, his gait dispirited. Running a finger over her tender, throbbing lips, Blanche found herself wondering for the first time whether what Jacques felt for her might be more than pity.

After he left, she walked off toward one of the greenhouses, still consumed with turmoil. Then she caught her reflection on a cold pane of glass—a pitiful freak with tears streaming from her eyes, coursing down her swollen, hideously scarred face.

Blanche hurried into the safety of the greenhouse, slamming the door behind her. Her sobs were raw and soul-shattering. In her torment, she grabbed a potted plant and hurled it onto the floor. Then she hurled another and another and another, until none was left whole.

CHAPTER
Twenty-nine

The following afternoon, while Roland was gone at a meeting of the Planters Association of St. Charles Parish, George Bentley came calling. Angelique was grateful that George had come for his visit while her husband was away; she still felt she had every right to receive him. Yet she did become a bit uneasy when Blanche begged off having tea with them, claiming she had a headache, and left Angelique alone with George in the parlor.

Nevertheless, she had a grand time telling George all about the Jenny Lind performance and the reception afterward. He hung on every word she said.

When he was getting ready to leave, he said, "By the way, Mrs. Delacroix, may I trouble you for the cuttings and bulbs we spoke of yesterday? As I mentioned, we lost practically everything in that bad frost—all the begonias and gladiolas, even the trumpet vine."

Angelique frowned. "Of course I'd be delighted to help you, Mr. Bentley, but I'm not sure which greenhouse those plants and bulbs are kept in. Blanche would know, but as you're aware, she's indisposed at the moment—"

"No problem," George returned with a grin. "Most of what I want will be in the greenhouse due south of the house, nearest the swamp. As I mentioned yesterday, Blanche has helped us with our garden before. I'd be delighted to see to the matter myself—with your permission, of course."

Angelique waved him off. "Oh, I wouldn't dream of not accompanying you."

Angelique grabbed her cloak and bonnet. On their way out of the house, she told Benjamin to have Mr. Bentley's carriage brought around to the south side of the house, and to see that the gardener, Eben, met them at the greenhouse.

Angelique and George went outside in the bracing coolness of the cold, sunny January day. As they headed southward to the greenhouse, she glanced back toward the house and thought she saw a curtain moving, almost imperceptibly, in the parlor. Had Blanche already come back downstairs? She frowned.

Inside the building, both Angelique and George gasped, looking around in horror at the wholesale destruction greeting them. Everywhere were broken pots, shards of pottery mixed in with clumps of dirt, roots, and wilting plants. The smell of the squashed, lacerated greenery was cloying in the damp warmth of the enclosure.

"My God—who could have done this?" George asked incredulously.

She shook her head in bewilderment. "I've no idea. Perhaps a wild animal of some sort—a fox or cougar?"

"Who had a taste for flowers and shut the door behind him on his departure?"

She frowned. No explanation seemed to make sense. "Well, whoever did this, I must apologize for the disorder. I suppose poor Eben will have to contend with it." Glancing at him apologetically, she added, "Why don't you come back tomorrow, when things are more in order—"

Yet George was shaking his head adamantly as he leaned over to pick up a wilted clump of lavender. "I'm afraid Eben will be utterly bewildered by this disaster. He's a good gardener, but he's quite old and arthritic, and he'll have no idea how to set this to rights." George's jaw was set in a determined line as he glanced around and added, "Unless we get these plants carefully repotted and watered at once, they'll be dead by tomorrow." Setting down the lavender, he removed his hat, greatcoat, and frock coat, hanging them on a nail, then rolling up his sleeves. "I'll see to it."

Angelique nodded, knowing George was right. "How can I help?"

She, too, removed her bonnet and cloak, for it was quite warm in the greenhouse with the sun beating through the glass panels. They cleared a work area on a large table, then she helped George carefully extricate the plants from the heaps of broken clay and dirt. Momentarily, silver-haired Eben lumbered in, his posture painfully stooped. His eyes widened as he viewed the devastation. George explained to him that someone had vandalized the greenhouse, and that he and Mistress Delacroix would help set things right, time being of the essence. Eben nodded, making no comment as he took up the broom and began sweeping up smashed pots and dirt.

George took a stack of empty pots down from a shelf, then he and Angelique carefully repotted the plants, laying aside various cuttings for George in a damp cloth. Angelique enjoyed working with the plants, whose smells ranged from tart and tangy to sweet or pungent. She was oblivious to the fact that her frock became smudged with black grit, and that she tore her skirt on a nail protruding from the workbench.

Once they'd corrected the damage as best they could and had watered everything, Angelique turned to Eben, who was still sweeping up. "Can you finish up here, now, Eben?"

"Yes, mistress," he replied respectfully.

Donning their cloaks, Angelique and George left the greenhouse and walked over to his waiting carriage. He tossed the bundle of cuttings and a bag of bulbs onto the seat, then turned to smile at her. "You're quite a gardener, Mrs. Delacroix," he said with a laugh as he looked her over. "You should see yourself—your coiffure's askew and there's a smudge down one cheek." He reached out to touch her face with his gloved hand, flicking away several specks of dirt.

"I suppose I must be a sight," Angelique laughed back. Such a sense of camaraderie had built between them during the last hour that she did not feel the least bit affronted by his casually brushing off her cheek. George seemed like a brother to her.

But unfortunately, even as they were laughing and talking, Roland was coming around the side of the house in a black temper. He'd just returned home, only to be informed by Blanche that his wife was out at the greenhouse with George Bentley! The girl had defied him twice—first, by not writing

the note to George, and secondly, by receiving him. Worst
treason of all, she'd gone to the greenhouse with him—alone.
What on earth had the two of them been doing there?

Now, the sight of them together confirmed his worst suspicions. They stood next to George's carriage—Angelique
laughing at Bentley like a shameless flirt, her hair disheveled
and her face smudged. And George was caressing his wife's
cheek with his foul, lecherous hand!

Never in his life had Roland felt closer to committing
murder, though whether he would kill Angelique or
George—or both of them—he wasn't sure. He still held his
riding crop in his hand, and he snapped it angrily as he strode
toward them.

Here, he'd believed his wife was such an innocent, he
thought bitterly. What an idiot he had been. The girl had run
away from him twice, had disobeyed him again and again,
had blatantly seduced the attentions of practically every man
on God's earth with those eyes of hers, that voice, that traitorous smile. Obviously, he'd been altogether too lenient with
her, behaving like a besotted fool; this time, he would mete
out a remedy that would bend her to his will forever—and
would have her sitting on pillows for at least a week.

When he was within ten feet of them, they both whirled,
spotting him in a mixture of shock, fear, and yes, guilt.
Roland stopped to glower back, and he barely recognized the
blood-chilling timbre of his own voice as he told George,
"Bentley, get the hell off my property. If you ever again
possess the imprudence to appear hear, consider yourself
challenged."

A look of stark fear flashed across George's face at Roland's ruthless ultimatum. For some reason, he thought, Delacroix was assuming he was chasing after Angelique—which
couldn't be farther from the truth. But obviously, this was
no time to appeal to the man's nobler intellect; one misstep
and he'd clearly be at the receiving end of Roland's pistol.

Thus, nodding stiffly to Angelique, George hopped into
his buggy and drove off. In the terrible silence that followed,
Angelique stood staring murder at Roland. His answering
glare was every bit as formidable as he stood across from her
with booted feet spread, every inch of him oozing a lethal
menace. It was on the tip of her tongue to upbraid him for

his unforgivable arrogance and rudeness and mistrust, to tell
him that she'd done nothing wrong. Yet some instinct for
self-preservation—or perhaps it was the unspeakable violence
in his eyes—warned her that this was not the time to speak.

"You," he said, pointing his riding crop at her, "come
here."

That's when Angelique's fear became wanton panic.
"No!" she cried, racing off, tearing into the woods that lined
the bayou, clawing through a stinging tangle of dead brush
and thorny vines. She glanced wildly behind her, and just as
she'd feared, Roland was following her, closing rapidly. Even
as she was turning to look ahead, she missed her step and
screamed—

The next thing Angelique knew, she was over her head in
ice cold, stagnant water, her mouth and lungs filling with the
odious ooze, her skirts and heavy cloak tangling about her
legs, dragging her down. Within seconds, her lungs were
bursting as she flailed ineffectually for the surface.

Then steely fingers grabbed her arm, and she was hauled
violently from the murky water, dragged onto the bank. Frigid
air lacerated her body and for a harrowing moment, she
couldn't breathe. As she struggled in helpless agony, her
waterlogged cloak and bonnet were ripped off her, then
she was thrown forcefully across Roland's knees and he
was pummeling her back. "Breathe!" he commanded.
"Breathe!"

Angelique choked, coughing out water and gasping for air.
The instant her gagging subsided, Roland lifted her into his
arms and tore off for the house. When she dared to look up
at his face, she saw a look of utter terror in his eyes.

CHAPTER
Thirty

"You little idiot!" Roland snapped.

It was half an hour later, and they were in Angelique's room. She was sitting naked before him in a hot tub of water near a blazing fire. Earlier, when Roland had raced in the door of Belle Elise with his wet, convulsively shivering wife, he'd bellowed at the servants to fetch hot water and wood, but he'd allowed no one but himself to touch Angelique. He'd literally ripped the clothes off her trembling body, wrapping her in a quilt until she could be deposited in the hastily brought bath. Now, sitting in the steamy water in the toasty-warm room, she was no longer shaking, but she couldn't have felt more vulnerable and exposed, displayed before Roland this way as he paced fully clothed and in a murderous rage.

When she didn't answer, he whirled on her. "Why did you run away from me?"

"Why?" she repeated with an incredulous laugh. "You looked ready to murder me—"

"Beat you senseless," he amended savagely. "And don't delude yourself that you've escaped my wrath yet."

"I did nothing wrong by receiving George!" she cried.

"No, you only defied your husband not only by receiving Bentley, but also by taking him out to the greenhouse for a little—tryst—"

"It was not a tryst!" she cried, almost choking in her rage. "George's garden froze and he merely wanted some cuttings—"

Roland stopped to glare at her. "How very ingenious of Bentley. But perhaps I do not care to share with him the fruits of Belle Elise—or my wife."

"You shared much more than that with his sister!"

At her ruthless barb, he took an aggressive step toward her, breathing hard. "Angelique, what happened between Caroline and me was before we got married—"

"Indeed? Is that why you ogled her that day in the parlor?"

"I didn't ogle. And furthermore, I didn't invite her here—"

"And neither did I invite George!"

"Nor did you obey me when I told you to warn him off. Or is that just another wedding vow you're reneging on, such as 'to love and to honor'?"

"Roland, I didn't do anything wrong!" she half-screamed. "And I don't think *le bon Dieu* ever intended for me to obey stupid orders."

His eyes blazed at her. "Stupid? I should have you over my knee for such insolence."

"Why not?" she railed back. "You've controlled my life in every other way—why not beat me again, as well?"

They glared at each other in the terrible silence, then the strain had Angelique choking on the swamp water still clogging her lungs. At once Roland was on his knees beside her, rubbing her back gently and easing her head downward. "Easy, love, easy," he said as she coughed up the water, and his tenderness, more than anything else, made her want to burst out screaming.

Once the spasm subsided, he pulled her to her feet and began briskly rubbing down her body and hair with a towel. "You've swallowed half the goddamned swamp and Lord knows what you'll catch now," he said as he carried her to the bed, placing her naked between the sheets and heaping blankets on top of her.

She felt very small as he stared down at her grimly. When he spoke, the very calmness of his voice was frightening. "Angelique, I'll tolerate your willfulness no longer. For now, you are to rest, but first thing tomorrow, you and I will settle everything in my study. You will admit you were wrong and you will promise never again to disobey me."

"Or?" she asked in a rising voice.

Now his tone grew ominous. "Or you'll accept the consequences."

"I'll do neither!" she hissed.

He made no comment on her rebellion. "Let me know when you've made your decision."

And he squared his shoulders and strode out of the room.

The next morning came and went, and Angelique did not go to Roland's study to meet with him. Nor did he come to her bed that night. She considered going to him, for the distance between them hurt like a festering wound. Yet she knew that going to him now would signal her capitulation to his will.

She wouldn't have thought he could force her to make a choice this way—but he was. He was holding her off with an anger icier and more lethal than the swamp into which she'd stumbled. His words, and his actions, said: *Choose. Humble yourself to me or accept the consequences.* She knew she would never admit she'd been wrong, for she hadn't been. Theirs was no marriage if there was no trust between them —if she wasn't even allowed to receive male callers in their home. There she knew she must make a stand. Being married to Roland did not give him license to swallow her up as a person: she had a right to her own identity, her dignity. Thus she would not give in to his threat—even though the impasse between them was breaking her heart.

While Angelique was not aware of it, Roland felt equally tormented following their disastrous fight. He stayed up late in his study at night, drinking absinthe and brooding. He was still furious at Angelique for defying his orders and receiving George, yet he also deeply regretted chasing her into the swamp. He was not proud of himself for frightening her into flight, and he was terrified that she might become seriously ill as a result of her accident. And when he had questioned the gardener, Eben, concerning what had transpired in the greenhouse, the slave had confirmed Angelique's story regarding the innocence of her and George's time there. This only exacerbated Roland's guilt.

Still, why had the girl flouted his wishes? Perhaps his dictate had not been entirely fair, but she should have obeyed him, nevertheless. He was sick to death of watching other men play up to her and devour her with their eyes. George's actions may have seemed innocent on the surface, but Roland

was convinced that his ultimate intentions toward Angelique
were far more dishonorable. And for the life of him, he
couldn't figure out whether his bride was aware of this mesmerizing effect she had on men. Was she deliberately playing
the seductress, or innocently flirting with disaster?

Whether her actions had been innocent or carnal, she
should have honored his wishes. Yet knowing he was right
in this did not obliterate one bit of Roland's pain—nor did
it soothe the ache in arms that longed to hold her. Sometimes
he hungered for her so much, it didn't seem to matter who
was right and who was wrong.

On the third night following Roland's ultimatum, Angelique was restless and couldn't sleep. She'd toss off the covers
one minute, only to shiver the next. Her eyes were swollen
from weeping off and on, and her throat ached from still more
unshed tears. She didn't think she could make it through
another night without Roland's comfort.

She got up and paced in the cold darkness, feeling strangely
wobbly on her feet. A glint of silver on her dresser caught
her eye and she went over and picked up the hairbrush.
Gripping the edge of the bureau to steady herself, she remembered the time she'd thrown a similar brush at Roland
in New Orleans, cracking him across the jaw.

Let him hurt her, then, she decided fiercely. She would
never, ever say she was wrong, but she'd much rather accept
his "consequences" than watch his anger destroy their love.

She crept into his room in the darkness, only to watch the
moonlight flicker over the smooth counterpane. He was gone.
Praying that he hadn't left the house, she tiptoed downstairs
in the cold silence, hanging onto the banister to keep her
balance.

She found Roland in his study, sitting in the darkness, his
booted feet on the coffee table and a near-empty decanter of
absinthe nearby. Staring at him, she gasped. It was just like
that other night when she'd come down here and kissed him.
Remembering how feral his passion had been that night, when
he'd also been drunk, she shuddered at the thought of how
violent his anger might be tonight. Even as he slept, the
suppressed power in his hard, muscled body was very evident.

Yet she had to confront this barrier between them. This had to end.

She shook off a new wave of dizziness and approached him, noting with a sudden catch in her heart that his shirt was askew, his hair unkempt, his face heavily bearded. He'd been suffering, too, she realized. Leaning over, she shook his shoulder gently.

Roland squinted up at her in the silvery light. "Angel?"

His tender word was practically her undoing, and it was all she could do not to throw herself into his arms. Obviously, in his befuddled state, he wasn't immediately recalling his terrible anger toward her.

Her heart pounding, she thrust the hairbrush into his hand. "I'm ready to accept your consequences now."

"What?" he repeated, his voice barely audible.

She tilted her head proudly. "I'll not say I was wrong to have George in, because I wasn't. I've never, never betrayed you, Roland, nor have I even considered it. It's just that—" her voice broke, then she stiffened her resolve and forged on "—you've never trusted me. However, if you must beat me for this to end, go ahead. It will be much less hurtful than letting you kill me with this anger."

"Kill you?" he repeated in a strangled whisper.

"Just get it over with," she said.

He shook his head in bewilderment. "You would let me hurt you, all the while feeling that you had done nothing wrong?"

She again recalled the time she'd struck him across the jaw in New Orleans. He still had a thin, pale scar across his chin. "I hurt you once—and you had done nothing wrong."

He was silent for a long moment. "Then come closer, Angel," he whispered at last, his voice laced with a confusing tenderness.

Trembling, she drew closer to him, and his free hand reached out to touch her thigh—his hand was hot on her flesh, even through her gown. A shudder ripped through her, then he whispered, "Angel, I think we can find a much better use for that sweet bottom of yours."

She heard the hairbrush go scuttling off and then she was hauled down into his lap. She was sobbing with joy, her arms tight around his neck as he kissed her violently, his bearded face abrading her softness. He hiked her gown about her waist and ran his hands roughly over her bare hips and thighs. Rapturously, she returned his kiss, moaning and clinging to him.

"Oh, my sweet Angelique," he said in a breaking voice. "I've been such an ass. So crazed by jealousy, anger, and pride." His hand slipped between her thighs, stroking her welcoming wetness. She arched convulsively as his mouth caught hers in another searing kiss. "Oh, God, woman, you're so sweet, so hot and—"

Abruptly, he froze, his lips against her cheek. "*Mon Dieu*!" he cried. "You're burning up with fever!" Wildly, his hands felt her forehead, then slid down her legs to her bare feet. "And you're down here in the middle of the night, with nothing on your feet!"

Instantly rendered sober, Roland sprang to his feet with Angelique still in his arms. Clinging to him as he hurried up the stairs, she swam in a joy that was rapidly becoming delirium.

Within half an hour, Roland had a fire blazing in Angelique's room, and he had summoned Blanche to sit with her while he went for the doctor.

By the time Blanche arrived in Angelique's bedroom, the girl had drifted off into a delirious sleep. "What is it, Brother?" she asked, glancing anxiously at the bed, where Angelique was now moaning and thrashing about.

"She obviously caught some malaise when she fell into the swamp the other day," he replied, distractedly shaking on his frock coat. He stared at his wife with tortured eyes. "If something happens to her, Sister, I care not to see another day."

"No Roland, you mustn't say—"

But even as Blanche reached for him, he dashed out the door.

Miserably, Blanche sat down by Angelique's bed with her rosary beads in hand. The girl did, indeed, look deathly ill —there were bright fever spots on her cheeks, and her eyes looked sunken as she continued to shift restlessly and tear at the covers. Blanche stood, gently drawing up the counterpane the girl had tossed off. Then she sat down, biting her lip.

Blanche knew this was all her fault. When Roland had come storming into the parlor three days ago, demanding to know where Angelique was, Blanche had rashly told him that his wife was out in the greenhouse with George. At the time, she'd recklessly lit a match to a powder keg to cover her own guilt for having destroyed the plants. She'd been too ashamed and frightened to really consider the impact of her words on her stepbrother; her sole purpose had been to draw Roland's attention away from her own misdeed.

And she'd accomplished this, with a vengeance! From the moment Roland had come rushing back into the house with his shivering wife, Blanche had been consumed with the same sick fear that had been in his eyes ever since. Everyone knew that the contagion of a hundred dire maladies lurked in swamp water. The girl was young and strong, but stronger ones had died before her after coming in contact with the miasmic ooze.

Blanche clutched her rosary beads and stared shamefaced at her lap. Angelique had done nothing to deserve such betrayal at her hands. Blanche had hurt both Angelique and Roland—perhaps irrevocably—with her treachery. Now if the girl passed away, it was she who deserved to die, not Roland.

If Roland knew of her perfidy, he would doubtless cast her from the house—and justly so, she mused. With tears in her eyes, Blanche prayed for Angelique's recovery. And she vowed before God that if only He would bring the girl back to health, she'd never again do anything to bring her harm.

Roland brought in the local doctor, a thin-lipped, ill-humored man who laconically pronounced that Angelique had contracted a billious fever. The physician could think of little to do for her except to bleed her with mechanical leeches, which Roland refused to allow. The man shrugged, clicked shut his bag, and prepared to leave, saying, "Try to get some liquids down her. It should pass in three days—one way or another."

Roland banned everyone from the room and sat vigil with

Angelique. His face grew heavily bearded, his eyes red and crazed with fear. She drifted in and out of delirium, clawing at her covers, her fever always high. Occasionally, she mumbled or cried out. Roland hurt with the pain she felt and would have given his life to take it away. He sponged her off and meticulously saw to her needs. Occasionally, in her more lucid moments, he was able to get a few spoonfuls of broth down her.

She was going to die, just like his father and stepmother had, somehow he knew this. Terror and guilt gnawed at his stomach like a thousand sharp razors. When she died, he would bury her, then he would go to his study, get his pistol and blow out his miserable brains. There was nothing left for him in this world without her. She was everything sweet and good and selfless he had ever known. And he had destroyed her.

Damn his asinine pride in forbidding her to receive George! The entire incident seemed petty and stupid now. Angelique had always been a loyal wife, and he'd had no real cause for his high-handed directive. Yet he'd wanted more from her —her heart, her soul. He'd wanted her never to cast that beautiful smile on any man but himself. What a fool he'd been to think he could force her to love him. Now his demands and mistrust were threatening her very life.

On the third day of her illness, Roland found the doctor's prophecy coming true. Angelique had an alarmingly high fever one minute, then shook with chills the next. Deep circles rimmed her eyes, and she looked thinner, drained by her ordeal. Roland knew that by tomorrow, she would either shake off the malady or succumb.

Roland sponged her off when she was burning and heaped blankets on her when she shivered. Occasionally, he held her upright and gently patted her back as she coughed up more fluid.

By that night she was flailing about, so wild in her delirium that he feared she would do harm to herself or die from utter exhaustion. When an uncontrollable fit of shaking consumed her and he couldn't get her warm, in desperation he threw off his clothes and climbed into bed with her, drawing her shivering body close.

At once he was hit by unendurable sensations—how heav-

enly she felt in his arms, how elusive sanity was becoming
for him, and how exhausted his own body felt. When he
thought of how he might never again hold her this way, it
was his undoing, and sobs racked his body. After a moment
he glanced down at her and found she was staring up at him
with glowing, delirious eyes that had never looked more
beautiful. Her face looked radiant, it was so flushed and
bright.

"Roland," she whispered, "you're crying."

"Oh, *ma chére*." He held her close and wept without
shame.

"Please, Roland, don't cry. I love you. I want to have
your baby."

Her words tore his heart to shreds. They'd sounded so
lucid, yet he realized they couldn't be. She'd said she loved
him, yet surely that was the fever speaking—

Still, he remembered that emotional morning back in New
Orleans, when she'd wept in his arms because she wasn't to
have his child. The memory shattered what remained of his
self-control. He buried his face in her hair, trying not to alarm
her with his sobs.

Angelique was indeed delirious. Yet even in her befuddled
state, she found Roland's pain tearing at her heart. Some-
where in the back of her mind, she realized that there was
an aching gulf between them, a chasm that must be bridged.
Another world was calling her, yet she didn't want to go.
She had so much left to resolve here.

"Roland, please, don't cry," she whispered. "Let me love
you."

Now she was squirming against him in a very womanly
way, burning with fever again. Burning *him*. He drew back
with a sharp gasp and stared down at her. "Angel, we can't.
You're ill."

His words did not register on her fever-bright eyes.

With a groan, Roland left the bed and blew out the lamps.
He climbed back under the covers, resolving that he had to
make her rest. And if she slept, so could he. He rolled her
onto her stomach, fearing she'd start choking again in the
night, and half-covered her body with his to force her to lie
still. He threw an arm across her shoulders, and gently but
firmly pinned her hand down on the sheet. "Sleep now,

Angel,'' he whispered, kissing her ear. ''Please, you must sleep.''

At first she seemed content to lie passively beneath him, but then she grew wild again, driving him insane as her bottom squirmed against his manhood. She struggled to get free of him, demanding, with a ragged sob, ''Love me. Oh, please, Roland, love me. You're killing me with this distance.''

Killing her, he thought. Yes, he was killing her! He had brought this catastrophe crashing down upon her. And now —*mon Dieu*!—she was reliving the last few days, all the pain of their separation. And through it all, she was begging him to love her! Her torment clawed at his heart, even as her wild, uninhibited movements sent hot desire traitorously shooting through his loins.

Roland cursed his own carnal weakness, vowing that he could not, would not, take Angelique this way. He struggled to contain her beneath him, moaning a silent prayer: *Please, don't let her die. Let her rest now. Don't let her die.*

They grappled there for what seemed an eternity. Memories, poignant and remorseless, assailed him: Angelique, enchanting him with a lovely song; Angelique, laughing as he twirled her about in the garden; Angelique, beckoning him with her vibrant eyes—

Angelique, running away from him, terrified . . .

And still she writhed beneath him, begging, ''Love me. Please, Roland, love me,'' her anguished words rending his very soul.

He resisted her until he feared madness would overtake him. Yet when she insinuated a hand between them, clenching her fingers around his painfully swollen manhood, the part of him that was all ruthless male could endure no more. He burrowed between her thighs, lifting her hips slightly and piercing her womanhood with the hard, aching tip of his need. *Mon Dieu*, she was so hot, burning inside, so taut around him that he was on fire with the sweet constriction of her. He surged in deep and tight and heard her answering moan of pleasure. Belatedly he realized his insanity and tried to withdraw, only to hear her strangled ''No!'' as she arched against him.

Roland lost all control. He might lose her tomorrow, but

he would love her tonight, without restraint. He pulled her back onto her knees with him, draped his body over hers and plunged deeper. They hung there, two souls determined to merge, defying the impossibility and the pain.

Angelique awakened the next morning on her stomach. Roland was lying half on top of her, one leg draped possessively over her back.

She had a vague, provocative memory of mating with him last night like some barnyard creature. When she moved, the slight soreness between her thighs confirmed that she hadn't imagined the incredible depth and pressure of him as he'd thrust against her womb, spilling his seed deep inside her. Her breasts felt tender from where his hands had kneaded, and one side of her face and the back of her neck felt rope-burned from his beard. Roland had taken her with desperate, powerful, and violent passion. It had been devastating and wonderful. And perhaps even now a child was growing inside her at last—a child born of their sweet, wild need last night.

She moved again and Roland jumped awake, rolling off her. Frantically, he put his hand to her face. "Your fever is gone. Oh, my angel!"

There were tears in her eyes as he drew her into his arms. They held each other for a long, emotional moment, then Angelique whispered, "Uh—Roland?"

"Yes?"

"Do I remember what I think I remember?"

He drew back and stared down at her contritely. "Angel, I tried my damndest to resist you last night. But I'm afraid you were—ah—very wild and provocative. As it turned out, making love to you was the only way to subdue you. And you," he paused to smile sheepishly, "rather demanded that I do just that." Searching her face anxiously, he added, "Are you sorry, Angel?"

"I'd be sorry if we hadn't." Hearing his ragged moan, she buried her face against his neck.

"Angel, I love you," he said brokenly, for the first time since New Orleans.

"Roland, I've never felt closer to you," she whispered back, feeling his tears trickle down her face.

While Roland and Angelique were celebrating her recovery, Blanche was sitting in her stepbrother's office downstairs, consumed by guilt.

Angelique was doubtless dead by now, God rest her soul. Blanche had seen that unspeakable finality in Roland's eyes when he'd spoken with her briefly last night, informing her that his wife's condition had worsened. Blanche hadn't had the heart to summon the priest for extreme unction. She was sure that any moment now, Roland would come downstairs to inform her that his beloved Angelique was gone.

And it was all her fault! She'd now destroyed two marriages for her poor stepbrother. Granted, she may have had cause with Luisa, but she'd had no cause with Angelique. She had distrusted the girl from the start, willfully misinterpreting her every kindness. And the girl had been goodness incarnate, had never done anything to bring Blanche harm. Yet she'd been blinded to Angelique's virtue in her own terrible fear and insecurity.

Blanche realized her fatal error now—now that it was too late. Now that she'd destroyed Angelique's life and had shattered Roland's happiness forever.

Blanche went over to Roland's desk and opened the drawer, staring at the pistol. It was the gun that had killed Luisa, and it was only poetic justice that she use it now to atone for her unspeakable sins. What God had joined together, she had put asunder—forever.

Even as her hand was moving to clutch the handle, the door flew open. She glanced up sharply, automatically closing the drawer as Roland burst into the room, his eyes wild with joy.

"She's well! Oh, Sister, Angelique is well!"

With a cry of exultation, Blanche flew across the room into Roland's arms. They clung to each other, both shamelessly succumbing to their tears.

CHAPTER
Thirty-one

During the next weeks, Roland watched over Angelique like a fanatic. He wouldn't let her out of the bedroom for a full week; and even then, it was only to carry her downstairs and place her, heaped with quilts, before a roaring fire.

Blanche, too, hovered over the girl, bringing her special broths and reading to her. Angelique became cantankerous at all the unneeded attention, which only made Roland and Blanche fret over her all the more. A full two weeks after her fever had broken, she would start to get up to fetch some item, only to have one of them—more often, both—dash up to get it for her. "You're treating me like a porcelain doll!" she railed at Roland one night, after he sprang up to grab her knitting for her. But when he merely grinned back at her and handed her the half-finished afghan, she couldn't protest further. He'd looked so happy in that one unguarded moment; and most of the time these days, he looked quite grim and preoccupied, for a reason she couldn't fathom.

He insisted that she continue to sleep in her old room, and this made her feel hurt and confused. Three weeks after she'd shaken the malaise, she went into his room one night. He was undressing near the bed and looked up at her, startled. He looked so handsome in his shirt and well-fitting trousers, the lamplight outlining the chiseled planes of his face and shining in his thick, black hair. Her heart did a lurch as his deepset blue eyes locked with hers.

"Don't you think it's time for me to move back in here with you?" she asked tremulously.

For a fleeting moment, she watched a terrible pain and need cross his eyes. Then he shook his head, "No, Angelique. You're still recovering and I might—hurt you in the night."

He started toward her with a kindly smile. "Here, let me help you back to bed before you take a chill."

Then Angelique did something that startled even herself. She whirled about and exited the room, slamming the door in his face.

In her room, Angelique threw herself across the bed and sobbed herself to sleep. She was feeling so emotional these days. Perhaps Roland was right that she still hadn't fully recovered. But that was no reason for him to withhold himself from her. At night she ached for his warmth and his love. Hadn't he said he loved her that morning after they'd taken each other with such sweet violence?

Maybe that one episode was at the root of her husband's withdrawal. She thought back to that wild, delirious night. She had a hazy memory of squirming against Roland wantonly, of *demanding* he make love to her. Perhaps the passionate side of her nature that she'd revealed had put him off. Perhaps he'd considered her conduct lurid for a proper wife.

Well if he did think that, he could just go rot! Angelique had no regrets regarding the beautiful, desperate night she and Roland had shared. They were husband and wife, they belonged to each other now, and nothing they had done was wrong.

When Angelique awakened the next morning feeling nauseous and dizzy, she initially feared that her malaise had returned. But even though she retched at the basin for several minutes, the episode quickly faded, and she felt fine the balance of the day.

Yet the next three mornings brought a return of the perplexing nausea. Again, each time, Angelique felt fine afterward. On the fifth morning of the recurring malady, she thought over the past weeks, and a realization dawned on her, filling her with fierce joy.

Grabbing her dressing gown and slippers, not even pausing to rake order through her disheveled hair, Angelique hurried downstairs. She burst into Roland's study and he stood, startled, dropping his pen.

"I'm pregnant!" she cried.

For a moment, a look of pure joy flashed in his eyes, then

that horrible, worried look again gripped his features. "How can you know?"

"I just know!" she cried exultantly. "I'm never . . ." Despite the blush heating her face, she finished, "I'm never late."

"Perhaps with your illness—"

She shook her head, crossing toward him. "No. I'm pregnant. I just know it. No other explanation makes sense. I've awakened positively green for five mornings in a row, and then I feel fine the rest of the day. Oh, Roland, we're really, truly going to have a baby! It happened—" she blushed, then smiled at him radiantly. "It happened that night."

Roland swallowed hard. They both knew precisely what night she was referring to. "Angelique, you should be in bed."

Hurt by his distance and guardedness, she was tempted to stamp her foot. "Aren't you happy?"

He came to her side and gently took her into his arms. His smell and nearness were such sweet torment to her senses, she wanted to rail out at him and demand that he love her all at the same time. Even as he held her, he still seemed so remote, unreachable.

"Of course I'm happy," he murmured, stroking her tumbled hair.

But his voice lacked conviction, and bitter tears welled in her eyes.

After Angelique left the room, Roland collapsed on the leather settee, feeling shaken, overwhelmed by warring emotions.

When Angelique had told him she was pregnant, at first he'd wanted to grab her and kiss her senseless, so complete was his joy.

But then sanity returned, reminding him of how ill she'd been, of how they'd conceived this child in the desperation of that night she had almost died, at the very height of her delirium.

Now, he saw Angelique recovering her strength too slowly. She was quite thin, and there were still dark circles beneath her eyes. Guilt over his wild, torrid passion that fateful night gnawed at him endlessly. Guilt was the very reason he hadn't come to her bed since then. The experience had demonstrated to him his utter powerlessness over his raging need of her— a need strong enough to consume them both. Looking back, he still couldn't believe how totally he had lost control, how rapaciously he had devoured her slim, beckoning, fever-wracked body.

He wasn't sure she was up to handling a pregnancy now. She was still seventeen, wouldn't be eighteen until late this spring. And would the baby be healthy, conceived when its mother was so ill?

She seemed so happy about the child, and of course this pleased him. He'd been well aware that she'd wanted a baby for some time, and it was gratifying to know he'd granted her wish. In a sense, they were bound together now through the tiny life they shared.

She wanted his child, but did she really want him? She'd been so cross with him during her recovery, seeming to resent his ministrations. Was she truly happy here with him, being his wife? Or was she missing their more exciting times back in New Orleans? He couldn't forget that he'd forced this marriage on her, and that she'd never, ever actually told him that she wanted to spend the rest of her life with him—

In the depths of her delirium she'd said she loved him. How he prayed it could be true! Had she meant the words, or had they sprung from the dementia of fever, from her wildness that night, her desire to create life even as she clung desperately to her own?

And then he thought again of his baby growing inside her, and guilt and worry could not contain the surge of joy that consumed him and filled his eyes with tears. Never had he loved her more! Never had she so dwelled in his soul.

And all that mattered now was to cherish her and keep her and their child safe from all harm.

While Roland's reaction to her pregnancy had baffled and hurt Angelique, Blanche's response was overwhelming. Never before had the spinster rushed up to give Angelique a warm embrace, much less plant a kiss on her cheek.

"Oh, Angelique, praise the saints!" Blanche cried jubilantly. In her transport, she issued rapid-fire questions that Angelique could not possibly answer all at once. "When is the blessed event to occur? Do you want a boy or a girl? We must start on the layette and the nursery at once! Oh, wouldn't it be wonderful if he—or she—has your splendid singing voice? And what did Roland say when you told him? I know he was beside himself with joy!"

Though Blanche's mention of Roland's reaction pricked Angelique's heart, she braved a smile, finding Blanche's excitement contagious. "I take it you're pleased, then?" she teased.

Blanche clapped her hands, her dark eyes aglow. "Oh, my dear! Just think—I'm to be an aunt!"

In her bliss, Blanche failed to see the shadow crossing Angelique's eyes as she poignantly recalled that Roland had never exultantly announced that he was to become a father.

After Angelique left the parlor, Blanche sat down at the desk and began making a list of supplies they'd need to order for the baby's room and layette. Of course she'd go over the list with Angelique and let her make the final decisions. But Roland's dear young wife would need much rest in coming months, and Blanche fully intended to help her every way she could.

A baby! Blanche's heart sang at the thought. Life, dormant for so many years, was at last renewing itself at Belle Elise. The coming child was truly a portent from God, Blanche knew—it was a sign that she'd been forgiven. The past was over now, dead and buried, and it was time to look to the future, to life bringing forth life.

Oh, she must go congratulate Roland! Surely he was so happy!

Blanche thought back to the emotional morning when Roland had told her that Angelique would live. Later that same day, Blanche had gone to the village church and had confessed her sins, her interfering in Roland's marriage, to the priest. She'd done her penance and had vowed before God to make things up to Roland and his wife. Now she would devote herself to being the best friend and helpmate Angelique had ever known—and a loving aunt for the child.

Of course, marrying Jacques was out of the question now. Thinking of her beloved, Blanche ignored the sudden lump in her throat, the stinging in her eyes. She turned her thoughts to imagining what her tiny, precious niece or nephew would look like.

By the next night, Angelique had had enough of Roland's exiling her to her former bedroom.

He had her so confused! She couldn't be sure whether his withdrawal was due to concern over her health, or whether his distance was spurred by something more serious and insidious. He didn't seem at all excited about the baby, and this hurt terribly. It made her recall those awful rumors Blanche had mentioned—that Roland might have actually fathered Phillip.

Did he not want a child now because he already had one? Or had the news of her pregnancy spurred guilt due to his own, earlier transgressions?

Whatever had happened in Roland's past, Angelique knew in her heart now that he'd been faithful to her since their marriage. With their child growing inside her, she was filled with a unshakable resolve to put the past behind them and to look to their future.

She recalled his saying, on several occasions, that he didn't want to share her. Could he actually feel jealous of the baby? This thought made her face grow warm. Roland's possessiveness was provocative in one sense, yet unsettling in another.

Well, whatever their difficulty was, the only answer was to love him unconditionally, to help him adjust to the coming of their child. And, whatever the problem was, it would never be solved in separate bedrooms.

Angelique brushed her hair until it shone, then donned a very thin, revealing nightgown—a powder blue, lacy affair tied at her shoulders with satin bows. Determinedly, she crossed the dressing room connecting her room with Roland's. She entered his room without knocking.

He was seated in the chair by the window, a book in his lap. At the creaking open of the door, he glanced up sharply. He stared at her in the diaphanous gown, his eyes fervid, fiery. Whether he was furious, or aroused—or both—she couldn't really tell.

"Angelique—go to bed at once!" he ordered in a hoarse, trembling voice. "You'll take a chill."

"I'm tired of sleeping alone," she retorted petulantly.

Roland actually fought a smile as his gaze continued to rake over her lush curves, enhanced by the very suggestive gown. "Go to bed, little siren," he scolded unsteadily.

She held her ground, tilting her chin in a familiar attitude of defiance. "If you want me to go to bed, Roland, you'd best plan to take me there. And if you want to keep me there, you'd best plan to stay—just like you did that other night."

"Angelique—oh, Christ, please don't do this to me." His words came raggedly, his eyes emitted a desperate plea and she watched his hands tighten on the book until his knuckles turned white.

"No! I refuse to be banished like—like some invalid child! You say I'll catch cold, but I'm cold every night without you!"

And, ignoring Roland's anguished groan as he buried his face in his hands, she untied her gown and let it slide to the floor.

At once his head snapped up. "*Mon Dieu!*" he cried, his eyes devouring her nakedness.

Remorselessly, she continued, "Well I'm cold now, Roland—shivering—and what are you going to do about it?"

In a flash, his book slammed the floor and he was standing beside her, hard, aroused, hauling her into his arms.

"Oh, Roland!" she cried joyously. "This is no time for us to be apart. This is a time for us—"

But then his lips were roughly silencing hers, his strong arms lifting her, carrying her to his bed. His eyes blazed with need as he lowered himself upon her . . .

To share, her heart cried out joyously as she gave herself over to the man she loved. *This is a time for us to share*.

CHAPTER
Thirty-two

Almost three quarters of the year had passed, and summer was straining on toward autumn, by the time Jacques Delacroix returned to New Orleans.

The day after his arrival, Jacques planned to lunch with his friend André Bienville. That afternoon, he intended to travel by horseback to Belle Elise, there to solicit Blanche's long-awaited answer to his proposal of marriage. During his months in New York, Jacques had missed Blanche dearly, and had prayed that she would have a change of heart.

Jacques was preparing to leave for his luncheon engagement when his son came up to him in the hallway with a letter in hand. "Father, you were so tired last night that I thought I'd wait and give this to you today."

"Thank you Son," Jacques replied, taking the envelope from Jean Pierre with a feeling of impending doom.

Jean Pierre tactfully withdrew and Jacques laid down his hat and cane. He read the correspondence from Blanche, dated a month past:

My dearest Jacques,

I'm writing you in care of Jean Pierre, knowing that you should soon be returning to New Orleans.

We've wonderful news here at Belle Elise. Roland and Angelique are expecting their first child in early September. I am to be the baby's godmother, and Angelique and I are quite busy making preparation for the blessed event.

With the coming of the child, it is more than ever impossible that I should wed you, Jacques. I am greatly

284

needed here. You must know that I am very fond of you; but our sensibilities would never be compatible.

Forgive me for not being the right woman for you, and I pray that you will find her one day. And I hope that you will still visit Belle Elise on occasion.

Affectionately,

Blanche

Finishing the letter, Jacques crumpled it in his hand. Blanche was still fighting him, grasping at any excuse to deny their love.

Well, he wouldn't give up. He just couldn't.

Over lunch at Antoine's, Jacques vented his frustration to his friend, André. "Now Blanche says she can't marry me because she must assist with my nephew's forthcoming child. It's all a smokescreen, André, to cover this nonsense about her face."

"Blanche seemed to do fairly well at the Lind concert last winter," André remarked.

"*Oui*. Yet the very next day, she ran home to hide at Belle Elise. *Pour l'amour de Dieu!* How am I to get through to the woman? I was planning to visit her at Belle Elise this very afternoon—now this!" Jacques sighed, flashing André an apologetic smile. "Enough of my personal tragedy. Tell me, *mon ami*, how is your lovely Hélène?"

The white-haired Creole grinned proudly. "She's pregnant again."

"Why, you old rascal!" Jacques teased. "That's the fourth child in so many years since you wed the girl. And I bet she thought she'd have an easier time, marrying a relic like you."

André chuckled. "When one has a child-bride, one must make provision that she remain well-occupied."

Jacques grinned, shaking his head. "Lord, man, how I envy you." Taking a sip of wine, he added, "How are things at the opera?"

"We're preparing to launch our season with *Les Huguen-ots*, as usual." With a crafty gleam in his gray eyes, André added, "It's a pity that your nephew's brilliant young wife cannot join our company. After *La Lind's* performance here, the community would welcome another prima donna of her stature. But alas, you say the girl is also expecting now, like my Hélène?''

''Practically any day now, according to Blanche's letter. There seems to be quite a rash of procreation in the region.''

André grinned. ''Considering how beautiful young Madame Delacroix is, and being aware of her husband's fiery temperament, I can't say I'm surprised. Still—I do hear that Barnum profited a clean half-million in his venture with Jenny Lind. Just think of what we might accomplish with a singer of Angelique Delacroix's beauty and brilliance—some time after her confinement, of course.''

Jacques waved a hand resignedly. ''I must tell you, André, that when I visited with my nephew and his wife last winter, I broached the subject of Angelique's singing at the opera. Roland's reaction was predictably scathing.''

André scowled. ''Still, don't you think we should give this another try? What if we emphasize to the two of them that we want Angelique for only one concert? We could make it a virtuoso performance, just like Barnum did with Lind. With this town's mania for opera—and the right publicity, of course—I can visualize tickets selling for upwards of fifteen dollars a piece.''

Jacques whistled. ''My God, André. You've given this venture considerable thought, haven't you?''

In typical Creole fashion, André shrugged, but the calculating gleam in his eyes was not lost on Jacques. Leaning forward, Jacques asked, ''Tell me, would you actually be content to have the girl for just one performance?''

''Of course not,'' André replied slyly. ''But it's a beginning—*n'est-ce pas*? Why don't we go see the girl, talk to her?''

''Then I'd have a reason to see Blanche again,'' Jacques murmured, brightening at the thought.

''Of course. As they say, *mon ami*, the perfect excuse.''

Jacques nodded, his brain humming. He was suddenly so consumed with excitement at having a pretext for seeing Blanche again, he didn't really consider the possible impact their request of Angelique might have on her marriage.

''And wouldn't you like to regain the face you lost in not underwriting Barnum with *La Lind*?'' André added cagily.

Jacques grinned ruefully. "André, you're ruthless."

"Utterly. So when do we visit Belle Elise, *mon ami*?"

At Belle Elise, Angelique was now great with child. The spring and summer had passed peacefully between her and Roland. He'd seemed altogether too protective of her, too fretful regarding her health. But he'd also been especially gentle and tender toward her during her pregnancy.

Roland had never told her that he truly welcomed the coming child, who was now so much a part of her—so huge and active in her belly. Yet on a recent night, as she'd undressed for bed and had felt the baby kicking her with exceptional vigor, he'd chuckled at her wide-eyed reaction. He had crossed the room and embraced her fondly, placing his hand on her stomach and feeling their baby pummeling against his palm. "He's quite a fighter—this child of ours," he had said with a proud grin. Angelique had smiled back at him radiantly, not correcting him when he'd referred to their child as a son. Somehow, she also knew their baby would be a boy.

Blanche had been a marvelous helpmate during the months of Angelique's pregnancy, helping her decorate the nursery and prepare the layette. Sometimes, Angelique actually thought Blanche was more excited about the coming child than she was—if that were possible. The spinster hovered over her as much as Roland did, constantly monitoring her diet and urging her to rest more during the day. At first Angelique had rebelled against all the coddling; yet both Roland and Blanche had been obdurate, and finally she had come to accept their pampering her with good-natured resignation.

The only sad note to sound during past months had come last spring, when Coco's baby had been delivered stillborn. The child, more white than black, had been buried in a quiet graveside service on plantation land. Only three weeks later, Coco had married one of the slaves, handsome young Reuben, and the two were already expecting their own child. Sometimes Angelique couldn't help but feel that the stillbirth of Giles Fremont's illegitimate progeny had been for the best. Still, it wrenched her heart every time she thought of that poor, lost little soul they had buried.

On a morning late in August, Angelique awakened with a pain low in her belly. The contraction faded, only to recur again a quarter hour later. She wondered with sudden joy if her labor was beginning, if she might hold her beloved child in her arms by that night. Yet she'd been visited by all sorts of weird aches and pains lately; and otherwise, she felt quite energetic. Perhaps her time had not come as yet.

Late that morning, as she and Blanche were knitting booties and baby blankets in the parlor, they heard the sound of a carriage approaching. Moments later, Benjamin ushered in Jacques Delacroix and André Bienville.

While Angelique smiled in pleasant surprise at the unexpected visitors, Blanche looked frozen in her seat as she watched Jacques stride into the room.

"My dears, my dears!" Jacques cried, warmly kissing each woman. "Now don't get up, either of you! How good it is to see you both! Blanche, you look beautiful, as always. And Angelique, congratulations on the blessed news. You're truly aglow." Gesturing toward André, he added, "You both remember my friend André Bienville of the New Orleans Opera?"

Angelique and Blanche politely greeted André, then Angelique took charge as hostess, asking the men to seat themselves and ordering tea. She noted that Blanche still looked stiff as a porcelain figurine as she sat in her chair across from Jacques, tensely staring at him. Angelique was grateful that Roland was out overseeing the fields with Mr. Jurgen, since she had a feeling her husband wouldn't have greeted their guests graciously.

Over tea, Jacques delighted them with tales of his recent riverboat excursion up the Hudson River with friends from New York. Angelique noted that Blanche was beginning to warm up as she listened to the glowing details of Jacques's journey.

After small talk had been exhausted, Angelique turned to André, whose presence had greatly aroused her curiosity. The white-haired president of the New Orleans Opera looked quite distinguished today in his black suit, crisp white shirt linen, and ebony studs and cufflinks. "Well, M'sieur Bienville, we are quite honored to have you as our guest today."

He chuckled. "I'd wager, my dear Madame Delacroix, that you're quite perplexed as to why I've intruded on you."

"Oh, but you haven't intruded at all, M'sieur Bienville."

"You are too charming, Madame Delacroix," André gallantly returned. "Actually, when Jacques mentioned that he was planning to visit Belle Elise, I begged to come along so that I might persuade you to favor us with a song. Surely after I've come all this distance, you won't disappoint me?"

Angelique laughed. "You came all this way just to hear me sing, M'sieur Bienville?"

"Heaven is much farther, Madame Delacroix, but I would have to travel at least that far to hear a voice such as yours."

Angelique again laughed, shaking her head. "How can I refuse the request of a man of such—eloquence?"

"Indeed," André concurred with a smile.

Blanche was persuaded to accompany Angelique. She sang several lovely songs for the men, including some challenging Mozart arias, which she executed perfectly.

Afterward, André and Jacques exchanged a look of reverent amazement. Then André turned to Angelique and got straight to the point. "Madame Delacroix, a voice as brilliant as yours must be shared with the world. I'm begging you to come to New Orleans some time in the fall—entirely at your convenience—to do just one virtuoso performance at the St. Charles. Should you agree to this, I can guarantee you a full house and a generous fee for your services. Think what a nice little nest egg this could be for your child."

Angelique, taken aback by Bienville's proposal, didn't at first know how to respond. Observing her momentary confusion, Jacques put in earnestly, "Angelique, please, give André's proposal some thought. You'd be giving the opera-goers of New Orleans an experience they will never forget."

But by now, Angelique had recovered her self-possession and was shaking her head. "M'sieur Bienville, I'm quite touched by your confidence in my abilities. But for personal reasons, I must decline. Furthermore, I'm afraid my husband would never—"

"Let two scoundrels steal his wife from beneath his very nose," an ominous male voice finished.

There was an collective gasp as all four turned to view

Roland standing in the archway, his tall, muscled body rigid with anger, his expression thunderous.

Coming into the house moments earlier, Roland had heard the sound of male voices, which compelled him on toward the parlor. Standing at the archway, it hadn't taken him long to determine that Jacques and André Bienville were trying to persuade Angelique to sing at the opera—and the knowledge of their perfidy had filled him with unspeakable rage. Now, all he could think of was that his uncle, fully aware of his feelings, had betrayed him. All he could think of was that these too cads were trying to steal his wife—a pregnant wife whom he loved and about whom he felt fiercely protective.

At once, Jacques tried to defuse the volatile situation. "Why Nephew! How good it is to see you—"

"A bald-faced lie if I've ever heard one," Roland cut in ruthlessly, striding into the room. He continued to address Jacques with barely suppressed fury. "Evidently you have an impediment of memory, as you mentioned this lunacy about Angelique's singing last winter. My answer was no then, and it remains no now. Yet you and your grasping friend have had the unmitigated gall to go behind my back to try to secure my wife's consent. Due to your unforgivable treachery, neither of you is welcome in this house—ever again."

At Roland's words, the women gasped in horror. Jacques stood, drawing himself up with dignity. His eyes gleamed with affronted pride as he said tightly, "If those are your sentiments, Roland, André and I bid you goodday."

There was absolute silence as the two men squared their shoulders and strode out of the room. Afterward, Roland turned to Blanche. "Will you excuse Angelique and me for a moment?"

"Of course, Brother," Blanche said stiffly. Throwing Angelique a compassionate look, she hurried out of the room.

Roland glanced at Angelique. Her face was so white, it was virtually expressionless as she stared back at him. He was very much afraid that the intrusion of the two men had overtired and upset her. Gently, he asked, "My dear—are you all right?"

Thus, great was Roland's astonishment when Angelique sprang to her feet and cried, "How dare you, Roland!"

"How dare I what?" he asked confusedly.

Her dark eyes blazed with rage as she shook a fist at him. "How dare you cast your uncle and his friend from our home! How dare you say they acted unforgivably! They did nothing wrong! It was you who acted unforgivably!"

"Indeed?" Roland retorted, unable to believe his ears. "How can you say that, when those two cads tried to steal my wife?"

"They didn't try to steal me!" she railed, clenching her teeth. "They made a simple request, which I was quite capable of answering on my own! But you've never recognized that I was able to do anything on my own! Oh, no, you had to answer for me—in this and in everything! Damn it, even if they had wanted to steal me, they couldn't have done so had I not wanted to be stolen!"

"You're distraught," he said gruffly, as if that explained everything.

"That's right, I'm distraught," she retorted, "and I'm staying that way until you go after Jacques and M'sieur Bienville and beg their pardon for your despicable behavior."

"What?" he echoed with a disbelieving laugh. "Despicable behavior? I'm the wounded party here—"

"Wrong!" she cut in vehemently. "I'm the wounded party here—as are Jacques and M'sieur Bienville. And once again, I demand that you go after them and apologize."

"Apologize?" he repeated, flinging his hands outward. "You may as well wish for ice on the river by sunset."

"You'll apologize," she said in a deadly calm voice, "or I'll go after them and do so in your behalf." Tilting her chin at him rebelliously, she added, "And I swear, Roland, if you don't right this personally, I'll sing for them in New Orleans."

"Over my dead body, you will," he ground out.

Yet Angelique was unheeding as she shoved past Roland and hurried out the front door, intent on finding the two men and begging their forgiveness.

For a moment, Roland stood paralyzed, unable to believe Angelique had defied him so soundly. Then he cried out, "No!", and hurried after her.

He tore down the front steps of Belle Elise, watching his wife race toward Jacques' departing carriage. "Damn it, Angelique, don't run. You'll hurt yourself or—"

Then his voice froze in helpless horror as he watched his wife stumble ahead of him, falling on the lawn.

CHAPTER
Thirty-three

Roland raced toward Angelique.

Never in his life had he known such stark fear. Watching his wife stumble on the lawn was ten times worse than the day when she fell into the bayou. The fact that she had fallen facedown and was lying so still only exacerbated his terror.

Arriving at her side, he turned her gently, anxiously scanning her face.

"My water broke," she told him tonelessly.

"*Mon Dieu*," he cried. He scooped Angelique up into his arms and hurried for the house as fast as safety would allow. Behind them, Jacques's coach continued, unheeding, toward New Orleans . . .

Roland took Angelique up to bed, then dispatched Reuben for the doctor. In the meantime, Blanche and Coco took charge of Angelique's labor. Blanche banned Roland from the bedroom, and thus it was his lot to sit downstairs, helplessly listening to his wife's screams, cursing the tradition that banned husbands from the birthing room.

When the doctor finally arrived four hours later, Roland was ready to throttle the man. Then, mere minutes after he went upstairs, Roland heard Angelique's worst scream yet, and it tore at his heart. He raced upstairs—tradition be damned—and burst into the bedroom. Dr. Monroe, after hastily throwing a sheet over Angelique, turned to him, livid. "We are under control here, sir. 'Tis a dry birth—which means more pain for your wife. But the course of her labor will also be mercifully foreshortened. Now kindly leave the room, sir, and let us attend to our duties.''

Roland was tempted to hit the man. But he knew that imposing himself in the room would not improve things for Angelique. With an anguished look at her pale, drawn face, he turned and left.

The hours after she fell on the lawn were nightmarish for Angelique, as well. When she turned her foot in a gopher hole and realized that she was going to tumble, she had managed to break her fall with her hands. Her stomach was not directly hit. Yet evidently the fall was enough to break her water, which came out in a single, terrifying gush. Even more horrifying was the look on Roland's face when he turned her over. The blood was gone from his features, and he looked frightened or angry . . . perhaps both.

After Roland deposited her in bed, her pains came with a vengeance—like merciless, tenacious tentacles, digging and clawing deep within her belly. The midday heat was cloying, only intensifying her discomfort, and the cold compresses Blanche kept applying to her brow seemed but a tepid encumbrance. There was really little Blanche or Coco could do to lessen her pain.

When the doctor finally arrived, he was no real help or comfort. Dr. Monroe was rough in his ministrations, tersely informing her that her pelvis was barely adequate for the child to pass. Angelique was well aware of her own difficulties. She tried not to cry out as the contractions became more frequent and agonizing—fearing she would alarm Roland—but that resolve proved impossible to hold onto. Then, after a particularly excruciating pain tore a scream from her lungs, her husband burst into the room—his eyes crazed, tortured . . .

Angelique had been furious at Roland earlier, up to the moment when she'd fallen. Thereafter, fear for her baby's safety had overtaken her rage. But now, during the brief, haunting moment when he stood at the portal staring at her, she realized that he was suffering every bit as much as she was. She wanted to cry out to him to stay with her, but realized the doctor would never allow this. After he left, she

managed to swallow her next scream, tearing at the sheet
with her hands . . .

Later, during the moment of birth, even the pain was beautiful for Angelique. She wept with joy as she held her and
Roland's child for the first time. The baby was so beautiful,
tiny and perfect, his skin as pure and pale as porcelain, his
hair the familiar midnight black of his father. Gazing down
at the small miracle in her arms, Angelique again wished
Roland could be with her at this moment—for she instinctively knew that if only they could share this experience as
a family, then nothing, ever again, would tear them apart.

Roland had a son. Six agonizing hours after Angelique
tripped on the lawn, it was all over. Blanche came down to
the parlor, beaming, with a tiny bundle in her arms. "You
have a son, Brother. Come see how beautiful he is."

Roland jumped up from the chair where he'd sat, distraught
and powerless, as Angelique labored. He hurried to Blanche's
side and stared in awe at the baby. "Is he all right?"

She nodded. "The doctor says he's a bit on the small side,
but strong and in perfect health."

Blanche placed the bundle in Roland's arms. Tears stung
his eyes as he looked down at his tiny, perfectly formed son.
"Angelique?" he asked hoarsely.

"The doctor says she'll be fine, as well," Blanche said
gently. "I'll leave the two of you to get acquainted," she
added wisely.

Roland sat down with the infant. Never in his life had he
seen a child so small—or so beautiful. He studied the precious
little face and tiny features, the thin crowning of black hair
on the baby's head. His own son—his and Angelique's.
"You certainly put your mother through enough," he told
the infant with a tender smile.

At his father's words, the baby yawned, opened solemn
blue eyes and stared up at his father intently. Then he
promptly feel deeply asleep again, his little mouth quivering.

Roland held the baby close and shut his eyes in silent
gratitude. Thank *le bon Dieu* it was all over and both mother
and child were fine. Not that he deserved it. He deserved to
have lost them both.

Looking back, Roland could now see the destructiveness of his behavior toward Angelique—his deadly pride, his jealousy, his terrible anger. Twice he'd put her very life in peril with his crazed possessiveness, and this last time, he'd risked the life of their precious son, as well.

He was wrong for her—he could see that now, with a vengeance. His love was an insidious poison that would destroy her one day.

Upstairs, Angelique started awake as Blanche stepped into the room. Glancing at the empty bassinet near the bed, she tensed. "Where's my baby?"

"There, don't fret yourself, Angelique," Blanche said soothingly. "I took the baby down to meet his father. Roland has suffered so during the past hours, and I thought you'd want him to know that both of you are all right."

"Of course," Angelique said. "Was Roland—happy?"

"Oh, yes, certainly he was," Blanche said as she stepped forward. "We're both overjoyed, Angelique. Now you must rest. I only came up to see if there's anything you're needing."

Angelique shook her head, then again glanced at the empty bassinet. "Roland will bring him back soon?"

"Indeed—I'll see that he does."

Angelique closed her eyes as Blanche slipped from the room. She felt drained, both physically and emotionally, yet she was also swimming with joy to have the baby she had so longed for.

She still felt somewhat confused and hurt regarding Roland's behavior earlier that day. But she dearly hoped that the two of them would be able to resolve their troubled relationship—for the sake of the child, and their love.

She was drifting off to sleep again when Roland entered the room with the baby. "How are you feeling?" he asked.

"Fine," she answered, her eyes riveted on the small bundle in his arms. Then she glanced up at him, and the anguish in his eyes brought tears to her own. She bravely blinked them back. Was he truly happy about the child? She couldn't tell.

"Shall I put him back in the bassinet?" he asked.

"No," she managed to whisper. "I want to hold him."

Angelique pulled herself upright, wincing at the pain. Roland handed her the baby, then gently wedged some pillows behind her back. "Comfortable now?"

"Yes," she lied. Studying Roland's drawn face, his forced smile, she realized they were like strangers together.

He sat down in a chair next to the bed. "He's beautiful, you know," he remarked, glancing at the baby in her arms.

She smiled, feeling warmed by his words—though the torment in his eyes still made her feel off balance. "I thought of calling him Justin—for your brother. And Paul—for the saint."

"Justin Paul," Roland repeated. "Yes, I like that very much."

"We must have him christened properly, of course," she added.

"Of course," Roland agreed solemnly, "as soon as you are better." He watched his wife shift slightly in bed, and the glimmer of pain in her eyes was not lost on him. He stood and gently took the baby from her arms. "You must lie down now, my dear. Sitting up that way is causing you pain."

Angelique nodded weakly. As much as she wanted to hold Justin, she was in too much discomfort to protest. Roland placed the baby in the bassinet then gently helped his wife scoot down under the covers. He kissed her brow tenderly and whispered, "Thank you, my dear—for our son."

His words brought a new welling of emotion, making Angelique's eyes sting, her throat ache. As he turned to leave, she called after him tentatively. "Roland?"

He turned to her, and again she glimpsed that haunted pain in his eyes. "We'll talk when you're better," he said.

Six weeks passed. Angelique recovered, and Justin thrived on her milk, which Angelique's slim young body provided in startling abundance. Three weeks after her confinement, the baby was christened at the local church, with Blanche standing up with Roland and Angelique as the child's godmother.

Roland visited with Angelique and the child daily. Yet their moments together were awkward, and he was distant, sleeping in a guest room upstairs. At first Angelique didn't mind, since she was very sore from the birth as well as up at all hours feeding Justin. But as the weeks passed and her health returned, as Justin mercifully settled in to sleep for a six-hour stretch each night, she longed for her husband's comfort and warmth. She longed for this emotional impasse between them to end.

When it did, it was far from in the way she'd imagined.

Roland had privately continued to feel tormented during every day of his wife's recovery. He couldn't bring himself to ask for her forgiveness. For as far as he was concerned, what he'd done that fateful day of Justin's birth was unforgivable, thus making a reconciliation impossible. He kept agonizing over their argument, right before Angelique had fallen and gone into labor. She's said that if he did not apologize to Jacques and Bienville, she'd go to New Orleans and sing for them. Increasingly, he felt that she must have expressed what she'd truly wanted in that moment. She'd tried to be a dutiful wife to him, but in that one unguarded instance, the mask of her pretension had been stripped away.

After all, no one had ever asked her if she wanted this marriage—it had been forced on her against her will. When they'd stayed in New Orleans for those long weeks last winter, he'd feared the glamorous world of Creole society and the opera might lure her. Why shouldn't she want to pursue some dreams of her own? Whenever had he asked her what she wanted at all? Just as she'd accused, he'd tried to dictate her every move, had refused to trust her—

And in the process, he'd almost destroyed her. He had no right to hold her now. She had never been his, not really. All his efforts to hold her had surely smothered and alienated her.

He knew, now, that the only way to keep her would be to offer her her freedom. As much as the thought of being without her and his son agonized him, he recognized that he had no other choice. He knew how proud Angelique was and realized that any day now, she would surely inform him that she would be going on to New Orleans to perform for Jacques and Bienville. His only hope was that just this once, he not try to control her, that he go to her first and let her go. He would pray that if he didn't stand in her way, she would choose to stay of her own free will. Yet if she did go, so be it. He couldn't blame her and it was certainly everything he deserved.

Thus, with a heavy heart, Roland visited his wife's bedroom one day early in September. He found Angelique sitting in a rocking chair near the window, rocking their sound-asleep babe. Never had she looked so beautiful. The sun streamed down on her raven hair and outlined her radiant face. How many times had he longed to touch those lush breasts that now strained so fully against the fabric of her lovely red frock?

He cleared his throat and she turned, smiling at him tentatively. He went to sit on the edge of her bed across from her. "The child is thriving," he said, nodding at young Justin, who, at six weeks, had totally compensated for his early birth and was now well-rounded and healthy.

"Your son grows more ravenous every day," Angelique told him. "In fact, every time I nurse him, I feel drained . . ." Realizing that her statement had been indelicate, she blushed and lowered her eyes. "At any rate, he does not suffer from lack of appetite."

Roland barely managed not to groan aloud. His son was not the only one ravenous for his wife—though his own appetites were of a much darker nature. It had been over two months since Roland had bedded Angelique, and never had he been more conscious of that fact than he was at this moment. Indeed, the painful tightening in his loins almost prompted him to abandon his nobler intentions. He realized that he even felt jealous of his young son for having her undivided attention—

Another reason to dislike himself, added to weeks of self-recrimination and layers of self-loathing.

He cleared his throat and said, "I suppose you'll be wanting to go to New Orleans now, to sing for Jacques and Bienville."

Her head shot up and for a moment, she looked stunned. "I beg your pardon?"

"I said I suppose you'll want to sing in New Orleans now that you're better." Stiffly, he added, "That's what you said you would do."

She tilted her chin slightly in that attitude of defiance he recognized so well. "Yes, that's what I said I would do."

"Well . . ." He braced himself, and then, staring at the floor, he whispered, "I think you should go."

"Oh?" He could hear her voice rising slightly.

"You said you would go if I didn't apologize to Jacques and Bienville—and I haven't apologized."

"That's true." A horrible silence stretched between them, then she asked, "What about Justin?"

Roland ventured a glance at her. Her eyes were deeply dilated, gleaming, yet her true emotions were impossible to read. "You're nursing him. So I presume you'll be taking him along."

"You presume correctly," she replied tersely.

"Of course I'll want to see him," he added awkwardly. "We'll have to arrange something there."

"Of course," she repeated woodenly.

He sighed. "I'll dispatch a letter to Emily to tell her you are coming, and I'll settle a suitable sum with Maurice's firm to be available for your needs." He smiled bitterly. "Jacques will be delighted—he'll have his day to shine now, his angel to sing."

As he started for the door, she called after him. "Roland?"

He turned, staring at her with anguished eyes.

With her heart in her voice, she asked, "After the concert—what then?"

He could only shake his head sadly as he turned to leave her,

After Roland left, Angelique succumbed to her tears, shaking with silent sobs as she held her precious baby. Roland didn't want her or Justin—he'd just made that brutally clear by sending them away. The pain in his eyes as he left the room had demonstrated that he could barely stand the sight of either of them.

Doubtless, she had committed the unforgivable in his eyes that day when she'd defied him so recklessly and had raced after Jacques and Bienville, thus endangering the life of their child. She had wanted to forget that day and her angry ultimatum to her husband, to look toward their future and a true reconciliation.

Yet obviously, Roland wasn't willing to forgive or forget. If only he had railed out at her for her foolishness—anything to show that he cared. But he hadn't. There was nothing between them—no loving, no recriminations.

And Roland had reminded her that he still hadn't apologized to Jacques and Bienville concerning that terrible day, and that meant that he continued to regard himself as blameless. He wasn't willing to meet her halfway, to give at all from his former, peremptory behavior. If she stayed, they would continue to claw at one another until they destroyed every positive emotion between them. And for the sake of their child, this must not happen.

She would go then. He was sending her away, anyway. Even now, as always, he was offering her no choice. If only he'd asked her to stay, she would have, gladly, burying the past and rushing back into his arms. But he hadn't. Her marriage was over.

CHAPTER
Thirty-four

On an October afternoon four weeks later, Angelique sat in a rocking chair in her room at the Miro townhome, nursing young Justin. At two and a half months, the baby continued to thrive. His body was pink and well-rounded, and he sported a shock of black curls. Often when he stared up at her with his solemn blue eyes, he reminded her poignantly of Roland.

Angelique smiled as her son nursed hungrily, pummeling a small fist against her breast. She welcomed these quiet moments with him. It was hard for her to believe that her life had changed so radically in just a few short weeks.

Only two days after she and Roland had their momentous talk, Angelique had departed for New Orleans with Blanche, Coco, and Reuben. Roland had urged Blanche to accompany Angelique; and ultimately, the spinster couldn't bear the thought of being away from young Justin, whom she adored. In past weeks, Blanche and Coco had shared babysitting

duties while Angelique practiced for her forthcoming concert
at the St. Charles Theater.

Angelique could hardly believe that in less than a week,
she would be performing solo before thousands of opera af-
icionados! She well knew that Creoles were true epicures of
opera, and that her audience next week would never tolerate
a substandard performance.

Madame Santoni had increased Angelique's confidence regarding her upcoming initiation by fire. André Bienville had
invited Madame down from St. James, offering her a suite
at the St. Louis and a generous weekly stipend as Angelique's
vocal coach. To Angelique's surprise, Madame had accepted;
her husband, Antonio, remained behind in St. James to care
for their business.

Time being of the essence, Madame had helped Angelique
select a repetoire at once. Each day, Angelique and Madame
met at the theater for morning and afternoon practice sessions,
and Blanche augmented these by accompanying Angelique
for additional practice at the Miro townhome. Under Madame's tutelage, Angelique had soon slipped into the familiar
practice rituals of her childhood—the endless scales, the cadenzas, the trills.

Soon after her coaching sessions with Madame began,
Angelique had confided to her teacher her misgivings about
performing before an audience, for profit. Madame had nodded wisely, and had told her, "I know you were raised to
believe that a proper young woman simply does not appear
on stage. I fear I also fostered that belief in you at an early
age, by urging you to sing only in church, to praise God.
And while I never said so in so many words, I also made
you believe that singing on stage was wicked." There had
been tears in Madame's eyes as she continued, "I did so
because of my own guilt, *cara*. I always felt that the tragedy
that befell Antonio and me back in Italy was God's punishment for my vanity in appearing on stage. But when I heard
Jenny Lind perform last winter, I had a change of heart. You
see, Fraulein Lind also sees her voice as God's gift, but that
does not keep her from sharing her incredible talent with the
world." Madame had squeezed Angelique's hand as she finished passionately, "Your gift, *cara*, is even greater than

hers, and to keep that bright flame hidden forever would be
the true sacrilege. And I realize now that what happened to
Antonio and me back in Italy was just a tragedy of circumstances.''

Angelique smiled as she recalled the emotional moment
when Madame had made her revelations. Afterward, she had
hugged her teacher, and at last, she had known peace in her
heart regarding her decision to perform.

Practical considerations had also prompted Angelique to
do the concert. André Bienville had already offered her a
permanent, generously salaried position with the opera.
Angelique was seriously considering accepting his offer, although she would wait and see how she was received at her
debut. After all, she had a son to support now. As far as she
knew, she and Roland were permanently estranged, and while
he had set up a generous account for her with Maurice's firm,
she disliked spending his money.

Looking down at her precious Justin, now fast asleep at
her breast, Angelique felt a catch in her heart as she thought
of how much she missed her child's father. At night as she
lay in her lonely bed, she ached for Roland's warmth, his
embrace. Their love life had been very intense, and as much
as her heart hungered for his companionship and emotional
support, her healthy young body was ravenous for the physical release only he could bring her. Their separation had
made her realize as never before that she needed him on every
level—emotional, spiritual, and physical.

If only he missed her a fraction of the amount she missed
him!

Blanche had several times urged Angelique to return to
Belle Elise and seek a reconciliation with Roland; but, as
Angelique had reminded her, it was Roland who had provoked the estrangement, by sending her away. Now it was
up to him to make the first move. And so far, he had made
no overture in her direction, and this hurt deeply.

Yet Angelique refused to let herself dwell on the tragedy
of her failed marriage; despite her inner pain, she forced
herself to look forward, to maintain a positive facade, for her
child's sake.

A discreet knock now sounded at Angelique's door. After
she covered herself and called out softly, "Come in," Emily

Miro stepped into the room, looking lovely in a gold silk gown. A newspaper was tucked under her arm. "Well, how is our precious little boy this afternoon?" she asked with a smile.

Angelique smiled back at her hostess and friend. Emily had been the soul of gracious hospitality these past weeks. "He's sound asleep, with a very full stomach."

Emily opened the paper and extended it toward Angelique. "Here, look at this while I put Justin down in his cradle."

Angelique nodded, carefully transferring the baby to Emily's arms and taking the newspaper. She stared down at André Bienville's huge advertisement in the New Orleans *Crescent*. "Come hear the Cajun Angel," it proclaimed. "Only a few choice seats left."

Angelique sighed, setting the paper aside. Emily, across the room, turned from the cradle. "André is doing a marvelous job of promoting you. All over the Quarter, everyone is buzzing with excitement regarding your debut."

"So I've noticed," Angelique replied, recalling how, during recent days, several Creoles had actually stopped her on the streets to ask if she were indeed the "Cajun Angel." Ruefully, she added, "Now if only I can live up to André's expectations."

Emily waved her off. "Oh, Angelique! Anyone who has heard you sing would never have doubts there."

Angelique was pensively silent for a moment, then asked, "Has Blanche left with Jacques for their dinner engagement?"

Emily shook her head. "Not yet. She's down in the court-yard waiting for him." Emily's eyes glowed as she continued, "Angelique, your teaching Blanche to use stage makeup on her birthmark was a true stroke of genius. I note that every time Blanche goes out with Jacques now, she wears an even lighter veil."

There Angelique had to smile. When they'd first come to New Orleans, Blanche had sequestered herself at the Miro townhome, refusing to see Jacques and claiming she must look after Justin. Then, as the costume mistress at the St. Charles began training Angelique in the application of stage makeup, it occurred to her that the heavy grease paint would be the perfect mask for Blanche's birthmark. Angelique had brought home a paint kit, and had prevailed upon Emily to offer support in approaching Blanche. At first, Blanche had balked at the idea of using heavy paint, which was the earmark of actors or women of the streets. Finally, through laborious persuasion, Emily and Angelique had convinced Blanche to let Angelique experiment with various shades. They'd found the perfect blend for Blanche's cheek, subtly covering the paint with magnesia powder to affect a flesh tone. Following the application, the birthmark was still discernible, but much paler. The look in Blanche's eyes as she stared at her transformed visage warmed Angelique's heart. For the first time in memory, Blanche looked truly beautiful, not because the mark was masked, but because she glowed with inner happiness.

Nevertheless, Blanche had been a nervous wreck the first time she went out with Jacques with the paint on her face. Yet hours later she'd come home, radiant, telling Emily and Angelique of her success. "Jacques didn't say a word about my face. He didn't even seem to notice—nor did anyone else!"

"That was the entire idea, *n'est-ce pas*?" Emily had put in, and the three women had laughed, huddling in a joyous embrace. Since then, Blanche had seen Jacques several times each week.

How Angelique wished she could see Roland that often! The thought brought a cloud to her eyes. Emily, observing her suddenly pained expression, asked, "Thinking of Roland, dear?"

Angelique nodded, braving a smile at her friend. Emily had been a marvelous confidant during past weeks. "He's never really out of my thoughts."

"Do you truly think it's hopeless, dear? When the two of you were here last winter, you seemed so in love."

Angelique sighed, recalling those beautiful days with intense longing. "Roland has just never thought of me as an individual, as a full partner in the marriage. He's always dictated my every move, and I suppose I'm just not capable of becoming a subservient wife. This last time when I defied him, I fear I destroyed any chance for a future between us. There's no trust there, Emily, and without trust, a marriage is doomed."

"If only he would come down for your performance," Emily said fervently, "then perhaps the two of you—"

"He won't come," Angelique cut in, and for the first time, there was deep bitterness in her voice.

CHAPTER
Thirty-five

Down in the lush courtyard, Blanche was drinking lemonade at the wrought-iron table and anxiously awaiting Jacques's arrival. She glanced about at vibrant flowers spilling from the formal beds; she inhaled the intoxicating aroma of nectar, and smiled as she listened to the singsong patois of a cala lady drifting in from the street. How beautiful was the world—her world!

Though Blanche had come to New Orleans feeling depressed due to Roland and Angelique's estrangement, in other ways, the trip had radically changed her life. Since the day Angelique had brought home the paint kit from the theater and had convinced her to use the makeup on her birthmark, Blanche hadn't been as terrified to go out in public. She'd been able to see Jacques several times each week, and, despite some residual discomfort, she'd enjoyed the outings more than she ever would have dreamed. Together, she and Jacques had attended concerts and operas, they'd gone shopping and to museums, even out to the lake. Though Blanche had never before considered herself a prisoner, she realized now that she was beginning to feel free for the first time in memory.

Blanche still doubted there could be a future for her and Jacques—she wasn't quite ready to become a world traveler with him. And besides, she'd already vowed before God to devote herself to improving Roland and Angelique's marriage and being a faithful godmother to young Justin. Considering the estrangement between Roland and his wife, she had her work cut out for her there.

Hearing the gate creak open, Blanche stood, smiling as she watched Jacques stride through the archway. Her heart quickened as she studied him in his black suit, ruffled shirt and top hat; his gold-hilted walking stick clicked on the tiles as he neared her. She blushed as his dark gaze flicked over her approvingly. She was wearing a new dress just picked up from the *couturière*—it was fashioned of emerald green satin brocade, full-skirted, with a rounded neckline revealing a daring hint of cleavage. Her outfit was completed by a pearl necklace and matching earrings, and a deep green velvet hat and light veil.

Blanche didn't resist when Jacques embraced her warmly. "My dear, you look heavenly in that vibrant green. Are you ready to depart for our evening?"

"Of course," she said with a shy smile. "And you look so handsome yourself, Jacques."

She took the arm he extended, and they walked down the stone corridor to the open gate, where the coachman awaited them. Inside the carriage, they sat close together. "Well," Jacques began, squeezing her gloved hand, "how are the Miros, and Angelique and her baby?"

"The Miros are fine, and young Justin is thriving," Blanche replied with a proud smile. Then a shadow crossed her eyes. "Angelique is doing—as well as can be expected under the circumstances."

"My stubborn nephew has still made no move in her direction?"

Blanche shook her head sadly. "Several times, I've urged Angelique to go back to Belle Elise, to talk things over with Roland. But she refuses to make the first move. She insists that Roland sent her away in the first place, and says she won't return home until he comes to New Orleans and asks her and the baby back. I told Angelique I was sure my stepbrother never intended to give her the impression that he was sending her away—but she remains adamant."

Jacques sighed, thinking of his own guilt regarding his nephew's estrangement from Angelique. "I wonder, can nothing be done to effect a reconciliation?"

"After Angelique's performance, I intend to return to Belle Elise and beg my stepbrother to come to New Orleans and ask her back."

A trace of suspicion flickered in Jacques's eyes. "And are you again going to sequester yourself away at the plantation?"

Blanche avoided Jacques's eye. "I—I don't know, Jacques. Angelique and Roland do need my help."

He drew a ragged breath. Blanche had seemed a changed woman since she'd started wearing the theater paint. Jacques had noticed the skillful application of makeup the first time she'd worn it, but he'd wisely made no comment. As far as he was concerned, her birthmark was nothing to be ashamed of; but if wearing grease paint put her more at ease in public, so much the better. Indeed, the makeup had drawn them closer—

Yet now they could so easily be wrenched apart again. Angelique would soon perform, then Blanche would surely return to Belle Elise. She wouldn't be content until she managed to get Roland and Angelique back together. Then she'd resume her permanent role as helpmate to Roland and Angelique, and doting godmother to the child—and she'd throw away any chance for their future happiness!

It was all becoming exquisite frustration for Jacques. And thus he knew he'd been right in deciding to make his move tonight. He refused to let the woman he loved slip through his fingers!

Tonight, he would propose marriage again, and if Blanche refused, by the saints, he would take the decision out of her hands—

He would compromise her. Reprehensible though it was, Jacques was a desperate man. Blanche loved him, he loved her, and love had brought him to this madness. He vowed that before this night was out, he would secure her consent —one way or another.

Thus, with grim resolution, he took her hand. "My dear, do you remember the question I asked you last winter?"

Blanche avoided his eye. "Yes, Jacques. But I wrote you—"

"I consider that letter of no consequence. I would hear the answer from your lips—now."

Miserably, Blanche stared at her lap. "Jacques, I've enjoyed these past weeks with you, but as I already mentioned, Roland and Angelique do need me so, and—"

"Have you thought that it might be best to let the two of them solve their own problems?"

Blanche drew herself up with dignity. "I'm godmother to young Justin, as well. Therefore, my marrying you is out of the question."

"I see," Jacques replied tersely. While her negative response brought a wave of disappointment, he'd anticipated it earlier and had already made provision to bring her around. Clearing his throat, he announced, "We'll be stopping by the house on St. Charles before going on to dinner. I thought we'd ask my son to join us tonight."

Blanche glanced at him, startled. "Certainly—if that is what you want, Jacques."

My sweet, if you but knew what I want. What I will not be denied this night, Jacques thought to himself ruefully.

At the house on St. Charles Avenue, Jacques unlocked the door himself after their knock brought no response. While Blanche glanced about the deserted downstairs in rising perplexity, he smiled to himself. Just as Jean Pierre had promised, no one was about.

"Where is everyone?" she asked.

He shrugged, feigning innocence. "Considering my son's unpredictable nature, there's no telling."

"Then shouldn't we go on to dinner?" she continued nervously.

"Of course," Jacques returned with a smile. "But first, dear—I fear your hat has been tugged askew by the breeze. Perhaps you should go upstairs and make an adjustment?"

"Oh, of course." Blanche, so painfully conscious of her appearance, at once started off. "I'll be right back."

Jacques grinned to himself as he watched her voluminous skirts sweep up the stairs. So far, she'd been putty in his hands. She never should have pitted herself against a man of his determination.

After a moment, he followed her. He walked down the upstairs corridor until he discovered an open bedroom door. Blissfully unaware of his presence, Blanche stood at the dressing table, her hat and veil removed as she touched up her coiffure with a comb.

Jacques entered the room and shut the door, throwing the latch.

She gasped, whirling to face him. "Jacques! Whatever are you doing up here? This is—"

"Improper? Scandalous?" he provided with a grin.

Blanche dropped her comb. "Jacques, you must leave this room at once. Otherwise, you'll—"

"Compromise you?" he supplied with a wicked chuckle. "But *chérie*, that's precisely my intention."

There was a moment of terrible silence as he steadily stalked her, his eyes gleaming lustily. Blanche's heart beat so hard, she was sure Jacques must be able to hear it. At last she managed to whisper, "Why are you doing this?"

"Why? To bring you to your senses, of course."

"My senses?"

"Yes." To her horror, he removed his frock coat, tossed it aside, then continued toward her. "Always living vicariously, aren't you Blanche? You've lived your life through Roland's eyes, through my travels, and now through Roland and Angelique's child."

"I—I'm sure I don't know what you mean."

"You know precisely what I mean." He paused and gazed at her almost sadly. "Sometimes, *chérie*, when we cannot see what is best for ourselves, others must force us to see reason." Her eyes grew huge as he untied his cravat and then began working on his studs. "Therefore, tonight, my dear, you will taste life on its own terms—on my terms."

"No," she denied hoarsely, backing up against the dressing table.

Jacques's dark eyes blazed with passion and determination. "No? You would deny me, sweet? Don't you think you owe me more than that for all these years of loving you?"

She stared miserably at the floor, and her voice was choked with tears. "You don't love me. You pity me."

That angered him and he grabbed her by the shoulders, shaking her. "Blanche, for once and for all, get it through your head that what I feel for you is not pity. But since you're so loathe to believe me—perhaps a more physical demonstration is in order."

Blanche swallowed hard. Even his fingers, hard and hurtful as they dug into her shoulders, made her reel with debilitating desire. "Jacques, please, you're being unfair. When you touch me this way, I can't—"

"But I'm counting on precisely that, *chérie*," he said with an implacable smile.

"Jacques, you're ruthless," she whispered weakly.

"Indeed," he replied as he dragged her close and kissed her.

Blanche trembled, aching with desire as Jacques's lips ravished hers. His tongue invaded her mouth and she moaned, clinging to him. But when he moved to kiss her birthmark, she automatically stiffened. At once he pulled back, scowling at her.

"Stop this nonsense," he growled. And he slapped her once, sharply, on the derriere.

"Oh!" Blanche cried, more aroused than angered by the sting of his hand. Yet further speech was smothered as he crushed her close and claimed her mouth again. This time, when his lips moved to her birthmark, she didn't resist.

From that moment on, Blanche was lost. Jacques was impatient and passionate, having been true to his love both mentally and physically for too many long years. He also knew that he must overwhelm her, take her quickly, allow no opportunity for second thoughts to seep in.

He should not have worried, for she was powerless to resist him—so ready, after years of loving him, wanting him. She wept with joy as his feverish hands removed her jewelry and unbound her hair. Then he was undressing her and kissing her all at the same time. "You're beautiful," he whispered as he lifted her naked body onto the bed. "So beautiful."

Blanche stared up at him with eyes shining with adoration. At that moment, she felt filled with love to her very soul, and beautiful for the very first time in her life.

Jacques shed his own clothes quickly. Blanche's eyes widened as she glimpsed his naked, hair-roughened body, but he allowed her no time for panic. When he joined her on the bed, he at once burrowed between her thighs. He knew that this first time, the consummation was critical.

Their joining brought fresh tears to her eyes as he claimed the tight virginal passage that had lain dormant for half a lifetime. Yet even the pain was beautiful—tearing her apart yet making her whole again, making her one with him. Soon rapture overwhelmed the hurt, and Blanche found herself consumed with shockwaves of ecstasy as Jacques deepened his thrusts and pressed his mouth into hers.

As he moved powerfully toward his climax, he stared down into her eyes and whispered, "I love you. Now I shall hear it from your lips."

"I—love—you," she whispered convulsively, each word met by a riveting, deep thrust, and then he was at rest inside her.

For a long moment they were quiet, glorying in their shared love. Then sanity returned for Blanche and she pushed Jacques away.

"*Chérie*, what is it?" he asked. "Did I not please you?"

"No—it's not that." She blinked back tears, feeling ashamed of her own wantonness. "Please, just take me home now."

"But you do not seem to understand, my love," he whispered. "Your home is with me now. We'll be married at once, of course."

Blanche turned to him, her eyes huge, alarmed. "Jacques, surely you can't think that now . . . My God! You planned this, didn't you?"

"To the letter," he returned proudly.

"Well, I won't marry you!" she snapped.

Jacques merely shook his head and laughed. "My poor darling. You're such a guileless innocent. Don't you understand? I've ruined you now. You have no choice but to marry me. And should you still have the imprudence to refuse my suit, I'll simply keep you here with me until Jean Pierre returns at dawn. When the news gets out, that ought to bring my nephew running with a shotgun soon enough, *n'est-ce pas*?"

"Why that's—depraved!" she said indignantly.

"Think, Blanche," Jacques said. "What if there is a child?"

"Oh, my God!" she cried. "It could have my birthmark!"

Her words brought thunderclouds to Jacques's eyes, and he regarded her sternly. "If our child has your birthmark, I will only love him more because he reminds me so much more of you." He drew her trembling body close. "Listen to me, *chérie*," he whispered, stroking her arm. "I just made

passionate love to you. Do you really think I could have done
that with a woman I pitied?''

''Oh, I don't know!'' she cried. ''I'm so confused!''

''Unfortunately, my dear, I'm no longer willing to tolerate
your confusion or your denial of our love. We'll marry as
soon as the banns can be read, and then we're leaving on an
extended tour of Europe.''

Blanche looked up at Jacques with forlorn hope—he had
just promised to fulfill all her dearest, most secret dreams.
And yet . . . She sadly shook her head.

''What is it now?'' he demanded.

''Jacques—I'm not worthy to be your wife.''

''By the saints! Must I have you over my knee to end this
lunacy?''

She gripped his arm and spoke earnestly. ''No, you don't
understand. I can't marry you because of—a vow I made.''

''Pray, continue.''

In a voice thick with emotion, Blanche confessed, ''I—
I've done wicked things, Jacques, and now, I must spend the
rest of my life atoning. When you hear what I've done—
you'll never want to marry me.''

Jacques laughed shortly. ''My dear, you seem to know
nothing of my determination—or my absolute faith in you.
Whatever is on your conscience, I'm sure it's of little consequence. But, pray, share it with me—for from this moment
on, we shall share everything together.''

His devoted words gave her the strength to continue. ''It
concerns Roland and Angelique,'' she began.

CHAPTER
Thirty-six

On a mild afternoon two days later, Jacques and Blanche
were admitted to Belle Elise by Benjamin. Jacques tried his

best to buck up Blanche's courage as they sat in the parlor awaiting Roland.

"Oh, Roland shall never forgive me when he hears what I've done," Blanche lamented for the dozenth time that day.

Jacques squeezed her hand and spoke sternly. "My dear, we've been over this again and again. What you did was perfectly understandable under the circumstances, and I'm sure my nephew will agree. We've only come for this confession due to your insistence on marrying me with a clear conscience." Ruefully, he continued, "Actually, if anyone should apologize to my nephew, I should. That day I came here with André, I was obsessed by the idea of convincing Angelique to perform in New Orleans, knowing that you would likely be asked to accompany her there. I didn't realize that I might drive a wedge between Roland and his bride—which, it turned out, I did with a vengeance. No wonder my nephew banned me from his home."

"Oh, Jacques. I'm sure Roland didn't mean his angry words."

The two fell silent as Roland stepped into the room. He was immaculately dressed and groomed; his expression was strained. "Blanche—Jacques," he acknowledged stiffly.

Jacques stood and strode over to his nephew, extending his hand. "Roland, how good it is to see you again. I must apologize for my rather presumptuous behavior the last time I was here."

Roland at once accepted the handshake, smiling ruefully. "Actually, Uncle, I can't begin to tell you how much I've come to regret that day myself." He moved off toward Blanche, his eyes reflecting not a glimmer of shock at the makeup she now wore. "My dear, you look lovely." He kissed her cheek, then turned to Jacques. "Well, Uncle, let's be seated then."

After the two men were seated, Roland smiled kindly at his stepsister. "Tell me, Sister, have you enjoyed your time in New Orleans? I'm assuming Jacques volunteered to escort you home?"

Blanche glanced awkwardly at Jacques, and he cleared his throat and turned to Roland. "Actually, Nephew, Blanche and I have come for only a brief visit. I'll be escorting her back to New Orleans before nightfall."

"I see." With a frown drifting in, Roland added, "If you've come with some message from Angelique, you may tell my wife that I'll speak with no emissaries regarding our marriage."

"I, er—" Jacques coughed. "I'm afraid we've brought no message from Angelique."

For a long moment, Roland was silent, his jaw tight and his eyes gleaming with suppressed emotion. "I see. I presume that she and the child are thriving?"

"Indeed, they are," Jacques hastened to reassure his nephew.

"Then, pray, tell me why you and Blanche have come."

Blanche started to speak, but Jacques raised a finger to his mouth. "Nephew, Blanche has something she wishes to discuss with you. But first . . ." He paused to smile at Blanche, and she smiled back adoringly. "Roland, since you are Blanche's remaining male relative, I'm asking you for her hand in marriage."

To the couple's pleasant surprise, Roland broke into a broad grin. "Why that's wonderful news, Uncle. I've been aware that you two have been admiring each other for ages, and I'm delighted that you've finally decided to tie the knot."

"I presume we have your blessings, then?" Jacques asked.

"You do, indeed."

"There is one thing, Roland," Blanche put in tentatively.

"Yes, dear?"

Blanche twisted her fingers nervously. "As Jacques mentioned, there's something I must get off my conscience before I can wed him."

Roland scowled. "Oh?"

At this point, Jacques said wisely, "I believe I'll leave you two to your discussion and have a constitutional about the grounds."

After Jacques left the room, Blanche stared at her lap for a long moment. "Roland, I've come to beg your forgiveness, because I've—I've interfered in both your marriages."

He raised an eyebrow. "Indeed? In what way, dear?"

She stared at him through her tears. "It's a long story—"

"Then why bother? I'm sure that whatever you think you

did has simply loomed too large in your mind. It's best left
in the past—''

''No,'' Blanche interrupted vehemently, her fists clenched
in her lap. ''I must tell you or—or I can't marry Jacques.''

Roland listened in rising perplexity. ''Very well, Sister. If
your feelings are that strong, please proceed.''

Blanche nodded, meeting his gaze bravely. ''As you're
aware, fifteen years ago, your father married my mother and
I came here to live. For some time, I . . .'' Blanche's voice
faded to an anguished whisper, then she blurted, ''I fancied
myself in love with you. But—I knew you could never love
me back, because of my deformity.''

''Blanche—''

''Please, hear me out!'' she pleaded. After Roland reluctantly nodded, she continued. ''When you married Luisa six
years later, I was at first insanely jealous. I did try my best
to accept her. But Luisa—you never knew this, Roland, but
she belittled me constantly, calling me a freak. And from the
day she married you, she threatened to have me cast out of
the house.''

''*Mon Dieu*!'' Roland cried, leaning forward in his chair.
''Why did you not tell me this?''

Blanche gestured helplessly. ''Luisa said that if I told you,
she'd tell you I was in love with you and had been trying to
break up your marriage.'' Her voice trembled with bitter
emotion. ''Oh, how she could read my feelings, much as I
tried to hide them. And I did love you then, Roland—but I
never intended to act on that love.''

''Blanche, you should have told me what Luisa was
doing.''

''Would you have believed me?'' she asked in a small
voice.

''I would have,'' he gritted out.

Blanche sighed. ''At any rate, the longer you were married
to Luisa, the more she wanted to get rid of me. As you know,
she became insanely jealous of practically every woman in
the parish—anyone you ever looked at. She even thought
that you had slept with Justin's wife and had fathered young
Phillip—though we all knew what lunacy that was.''

Roland nodded dismally. ''How bitterly I do remember.

Luisa seemed to grow even more—unhinged—after Justin died, when Emily and Phillip stayed on, so desperately needing my help and guidance.''

"Tell me, do you recall the time when you went to New Orleans alone, just a few weeks before Luisa's death?"

He scowled. "Yes—that would have been harvest time."

"Well—while you were gone, Luisa finally made good her threat and cast me from the house."

Roland looked thunderstruck. "My God, Blanche! Luisa had absolutely no right to do that!"

Blanche shuddered. "I went to stay with Caroline Bentley, and then a few days later, Luisa came over and told me I could return home. She warned me that if I ever told you of her actions, it would be my last day at Belle Elise."

Roland gritted his teeth, just barely able to restrain himself from saying something very disrespectful about a dead woman. "Doubtless Luisa asked you back because she knew I'd raise holy hell if I came back and found you gone."

"Perhaps so. At any rate, on the day of the Harvest Ball a few weeks later, you may recall that Caroline and George Bentley came rather early for the festivities. Caroline, Luisa, and I were seated on the front veranda while you, George, and Phillip pitched quoits out on the lawn. Then—something terrible happened."

Roland's shoulders tightened as he leaned forward. "Go on."

"Right in front of Luisa, Caroline said something like, 'Just look at Phillip with Roland. The boy looks enough like him to be his son, not his nephew.' "

"By the saints!" Roland cried, falling back in his chair.

"I think even then that Caroline—fancied you. And I think she resented the way Luisa had treated me. Still—when she made her comment, she couldn't have known how obsessed Luisa had become with the idea that you and Emily were having an affair."

Roland laughed bitterly. "And she couldn't have known how obsessed Luisa had become with the idea of having a child of her own."

Blanche raised an eyebrow. "She was?"

"Indeed," Roland concurred grimly. "It all came out one night, when Luisa had too much to drink. You see, Luisa had a younger sister who drowned while in her charge—a favorite sister her parents doted on. I think Luisa's guilt filled her with an obsession to have her own child—I suppose in her twisted way, she thought she could atone to her parents that way. Anyway, when she told me of her frustration at her childless plight, she also accused me of being—sterile. In retrospect, I really think that was the true reason Luisa was—well, less then discreet during our marriage. She was seeking the child she was convinced I couldn't give her."

"Oh, my God!" All color had drained from Blanche's face. "Then Luisa must have really snapped when Caroline made her comment about Phillip—not that it was true."

Roland nodded. "Nevertheless, I'm sure the comment made Luisa conclude that she was the one who was barren. Considering her mental state at the time, it's not surprising that she went over the edge." Slowly, he shook his head, his eyes gleaming with painful irony. "You know, Sister, I'm glad you've told me about that day and Caroline's comment. For everything makes sense to me now. You see, later that same night, Luisa confronted me in my study. Then," he paused to clear his throat, "there was the accident."

"Yes."

"But there's something I still don't understand," Roland went on with a frown. "Why do you feel any guilt regarding this?"

Miserably, Blanche confessed, "Because I tried to retaliate against Luisa—in subtle ways, perhaps. I told her small lies, twisted things around and tried to come between the two of you—"

Roland cut in firmly, "Blanche, Luisa and I were already dead set on a collision course."

"I disagree. That day when Caroline made her comment, I knew—at least to a degree—the effect it would have on Luisa. Yet I remained silent."

"Of course you did! What else could you have done, considering the despicable way Luisa had treated you?"

"Still, I could have done better—"

He held up a hand. "Sister, I'll hear no more of this nonsense. Now tell me—what else is on your mind?"

Blanche drew a ragged breath. "After Luisa's death, I realized that I never really loved you—I mean, not in a man-woman way. And when Jacques started visiting Belle Elise, I realized it was he that I truly loved. Yet my guilt over your marriage and my deformity held me back. Then, when you married Angelique—''

"Yes?" he asked hoarsely.

Blanche spoke with great emotion. "Brother, I knew in my heart that the girl was goodness incarnate. But when she kept suggesting I go to New Orleans—really, just to help me—all those old fears crept back, and again, I found myself acting in a way that shamed me. I feared Angelique was trying to get rid of me, just as Luisa had. Thus, I—I tried to drive a wedge between the two of you as well. And now—now I've destroyed two marriages for you, Brother.''

With her last words, Blanche burst into tears. Roland rushed to her side and took her hand. Once she quieted a bit, he spoke. "Blanche, I must tell you that my not thinking of you in a romantic way had nothing to do with your birthmark. Even though we're not actually related by blood, I've always thought of you as a sister—a dear sister who will always have a place in my home.''

"Oh, Roland!"

She fell into his arms, and in that moment, years of suffering and pain began to heal for Blanche.

After the emotion subsided, Roland drew back and continued with a kindly smile, "As far as my marriage to Angelique is concerned, you're blaming yourself for things that are far from your fault. I think Angelique and I both knew from the beginning that you felt some very natural resentment of her. Why shouldn't you have? After all, you'd been mistress of Belle Elise for many years—and then I showed up, suddenly, with a new wife to take over your duties." Roland patted Blanche's hand and continued, "But you must know that what's going on between Angelique and me now has nothing to do with you. The girl simply does not want to be married to me.''

"Oh, Roland! That just isn't true!"

"Then why hasn't she told me as much?"

"She thinks you sent her away."

"That's not the case," he said grimly. "Indeed, on the day Jacques visited last, Angelique is the one who told me she would leave.''

Blanche had no answer there. Biting her lip, she said, "Roland, come to New Orleans next week and hear Angelique sing. It could be a new beginning for both of you."

Roland shook her head. "I will be going to New Orleans before long to see my son, but I won't be attending my wife's concert. I've afraid the next move is up to her."

"Oh, Roland." A tense silence fell between them, as Blanche frantically tried to think of some tack that might reach her stubborn stepbrother. At last, with desperation, she blurted, "You know, Brother, I ran into George Bentley at the theater the other day. He and Caroline are staying over for Angelique's performance. George said he can't wait to hear her sing."

The answering glower in Roland's eyes could have pulverized diamonds. After a long moment, he managed to regain control of himself and said with a forced smile, "Well, Sister, shall we go find that fiancé of yours before he grows unduly impatient? It's time to hunt up a bottle of champagne, don't you think?"

On the way back to New Orleans, Blanche was unusually quiet. Finally Jacques demanded, "Well, what is it, my dear?"

"Oh, Jacques, I fear I've sinned again."

"Indeed?"

She nodded dismally. "After vowing never again to interfere in Roland's marriage, I—I lied to him."

"What?" her fiancé thundered. He uttered a string of oaths in rapid French. "Must we now turn about and return to Belle Elise for yet another purging of your conscience?"

She wrung her hands. "No—I think that would only make things much worse. I'll just go to confessional and do my penance."

He slanted her a stern look. "Pray tell, what manner of mischief did you indulge in this time, my pet?"

"Well . . . I told Roland I ran into George Bentley in New Orleans and that he can't wait to hear Angelique sing at the St. Charles. And I'm afraid—well, that was a bald-faced lie."

Jacques howled with laughter. "It's a miracle my nephew

is not sitting here between us at this very moment, his valise in his lap.''

"Do you think Roland will come to Angelique's concert now?'' Blanche asked, her eyes gleaming with forlorn hope.

Jacques chuckled. "I think there's an excellent chance.''

"Oh, he must! The only way Angelique and Roland will get back together is if he sees her again.'' With an heavy sigh, she went on, "Angelique and Roland are both caught up in their pride. She won't come back because he hasn't asked her, and he won't ask her because she said she wanted to go. It seems a hopeless impasse.''

"Unless the proper nudge is applied,'' Jacques pointed out. "And from what you've just told me, what you just administered to my nephew was more like a swift kick in the pants. And eminently deserved, I must say.''

CHAPTER
Thirty-seven

On a mild fall evening six days later, Angelique sat in her dressing room at the St. Charles Theater, staring at her visage in the dressing table mirror. The air was sweet with the aroma of the dozen red roses Madame Santoni and her husband had sent her a few hours ago.

Moments earlier, Madame had departed the tiny room to join her husband out in the audience, after hugging Angelique and wishing her good luck tonight. Madame had wanted to stay with the girl until her curtain call, but Angelique had requested a few moments alone to say her prayers and gather her thoughts. Madame had understood.

Angelique had finished her prayers, and she felt relatively serene about what was to come. She studied her reflection critically. All her features stood out due to the application of stage makeup; her eyes, her high cheekbones, her mouth, were all vividly highlighted. Her ebony curls were piled high on her head, and a gold tiara, sparkling with rhinestones, added a regal touch. The rubies Roland had given her at New Years winked back at her from her neck and ears.

Her costume was of deep red brocaded satin, low-bodiced, tight-waisted and full-skirted, with a flowing train. The skirt was parted down the front to reveal a white lace underskirt; the edges of the scalloped opening were adorned with bows and small silk flowers. Except for her makeup, Angelique looked more like a queen about to hold court, than New Orleans's newest prima donna about to make her concert debut.

Last night's dress rehearsal, with full orchestra and chorus, had gone well. A few distinguished guests and representatives of the city's newspapers had attended, at André Bienville's invitation. Only this morning, the *Crescent* had heralded Angelique as "The opera's newest, brightest flame . . ."

Angelique sorely hoped she could live up to that lofty title tonight. Already, she could hear the muffled, discordant sounds of musicians warming up in the orchestra pit, reminding her that time was growing short. Her stomach fluttered, and she reminded herself for the dozenth time that she was doing this for her son.

Wistfully, she wondered how her beloved parents would feel—God rest their souls—if they could see her tonight. Would they even recognize their own daughter now? Her life had changed so radically in just a little over a year.

She sighed as her thoughts turned to Roland. Even though she felt he had wronged her grievously by sending her away, she still loved him and missed him terribly. Was he happy? Did he think of her at all? Despite the impasse between them, it hurt that he hadn't come to the city to hear her perform.

During past days, Angelique had tried to remain positive; she had continued to take her strength from young Justin. She had also been greatly cheered by the news that Blanche and Jacques would wed in just two weeks' time. This was no less than a miracle, she knew. Yet she also yearned for the days when she and Roland had known such bliss!

Angelique's musings were interrupted by a sharp knock at her door. She called, "Come in," and turned to watch André Bienville stride into the room, looking quite dashing in his formal black, the lamplight glinting off his shock of white hair. Kissing Angelique's hand, he said gallantly, "My dear, you are the most beautiful prima donna ever to grace our stage."

Feeling her cheeks warm, Angelique smiled at André. "Why, M'sieur Bienville! Were it not for your lovely wife, Hélène, I'd swear you were flirting with me."

He winked at her. "Were it not for my lovely wife, Hélène, you'd be right." As she stood in a rustle of skirts, he offered his arm. "Well, dear. Are you ready?"

"As ready as I'll ever be," she replied ruefully. "M'sieur Bienville, I just hope I can—"

"You'll be wonderful," he said vehemently, not even allowing her to voice a misgiving. "Now come."

As they left the room, Angelique asked, "Is the audience full?"

He laughed heartily. "There's not a seat left in the house."

In the wings, Angelique and André were greeted by the conductor, M'sieur Moreau, who also kissed Angelique's hand and complimented her lavishly on her costume. Across from them in the opposite wing, Angelique could see the chorus members, patiently waiting with music folders in hand. They would enter the stage after her first song.

M'sieur Moreau wished Angelique good luck then left to descend into the orchestra pit. Seconds later, Angelique heard booming applause. "*Mon Dieu*," she murmured to André. "The house must indeed be packed."

She waited in the wings during the opening orchestral selection, the first movement from Schubert's Symphony in B Minor. The music created an aura of hushed expectancy with its lilting, full-bodied melodies and dramatic violins in counterpoint. The finale was followed by more enthusiastic applause.

"Well, dear, it's time," André murmured to Angelique. Staring down at her kindly, he added, "Angelique, I feel as if you're my daughter. Therefore, would you indulge this old man with a hug?"

"Of course," she replied.

As she hugged him warmly, he kissed her brow and whispered, "Good luck, my dear."

"Thank you," she murmured as he released her. Angelique

squared her shoulders, turned, and started toward the stage, feeling bolstered by André's reassurance. The second she left the wings, she was met by deafening applause. At midstage, she turned and bowed deeply, and the attendees responded with hearty bravos and even louder clapping. Straightening, Angelique stared out into the theater, for a moment overwhelmed by the size of her audience and the scope of their adulation. André had been right—every seat in the house was taken. Thousands of formally dressed operagoers sat beneath dazzling crystal gaslights, applauding her and cheering her on. Angelique knew that every person attending tonight had paid at least fifteen dollars for the privilege. What if she couldn't live up to their expectations? They would ride her out of town on a rail!

At last the applause receded, the attendees raptly waiting for her to begin. The gaslights were lowered and the conductor glanced at her anxiously, watching for his cue. But Angelique continued to stare frozenly at the audience. Then a familiar face caught her eye. At first she couldn't believe what she saw, then realization dawned.

Roland! He was seated squarely in the middle of the fifth row, just two rows behind Madame Santoni and her husband. Angelique stared at him and their eyes locked for a long, emotional moment.

Out in the audience, Roland had been anxiously awaiting his wife's entrance. For weeks, he had agonized over whether or not he should attend this concert. Though his life had been sheer hell without Angelique and Justin, pride had held him back. Yet ultimately, when Blanche had told him that George Bentley would be attending tonight, he found he couldn't stay away. He'd arrived in New Orleans earlier today. Before coming to the theater, he'd stopped off at the Miro townhome to see his precious son, and the reunion had rocked him to the depths of his being. By the saints, he had missed that precious baby so!

Yet as emotional as that moment had been, it could not compare to the feelings raging inside him at the sight of his beautiful young wife walking onto the stage. Angelique was so captivating—she moved with such grace. Her costume was dazzling, the perfect showcase for her slim figure, her

lush breasts. When she dipped into a deep bow, the audience
went wild. Then she stood, holding her head with regal grace
as she waited for the applause to die down. Watching her
stand there, with such dignity and self-possession, Roland
felt his heart thudding in sudden desolation. He loved her so,
had missed her desperately. Yet still, she seemed so unreachable. Much more than physical distance separated them now.

Then she spotted him, and those vibrant, flame-bright eyes
locked with his in a moment of stark, unguarded emotion.
And joy overwhelmed Roland's pain. All he could think of
was that he loved her and he only wished her well in this
moment.

And Roland smiled.

When Roland smiled at her, Angelique smiled back, and
her heart leapt with joy. He had come, after all! Suddenly,
she was at peace. Despite their problems, all she knew was
that he was here with her now and she could do anything.
Whether tomorrow found them together or apart, they were
together in spirit at this moment. No matter what, they had
this—they had their love. It was real, abiding, eternal. They
both knew it, and no one could take it away from them.

Thus with confidence Angelique turned and nodded to the
conductor, and he launched into the orchestral introduction
to her first selection.

As her opening number, Angelique and Madame had selected an English translation, transcribed for soprano, of Wagner's "Song to the Evening Star." While both Madame and
her pupil had been uncertain as to how the Creoles would
receive Wagner—who had been hailed by some and damned
a heretic by others—Angelique had always been captivated
by the poignance and power of the German composer's music.
They needn't have worried, for as she lifted her voice in the
glorious aria, her audience listened, mesmerized by each
bright note.

Angelique gave herself over to the emotion of her music
—her voice eloquently expressing a passionate range of feeling, love and heartbreak, laughter and tears. Her voice was
strong, crystal clear, and unwavering. Several times as she
executed the aria, she glanced at Roland, and he stared back
at her with an emotion to match her own. As she reached the

song's bittersweet climax, more than one Creole in her audience dabbed at tears.

When she concluded, there was a long moment of total silence, and at first Angelique feared she had disappointed her listeners. But then the applause began—the bravos, the stomping and clapping so deafening that the floor of the stage shook. Bouquets were hurled at her feet. She picked up the lush flowers and beamed at her devotees as she took her first of many, many bows.

From that moment on, Angelique's concert was an utter triumph. Following Jenny Lind's lead, she and Madame had selected an eclectic repetoire—several classical arias, mingled with patriotic tunes and folk songs. The chorus joined in on a number of the selections, but the audience seemed most charmed by the songs Angelique sang solo in her dazzling, incomparable soprano voice.

At the conclusion of her program, Angelique's audience simply refused to let her go—applauding, cheering, heaping a sea of flowers on the stage and loudly demanding encores. She ended up singing five encores, an unprecedented number for the St. Charles. On her final curtain call, she chose her old favorite, "The Last Rose Of Summer." Her audience listened raptly to her shining, soulful rendition. Her rich, moving crescendos left more than one listener breaking out in shivers, or in tears. As she concluded the poignant selection, she stared at Roland, singing each note just for him. He stared back at her, his eyes filled with turmoil, and she felt a sharp twinge of disappointment when he abruptly tore his gaze away.

Following the exquisite song, her audience at last, reluctantly released her. She exited the stage into André Bienville's jubilant embrace. "My dear! My dear! Your performance was an utter triumph!"

He escorted her to her dressing room, all the while continuing his glowing review of her singing. At the door, he winked at her and said, "Best take a moment to freshen up, *chérie*, before the rush of your *afficionados* overwhelms you."

Thanking André, Angelique entered her dressing room and leaned against the closed door for support. After she caught her breath, she crossed the room to look at her reflection.

Her eyes were shining, filled with excitement, her face alive, glowing.

And all at once, she knew it wasn't because of the crowd's thundering adulation, or her own brilliant performance. It was because Roland had been there! In this moment as never before, she realized how much she loved him, how much she had missed him, how empty her world had been without him. All she wanted was for him to take her and Justin home. Her obligation here in New Orleans was fulfilled, and all that mattered to her now was her husband and son.

Surely there was hope for them! She'd seen it in his eyes at the beginning of her performance. Then a frown drifted in as she recalled how he had avoided her gaze during her final selection. Perhaps the emotion had simply been too much for him . . .

A knock came at her door, and a familiar voice called her name. *Mon Dieu*, it was him! She rushed across the room, flinging open the door, greeting him with love and joy in her eyes—

But as soon as she saw his face, she knew that something was terribly wrong. Something had happened to him during the performance—she could see it in his impassive eyes, in his detached, drawn features. Never had her husband looked more handsome—yet never more distant and unreachable.

He stood there staring at her, his physical proximity every bit as devastating to her as his emotional withdrawal. Oh, she'd forgotten what a magnificent figure of a man he was —how broad were his shoulders, how clean and decisive the line of his jaw. He was a masterful, intimidating presence in his impeccable formal clothes. And his eyes—she could barely force herself to gaze into those beautiful, yet chillingly remote blue eyes. How she wished he would touch her, drag her into his arms, crush her close and kiss her. But he didn't—and his rejection cut her to the quick.

"Roland, I—didn't think you would come tonight," she managed.

"And not miss the event of the season here in New Orleans?" Though his words were laced with cynicism, she detected a strange, underlying sadness. "You performed brilliantly tonight, *chérie*," he added as he stepped into the room.

His use of the endearment, *chérie*, set her reeling, yet she could detect no softening in his expression as he turned to look at her. "Thank you," she replied awkwardly, closing the door.

Roland cleared his throat and continued with a wry smile, "When you sang 'The Last Rose of Summer,' there was scarcely a dry eye in the house."

Suddenly she was angry with him, unreasonably angry that he had placed such distance between them for so long—and that he made no move to touch her now. "I'll bet your eyes were dry," she said bitterly.

He raised an eyebrow, staring at her intently for another long, charged moment. But instead of responding to her caustic remark, he said resignedly, "Obviously, you're well-suited to this life."

Angelique tilted her head, not liking the direction his remarks were taking. Was he glad she was well-suited to this life—thus relieving himself of the burden of a wife he did not want? "André Bienville has told me I can have a permanent position with the opera if I want it," she announced proudly.

"Indeed?" he replied tensely. "And have you thought of where our son will fit into all of this?" Before she could answer, he continued in a gentler tone, "I stopped off and saw Justin briefly at the Miros. He's looking wonderful."

"Thank you," she muttered, barely able to restrain a new wave of indignation. How dare Roland question her judgment in raising their son, when he'd sent both of them away! "Is there anything else?" she asked tersely, her eyes blazing at him.

His jaw tightened and he replied coldly, "I'm returning to Belle Elise tomorrow. You may do as you wish, but our son will be returning home with me, regardless."

Outraged by his arrogant assertion, Angelique was about to issue a blistering retort when abruptly, the door was flung open and Blanche and Jacques burst in.

"Angelique, you were *magnifique*!" Jacques cried, embracing the girl and whirling her about. Then, spotting Roland, who stood scowling at the scene, Jacques nodded to him. "Well, hello there, Nephew. Couldn't resist coming to hear your beautiful wife sing after all, could you?"

Roland smiled cynically, but his eyes were glowing oddly as he stared at Angelique and replied, "No. I couldn't resist."

Blanche rushed forward and gripped Roland's arm. "Oh, Roland, won't you join us at the reception André Bienville is hosting? Why, there's plenty of room for you and Angelique in Jacques's carriage—isn't there, Jacques?"

"Indeed," he concurred. "Blanche and I insist that you two accompany us."

Yet Roland shook his head. "Not tonight, thank you Jacques." He nodded stiffly to his wife. "Angelique—I'll call on you tomorrow to discuss our son."

Angelique stared at Roland's departing figure, trembling and blinking at tears as the Santonis and half a dozen other exuberant operagoers burst into the small dressing room.

Outside the theater, Roland stood beneath a streetlamp, lighting a cheroot and cursing himself a hopeless ass. Beyond him, across the shadowy sidestreet, was the door whence his wife would shortly exit. He'd come to this spot hoping to steal another moment alone with her—sheer lunacy, under the circumstances, as a crowd of autograph-seekers was already gathering.

Tonight when he'd watched Angelique enter the stage, he'd ached to have her back. At that moment, he'd been willing to get down on his knees and beg her forgiveness, if necessary. Yet that was before he'd heard her sing, watched the audience's response to her. She'd been brilliant, captivating everyone, including himself. Still, filled with forlorn hope, he'd rushed to her dressing room afterward. Then one look at her luminous face, her glowing eyes, had confirmed what he already knew—

She did not belong to him anymore. She'd never belonged to him, not really. She belonged to the glittery world of New Orleans and the opera. When he'd realized this, it had filled him with a sadness soul-deep and unendurable, and his cutting remark about taking Justin home had been a last, desperate attempt to hold on to her.

He sighed. They would have to reach some compromise regarding the child, that was clear. He'd missed his son terribly during past weeks, and he wasn't willing to live without him. Perhaps Justin's time could be divided between New Orleans and Belle Elise—

His jaw tightened. He knew that as Angelique's husband, he had every right to demand that she come home with him. Yet at what price? He realized that he loved her so much that he was willing to let her go, rather than crush her spirit. If this was the life she chose, so be it—

Then she emerged from the theater door, looking regally beautiful in her stylish felt hat and fur pelisse, and his resolve almost melted. Oh, he was so tempted to grab her, take her away with him, even if she never loved him—

Yet quite obviously, she did not need him at all. She was laughing with the crowd, gaily signing programs. In fact, there were so many fans crushing, clamoring about her that were pushing her into the street—

Mon Dieu! With eyes wild, Roland whirled to watch a carriage race toward them from the opposite end of the street—its noise not heard, except by him, in the tumult. Dear Christ! The carriage was bearing down with deadly precision on the very spot where Angelique now stood—

Roland threw down his cheroot and raced toward her—as if running for his very life. For she was his life—he knew that now—and she was about to be crushed to death before his very eyes!

Sweet Jesus, could he get there in time? The carriage was closing in so fast, just like—

"Justin!" he screamed as he lunged for the woman he loved.

CHAPTER
Thirty-eight

Angelique scarcely knew what hit her. One minute, she was signing the programs her excited fans were extending, then the next minute she heard her husband screaming the name of Justin, her son.

The next thing she knew, she was hurled back, forcefully, onto the banquette, the breath knocked from her lungs. Roland's strong body was covering hers, and she knew a split-second of excruciating, helpless fear and rage that he would do such a thing to her, humiliating her in front of her well-wishers.

Then, as oxygen at last stabbed her lungs, she watched a carriage roar by in the street, mere inches from her toes, and realized that Roland had just saved her from certain death.

Luckily, no one else in the throng had been hurt.

A hush fell over the crowd. Angelique's fans backed off, whispering to one another in shocked undertones as Roland struggled to his feet. He looked down at Angelique, his features grimly white as he extended his hand. "Are you all right?"

She nodded, swallowing convulsively.

He pulled her to her feet, brushing her off then retrieving her hat from the banquette. "You're coming with me," he said.

As he led her away, she looked down and saw his hat, crushed flat as an omelet in the filthy street.

Moments later, Roland and Angelique were boarding a hansom cab. She heard him order the driver to take them to the St. Louis Hotel. She tried twice to start a conversation with him, but he answered only in terse monosyllables. She realized that he was hardly in a conciliatory mood. In fact, he looked furious as he stared out the window.

Next to her, Roland was, indeed, seething as the cab rattled through the cool, dark streets. At the moment, it was all he could do to contain his rage. Rage that his wife had gone off to New Orleans and had almost gotten herself killed. Rage at himself for ever letting her go. Here he'd been heaping guilt on himself, afraid his love for her was a curse that would ultimately destroy her. Well, he'd just saved her life, hadn't he? If he hadn't been there—perish the thought!—she'd be dead now. So obviously, his love for her was not a blight in any way. Why, then, had he tolerated this asinine behavior, this willfulness on her part? She was his wife, by God, and before this night was over, she would be mastered and made to see reason.

When they arrived at the St. Louis, Roland helped Angelique out of the carriage. He glanced at her only when necessary as he led her briskly past the columned, gaslit facade and into the elegant lobby. His fingers dug into her arm as they climbed the stairs.

When they were at last sequestered in his room on the second floor, he tossed down his key, doffed his greatcoat and turned to face her. Angelique calmly took off her pelisse and hat and laid them across the foot of the bed. She met Roland's angry, gleaming gaze unflinchingly, though it was difficult. His entire body was taut, rigid with indignation, and he was breathing hard. Never had he looked more threatening—or more provocatively male.

"You," he growled at last, pointing at her, "are coming home with me tomorrow."

Angelique was too stunned to reply.

Roland's voice rose menacingly as he began to pace, gesturing his exasperation. "I've had it with your willfulness and your independence. Hell, you can sing, *chérie*, sing brilliantly. And doubtless you enjoy your scintillating life here in New Orleans. But I'm afraid your neglected husband has decided to curtail your fun. Damn me a selfish bastard, but you're mine!" He crossed to her quickly and took her by the shoulders, his eyes blazing down at her. "You're mine, I tell you, and I'll not allow you to go get your fool self killed! You're my wife and I've been without your services quite long enough, thank you. Now take your clothes off, get in that bed and let's get on with this marriage."

At last Angelique wrenched herself free. "Why, you big oaf!" she practically screamed at him, trembling at his unmitigated audacity. "How dare you even speak of your husbandly rights, when you gave up those rights! How dare you demand that I come back, when you're the one who sent me away!"

"You're the one who said you wanted to go!" he thundered out.

"No I didn't! I only said I would sing at the opera rather than tolerate your despicable behavior toward Jacques and André Bienville."

"Hah!" He flung a hand outward, his voice sizzling with fury. "Your ultimatum was merely an excuse to leave me! You never really wanted to be my wife."

"That's not true!" she cried desperately. "I did want to be your wife! But as always, you made all my decisions for me. You sent me away!"

"Damn it, I didn't—"

"Yes, you did!" Angelique could no longer contain the hot emotion stinging her eyes as she went on, "Even as my heart was breaking, crying out for you to make a move in my direction, you told me to go away!"

He blinked rapidly, the truth at last beginning to dawn on him. "But—but I thought you wanted . . . Don't you know it broke my heart to tell you to go?"

"Then why?" she cried.

"Because . . ." Helplessly, he ran a hand through his hair. "I thought I was bad for you. Twice, my anger endangered your life—"

"But your vigilance saved it tonight," she pointed out.

"Yes," he said vehemently, seeming to remember his righteous anger. "So it appears I'm not bad for you, after all. You obviously need the protection, guidance—and discipline—of a strong husband. Thus I'm taking you back."

"You're taking . . . ! Don't you understand anything?" she railed. "All you've done since the very day you met me was to order me about, to dictate to me in everything. You never trusted me to think for myself or to make the smallest decisions on my own. You never trusted me to be faithful to you. And even when it came to my singing at the opera, you took that decision out of my hands, too, and told me to come here."

"I . . ." His voice trailed off and he seemed momentarily at a loss. "What was it you wanted, then?"

In a voice hoarse with emotion, she said, "All I ever wanted, Roland, was for you to offer me a choice."

"A choice?" he repeated with a bitter laugh. "A choice about whether or not to be my wife? You really think I should have—could have done that?"

She nodded.

"And if I'd offered you this choice?"

"I would have chosen you."

"Oh, Christ." In an instant, he had her in his arms, clasping her tightly to his heart. His anger was gone, replaced by vulnerability and stark anguish. Tears stung his eyes as he whispered, "*Chérie*, forgive me. As usual I have been a consummate fool. I've let my pride and anger get in the way of the things I truly want to tell you." Looking down into her eyes, he whispered soulfully, "I love you, Angelique."

"Oh, Roland!" she cried. "I love you, too. So much!"

They kissed—deeply, ravenously. And in that moment, the emotional distance of months crumbled away, and their need for each other could no longer be contained. Feverishly they tore at each other's clothes, still kissing, tasting, as the layers of garments, of inhibitions, fell away.

"Say you're mine," he groaned into her mouth.

"I'm yours," she gasped back. "Always yours."

Roland swept Angelique up into his arms and carried her to the bed, laying her down tenderly then joining her there, feasting his eyes on her lovely nakedness. "My angel, my love," he whispered hoarsely as he lowered his lips to hers.

"My husband, my love," she whispered back. She gloried in the masculine feel of him, running her hands over the strong muscles of his back, his hard buttocks, his sinewy thighs. He groaned and his lips hungrily sought the fullness of her breasts. She bucked in ecstasy as his mouth took her nipple, as his rough, slightly bearded cheek pressed into her soft bosom. She ran her fingers brazenly down his chest and lower, much lower. She gripped his turgid manhood and squeezed it lovingly—

His reaction was immediate and fierce as he parted her thighs and buried himself in her moist, throbbing recesses. He was huge inside her, hot and charged. Her womanhood gripped him in a seizure of rapture so intense, she tossed her head violently. He uttered a ragged, "*Mon Dieu!*", then his mouth crushed deeply into hers. She wrapped her legs about his waist and met him, her body passionately demanding everything he could give her, her abandoned movements giving him back ecstasy in equal measure. They cried out their love as he plunged deeply, so deeply, until she become liquid, hot and tight about his pumping shaft. Then came the convulsive thrust that lifted them off the bed, and they were one, exploding together.

*   *   *

"Content?" he asked long afterward.

"Almost," she whispered.

He rolled off her, scowling. "Did my lovemaking leave you lacking in some way?"

"Never," she assured him with a smile, amused by his irate expression. She sat up against the headboard and turned to him solemnly. "But I must know something, Roland. When I go home with you, will things truly be changed? Will you try to trust me this time?"

He sighed as he sat up beside her, staring away at the wall.

Gently, Angelique continued, "I never could understand why you were so jealous, so possessive. I never did anything to merit such a lack of faith. Were you truly afraid I'd betray you, like Luisa did?"

He turned to smile at her, yet an inner turmoil shone in his eyes. "In my heart, I knew you never would. But after we married, I suppose some of the old fears did creep back. You see, in my first marriage, there was no love, no trust—only anger and betrayal. I suppose that's why, when we were first wed, it was so hard for me to trust either you or myself." He twisted one of her raven curls about his finger and continued ruefully, "And Angel, having you for a wife did not make things easier for me. Your guileless beauty made every man who saw you fall in love with you. When you sang, it was ten times worse. Quite frankly, I had a damnable time trying to control my passions."

"I was always true to my vows to you, Roland."

"Ah, yes," he murmured ironically. "From the beginning, you made it clear just how much your duties meant to you." Stroking her cheek, he whispered tenderly, "But, *chérie*, you never told me you truly wanted to be my wife. The marriage was forced on you against your will. And if I never offered you any choices, it was because I was afraid if I did, you would have turned away from me."

"I wouldn't have," she whispered straight from her heart.

"I know that now. Yet not knowing for so long may have been at the root of my high-handed behavior. Though, of course, it was no excuse." He was silent for a long moment, then took her hand, staring at her searchingly. "There's something else I want you to know. Something I couldn't bring myself to tell you before.''

"Yes?''

He intertwined her fingers with his, and she could feel great tension in his grip. "Remember when I told you how Luisa died?''

"Yes.''

He sighed, glancing off at some point in the space. "I'm afraid I didn't tell you the entire truth. There's someone I've been protecting.''

"Oh?''

He nodded, turning to face her. "First, I must ask you something. You heard the rumors, didn't you—about me and Emily?''

She met his gaze bravely. "Yes.''

"Did you believe them?''

At one time, Angelique would not have known how to answer that question, yet tonight she could say truthfully, earnestly, "No.''

"I'm glad,'' he whispered back fervently, squeezing her hand. "Because the rumors were completely false. I'll admit that I wasn't totally discreet during my first marriage, but I never would have slept with my own brother's wife!''

"I know that, Roland,'' she whispered.

"Nevertheless, I'm afraid Luisa became obsessed with the idea that I'd been sleeping with Emily and had even fathered Phillip. You see, Luisa very much wanted a child of her own, to an obsessive degree. And our marriage bore no progeny. Then, on the very day she died, Luisa overheard someone remarking about how much Phillip and I resembled each other. Looking back, I'm sure she must have snapped at that moment. And tragically, that very night, she found me in my study with Emily and young Phillip.''

"Wait a minute!'' Angelique cried, leaning forward to stare at him in amazement. "I thought the argument that resulted in Luisa's death was just between the two of you!''

"No. That's the story I insisted that we tell the world— but actually, both Phillip and Emily were with me at the time.''

"Then it's Emily you've been protecting all this time?''

"Yes." He sighed raggedly. "Emily frequently sought my counsel in that first year after Justin died. On the night of the party, she had come to my study to ask my advice in the matter of Phillip's future schooling. Then Luisa burst in, drunk, and evidently convinced that she'd interrupted a romantic tryst. When she spotted Phillip there, she went crazy. I think that's what ultimately drove her over the edge—not just seeing the three of us together, but being confronted with ostensible proof that I had fathered a child, that she was the one inadequate, barren, in our marriage. God, if only she could have known how wrong she was!" His fist slammed the mattress, and he took a moment to regain his composure. "Anyway, before I knew what was happening, Luisa had grabbed my pistol out of the desk drawer and was aiming it at Phillip, screaming out that she would kill the little bastard I'd fathered."

Angelique was stunned. "Oh, no! How could she!"

"She must have truly lost her mind, to try to take out her wrath on an innocent child. Of course I went rushing in to take the pistol away, but Emily was quicker. She must have deflected the gun just as Luisa was pulling the trigger. Then Luisa slipped to the floor, mortally wounded. The rest . . . you know."

"*Mon Dieu*," Angelique murmured. "So you've pretended you killed Luisa all these years to protect Emily and Phillip?"

"Of course. Think of what it would have done to Emily's reputation if the entire sordid little episode had been revealed. She'd already suffered enough due to my brother's drunkenness and his asinine, untimely death. I was unwilling to let anything stand in the way of Emily's or Phillip's future happiness."

"Oh, Roland!" Angelique cried, embracing him. "I love you so much for doing that. Did Emily feel—badly afterward?"

"She did for a time. I think she felt the most guilt because I refused to let her take any of the blame. But as far as the accident itself was concerned, she soon realized that she had no choice."

Angelique nodded solemnly. "Of course she had no

choice. I would do precisely the same thing if anyone should ever threaten Justin.'' Hugging Roland tighter, she added, "Oh, *chéri*, I understand everything now. So that's why you and Emily have always had such a special relationship?"

"Yes. Do you mind?"

"No, of course not. I trust you with her.'' After a moment, she went on, "But the question remains—will you trust me?''

"My love, I vow to try my damndest," he said ardently, kissing her cheek. "But I'll always be a passionate Creole, and I'll always demand your fullest attentions. However, if I should fail,'' he smiled suddenly and ruffled her hair, "feel free to hit me over the head with your slipper."

She laughed ruefully. "Oh, I will—but I may use a cast-iron skillet instead. You're very hard-headed, Roland.''

He chuckled, his eyes roving over her lovely nakedness. "Well, my pet, you're deliciously mussed now, and I've effectively kept you away from your reception. Are you sorry? Shall we make a late appearance?''

She shook her head happily and kissed him. "No, let's not.'' Wickedly, she added, "Anyway, it was much more fun to be dragged off by you—and ravished.''

"Ravished?'' he repeated indignantly.

"Willingly ravished,'' she purred back.

He grinned and snuggled her closer. After a moment, he asked almost wistfully, "Are you sure you won't miss what you knew tonight—the opportunity to become a world class prima donna, to go on tour like Jenny Lind did?''

"No, I'll not miss it—though I'm glad I had the opportunity to experience it this once. There's probably never a thrill quite like the first time—though nothing would ever compare with the thrill of falling in love with you, Roland.''

He pulled her into his lap and kissed her. "Oh, *chérie*, you're turning me to putty in your hands.''

"About time I took charge of you a bit,'' she said with a chuckle, kissing him back.

"When did you know you loved me?'' he asked.

"I think on the day I saw you with Caroline in the parlor, the day I ran away," she said, a mock pout forming on her lovely lips. "I was so angry that you didn't want me.''

He howled with laughter. "When actually, my desire for

you was driving me insane." Kissing her pout away, he added, "I think I fell in love with you the moment I laid eyes on you in the French Market."

"You did? Oh, Roland." Then, with feigned indignation, she added, "But you were such a menacing brute that day!"

"Indeed—but now the beast has been tamed." Many kisses later, he asked, "You're sure you won't want to return to the opera someday?"

"Oh—maybe years from now, when our children are grown." As his mouth closed on her nipple, she added breathlessly, "Then again—maybe not."

"And you're sure you don't want to go to the reception —bask in those final moments of glory?"

"I've all the glory I want right here." Curling her arms lazily about his neck, she whispered seductively, "Now tell me, my darling husband. What do *you* want?"

Looking down at her, he surprised her by saying tenderly, "I want to get our baby and bring him back here with us, to share our happiness. Our family has been apart too long."

"Oh, Roland."

With a devilish glint in his eyes, he added, "However, before we go . . ."

Angelique moaned with pleasure as he rearranged her on his lap, then filled her once more with the solid proof of his love.

Two hours later, they finally returned to the hotel with Justin, after going to the Miro townhome and taking him away from a startled Coco. They donned their nightclothes and placed the baby on the bed between them. Roland watched Angelique feed his son, and listened to her singing the baby a sweet lullaby. Never had he felt so filled with love as at that moment.

Afterward, they watched the baby kick and coo happily as he stared up at his parents with his father's solemn blue eyes. Roland reached over his child to stroke his wife's cheek. "You know, you do have the voice of an angel," he whispered.

"All yours, my love," she whispered back.

About The Author

Eugenia Riley is the author of numerous historical and contemporary romances. A native Texan, she is a magna cum laude graduate of Texas Wesleyan College in Fort Worth, a former English teacher and editor of *Touchstone* Literary Quarterly. She lives in Houston with her husband and two daughters.

Ms. Riley is also the author of *Laurel's Love*, *Sweet Reckoning*, and *Mississippi Madness*, all published by Warner Books.

Ms. Riley welcomes mail from her readers, and would be happy to answer any questions you might have. If you would like a free newsletter and bookmark, a SASE would be appreciated. Please write to:

Eugenia Riley
P.O. Box 840526
Houston, TX 77284-0526